PREY FOR THE
ABYSS

PREY FOR THE ABYSS

A Alex Come'

ARPress

ILLUMINATING IDEAS,
EMPOWERING VOICES

ARPress
45 Dan Road Suite 5
Canton MA 02021
Hotline: 1(888) 821-0229
Fax: 1(508) 545-7580

Ordering Information:
Quantity sales. Special discounts are available on quantity purchases by corporations, associations, and others. For details, contact the publisher at the address above.

Printed in the United States of America.

ISBN-13:   Softcover   979-8-89330-857-0
                eBook   979-8-89330-859-4
                Hardcover 979-8-89330-858-7

Library of Congress Control Number: 2024902475

TABLE OF CONTENTS

Dedication:

Dedicated to all readers of Killing Blue Eyes. To those it thrilled, those it frightened, and to those who requested what has been created in this, the second of a three book series presentation. To all readers, may you enjoy, shreek, laugh and keep the lights burning for every moment captured within the light and the darkness of these pages. Enjoy the read!

CHAPTER 1

**Tecumseh Correctional Institution
State of Nebraska
Death Row: cell 10**

**December 20th
3:00am**

The Nebraska Institution's most infamous prisoner keeled sweeping the charging child into his arms. As always, the very sight of him sent the Death-Row icon into a smiling rapture. The welcomed embrace lasted but a few seconds before the thick iron door closed behind them.

Pushing his son to arm's length the happy father known throughout the prison as, Blue Eyes, looked him over dotingly. "And how has my little Cain been?" He asked.

"I am learning much, father." The youngster told him proudly.

"I knew you would," Blue Eyes chimed widening his smile. Embracing the boy once more he whispered softly into his little ear, "Did you summon them my son?"

Placing his mouth close to his father's ear, Little Cain whispered back, "They are there as we speak."

Following one last tender squeeze, the seven-year resident winked at his son then stood and turned to his wife. Pulling her close they kissed passionately. Knowing what her husband liked, Nicole slid a hand to his crotch and rubbed him as Cain moved to the bed where he sat waiting patiently.

Three floors above in the Prison's Communication Center, Sergeant Billy James adjusted the room's observation camera for a close up of Nicole's hand. Watching for only a few seconds he quickly pulled his eyes away. His heart was racing. Both anger and guilt were mixing like a mental poison in his head. Billy had grown to know the prisoner called Blue Eyes quite well. He had befriended him and admired his extraordinary intellect and charming persona.

Leaning back in his swivel chair Billy sighed; he had also been sleeping with the man's wife for the past year; and worse, he had fallen in love with her and she with him. And tonight, Lord help him, he would be putting the depth of that relationship to the test.

Ending the embrace Blue Eyes moved to his stainless-steel desk and sat. Nicole walked to the bed, kissed her son on the top of the head then sat beside him. She loved her little boy, although sometimes in secret she'd find herself sobbing; even trembling over the strange dark power his father held over him, actually power he held over the both of them. Yet, regardless, if that was her price to pay then so be it. This beautiful little bundle of joy had come from her very womb and there would never be another.

Never would she have guessed that night seven years ago in New Orleans, while high on crack, the conception of such an adorable little being would come to be. His father's seed had been as powerful as his eyes were beautiful. Doctors had told her of the miracle. Two years prior she had undergone surgery for cancer of the Uterus, informed she could never have children. Then bang, one night with his father and along came the miracle of miracles. Not realizing, Nicole was staring at her son while stroking his long blond hair.

Blue Eyes sat gazing at them; but it wasn't his wife and son he was seeing. Nor did he realize his mesmerizing eyes of blue were undergoing their peculiar, ever-increasing metamorphosis. Their rich cerulean beauty began fading, replaced by a slow-moving shimmering blackness; a transformation of power; human eyes giving birth to an evil malevolence; the creation of dark portals through which wicked things could look out.

Focused on her son, Nicole did not see, nor would have recognized the image of the man reflected upon the now darkened orbs of her husband's staring eyes. She may, however, have noticed the hint of a smile showing at the corners of his mouth. And perhaps heard the faint gleeful, child-like chuckling of his whisper, "Here I come, Clay. Ready or not."

The bazaar manifestation had lasted only seconds. And upon his eyes returning to their stunning color of blue, he crossed one leg over the other and smiled, "Nicole", he said, "if you can refrain from ogling our son long enough, perhaps you can find time to talk with me."

Pulling her eyes from the boy she apologized, "I'm sorry Quinton". Then glancing quickly back at the youngster, added, "it's just that he is so darn cute." Following a loving wink her eyes returned to her husband; expression growing somber. "So how are you holding up?"

"Very well considering the circumstances," he said. "Do you have everything in order?"

Nicole gave a nod. "I have all the arrangements made: financing, contacts, everything."

Changing the subject, she forced a smile. "As usual, you saw I did not wear a Bra."

"Yes, and did my fellow prison mates notice?"

Nicole grinned. "Oh yes, and so did the guards; all pretending they weren't looking, but all wanting a touch."

Pleased, Blue Eyes looked to Cain, "I could use another hug little man. How about it?" Hopping off the bed the youngster hurried to his father's side where he was lifted upon his knee. Giving the boy another tender squeeze, Blue Eyes again whispered into his ear, "So, my dearest little son, just how might Mrs. Parks be doing about now?"

Placing his mouth to his father's ear Cain replied softly, "The police found Mrs. Parks two days ago and she lies in the hospital unconscious. Mr. Parks has not left her side."

The remarkable blue of the killer's eye's sparkled; "And so it begins"!

CHAPTER 2

City Hospital
Lafayette, Indiana

December 20th
3:00 am

Ron Parks sat beside the hospital bed dozing in a green, high-back chair. He had nodded away holding his wife's hand. The IV's of normal saline and nutritional liquids flowed steadily through their lines and into his wife's comatose body.

It had been nearly forty-eight hours since the discovery of her unconscious form lying naked upon the marbled steps of the Lafayette Courthouse. From the moment they had called him he remained at her side, holding her hand, occasionally stroking her hair and whispering words of encouragement he was confident she could hear. And more times than realized, he had wiped away the tears falling from his own eyes and onto the soft cataleptic features of her expressionless face.

An array of feelings zapped endlessly through his brain like charged electrical currents, their relentless assaults leaving him angered and frustrated. Hospital labs had identified the meth overdose. Had it not been for the anomalous 911 call and quick response of paramedics, she would have been found DOA.

None of it made sense to Ron. Michelle had never touched any drug except those prescribed by their doctor. Someone had intentionally pushed the poison into her veins; and they had raped her. It was all so overwhelming. For seven years, he had not felt such anger, not since those horrific days involving the Blue Eyes Killer. But this could not be him, he was sitting on death row waiting to die in six days. It had to be something else.

A wisp of noise awoke him. Opening his eyes, Ron took a moment to clear his sleepy mind. He looked at Michelle draped motionless beneath her bed sheet. Her slumbering form like everything else in the muted room lay buried in shadows.

Rising, Ron kissed her forehead, stretched, yawned into the semi-darkness and glanced at his watch, 3:00 am. He disliked the wee hours of morning. Walking to the open door, he glanced up and down the hallway. Some rooms were open, some closed. The nurse's station located six rooms to his left appeared abandoned, but of course, someone was around somewhere. He yawned again. What he needed was a good cup of coffee.

A brooding stillness lay interwoven within the dim-light of the hallway, and somehow, in some way things didn't feel right. Sure, it was three in the morning, patients were sleeping, and the nursing staff had been reduced to basic bones, and yes, it wasn't unusual that lighting had been dulled for an atmosphere of slumber. All of it made sense, yet to Ron Parks something felt wrong.

Ron sighed again. Sometimes he hated being a cop, living beneath that cloud of never-ending suspicion. "Knock it off, Parks," he admonished himself. Leaned against the door jam he slipped his hands into the pockets of his jeans. He was tired, so much so, his eyes burned as though filled with little shivers of glass.

In his state of early morning lethargy, he spoke once again to the only person capable of hearing him talk; himself. "So, Ronnie Suspicious, what say we go find us a cup of coffee: black, hot, and caffeine charged? It'll wake us up."

Glancing back at his sleeping wife, Ron pressed his lips tightly together. What he really needed, wanted, was for his sweet Michelle to wake up and squeeze his hand, then smile and say let's go home.

Something far down the hallway to his right, moved. He turned quickly but saw nothing. One of the Nurses must have slipped into a room. The movement had been quick, barely catching his peripheral.

Forcing a smile to help hide the embarrassment of cop paranoia, Ron stepped into the hallway. Turning left, he walked to the nurse's station. With luck, he'd find a pot of coffee brewing there, and if so, it would save him a trip to the vending area two floors below.

He found the station deserted. Where was everyone? Taking liberties; he scanned two open charts lying on the counter-top; neither were his wife's, so his eyes roamed on. Six books, held upright by black metal bookends, stood to the far left and a half drank cup of coffee, still steaming, rested on a blue napkin. He winked at it. "Yeah baby, you're a good sign".

Centered on the wall behind the nurses-counter hung the callboard for all rooms. He searched for Michelle's number and located it left center, 2221. To the right of the big board were three doors, and if his cop savvy were correct, he'd find a brewed pot of coffee behind one of them.

In the foyer down the hall, he heard an elevator bell ding and doors open. Turning to look, he made a face, the car opened but no one exited; then the doors closed, and he heard the sound of hydraulics taking the car to another level.

Shrugging, Ron moved behind the station and opened the first of the three doors; it turned out the soiled linen room. Disappointed he closed it and moved to the next room; he struck gold.

"Eureka!" he said, scanning the small nurse's lounge with thankful eyes.

Against the wall, sitting beside a Navy-blue loveseat, a round end table held a stack of Styrofoam cups and a ten-cup coffee pot, nearly full. Grabbing a cup, he filled it to three quarters and sipped. It tasted fabulous and he raised the cup to toast the brewer, "To you Ms. Nightingale, wherever you may be."

On his third sip, the callboard outside the door began to chime softly. Leaving the lounge, he walked to the desk and glanced up and down the hallway. He saw no one.

Shaking his head Ron turned to the callboard. The coffee cup dropped from his hand striking the floor. Its hot contents leaped into the air then rained back to earth splattering his shoes.

The chime continued with a steady blinking light indicating the room. Somehow, he managed to mumble the number… "2221." Ron Parks shouted loud enough to wake the entire floor… "Michelle."

CHAPTER 3

Home of Janis Barr-Lemus, Private Investigator
Alexandria, Louisiana

December 20th
3:00 am

Janis opened her eyes as if her lids had been pushed up by small, steel springs. "Here we go again." She mumbled. The bedroom lay like a black sky void of moon and stars, and she realized the bed was empty; a small sigh expressed disappointment.

Rolling onto her side, sleepless eyes gawked at the alarm clock; 3:00 am. Although the heated waterbed felt therapeutic, it did little in easing her unexplained bout of restlessness. Frustrated, she flopped onto her back and whispered into the blackness, "crocks, crooks and crapola."

The petite strawberry blond had no idea why, but for over a week she had been tossing and turning, eating less and feeling edgy. It perplexed her. She didn't feel sick, Per Se, her love-life was great and financially she was stable; yet something was just not right.

Maybe she needed a challenging case, or perhaps a vacation; a week or two in Cancun maybe. Regardless, whatever was wrong it needed fixed. Her zeal for life had made a U turn and was running full speed the wrong way. Even her two cats, Bounty and Hunter were in on it.

They had cut back on litter box use; thus, requiring she empty it less often; Janis missed the ritual of grumbling at the little meowing fur balls; "A sad state of affairs," she had scolded them, "when your own frigging cats turn on you."

Climbing out of bed she made her way to the bathroom. She hit the light switch and the sudden brightness hurt but awoke her senses. At the sink, she splashed water on her face then went pee. While washing her hands she decided a cup of green tea would be most befitting this early sleepless morning.

Slipping a housecoat over her blue, silk-nightie, she made her way to the kitchen and filled a teakettle with water. Yawning, she lit the burner and placed the kettle over the flame.

When she turned, they were standing at the opposite end of the kitchen table. Their unannounced presence startled her and she screamed, but it was more like a short yelp. There were six of them, all strangers dressed in black, and young; mid-twenties maybe; each staring in silence. Janis scrutinized the group with quick assessment.

There was one woman, and she, along with one of the men were holding Bounty and Hunter. The animals lay straddled their arms being stroked. Janis frowned; the damn traitors were purring.

Janis inched away from the stove to the adjacent counter, positioning herself near a woodblock of cutting knives. One of the six strangers stepped out from the others. He spoke, his voice enunciated with a slight foreign accent; perhaps French.

"Janis Barr, we have not been summoned to hurt you. Only give warning."

Janis frowned again "Warning?"

"It is regarding your friend Clayton Cooper. Soon the forces of darkness will come against him. When that happens, you are not to help this time. We know of your reputation; give us your word and we will leave without incident."

Janis took a deep breath, "Well, Mr. whoever you are, it certainly appears you have me by the short-hairs."

The speaker gave a nod, "Then you agree?"

Janis gave him a smile. "I didn't say that. Like you said, Clayton Cooper is a friend, so I'm afraid that if he asks for my help, well; quite frankly, I'll help him."

The one with authority nodded, "I see. Then understand this, if you aid him in anyway, you will be given to us and become our prey; to us it will be a game, to you it will not. You will know little rest until the day we chose to drain you."

Janis showed surprise. "What the hell is that supposed to mean?"

Smiling now himself, the orator raised his face to the ceiling.

Janis glanced up, speaking aloud, "What, do I have cockroaches?"

When he lowered his face, so did Janis. Their eyes locked and she caught her breath. As though straining to see more clearly, she squinted; more a reaction to the shock of what she was witnessing. The man standing less than eight feet away was changing, physically altering. It was a metamorphosis, some form of transmutation. What the hell ever it was it unnerved her, and the words slipped from her mouth, "what the fuck are you?"

He snarled, a low guttural sound, a deep-throat-ed growl that seemed to resonate as if they were standing in a void. Janis watched astounded as two white fangs descended from his gums. They lengthened to well over an inch narrowing to pinpointed sharpness and curved slightly inward. In Janis's head flashed an image of Bella Lagosy's Dracula. Shaking her head, she told herself, "This is just a freaking nightmare, wake up before you wet yourself."

Her stare moved from the teeth to his eyes. They too had undergone change. The whites had yellowed, and his pupils constricted to barely noticeable dots.

The two holding Bounty and Hunter set them gently on the woodblock table: the only thing separating these weirdos from her. Janis's eyes darted to the cats then back to the man with the dagger teeth and haunting eyes.

The two stared exchanging no conversation. Then the transformation began to reverse; the long fangs receded and the yellow of his eyes faded back to white. The pupils re-dilated.

The eeriness of it caused Janis to shake her head for lack of understanding. For the first time in a long time, she found herself speechless; but the man now back to human form was not and he told her, "As mentioned, we have been instructed that should you refuse our offer, Janis Barr, we are to apply a certain amount of persuasion."

Janis's speech found its way back. Never removing her eyes from the man out front, she pulled two brown-handled butcher knives from the woodblock. "You know," she said, "I have to tell you, you just scared the living shit out of me, and you better hope to hell none of it got on my favorite nighty, I also feel it necessary to tell you three more things: First, I find forced persuasion most exhilarating; second, you take even one more step and you're gona' bleed. And thirdly; and you're gona' love this one; there is a very intense, incredibly handsome, African-American man standing right behind you with a .45 pointed at your very weird, freaking head."

CHAPTER 4

Lafayette City Hospital

Ron Parks sprinted down the hallway. His legs could not carry him fast enough to room 2221. His Michelle, his sweet Michelle was awake, alive; she was back. Praise God, she was back!

Reaching the room, he grabbed the door jam to keep from sliding past the doorway. Rushing in he struck the light switch and the room burst into brilliance. Elated, he couldn't wait to see those beautiful baby blues and that one of a kind, brighten the world smile. There were a million things he wanted to tell her, to share with her, but most of all he just couldn't wait to squeeze her tight.

However, Ron Parks did not get that pleasure. Michelle was lying supine just the way he'd left her, motionless beneath the sheet, still asleep in that horrid cadaver-like form. She had not moved. His heart sank and he cried out in despair…" For the love of God!"

Distraught eyes searched the room, but no one was there. How could that be? Who had pushed the call button? Ron frowned. His wife had to have moved, it had to have been her. Pulling Michelle into his arms he pleaded while squeezing her tight. "Speak baby. Please talk to me!" Cradling her head against his chest he blinked at the tears filling his eyes.

This was cruel, impossible to bare. Now sobbing, he begged her to open her eyes, but his pleading fell only to the shadowy deafness of the room. It was with a loving tearful kiss to her cheek he saw them. Slowly he lowered her flaccid body back to the bed, carefully rolling her head away from him and leaning in for a closer look. On the side of her neck were two small puncture marks, blood oozing slowly from the holes. Ron blinked; confusion over taking his mind." What the hell?"

Quickly pulling a handkerchief from his pocket he applied pressure over the wound site. With his free hand noticeably shaking, he pushed the nurse's call button. What the hell was going on here?

Raising his eyes he glanced to the doorway, waiting, but no one entered. Again, he pushed the call button, then pushed it again and again and again. Where were those frigging nurses? He yelled loud enough to be heard clear to the station, "In here, 2221, HELP!" Continuing to apply pressure he waited, seething, growing impatient, but still no one responded. He knew there were three nurses on this floor and not one fucking one of them was responding.

The hallway lay a desolate dimly lit passageway. He yelled a second time, now practically screaming... "One of you, somebody, get your ass in here NOW." Nothing!Frustration pounded in his head, building to a crescendo of explosion. "Shit. Shit!"

Carefully Ron removed the handkerchief and checked the puncture site; the bleeding had stopped. He sighed. Placing the hankie beside Michelle's head he stormed to the door, glaring up and down the corridor, he saw no one. His jaws tightened.

Glancing back at his wife he took a deep breath then stormed out. If it meant searching the entire Hospital, every floor, every mother-fucking room, he'd find a Nurse or a Doctor and drag their slowpoke medical ass back to Michelle.

Ron's heart was pounding, anger had reddened his face and his blood pressure was skyrocketed. These people were supposed to be professionals, caring, driven by their compassion for others...so where the Hell were they?

He had been moving briskly toward the nurse's station when suddenly he stopped, pausing there in the dim-lighted hallway. In all his law-enforcement years, seeing all the horrible things there are to see, investigating events and oddities that could not be explained, and constantly living with the awareness that death walked beside him… waiting; he had over the years; developed a natural sense of knowing when something was not right. That feeling was stirring now, and this time it wasn't cop paranoia.

It was a feeling, perhaps a subconscious glimpse of something, a glitter, a minuscule movement, a seconds worth of sound…something!

Ron remained motionless, facing the elevators, but it was not what lay in front of him that set off this awareness, rather, someone, or something was behind him, watching.

Whatever it was, it caused the hairs on the back of his neck to rise. The strange, alarming sensation had happened before; seven years prior in an old, abandoned Louisiana Mansion-when the gates of Hell had opened, and the forces of darkness had gathered there.

Slowly he turned. There were five of them, three men and two women, all dressed in black. One in particular stood slightly in front of the others. All of them were silent, their faces sober and staring intently at him. And there was something else; the one out front with long black hair, wearing a long western style duster and black Stetson -was holding one of the Nurses; she was frightened and pale with fear.

Ron considered going for the ankle weapon strapped to his right leg, a snub-nose .38. But he waited. What it was these people wanted he did not know, but they were there for a reason, and he was somehow part of it. Fifty or sixty feet of hallway separated them. They stood directly in front of the open door to Michelle's room. There was no way of knowing if that had any significance, but he wasn't willing to take the chance; he broke the silence.

"So, what gives? Who are you and what do you want?"

The one out front holding the nurse continued to stare a moment, considering his words, then said. "We are here because we were summoned. Our purpose is to inform you the power of Hell approaches; its destination is your friend Clayton Cooper. You are not to help him. Give us your word and we will return your wife just as she was prior to the accident. Refuse and she will never again experience the wonder of consciousness. As for you, you will become a plaything to us, and trust me; that is something you do not want."

The group consisted of all young people, late twenties, or early thirties.

"Who summoned you?" Ron asked the question more as a means of stalling rather than expecting an answer. He needed a strategy, a plan, and that required time.

"I am at liberty to tell. So, tell you I shall. We were summoned by Young Cain."

Ron frowned. "Cain?"

"Cain is all I know. So, tell us, Mr. Parks, what will it be; your wife alive and well, or forever gone?"

Ron bit thoughtfully at his lip. If only they weren't standing in front of Michelle's door. He wondered if he could reach the .38 before they entered her room. Nodding: merely feeling his way, he told them.

"Of course, I want my wife back, but Clayton Cooper is my friend."

"Life, Mr. Parks," the stranger replied, "is full of choices, and you must make one now."

Ron stared at him a moment, then asked.

"What if I refuse? What if I come down there right now and kick all your black-dressed asses?"

"Because, by the time you reach us, Mr. Parks, and even if you were capable of eliminating the entire group, by the time you finished, your wife would be dead. Observe." The one speaking fell quiet; raised his head and slowly opened his mouth. Two long, canine incisors descended downward out of his gums. Despite the shadowing of his face from the Stetson, Ron could see the color of his eyes changing.

Ron's own eyes widened. What he saw were fangs, white and narrow; slightly curved inward, no doubt designed to ensure grip of the flesh. There was no time for reaction.

The frightened nurse never saw it coming. The two sharply pointed teeth came down hard, plunging painfully into the side of her neck.

In the same instant, the biter's hand clamped her mouth, reducing her agonizing scream to a mere mumbling. Blood poured down the side of her neck soaking into to her teal-green scrub-top. She struggled to pry free of the impalement, but his grip was too powerful. His eyes, now yellow, stared haughty into Ron's as he bit. Ron could hear him sucking away at the woman's life-giving blood. Gripped by a state of disbelief, Ron Parks felt helpless.

The incident lasted but a few seconds; the nurse twitched twice, then went limp. The biter released her, and the body slumped to the floor. His teeth began to recede.

Ron glanced at the lifeless form then back. "As you observed only minutes ago, Mr. Parks," the killer said, "we have already tasted your sweet, Michelle. Refuse us, and we will drain her. We are all hungry, so do not toy."

Ron shook his head, unable to say anything, disbelieving what he had just seen. His eyes moved once more to the nurse lying crumbled on the floor, blood pooling beneath her head. Looking back to the biter the only thing Ron Parks could do was to stare.

The killer wiped his lips with a finger, then sucked it free of blood. "You thought we did not exist," He laughed lightly. "They have known along time that we do, but have kept it quiet, concealed it from the world. In unspoken agreement, we have not greatly enlarged our numbers and feed discretely. Trust me Mr. Parks, we are very real."

Ron Parks had not felt such a run of fear since those days in Louisiana. He thought, had hoped, such dark things were in the past now; buried with the bodies and horror left in the wake of the capture of the Blue Eyes Killer. Apparently, they had been reawakened.

"Decide, Mr. Parks," the killer said, "Which will it be, your wife or Clayton Cooper?"

CHAPTER 5

House of Janis Barr-Lemus

Pulling his eyes from Janis, the man dressed in black glanced over his shoulder and smiled, "Ah, yes,' he said with a tepid smile, "Agent Robert Langley Lemus, serial-killer specialist, retired. It has been a long-time agent Lemus. What, five, six years?"

Lemus nodded his recognition. "Six years, three months and two days. Who authorized you to make a contact?"

"Sometimes agent Lemus," the man starring at him said, "we find it…refreshing, to step out of the box. The FBI is not the only ones who require our kind of services."

Janis's face showed her confusion. "Bob, you know these people?"

Lemus nodded. "Only him," He motioned with the barrel of his weapon toward the one out front. Lemus spoke again. "What are you doing here, Louis?"

"We have come to talk with Ms. Barr, Mrs. Lemus now; and you; to give warning. They are coming out of the darkness for Clayton Cooper, and you must not assist him. We have been hired to hunt anyone that docs."

"Bullshit." Lemus said, "You take orders from NASIF and no one else. The agency would never allow it."

The man out front nodded. "Yes, agent Lemus, most of our kind still do take orders from NASIF: however, a handful of us have formed our own business. We've become independents, businesspersons, entrepreneurs if you will."

"Entrepreneurs my retired ass. It's more like blood-sucking assassins."

Louis grinned again, "Isn't that calling the kettle black, agent Lemus. You know very well what we do for NASIF. And each time we do it they turn a blind eye?"

"That's different, we're talking National Security."

"Murder is murder, agent Lemus. When someone dies, they are dead, and dead is dead, no matter what the reason...or the how."

"That's horseshit and you know it." Bob Lemus was growing angry. "I'm telling you right now. Fade back into the shadows where you belong and leave Cooper alone. If you don't, NASIF will track you down and put an end to your sick, disgusting life."

Louis stared at Lemus a long while before speaking again. "Until you retired agent Lemus, there was only one man with the resilience to turn the hunt against us, and you're gone now. You know a great deal about us, that I admit, however, you no longer have privy to current information or access to the store. A lot has changed since you were a player."

Bob Lemus told him coldly. "I will tell you only once. Get out of this house and never come back. Whoever it was that hired you, go back and tell them you changed your mind. And you can take this to the bank; if you fuck with Clayton Cooper, you'll bring me out of retirement. You know me, Louis. You don't want that."

Louis casually pulled his stare from Bob Lemus and looked at Janis. "You have been warned." The group exited filing through the kitchen door and fading into the early morning darkness.

The teapot began to whistle. Saying nothing, Janis quietly slid the knives back into the block, poured hot water into two cups, dropped in a teabag each and handed one to her husband. "Follow me." She said.

They walked to the living room and sat on the sofa. Following a few more seconds of silence, Janis blew on her tea and asked. "Okay, you don't have to tell me if you don't want too, or can't, but I have to ask. "Who in the hell were those people?"

Lemus took a careful sip from his cup. "Are you sure you want to know?"

Janis nodded. "Of course, I'm sure. They threatened me."

"Okay," he said, "you asked. They're Vampires."

Janis remained expressionless. She blew on her tea some more and took a sip. "You know Bob, if you were anyone else and tonight hadn't happened, I'd laugh at that. But okay, for right now I'll accept it. Next question, what is NASIF?"

Bob pressed his lips together thoughtfully. "Now that's something I really can't tell you."

Janis batted her eyes playfully, pretending to pout, "Please Bobby. I'll keep it secret; I promise." She raised her right hand "I swear by girl Gumshoe honor."

He smiled at her, "Okay, I'll tell, but not because I trust you, because I won't get any sugar for a month if I refuse."

Janis took another sip, hiding her grin.

"NASIF stands for National American Security Internal Force."

"Never heard of it. What's the purpose?"

"They investigate things of the paranormal."

"Like ghosts and flying saucers?" Janis asked.

Lemus nodded, "Right! Ghosts, UFOs and anything else that can't be explained; but might be a threat to national security."

Janis dabbed her teabag a few times. "Okay," she nodded thoughtfully, "so Vampires really exist, and they work for this NASIF? As assassins, I gather?"

Lemus nodded, "A handful do, yes. And in exchange for their services, they have been left alone with the understanding they are limited to two children per family and can only kill NASIF targets."

"How many of these freakies are out there?"

Lemus puffed his cheeks thoughtfully, "Oh, fifty-thousand, give or take."

Janis frowned. "How do they feed? They do drink blood?"

"Yes. They obtain blood two ways: through secret federally funded blood-banks, or, they feed on Hucs, *Human uncomplaining collaborators*; people who agree to give or sell to them their blood, via blood-draw or actual biting. Biting pays more."

"Holy, Crapola!" Janis said, "Do these things ever attack just to drink blood, like Count Dracula?"

Bob shrugged. "Every now and then one will stray. But they have their own police force. So, when it happens, we assist them in eliminating the perp then cover it up."

Janis took a sip. "I don't understand how they've been kept secret? If the world got wind of these things, there would be global panic. And worse, what if they're secretly multiplying, growing an Army?"

Bob sighed. "It would be chaos I know. But they're watched."

Janis made a thoughtful face, "You know Bob," she added following a sip of tea, "all this put aside I am worried for Clay and Nancy Cooper. Secret or not, we need to pay them a visit and give a heads up…if it's not already too late."

Bob sighed rising from the couch. "Absolutely sweetie, but it can't be discussed over a phone. And as much as I hate the thought, first I need to fly to Nebraska and visit with the blue-eyed devil. Despite his being locked down tight on death-row, he's somehow behind all this. Would you call the airline and arrange for a ticket and car rental while I shower?"

Janis dunked her tea bag a few times and took a sip. "Sure. And when I'm finished, I'll join you in the shower. Will you wash my back?" She was batting her eyes again.

Bob looked at her. "Jan, are you sure you understand the gravity of what is happening here?"

"Yes, I do, Bob." She cooed.

He stared several moments then handed her his cup. "Well okay than. I will wash your back; every beautiful inch of it."

CHAPTER 6

Lafayette City Hospital

Thoughts were running wild through Ron Parks' head. What to do? Were all the others in the group like this deviant, bastard? There were two unaccounted for Nurses; had they been killed in the same way? And how badly had they already hurt Michelle? Also, within the turbulent swirl of questions, Ron wondered of Clay; were the same kind of - whatever these people were - at his house as well?

Ron was confident the .38 would drop two of the five before they scattered; the problem was, would the remaining three make it into Michelle's room before he reached the door.

Ron stared at them with intensity, trying to make sense of what was happening. He had never before seen anything like the teeth that descended from the mouth of the one dressed like Marlboro man.

Ron was a veteran Indiana State Police Officer. If Vampires existed, he would have been informed. Whatever their origin, these people, things, were not human, at least not entirely. And if he had learned nothing else seven years ago in Louisiana; he had come to realize the things of the dark, those beings not of flesh and blood were virtually unstoppable by conventional means, no police force or military in the world, regardless how elite, could stop them. The battle with unearthly evil could be won by one weapon alone, and that weapon was the power of God.

To Ron it was spontaneous; a plan had formed. Dropping to his right knee, he pulled the .38 firing from that position. The killer of the nurse and a man standing just behind and slightly to the right, staggered backward through the others, falling to the tiled floor. The remaining three dashed into Michelle's room before Ron could get off a third shot.

Scrambling to his feet, he sprinted the sixty-foot stretch of hallway leading to what he hoped would be the rescue of his beloved Michelle. At the door he pressed his back to the wall left of the jam, took a deep breath, then charged into the room ready to fire. The Adrenalin rush was short lived.

At the end of the room, the large window stood shattered, sharp jagged fragments outlining its frame. Frigid winter air was howling and whipping the curtains. Michelle's bed was empty; she was gone along with the others.

Cursing, Ron charged the window and looked out. The cold nipped at his face. It was beginning to snow. Leaning out he looked to the left, right, then up and down. Nothing! Room 2221 was two stories up, one hell of a jump; yet no one was in sight.

Ron shouted Michelle's name into the howling wind, tears filling his eyes. And out in the hallway, although he could not see, did not care to see; the two men he had just shot; were also gone.

CHAPTER 7

Nebraska High Security Prison
Death row, cell 10

Saturday 21st
10:22 am

Bob Lemus, bordered by two guards armed with raised shotguns, stood ready while a third unlocked the thick iron door. Blue Eyes stood at the back of the room as was customary. Since the start of his incarceration only his wife and son had come to visit, so although he had no idea who he was about to meet, he found himself excited.

The door opened and Bob entered, "How are you Blue?" He said.

Blue Eyes could not stop the smile, "Agent Bob Lemus, you old son-of-a-gun, how have you been?"

"I've been Fine."

"How's that ulcer?"

"All healed up, thank you."

"Good. Glad to hear it. And how are Clay, Nancy, Ron and Michelle?"

"Three fine, one not so fine." Lemus told him.

"Oh," the killer expressed with furrowed eyebrows, "and who is it that is not doing so well?"

"Michelle Parks. Someone drugged and raped her."

"Oh goodness, that wasn't very nice now was it? And what about that cute little blond investigator, Janis?"

"Fine as well. Said to tell you she recommends the fried chicken for your last meal."

Blue Eyes took six steps stopping directly in front of Lemus. Leaning forward he sniffed softly. Then straightening, stuck his hands into the pockets of his coveralls and smiled. "Yes, I suspect she is doing fine. I can smell her on you. So how long have you been fucking her?"

Lemus ignored the remark. "I came to talk about Clayton Cooper."

"Oh. And what about my favorite Town Marshall, is something wrong?"

"There is and you know it. I want you to leave him alone. Call off the evil henchmen."

Blue Eyes faked a frown. "What do you mean?"

"I mean the Vamps. They have already visited me, and I know all about the things crawling out of hell again. Somehow, you're behind it all and I want you to end it."

"Bob," Blue Eyes said pulling his hands from his pockets and gesturing, "how could I possibly do anything from in here. Other than my wife and son, I haven't seen nor spoken to a visitor in seven years."

"I don't know how you're doing it, but you are." Lemus argued.

Blue Eyes folded his arms, "Well Bob, in just a few days you'll not have to worry about it any longer. I'll be dead and buried, gone, kaput, stiff, lifeless, bloodless, embalmed…"

"Knock off the shit-filled theatrics, Blue. Are you going to leave him alone or not?"

Blue eyes grinned again, "Are you asking, pleading, or ordering, Bob?"

"I'm telling. You allow one hair on his head to be harmed and -"

"And what, Bob? What can you possibly do to a man who is going to be dead in just a few short days?" Following a short pause of silence and cold stares, Blue Eyes walked to the bed and sat. Gesturing his hand toward the chair at his desk he said calmly, "Please Bob, sit."

Lemus pulled out the chair and lowered himself into it. He was angry with himself for losing his temper. Calming his voice, he said, "Look, like you said, you're going to be dead soon, anyway. Why can't you let it go?"

"Because Bob, seven years ago I warned Marshall Cooper, if he did not perform the simple ceremony as I requested, hell itself would come against him. Well, obviously he did not do as I said. So consequently, he will now reap his due reward. The doors have opened, and I will not stop it."

Lemus stared hard saying nothing. Then rose and walked to the door where he tapped three times on the little round peephole. Beyond the door, an officer nodded, and keys began to jingle. Lemus turned and looked back to Blue Eyes, "You know Blue," he said, "in my career I've learned to play hardball with the best. You were at the top of that list. But understand this, anything happens to Cooper, and I will take a personal interest in your son."

Blue Eyes rose slowly from the bed. "That agent Lemus, is something you had better never do."

The door swung open, and the two guards stood with shotguns raised, but before exiting Lemus glanced over his shoulder with a smile, "are you asking, pleading or ordering, Blue?"

CHAPTER 8

**Clay & Nancy Cooper's Home
Brooke Indiana**

**December 23
2:15 pm**

When the doorbell rang Clay was in the basement working on the dryer–the machine had quit producing heat and he had it torn apart. Nancy was vacuuming so neither heard the bell ring.

Outside, the winter day was unseasonably rare. A light snow was falling, the sun was shining, and white-fluffed clouds sat amid a crisp cerulean sky. Staring up into the cascading flakes Janis smiled. "Isn't it a gorgeous day, Bob?"

"Lemus glanced up for a moment then back to the door. "Yes, but I'll take the tropics." He pushed the bell again looking at Janis, "apparently they're not home."

Peering through the window beside the entrance-way and seeing no one she told Bob, "Try the door, handsome, maybe it's unlocked."

He tried. "Locked."

"Let's go around back." Janis suggested.

Bob frowned, "The snow has to be a foot deep back there."

Janis kissed him on the cheek. "We want the glass half-full, Bob, not half-empty. If they're not home, we'll build a snowwoman."

Still frowning Bob followed her around the house. At the door he grumbled, "Damn it Janis, I hate wet feet."

Glancing over her shoulder she smiled, "Well I don't hear you complaining when that other foot of yours is getting wet."

"Of course not," he told her, "That one stays warm."

Grinning to herself she tried the door, and it was unlocked. Both stepped into the kitchen. "This feels much better." Bob said, tapping snow from his shoes.

They could hear a vacuum running so Janis shouted. "Hello." Immediately the machine began whining down. Janis yelled again. "We're in the kitchen."

When Nancy rounded the corner, she yelled out in happy surprise, "Oh my God!" Immediately the two women embraced, then Nancy hugged Bob. "What in the world are you two doing here? Why didn't you call? Did you fly in; we'd have gladly picked you up at the airport."

"We know you would have," Janis said, "but we wanted to surprise you. When you didn't answer the door, we walked around back and came in. I hope it's okay."

"Absolutely," Nancy said, "you two are family. Listen, Clay's in the basement working on the dryer. Why don't you give me your coats and relax in the living room. I'll go get him. He'll flip when he sees you two."

When Nancy was gone, Bob and Janis settled on the sofa admiring the six foot beautifully decorated Douglas fur sitting in front of the bay window. "Now that's a Christmas Tree, Bob." Janis said.

Dozens of presents lay stacked beneath it and Janis squeezed Bob's hand, ""you know, I remember as a kid how Christmas was at our house. So beautifully decorated and full of colors and life." Pausing she took a deep breath then turned to Bob, "ya know, maybe it's time we think about a baby."

Bob rested his arm across the top of the sofa behind her. "A baby?"

"Yes, a baby! "Janis said.

"You are referring to one of those little things that cry, get sick all the time and poop and pee all over you. Am I right?"

"Yes, you are. And I don't mind if it's a girl or a boy."

Bob glanced away thinking. Janis felt a twinge of nervousness.

Several seconds passed and Bob finally turned back to her. His face was expressionless. The two stared. Then a small smile showed at the corners of his mouth," Jan," he said, "I think it's a wonderful idea."

Janis almost shouted loud enough to be heard throughout the house, "Yeah!" Kissing Bob on the cheek she said with a great big smile, "I love you, Bob Lemus. And as soon as we get back to the Hotel, I just may let you start working on the creation process."

Bob nodded his approval, "Yes. Absolutely. I know this is very important to you, so you have my word, we will work on that process every chance we get."

The voice came from behind, "Hi."

Their eyes shifted forward where a small boy rounded the end of the sofa stopping in front of them. Offering his hand to Bob he said, "I'm Michael."

Lemus took his little hand, "I'm Bob."

The youngster than shook Janis's hand. She smiled and he smiled back; dimples showing. Studying the youngster's features; Janis' thought there was no denying he was the perfect mix of his mom and dad, with his dad's wavy auburn hair and boldness, his mom's blue eyes and polite, open personality. "Are you friends of Mom and Dad?" He asked releasing Janis's hand.

Bob nodded. "Yes, for several years, ever since your mom found out she was going to have you."

"I don't believe it!" Clay entered the room with Nancy beside him.

Bob and Janis rose from the sofa gazing into the face of Clayton Cooper for the first time in seven years. Clay hugged them both, squeezing tightly. "It is so great to see you guys." He said stepping back and looking them over. "You two haven't changed a bit." Are you working a case together?"

"Sort of," Lemus told him glancing at Janis than back.

"Well sit back down and relax." Clay said excited. He couldn't stop smiling. "I just can't believe this," he said lowering himself into his recliner, "Bob Lemus and Janis Barr. Wow."

Janis and Bob glanced at one another, "Actually," Janis said, "its Bob and Janis Barr-Lemus now," Clay's expression showed the shock as Janis added, "No big deal, I just felt sorry for him after he retired, so I agreed to marry him." She did her level best to try and look serious.

Clay and Nancy sat speechless; their mouths open with happy surprise. Finally, able to form words they said it together in perfect harmony, "Well congratulations" Clay added teasingly "you know we must have lost the invitation, because you two sure as heck would have invited *us* to the wedding."

"Actually," Bob said on a serious note, "we were married in a quiet, private ceremony. I don't want it to sound sleazy, but we tied the knot in Vegas five years ago."

"And just for the record," Janis interjected, "we were both sober at the time."

Nancy laughed, "Well it really doesn't matter where you say, 'I do'. Love is love and it's the most beautiful thing in the world," she pretended a sober look, "hey, wait a minute, you two crazy kids *didn't have to* get married, did you?"

Bob nodded with a sigh, "Truthfully Nancy, yes we did." Nancy had made the remark kidding and now she flushed with embarrassment. She and Clay both stared at Bob as he turned to look at Janis, "It was definitely a have to marriage. It was a matter of making Janis Barr, Janis Barr-Lemus, or my dying of a lonely heart."

Janis squeezed his hand. "Thank you, Bob, that was so sweet. She kissed his cheek and told Clay and Nancy, "You remember Bob from the old days? Well, he's growing up, learning to keep the glass half-full now."

Following a time of catching up Bob took advantage of a lull and glanced worriedly at Janis. He was dreading what had to be said but knew a moment could not be wasted. "Look Clay," he began, "I know we haven't seen one another for years, and I realize its Christmas, but we're here on business…involving you. It's happening again."

"What is?" Clay asked, although deep inside he feared he knew what the answer would be. Glancing at Michael, Bob smiled warmly. "Michael, would you mind if the four grown-ups talked privately for a few minutes?"

The boy looked at his parents and they nodded their agreement. "Sure." Michael said. He smiled at Bob and Janis "Nice to meet you." Then left the room.

Clay turned to Bob. "So, what are you talking about?"

"I'm talking about Blue Eyes. I'm talking about Hell and Demons; the whole shooting match all over again…only this time it's going to be worse."

Clay frowned, his face strained. "What do you mean? Blue Eyes is sitting on death-row?"

"Yes, he is Clay, and will fry in just a few days."

"Then what the hell are you talking about?"

"We don't know how he's done it, but they are coming after you."

Clay glanced worryingly at Nancy than back to Lemus, "It can't be. He's locked away."

"Somehow Clay," Bob said with frustration, "Blue Eyes has opened the gates and let them out again."

Staring long into Bob Lemus's face, Clay's mind regressed. Once again as if it were seven years ago; with his shoulders clutched within the claws of a winged demon flying him over Hell's sea of fire, its towering flames lapping inches beneath his feet and hearing the screams of lost souls, millions upon millions, all blind and wandering, feeling their way, begging deliverance from a place impossible to comprehend with the human mind. And worse, he could recall the horrid stench of sulfur and burning flesh.

Oblivious to the growing concern of those around him, Clay, just as he had seven years prior, began to cry.

CHAPTER 9

Michelle's eyelids fluttered as consciousness found its way back. Following a deep breath, her eyes opened. Clad in bra and panties, she lay atop the covers of an old sleigh-style bed. Emitting from an oil lamp dull light cocooned the room in gloomy, semi-transparent shadows.

Pale and weak, Michelle glanced arduously about. The lamp sat beyond the foot of the bed atop an aged dresser. To its right stood a towering wooden door. She could hear no sound coming in from beyond it. A frown garnished her face.

Left of the bed a narrow-elongated window framed a full moon and bright cluster of stars. She closed her eyes than opened them again asking herself, *where am I?*

Refocusing, she struggled to recall events leading up to now. Her head swam with dizziness, her thoughts foggy. She had been shopping at the mall. While returning to her car she was abducted and forced into a Black Van consisting of four assailants. She had resisted, fighting fiercely, managing to bloody one nose, and leave the impression of her latest dental work on the arm of another.

Michelle began to cry. She couldn't help it. Tears welled in her eyes, pooling and cascading down the side of her face. She wanted to go home, to escape the rest of the memory, but her mind kept it alive, reminding her of its horror and humiliation; first one man than the other, than a switch with the driver, the laughter, the cruelty. Had it not been for the mercy of the drug they injected into her body, she would have died of the pain and disgrace.

Sniffling, Michelle knew she needed to get control. She grew angry, more over lack of self-control than having been raped. She was stronger than that and yelled at her thoughts, "Shut up Mic, at least you're still alive. And it you're alive there's hope."

Refocusing, she once again scanned the surroundings. The walls, ceiling and floor consisted of huge block stone. The room was not large, ten feet by twelve maybe. An old English style padded chair and small bedside table to her right made up its remaining contents.

She had to get to the door. It was the one and only way out. She made an attempt to sit up but found it impossible. Her right wrist, right side of her neck and inside of her left upper arm felt as if they were burning. And she simply had no strength; why? The only thing able to move without effort seemed to be her eyes, and to a small degree her hands. The rest of her was there, she could feel everything, the remaining parts just wouldn't cooperate. She blinked and it hit home. *Anemic! I'm anemic. Why?*

Closing her eyes, Michelle took a deep breath. *Mic, you have to get out of here.* She attempted to lift her right arm. It came off the bed, but only an inch before dropping back to the mattress. No strength, her body felt void of muscle. She wiggled her toes and fingers. They worked. Closing her eyes, she tried again. Again, her arm lifted but quickly slammed the mattress. It was then the door opened.

Someone entered holding a candelabrum. Shadowed behind it, a dark, shapeless form seemed to be floating toward where she lay. At the bedside, who or whatever it was, set the twinkling light on the small table. The area beside the bed brightened and the carrier straightened.

Michelle's head turned slowly, and she got a clear look at her visitor; a young girl, twenty-five maybe, in a long black dress. She was pretty, her hair long and dark. The girl smiled pleasantly and spoke with gentleness. "It's so nice to see you're awake, Michelle."

"You know who I am?" Michelle asked.

The young woman nodded. "Oh yes. All of us do."

"Where am I?"

Ignoring the question, the young girl sat on the edge of the bed. "You may call me Carla."

"Where am I, Carla?"

"Sorry Michelle, I am not allowed to answer any questions. I have come only to piecemeal."

"What?"

"To piecemeal; to feed…but only a little."

Michelle looked at her, wide-eyed.

Smiling warmly, the young girl stroked Michelle's hair. "You're very beautiful, do you know that?I've asked if I can have you, but they've told me no; at least not yet anyway."

Michelle stared at her trying to make sense of what was happening. Finally, she asked."I'm at a loss here, Carla. What are you talking about?"

Again, ignoring the question, Carla stroked Michelle's cheek with the side of her hand, then ran a finger along her neck, zigzagged down her upper chest, over her soft Blue Padded T-Shirt Bra covering her left breast and down to her abdomen. She did not stop there; her finger glided slowly over Michelle's silk blue panties coming to rest on her left inner thigh. "What I'm talking about," Carla whispered while gently kneading the soft flesh, "is desire."

Michelle wanted to get up, to run from her, but she had no strength, no power. Carla laid both her hands on the tender skin of Michelle's thigh and rolled it gently so the inside of it was facing up. She then lowered her face and kissed the flesh tenderly. "You have such beautiful skin."

It was at that point Michelle, in terror, watched two long, sharp pointed teeth begin protruding downward from Carla's mouth. They extended until hanging like two white, slightly bent spikes. Her eyes metamorphosed, fading to yellow, the pupils constricting to tiny, pin-point dots.

The young girl dressed in black hissed, then plunged her narrow-spiked teeth into Michelle Parks' femoral artery. Michelle screamed at the pain; and far away, in Indiana, Ron Parks heard that scream in his heart.

CHAPTER 10

Cooper House

December 24
Christmas Eve

Nancy had gone all out for Christmas Eve dinner. Between her interruptions by pleasant chats with houseguests, she spent the day in the kitchen singing and whistling Christmas songs. She baked a Ham and Turkey, cooked homemade as well as stove-top dressing, made mashed potatoes and gravy, sweet potatoes, opened cranberries and corn, green beans and asparagus. And on the kitchen's long tiled counter sat a mouthwatering assortment of deserts. The Cooper house was as filled with noisy conversations and cheerful Christmas music, as it was with delicious aromas.

Guests included both Clay and Nancy's parents. Even Ron and the kids had come, although it had taken much prompting to get them to accept. Since Michelle's disappearance two days prior, Ron had spent every possible minute with Michelle and at headquarters combing through files and reopening cold cases.

Clay's deputy, Carl, his wife Sara and their fifteen-year-old twin girls, Lacy and Lynn were also there. Special guests, however, were Janis and Bob Lemus.

Clay and Nancy had persuaded the two to stay, ensuring them they were no imposition. Knowing the gravity of what was coming, Bob and Janis accepted, wanting more time to sit and talk anyway.

Dinner was served promptly at 6:30. The table required both leaves to accommodate the seating. Near his chair at the head of the table, Clay had set up a card table upon which Nancy set most of the bowls of food. With everyone seated, Clay asked that they give thanks. He asked Michael to do the honors and the boy accepted with a warm smile. Glancing about the table the youngster asked that everyone join hands and bow their head. When all eyes were closed and hands together, he began his prayer.

"We thank you Father in heaven for the food you have provided. We thank you for this special gathering of family and friends. And we remember with appreciation the reason we have gathered; to celebrate the birth of your son, our savior. We thank you for all you have done and pray you keep us safe. Amen.

Heads came up smiling, impressed by the eloquence with which the seven-year-old had prayed.

Clay began the happy chore of passing dishes around the table, moving counterclockwise. Serving spoons tapped against dishes, ice rattled in glasses, smiles flowed as smoothly as the tea and milk from their pitchers; and except for Ron Parks, chatter highlighted eager appetites.

Conversations varied until midway through dinner when Janis asked Michael what grade he was in.

"Academically, I'm in the eighth grade, but by my age I'm in third. That's because I'm home-schooled."

Janis smiled with admiration. "Wow. And what do you plan to be when you grow up, a rocket scientist?"

The seven-year-old took a drink of milk following a swipe with his napkin "I'm going to be a Pastor." Everyone paused to glance at the boy; each thinking the same; most seven-year-old boys want to be Firefighters, Policeman, or Soldiers.

"Really," Janis said surprised, "a Pastor. How wonderful. And what faith will you be?" She asked.

"It'll be Nondenominational." Michael told her matter-of-factually.

"Nondenominational," Janis said, "that's a pretty big word. Can you tell me what it means?"

The young boy looked surprised. "Yes, of course."

Janis glanced musingly at Michael's parents then back. "Okay," she said holding back her smile. "I have to ask, why will your church be nondenominational?"

"Well, I feel," Michael said, "to many of the other Churches have turned into boxes."

"Boxes?" Janis asked.

Michael took another drink of milk, another dab with his napkin. "As you know there are many different kinds of denominations." Janis nodded, he continued, "To name a few, Baptists, Catholics, Methodists, Christian Science, Assembly of God, Lutheran, Latter-day Saints; and others."

Janis made a thoughtful face. "So… you're referring to different denominations as boxes?"

"Sort of," Michael said, "you see, the different denominations sometimes perceive some scripture in their own personal way."

"But isn't that a good thing," Janis said quickly, "a variety of denominations, a variety of choices for the people. You know, different strokes for different folks. In the end, what really counts is that they believe in God, don't you agree?" Janis couldn't believe she was talking to a seven-year-old.

"Sort of," Michael shrugged, "do you read the Bible, Mrs. Lemus?"

Janis flushed. She hadn't been asked that question for some time. "Yes." She said, glancing once again to Clay and Nancy then back to the boy. "I read it, but probably not as much as I should."

Nancy interrupted, "Michael, I think we've talked long enough about religion."

Janis raised her hand, forcing a smile. "No, it's fine Nancy. I'm enjoying this."

"Okay," Nancy grinned back, "but I warn you, he's aggressive."

Janis winked. "Aggressive people are my specialty."

"I'm sorry if I embarrassed you." Michael apologized.

"You didn't Michael." Janis said turning once again to the boy. "Let's get back to the Bible. I really do read it from time to time."

"Great. Do you go to church?"

"You bet, Mass every weekend."

"And on a scale of one to ten, Mrs. Lemus, how would you rate your faith and trust in God, one being very little and ten a whole lot."

Janis flushed again. "Well…I don't know…a six or seven I guess."

Michael smiled for the first time. "If guessing, I'd say you're Catholic."

Janis was beginning to think Michael Cooper was a small version of a Secret Service Interrogator. "Yes," Janis said, "I am Catholic. Does that matter?

" No, not at all. Faith is simply a matter of believing in God."

Janis smiled somehow feeling a touch of relief. "Well, I believe in God for sure, so I guess I'll be going to Heaven."

"Actually" Michael replied, "the Bible tells us even Demons believe in God. Do you think they're going to Heaven?"

Janis thought to herself, *forget the Secret Service. This is Jesus himself come back as a little boy.* "No, Michael, I don't believe they will go to Heaven."

"Wonderful Mrs. Lemus," he said, "you have just discovered one of the many treasures buried in the pages of the Bible; that there is a big difference between believing and having faith."

Janis glanced at Nancy with raised eyebrows. "I told you so." Nancy said with a grin.

"May I tell you one of my favorite Bible verses, Mrs. Lemus?" Michael asked.

Janis nodded still surprised, "Yes, of course. Please do."

"After I tell you," Michael said with a smile, "I promise I'll try and say no more. It's a verse from the Book of James."

Janis stared dumbfounded at the little fellow sitting across from her; *Book of James, Demons, Nondenominational, faith, belief; so many adult words! Michael Cooper…*she said to herself, *who in the heck are you?*

"The verse Mrs. Lemus," Michael began, "is chapter two, verse seventeen. Promise me you'll think about the words after I tell you?"

Janis could only nod.

Michael quoted the verse without flaw, and everyone listened. *"Thus, also faith by its-self, if it does not have works, is dead."* For several seconds those sitting at the table remained stunned as if caught up in suspended animation, and this time all were thinking the same thing… who is this kid?

Out in the living room Dean Martin was crooning 'Let it Snow' from one of his Christmas CD's. The colored lights from the tree were blinking with a soothing softness, their glitter reflecting mellow in the glass of the large bay window. And on the other side of that window, beneath a steady cascade of falling snow, a horde of football-sized demons stood looking in.

CHAPTER 11

Tecumseh State Correctional Institution
Nebraska

Christmas Eve

Billy James walked into the communications center at 11:20 pm. A black leather sport bag hung over his shoulder, and he smiled at the guard he was to relieve.

"You ready to go home and set out cookies for Santa."

Officer Roger Pines returned the smile. "You bet, Sarge."

"Everything quiet?"

"Yep, hardly anybody here."

"That's why I love holidays." Billy replied.

Pines left his chair and Billy replaced him, setting the sport bag next to his feet. He scanned the monitors then turned to wish Pines a Merry Christmas. Pines returned the salutation and hurried away.

After making a fresh pot of coffee, Billy returned to his chair and watched monitors while it brewed. Of all the holidays to work, Christmas Eve had always been his favorite; a skeletal crew covered the prison, and he often became the highest-ranking officer within the complex.

Turning in his chair, Billy caught his reflection in one of the monitor screens. Pausing he studied the face staring back. This person was not the Billy James he once knew, once was, and it perplexed him. He still respected the law, loved his shield; and even now, twenty years later, he still enjoyed his job. Yet, he was about to do something unspeakable, unforgiving. Slumping back in his chair he made a soft sigh of frustration.

It felt as if his mind were imploding, twisting and bending, entangling right with wrong, turning everything upside down and painting it gray. Morality and sinning had begun to feel almost equal in their value. Billy shook his head and ran clammy fingers through his hair.

Rising from his squeaky chair, he trudged to the coffee pot and filled his cup then returned. He took a sip closing his eyes, savoring the warmth. It went down smooth. With reluctance, he opened his eyes and stared again at the man he once knew. "Billy James, Billy James, Billy James, he told himself, what the hell are you about to do?"

The monitors remained a wall of inanimate objects, hardly any movement anywhere throughout the complex. The hours crawled past, one slow, agonizing tick of the clock after another. Halfway through his ninth cup of coffee, 2:00 am struck. *It was time!*

Billy activated the camera to cell 10 as emotions knotted his stomach. For the first time since the incarceration of the prisoner known as Blue Eyes, Billy was about to meet him personally.

The camera brought cell ten into view. Blue Eyes was sitting at his desk reading. Several seconds passed before he laid the book down and looked up into the camera. He smiled. "And how are you doing this early Christmas morning, Billy?"

Billy hit a switch disabling the recorder to the communication's center. He wanted none of their conversation taped. Pushing the speaker button with a sweaty finger he said, "I'm fine, thanks."

"Wonderful." Blue Eyes said calmly. "And did you bring me a gift?"

Billy's finger remained on the speaker button, but he did not push it. Strain twisted his face. Nicole had assured him her husband had very willingly agreed to pay ten million dollars and safe passage out of the country - and give up his wife. All in exchange for helping him escape.

Billy took a deep breath and moved his mouth close to the microphone. "Yes sir. I bought you a gift."

CHAPTER 12

Tecumseh State Correctional Institute
FREEDOM

Outside the prison walls for the first time in seven years, the prison's most infamous death-row inmate breathed deeply, taking in the feel of the crisp winter air.

Daunting security lights caused the thick ice-covered concertina-wire to shimmer. The uninhabited parking lot in which he was standing – free - lay draped in a patchwork of dark and light shadows. The huge prison complex glowed with intensity, and he studied the amalgamation with wonder, imagining it a Great European Cruise Ship moored at some exotic port of call. Ah, he thought, the flavor of freedom! So delightfully delicious.

Feeling tingly, he pulled his eyes to the distant-muted tower and smiled for the guards he knew were watching. Rendering a smart salute he whispered, "au revoir" then climbed into the SUV and nodded to Billy. They pulled away with hard-packed snow crunching loud beneath the tires.

Staring into the side mirror the death-row killer watched as the sleeping prison shrunk slowly into oblivion. In a strange way, he was going to miss the place: it had been home for so long.

Darkness swallowed its last speck of light, and he pulled his eyes musingly from the mirror. While the Penal Complex had been a home in Hell, it certainly had not been the Hell Clayton Cooper would soon be sending him too. That Hell would be a sweet netherworld, his netherworld.

Ecstatic in his thoughts, Blue Eyes tugged playfully at his seatbelt. He could hardly wait. His soul would soar like a prized Raven into that dark Abyss, gliding with ease high above the great pit and over the towering flames, over the millions of lost souls endlessly burning in agony, screaming, their pain unbearable; an insufferable agony from which they would never know relief. He started to laugh but stopped himself; instead, he settled with a smile.

Closing his eyes, he envisioned his flight's end, landing amid the Cabrera surrounding the throne of his king and God, Satin.Kneeling there before him, watching as the mighty Prince of Darkness rose, approaching with his Dwarvan style Battle Sword, and feeling its weight laid upon his shoulder as the dark King Knighted him; he would become supreme Ruler of the Incubus, a General in the Evil opposing Army of The God of Christians. He could hear the cheers rising from the dark assembly.

Wind suddenly gusted rocking the SUV. The smile slowly faded and Blue Eyes took a deep breath whispering, *this time Clay there will be no mistakes.*

They turned onto the highway and Blue Eyes adjusted the rear-view mirror to stare at himself. "You know I like this look, Billy," he said, "the feel of being a Law-Enforcement Officer; the respect and authority that comes with it. Those guards watched us walk right out the door, no questions asked, all wishing us a Merry Christmas." Blue Eyes turned the mirror back, "of course that shouldn't surprise me. I do look dapper in uniform." Shifting his eyes to Billy, he quipped, "Don't you agree?"

Billy glanced at the man wearing his uniform, the man who had just turned his world inside out. "Yes," Billy said forcing a smile. "You look good." Hesitating a moment, Billy added nervously, "Everything is ready, right: the plane, the briefcase with the money, safe refueling stops all the way to Switzerland."

"Rest easy, Billy," Blues Eyes assured him, "I have everything taken care of. Soon you won't have a worry in the world. The plane is waiting as I speak, and Nicole as well I might add." Blue Eyes grinned, "your Nicole now.And remember, as far as the prison is concerned, you're going home sick. Your replacement is simply going to see a lump beneath the covers when he views my room. Blue Eyes patted his shoulder, "So relax. Within the hour you'll be flying free over the Canadian Rockies."

The SUV headlights cut through the cold darkness like long cylindrical lasers. To the East, crimson had begun to bleed through the dark sky and a light snow had begun to fall. Billy James' grip on the wheel had turned his knuckles white. Shift change at the prison would take place in less than two hours, and he wished the time frame was longer.

Occasionally the vehicle would slip on a patch of ice and Billy cursed quietly to himself each time it happened. The very thought of sliding into a snowbank terrified him. If he were arrested now, he'd be locked away the rest of his life.

"Don't you just love the winter season, Billy?" Blue Eyes asked joyous.

Billy didn't reply. His mind was mulling over all the things that could go wrong between the state of Nebraska and the country of Switzerland. Empathetic to Billy's concerns, Blue Eyes choose to remain quiet the remainder of the trip, respecting the man's fears. Billy had risked all to help him gain his freedom. Now, because of those efforts, Clayton Cooper would soon be sending him soaring into the bowls of Hell with the honors of a lifetime. All was good again.

By the time daylight had filtered in enough to illuminate the world around him, it was snowing hard. Through the cascading flakes, Billy pushed cautious and steady toward the airport, always watchful of the speedometer and rear-view mirror. As he drove, his heart addressed and readdressed the impact of what he had done, but always it came back to the same thing, right or wrong, ten million dollars and the rest of his life with Nicole made it all worthwhile.

At the airport, they parked the Van inside a hanger and boarded a private jet waiting out front. Billy was relieved but not ready to relax. Nicole was waiting inside the door and Blue Eyes kissed her quickly on the cheek than smiled as little Cain came running down the narrow isle smiling back.

Billy James climbed the aluminum steps, stooped through the doorway where Nicole smiled and kissed him passionately. She took him by the hand and led him to seats in the tail.

Billy noted three other people: the pilot and co-pilot sitting in the cockpit running a series of checks, and a young blond-haired male in a swallow-tail tux, who stood ready to be called to service.

Blue Eyes and Cain took seats across the aisle from Billy and Nicole and strapped in. The pilots completed their routine checks, and the aircraft began taxing to the end of the runway. Snow was still falling but to Billy's relief, it had not prevented their takeoff.

At the end of the runway the engines revved, the jet shook noticeably and, in an instant, they were being pinned against their seats racing forward. The aircraft lifted and they were on their way; Billy closed his eyes and sighed. At ten thousand feet, the pilot turned north flying toward Canadian airspace. At fourteen thousand feet, he leveled out and everyone unbuckled.

Blue Eyes grinned for Billy. "Fill better?"

Billy nodded. "Oh yeah, this is one hell of a career change."

"Well, it's one I appreciate."Blue Eyes sat back and relaxed asking, "So what do you think of my little airplane, Billy?"

Looking around, Billy James nodded approvingly. "Nice."

"She's a Gulf-Stream VSP. This lady can fly over six-thousand nautical miles before refueling, cruising at a speed of 560 mile per hour." Motioning to the young waiter, Blue Eyes ordered three glasses of Champagne and a Mountain Due.

Nodding politely, the attendant disappeared into a small galley located behind the cockpit."So, tell me Billy," Blue Eyes asked, "how persuasive was my wife in convincing you to help me?" Uncomfortable with the question, Billy glanced at Nicole then back. "She did a nice job convincing me, she's a great girl, and ten million is a lot of motivation."

Blue Eyes laughed, "Yes, it is, but you've earned your reward."

The attendant returned with a tray holding three glasses of wine. First, he served Nicole and Billy, then Blue Eyes and little Cain. Lifting his glass Blue Eyes proposed a toast, "To our freedom," The three tapped glasses and drank.

Blue Eyes glanced at his watch. "I'd say right about now we're directly over the Canadian Rockies. The attendant refilled their glasses. "Billy," Blue Eyes asked, "Have you ever jumped from an aircraft?"

This was another question that took Billy by surprise. He looked at Nicole, as if expecting an explanation of why he would ask such a question, but her expression remained dispassionate. Shrugging he turned his thoughtful look to Blue Eyes, "No, not really. I considered joining the Army once and becoming an Airborne Ranger, but it never happened."

"It's a thrill, Blue Eyes said, "makes you feel indescribably free, like an Eagle soaring through the clouds. I've made well over a hundred jumps; each as thrilling as the other."

Billy frowned, "To each his own. I see jumping out of a perfectly running aircraft much like a firefighter rushing into a burning house when everyone else is running out."

Blue Eyes smiled thoughtfully, "Yes, I guess there is some truth to that. But borrowing from an old cliche, "you shouldn't knock it until you've tried it."

Billy gave a silent nod then paused, shaking his head. He blinked his eyes repeatedly, suddenly feeling as if the glass of wine in his hand were his twentieth and not his second. Glancing from Blue Eyes to Nicole, he saw her gazing face blurring in and out of focus.

It was at that moment he realized what he had done. His involvement in freeing this killer was going to cost him everything. There was to be no ten million dollars, no happy life in Switzerland with Nicole, there would be no more life period. The wine glass fell from Billy's hand.

Seconds passed with consciousness fading. He heard the muffled sound of voices and felt his body lifted from the seat and dragged down the narrow passageway. He wanted to fight, to live, but his feet and legs were jelly. The movement stopped and strong arms held him suspended.

His hanging head watched the distorted shuffling of feet; then something was sliding, metal, then came a sudden blast of cold wind. It howled, blowing wildly through his hair.

Billy James could not stop what was happening but understand it clearly. Then he was free-falling, tumbling in absolute darkness through subzero temperatures. He thought of his life, his dedication to law-enforcement, to the people he served. Billy wished he could take all of this back. He also wondered if they would ever find his body.

CHAPTER 13

Christmas morning at the Cooper house was as a fun-crazy time. By eight all guests had meandered to the living room wearing pajamas and robes. The kids assisted Nancy in passing out presents and once done, it became happy-holiday mayhem.

Paper, bows and ribbons flew like graffiti, chatter and laughter added to the warmth of the soft flames dancing in the fireplace, and the snowflakes cascading past the windows made it a near-perfect Christmas. Every one's thoughtful support and respect of Michelle's absence made it endurable for even Ron and his children.

The remainder of the day lay filled with kids playing and running annoyingly through the house. The adults shared conversations, played board games, snacked on leftovers and stuffed themselves with sweets.

By two o'clock the Pepto Bismol had run dry, so guests began packing their treasures and heading home, each agonizing over having eaten far too much. Ron and the kids however, remained. Bob Lemus had asked him to stay.

Evening found the kids upstairs watching movies. Clay and Nancy, Bob, Janis and Ron sat in the living room sharing a bottle of red wine. This was a gathering Clay and Nancy were not looking forward too.

Resting his wine glass on his leg Bob Lemus grimaced thoughtfully, "Look" he began, "I realize what I have to say is far from adding to the Christmas Cheer, but it has to be discussed." Ron," he said turning, "I made a call late last night to the bureau for updated information concerning Michelle."

Ron said nothing as Lemus continued. "Tell me about the incident at the Hospital. I want to know everything that happened." Leaning back in his chair then, he crossed one leg over the other and took a sip of wine.

Ron looked down at the floor then into Lemus's face. "Four days ago, in the hospital, three men and two women showed up in the early morning hours. They were young, late twenties early thirties, all dressed in black. They killed a nurse in front of me."

Lemus uncrossed his legs and leaned forward, his face ascetic. "How did they kill the Nurse?"

Ron laughed lightly, a laugh that told of his disbelief. "One of them bit her on the neck…like a Vampire. They had bitten Michelle too."

Bob Lemus looked at Janis then back. "Was there a confrontation?"

Ron nodded. "Yes, I shot two of them."

"Did they fall when they were hit?"

Again, Ron gave a nod, "Yes, my drop-gun is a thirty-eight with hollow-points. They fell." Ron shook his head, his face strained. "As I fired, the remaining three rushed into Michelle's room. I was only sixty or seventy feet away. I charged the room running, yet by the time I reached it, in less than fifteen seconds, they had literally crashed through the hospital window jumping two stories below…with Michelle." Ron clenched his jaws, "No how in-the-hell could anybody do that?" he asked beginning to tear, "jump two stories holding a comatose body and vanish in less than fifteen seconds."

Bob swiped a hand over his face. "I have some explaining to do. But first I need to go outside and have a frigin' cigarette." He started to rise, but Nancy stopped him.

"Oh no you don't, Bob Lemus, you just keep talking and I'll get you an ashtray." When she left, Bob pulled a pack of camels from his pocket. Tapping one out, he lit it and inhaled deeply then sat back and blew smoke toward the ceiling. Nancy handed him the ashtray. "Now let's hear it." She said sitting down.

Taking a moment to look into each of their faces, Bob sighed. "Tomorrow," he began, "Blues Eyes will be escorted to the execution room, seated, strapped and zapped dead." He took another draw. "However, despite his having been locked up on death-row, he has somehow contacted Hell again and put a warrant on Clay's head. Whatever kinds of things are down there that we haven't yet seen, they're coming after him."

Clay shrugged, "We've dealt with demons before. We can do it again."

"Buddy," Ron injected "I wasn't going to tell you, but at the hospital, the one who killed the nurse said they had come to warn me."

Clay looked at Ron. "Warn you?".

"Yes. That when these things come after you, I am not to help in anyway. If I do, they will kill Michelle."

"Look Clay," Lemus jumped in, "the same kind of people who visited Ron came to our house, warning us too."

Clay felt a worrisome punch of frustration, "That son-of-a-bitch. Look," he said," I don't want anyone to get hurt. I love you guys so just stay clear; I'll handle it on my own." Focusing on Lemus he said, "Bob, if you can get me any information about this group, it'll help."

Lemus took another glance at Janis then back to Clay. "I'm afraid the situation is a hell-of-a-lot heavier than it looks." Clay didn't have to reply, his expression did the asking and Lemus went on. "These people dressed in black; while they're not demons, they aren't entirely human either." Everyone looked at Bob wanting an explanation. Lemus drew from his cigarette and exhaled into the air."The crew that visited Ron and us are in fact Vampires." Bob shrugged feeling awkward but added. "So, there you have it." Crushing out his cigarette in the ashtray he waited for the reply.

It took only a moment."Did you say what I think you just said?" Clay demanded.

"You heard right," Lemus said looking at him, "Vampires. Contracted to hunt us down and kill us if we assist you in anyway.

They're primary mission is to keep us occupied while the dark-brigade fucks with you." Lemus looked at Nancy, "Sorry, pardon my French."

Nancy waved her hand, "That's okay, but hold on here, Bob," she said, "The Bible tells of Demons, Wizards and Spirits, it says nothing about Vampires. They're Saturday Matinee Characters."

"Yes and no, Nancy."

"Yes, and no?" She asked questioningly.

"Let me tell you all a story," Lemus sat back placing the ashtray in his lap. "At the turn of the century in New Guinea there was an outbreak of an unknown disease. It originated from a group of people practicing Mortuary Cannibalism."

"People eating people, or more specifically, family eating family," Nancy said sounding more like a question.

Lemus nodded. "Exactly. That was how the disease spread, quickly becoming an epidemic. It was a neuro-degenerative disorder with horrific signs and symptoms: initially victims experienced unsteadiness of stance and gait, slow deterioration of speech and vision, body tremors and muscle loss leading to the inability to walk. They became bed-ridden, developed deep ulcerations, lost the ability to swallow, and suffered from urinary and fecal incontinence; all the while growing helplessly anemic."

Bob held his empty wine glass out to Nancy continuing to talk as she refilled it. "There mental acuity steadily declined to the point of delusional. In the end, every one of them died; or so it was believed. It turned out while still in the early stages, a few had migrated to the United States, Europe and Orient. Once discovered what had happened, most were tracked down and institutionalized. Under the strictest of isolation, they were treated…more like studied actually. Here is where it gets interesting."

Bob started to take a sip and the others shouted in harmony, "What!"

Postponing the drink, Lemus frowned, "They began to get better. It baffled science, they couldn't figure out why or how. Although international research was ruthless and covertly shared, the only common denominator found had been that something unknown was triggering Cerebral Atrophy."

"Brain-Cell-Death," Nancy injected.

"Yes," Lemus said continuing, "so with all lacking any explanation, the involved medical community labeled the illness, Kuru, a mysterious strain of Prion…a human semblance to Mad Cow disease if you will."

Bob paused polishing off what was left in his Wine Glass. Holding it out to Nancy again he went on, "Okay. So somehow without aid, they began getting better. The years passed changes came. And somehow, now, today, they've transformed into Vampires."

Ron asked, "Vampires or Cannibals?"

Lemus took a sip of Wine before answering, "Most are Vampires, only some remained Cannibals. But not Cannibals in the true sense of the word. Some cannibalism does still exist among them, but most of the lair is Vampire. Over the decades as the strain continued to mutate all developed a necessary need for human blood, but not so much flesh…at least not flesh for eating. They all, in a sense, developed a para-human physiology…adapting to survive; much the way sharks and cockroaches have for millions of years. These people still possess a hunger for the human body, only now it's for blood first…and near unmanageable sexual appetite second."

Ron spoke up again. "The two men I shot; they were gone when I exited Michelle's room where they were wearing vests or was it something else?"

Bob Lemus drank down the last of his wine and held out his hand again to Nancy. She filled the glass as he answered the question, "It was definitely something else."

Ron made a face. "Great! Now you can pardon my French. This just keeps getting fucking better."

Bob set the astray on the floor beside his chair and leaned forward, resting his elbows on his knees. "These, things, have developed a near superhuman Endocrine and Nervous system. Somehow, the two systems have merged and now function beyond sciences capability of understanding. Their bodies' possess a rapid, microsecond capability to maintain internal homeostasis; it's far beyond anything we have ever seen. They recover from life threatening wounds at remarkable speeds. For example, in a gunshot wound to the chest their body will repair itself within a matter of minutes…providing they have not been totally bled out or deprived of oxygen during the healing process.

"Then they can be killed?" Clay asked.

Lemus gave a nod. "Yes, but it's not easy. The bureau monitors them, and scientists continue with their poking and prodding. We continuously develop ways of killing them if necessary. A covert department called NASIF, National American Security Internal Force tracks them on a regular basis, insuring they do not breed without authorization. They are not to kill indiscreetly or commit sexual crimes. When they do, we, along with a Blood-Ferret; one of their own kind, a Bounty hunter if you will, join forces and track them down then dispose of the body or bodies."

Lemus took a sip of wine. "In addition to the tracking center, the department has what we call 'The Store'; a lab where weapons and devices are continuously created and developed just for that purpose."

"Do you still have access to this center now that you're retired?" Clay asked.

Lemus nodded. "Yes, I do, Clay." He then turned to Ron. "I can't grantee you anything, but if I were a gambling man, I'd bet a retirement check that by this time tomorrow, we'll know where Michelle has been taken."

Ron's reaction was a speechless gaze. He knew Lemus well enough to realize what he was saying was not to be taken lightly. Still, he stared intently into the man's eyes for reassurance. Seconds passed. The downstairs house lay quiet. From upstairs came the faint sound of the kids playing then a car splashed past the big bay window.

On Ron's face, the slightest hint of a grin began. It moved slowly at first, turning into a notable smile. Not removing his eyes from Lemus' and with a voice filled with hope, Ron said, "I have to tell you Bob, and I'm saying it in French again; I fucking love you."

CHAPTER 14

The following afternoon at exactly 3:06 the doorbell rang. All were sitting in the living room chatting and the ding stopped the conversation abruptly. Nancy flashed Bob Lemus a nervous smile and rose. Bob had informed them someone from the bureau would be arriving, and that that someone would be a Blood-Ferret, a Vampire.

Nearly completed with her PhD in Archaeology and minor in Anthropology, Nancy had insisted she be the one to answer - anxious for this near-overwhelming experience.

Her excitement soared with possibilities; envisioning escorting the creature to the college to show him off as if a great archaeological find. She imagined, although in a good way, herself scrubbed and prepped with a team of the world's most prominent surgeons preparing to cut the creature open for exploration. Few anthropologists, living or dead had ever suspected such creatures actually existed. Now, one stood at her very door.

Making her way across the living room, she paused glancing back at the others. Bob Lemus was grinning. Sighing, she turned and opened the door.

Holding a brown leather briefcase stood a tall man staring down at her. Wide shouldered, long shimmering black hair hung to his shoulders. Nancy guessed him to be around sixty *maybe three hundred and sixty*. Dressed in a brown Taupe Cotton Commando sweater, Adirondack Jeans, and tan combat boots, his brown eyes told of kindness hidden beneath a stoic, square-jawed handsome face. The sun was shining; Nancy marveled; he wasn't bursting into flames.

With a smile, his voice throaty in a gentle, masculine way he said, "Hello, my name is Ever. Is there a Mr. Lemus here?"

Nancy stared, not speaking. He looked like an ordinary man: no yellow bloodshot eyes, no vampire fangs or long black cape.

Realizing Bob Lemus had obviously explained who it was that would be coming; he widened his smile. "If Mr. Lemus is here, I'd like to come in. I promise I won't bite."

Nancy blinked, now embarrassed. "Oh, I'm so sorry, Mr. Ever."

"Just call me Ever, please."

Nancy forced a smile. "I didn't mean to stare, Mr. Ever... Ever. Please come in." She gestured with an open hand.

The man called Ever nodded and walked past her. From the couch, Bob Lemus rose and walked to greet him. When face to face the two embraced. It was obvious they were friends.

Bob led the way back to the group and introduced everyone. When seated he asked, "Did you get what we need?"

Ever set his briefcase across his lap and opened it. "Yes. They've taken her to South America." Lemus gave a nod. Ever pulled a map from his briefcase and closed the lid. He spread the map across the top saying, "This is a map of Bolivia. The assignment will prove rather difficult. Getting in will be easy, at least less challenging. But getting out with Mrs. Parks, well, that will prove quite exciting."

Lemus glanced at Ron. "You understand there will be risks?"

Ron gave a nod.

Placing a finger beneath the symbol of a body of water near the northeast corner of the map, ever said, "This is Lake Laguna San Luis." "We will land on this lake by amphibious aircraft. From there we take a boat up Lake San Miguel to the village of Magdalena. This part of the journey will not be difficult. But from the village we travel north by horseback, along the river for five kilometers, then we turn west into the jungle and follow a path to where they hold her, to Castle Blasonar de Racista."

Ever raised his eyes and slowly looked into each of their faces. "I will be honest, unless we kill everyone in the castle, they will stalk us once we've retrieved Mrs. Parks. And they will be relentless."

For a time, there was silence.

Outside despite the warm sunshine, it was snowing. Bob Lemus sat back in his chair and crossed one leg over the other. "Well," he said glancing out the window than back, "as for me, I've always preferred the tropics to cold, wet snow.I say we don't waist another minute. Let's go soak up some of that South American Sunshine."

CHAPTER 15

Ron made arrangements for his children to stay with his sister, explaining only that they had a lead on Michelle's whereabouts. Michael remained at home. Clay would have preferred sending his wife and son away as well, some place secret. But he could think of no one he'd feel safe sending them too, so he asked that Carl make frequent stops by the house while away.

In addition. Nancy would live with her Lady Laser .25 at her side. Clay and Nancy had also decided to sit down with Michael and explain all that was happening, as well as that which had happened in the past. His strong faith helped him to except and understand. At least they hoped so.

That night for supper Nancy and Janis teamed up to create a Yankee Pot Roast worthy of a master Chef's competition. All agreed to Christmas leftovers for dessert.

At dinner conversation turned to Ever as he explained a Vampire existence. "We." he began. "are not like your Hollywood bloodsucking monsters. In many ways we are like you. We thirst, hunger, feel too cold or too hot, we grow tired and need sleep. We can become sick, and we grow old and eventually die. We experience emotions just like you, love, hate, sadness, laughter, and even tears. And our hearts pump blood through our veins just like yours, our lungs depend on oxygen to sustain life. and we use the bathroom just like you. Biologically, yes, we do differ. Vampires recover quickly from even serious injury; usually healing within minutes. We eat the same foods as you, requiring their nutrition, and we enjoy their many flavors, just like you. The reason we are called Vampires, is that our bodies also require nutrient from human blood: for without it, we would slowly die of malnutrition. Understand our thirst for blood is not psychosomatic. To my race, human blood is as vital to our existence as the oxygen we all breath."

Michael studied the Vampire as he talked, curious of him. When a lull came, the youngster asked, "Mr. Ever, may I ask you something?"

Ever gave a nod, "Certainly. But please call me Ever."

Janis smiled to herself. *Here it comes Ever.*

"Michael?" Nancy spoke up quickly

The boy turned to his mother. "What Mom?"

"Let's not bother Ever with questions, okay"

"No, it is fine." Ever assured her. "The boy possesses as much curiosity as anyone of you."

Shrugging, Nancy glanced at Janis, trying not to grin. "Okay."

"Now Michael," Ever said, "what is it you wanted to ask?"

"I was wondering, do Vampires have souls and do they believe in God?"

Ever the Vampire Ferret, tracker, hunter and sometimes killer, paused thoughtfully. Every eye at the table stared, waiting. It was a question no one else would have asked, but all wondered.

Ever's reply was surprising, "Yes, on both of your questions. In our beginning, we were as human as you are. We were God's creation. Then a terrible disease came and began killing us. Somehow, our bodies began changing, defending itself against the disease. And now, decades later after all that changing, we have become what we are. Many of my kind go to church, they pray and work normal jobs. They just tell no one what they are.

"I see," Michael said, "so that's why you're nothing like the Vampires in the movies?"

"Basically, yes."

"Do you kill people for the blood you need?" Michael asked.

Clay spoke sternly from the end of the table. "Michael!"

Ever smiled warmly, "It is okay," he said glancing at Clay, then back to Michael.

"No Michael, I do not kill for my blood. Some have. That is wrong and why I am here. I help arrest the ones who do. I am like a Sheriff.

"Cool." Michael smiled. "Do you carry a gun like my dad?"

"I carry weapons, yes. But. . . "

The doorbell rang and Ever stopped in the middle of his sentence. Clay and Nancy exchanged glances, wondering who would be calling so late. It was now nearly 7:30. Clay excused himself and left for the door.

At the table, Michael continued with the conversation. "Are the weapons you use secret? Like laser guns, or do you use regular ones, but with bullets made out of silver or wood?"

"Our weapons are sort of secret," Ever smiled. "Let's just call them special weapons."

Clay reentered the dining room, and everyone turned; two men dressed in black suits were following close behind. Nancy rose slowly from her chair, surprise on her face she said aloud, "Well for heaven sake. I don't believe it. Agents Jones and Clendes!" Scurrying from her place at the table she hurried to them unable to hold her smile. "the whole darn family has come home." She said as they embraced.

When introductions ended and Jones and Clendes were seated, everyone turned to Lemus for an explanation. "I asked the Bureau if we could borrow them since the problem involves renegade Vamps. It's obvious the Brass said yes. But truthfully." he added with a grin, the two of them no doubt agreed to come because they, as always, were afraid to say no. They fear me."

Bob glanced their way, and they were wearing an expression of surprise. Bob intentionally lost his grin, "That's right boys, I knew!"

CHAPTER 16

It was established Clendes, and Jones would spend the night, sharing the pullout in the basement. And ever accepted the offer of bedding down on the couch. A little after 10:00pm, following Michael's bedtime, agent Jones assisted Ever in carrying in a wooden crate from his vehicle.

Back in his chair with the box at his feet Ever opened it explaining, "This container holds weapons issued by the Store. We must use them with caution for they will kill both Vampire and Humans."

The crate consisted of two trays. While they could not see what the tray beneath held, what lay on the top surprised them all. As if on museum display, a series of dark, knife-type weapons lay shadowed by light from the living room lamp; each weapon looking as if it had come from the Klingon Empire.

Ever retrieved the largest of the weapons. "This is called the Bat", he explained, "you grip the handle here in the center and the two slightly arched blades extending out resemble the wings of a Vampire Bat. As you can see these wings are sharp and partially serrated on each side, each wing is eighteen and a half inches in length. This weapon is designed to behead the enemy during combat. First you swing one way, then come back the other, ensuring the head is totally severed from the body. Remember, when killing Vampires, it is best you make certain the head is in no way left attached." Janis looked at Bob with a wrinkled nose.

Ever replaced the Bat and picked up another weapon. "This we call the Mustache. Again, you grip it here in the center. This weapon is a foot in length and somewhat resembles the handle-bar mustache of an old-time barber. The razor-sharp u-shaped ends are designed so that when you thrust into the neck with the blade straight up you then give a twist and pull. The idea is the blade slides in and through the neck behind the trachea, or windpipe, and when pulled free it hooks the windpipe slicing it in half. As you can see, we have been issued two Bats and four Mustache weapons. Obviously, both are used in hand-to-hand combat.

Replacing it Ever lifted the top tray and handed it to Jones to set aside. Pulling out the bottom tray, he told the others to fellow him and he walked with it to the Kitchen table. When he set it down, he turned to the others who had followed. "As you can see this weapon is less barbaric. Picking up a small framed semi-automatic handgun, he pushed a button releasing the clip. "This," he told them will hold twenty-five .22 Mag caliber rounds."

".22 caliber" Ron said, "I shot two of these freaks…no offense, with a .38 hollow point and didn't stop them."

Ever nodded, "Yes, I understand." Ever went on seeming to ignore Ron's remark. "In the bottom of this crate lay a handgun for each of you, along with two hundred rounds and five clips a piece. You see Mr. Parks, what makes the difference between your .38 and this small caliber is that each .22 Mag bullet contains one once of specially developed toxin so poisonous to the Vampire, it will kill them in seconds; providing the round hits them directly in the heart or brain."

Ever paused, placing the clip back into the weapon and returning it to the box. "Let us go back and sit". When all were seated and waiting, he told them, "When we reach the Castle, and our fight begins, there will be only three ways to kill those who will try very hard to kill you" all were listening closely, "And that" Ever went on, "Will be to shoot them with one of the toxin rounds, slice their windpipe in two, or behead them. Anyone of the three will disrupt oxygen flow so they cannot regenerate. If they are left able to breathe, believe me, they will live to hunt you again…and often within minutes".

Bob Lemus nodded, adding, "Trust him, he's right. These things just do not want to die." Lemus looked at Ever, "Enough for now, what say you I put on our woollies and go outside for a smoke?"

Following a polite nod, ever excused himself from the others and followed Lemus outside. The two stood talking in the driveway for some time; Bob smoked two Camels and Ever lit up a Romeo Y Julieta Belicosis Fino Cuban cigar.

No one knew what was being discussed but were sure it contained information they were not allowed to hear. When they finally returned, ever issued a .22Magauto with rounds and clips to each man and Janis. The fifth he kept for himself.

He and Ron also took possession of a Bat. Janis, Cooper, Jones and Clendes grabbed a Mustache. All knife weapons came with a quick-snap leather case that attached to a belt. The .22 semi-automatics came with a DeSantis Leather New York Undercover Shoulder Rig and four attached clip cases. The new weapons helped ease the tension of what was coming…but not entirely. With the exception of Bob Lemus and Ever, none had ever faced such an enemy.

At 11:12 Nancy was making the bed in the basement for Clendes and Jones. When finished she smiled goodnight and returned upstairs to make a final check of all the doors and windows. The light snow was still falling, and the temperature had dropped too below zero. Snowflake-like ice patterns were forming on the outside glass and created an appreciation for being inside. Turning out the lights, except for a small nightlight in the living room, she went upstairs.

Slipping quietly into Michael's room she ensured he was covered than kissed his cheek. She thought him asleep, but he opened his eyes and smiled. It wasn't a happy smile; it was forced, an attempt at hiding trouble and worry.

Nancy sat on the edge of the bed and stroked his hair. "Are you alright, honey?"

Again, Michael forced a smile. "Sure mom."

"I don't think so you little Tom Foolery. I've seen that look before. Something is troubling you. Now come on, spill the beans."

"I don't want to frighten you, mom."

Nancy frowned with concern. "Frighten me, what do you mean?"

"See. You're already frightened. I can tell it in your voice."

Nancy made a face. "No, I'm not. Now that's enough Michael Clayton Cooper. What gives? Tell me or I call in the big gun."

"They're coming tonight, mom."

"Who?"

"Demons."

"Michael, what are you talking about? No one is coming tonight. You're safe as a bug in a rug. Not only is your father here, but there are two FBI agents, a retired FBI agent, one Private Investigator and Ever. We couldn't be safer."

"They aren't coming to hurt us; just show us they are here."

"Michael that's silly. No one is coming. I just finished locking all the doors and windows. No one could get in if they wanted too."

"They don't use doors or windows."

"This is nonsense." Nancy said forcing another smile, "Now you go to sleep." She tucked the blankets up around Michael's shoulders and kissed his forehead as she stood up. "In the morning you'll see that everything is fine." She walked to the door, turned, smiled, and whispered, "I love you," then closed the door behind her.

Walking into the bathroom Nancy changed into her nightgown, brushed her teeth, then crawled into bed with Clay, snuggling close. Clay was reading and now laid down his book, slipping an arm around her.

"You, okay?" He asked.

"No. Clay, I'm frightened. I really thought all this was over."

"I know Baby."

"I just want it to stop" she said, "Little Michael is in his bed worried demons are coming tonight."

Clay grimaced. "It'll all end in just a few hours, just as soon as that Blue Eyed monster dies. We've all got the jitters with Michelle and the Vampire thing. But the moment that bastard draws his last breath, all of it will come to an end once and for all."

The phone rang out suddenly and Nancy jumped. Clay gave her a loving squeeze and kissed the top of her head. "Easy worry wart." He picked up the phone, "Yeah Hello?"

"Evening Clay, have you heard the latest? I'm free, out, flown the coop, walked, not going to fry, burn, toast, or roast."

Tossing back the covers Clay scampered out of bed scurrying to the window. Pulling back the curtain he glared down into the street seeing nothing but cold and darkness. He shook his head; his heart was racing. Truthfully, he wanted to cry.

"Hey buddy, are you there?" The voice asked.

Fighting to hide his anxiety he replied, "We've had this conversation before, I'm not your buddy."

"No, but I bet you're surprised."

"You got me there. How did you get out?"

"With a little help from my friends, but that's not important. What matters is that I am out, and we can finish what you screwed up seven years ago. And trust me, this time you will finish it. You will kill me, no errors, no bungling, and as your friends have already discovered, no interference."

The receiver clicked and the dialing tone sounded in Clay's ear. He turned to Nancy. Her face was pale, she knew by the conversation just who it was. Clay crossed the room and placed the phone back into its cradle. After staring at it a few moments he looked into Nancy's eyes, "Well...Hell! I better go tell the others."

CHAPTER 17

All had gathered once again in the living room. Bob Lemus immediately asked for the ashtray. Once in possession he lit a cigarette and paced the living room floor mumbling; "*How can this be? How in the hell can this be? The son-of-a-bitch was on death row. No one escapes from death row.*"

The others watched him pace, thinking it best they say nothing. Finally, after butting out his cigarette he approached them and sat.

"Okay, here's the plan. Jones and Clendes will remain here with Nancy and Michael, the rest of us will fly to Bolivia; we'll rescue Michelle, kill some mother-Fucking Vampires," Lemus glanced at Nancy, said sorry and continued, "then we'll fly back here and track down this blue-eyed bastard once and for all. And this time, and I swear to you on the sacred head of J. Edger Hoover, he won't be going back to prison."

It was agreed they'd fly out first thing in the morning. Lemus pulled Clendes and Jones aside warning them Blue Eyes would more than likely try and abduct Nancy and Michael. Should he gain possession of them there would be a less than poor chance of getting them both back alive. There would be no room for error.

Twenty-two minutes past midnight all were back in their beds. Sleep was long in coming for everyone. Each lay awake rationalizing, struggling to come to grips with what had happened and what was yet to come.

Outside the wind was picking up, it howled and pushed against the house, snow swirled, drifts amassed, and the temperature dropped beyond the reach of the thermometer.

Slowly each began to drift away - fading one by one into that trouble-free world of nothingness, a welcomed peace that tiptoed in without awareness. Time ticked as they slumbered; but at 2:30 a noise startled Janis awake.

Lying on her back, she stared into the darkness above. She lay quiet, listening to the noise which had awakened her. It proved disturbing and quickened her heartbeat. Every inch of darkness around her sounded as if it were filled with whispering voices, a mass of unrecognizable murmurings. What it was, or could be, she did not want to know. But she did realize it was not natural. Slowly, her hand eased out from beneath the blankets, and soundlessly, gentle, she grasped the .22 automatic Ever had issued too her. As was her practice, she had set it on the bedside table before crawling into bed. She pulled it beneath the covers and meticulously slid back the slide. Her heartbeat continued to climb.

She knew the importance of waking Bob. He was asleep beside her, lying on his side and snoring lightly. When she nudged him, he moaned. She nudged him again. The snoring stopped. "What?"

"Bob, something is in the room."

Bob Lemus, like Janis, opened his eyes to extreme darkness. His trained mind told him to lie quiet, to take seriously what he had been told. If it proved bogus later, that was fine. But until then the situation needed to be taken somberly. Not moving, he lay there hearing the same sound, wondering like Janis, what is it?

In the bedroom of Clay and Nancy, in Michael's room, around the couch in the living room and in the basement where Clendes and Jones lay on the sleeper-sofa, it was the same. All lay awake in their beds, motionless, surrounded by darkness and hearing the same strange nattering of indistinguishable whispers.

Clay, like Janis, had ensured the weapon Ever gave him lay close. He had placed it under his pillow. Now gripped in his hand he whispered to Nancy. "When I tell you, reach out and snap on the bed-lamp. On three." Nancy was frightened. Not only for what they were about to see, but for her son alone his bedroom. Michael had tried to warn her Demons were coming. Is that what was here now, or could it be Vampires staring at them through the darkness, waiting to feast?

Her thoughts flashed back seven years to the old Louisiana Mansion, to the horrible things she had seen there. The visions still haunted her. Clay began to count. Her hands were trembling. "One," Nancy reached out from beneath the covers. She had to force herself to move; for there was solace beneath the blankets. "Two." Her fingers touched the switch. Clay pulled the .22 auto free from beneath the covers. "Three!" Nancy threw the switch and instantly bright light filled the room. Clay raised the weapon poised to shoot, but nothing was there. The whispers vanished with the light…it was sudden silence. Glancing at one another they simultaneously threw back the covers and bolted into Michael's room, throwing on the light.

He lay awake beneath his covers propped against the pillows waiting for them. Moving to his side Clay and Nancy sat on the edge of his bed. Nancy squeezed him tight. "Are you alright little man?"

Michael nodded. "Yes. Did you hear them?"

Nancy nodded. "Yes, we did. But they're gone now."

Michael continued to stare at his mom. "No, they're not."

Nancy looked strained. "Michael, your dad and I have actually seen demons. Trust me, they are not here."

Michael took a deep breath. "Mom", he asked, "can we wake everyone and gather downstairs in the living room?"

Clay spoke up. "Why, Michael?"

The boy looked at his father. "Because of something I've been told to show you."

"Show us? Show us what?'

Michael reached out and squeezed his father's hand. "Them! You have to see them. There waiting and won't go away until you do."

Clay glanced at Nancy with an expression of total loss. "Okay, son," he said looking back to Michael "We'll get everyone up and meet in the living room."

Once gathered all admitted to hearing the same strange whispering. Now, sitting together they waited quietly. Michael told them what was coming, and Nancy asked, Michael, you told us what is coming, what we are to see. But you did not say who it was that told you to tell us. Was it the Devil?"

The boy replied with no hesitation. "It was God."

"God!" Nancy expressed with surprise.

"Yes mom."

Nancy let out a thoughtful sigh. "Okay," she said, looking around at the others, hoping they did not think her son was in need of psychiatric counsel.Looking back to him she asked a second question, "Michael, are the Demons her now?"

He nodded a silent yes.

Bob Lemus cut in, "if you can see them, why can't we?"

"Because you must see them through Spiritual Eyes."

Lemus's brow furrowed, "What do you mean, Spiritual Eyes?"

"You're trying to see them through eyes that can see only things of this world: like trees, cars, grass, other people, and all that stuff. What is here is not of this world. You can see them only through God's eyes."

Lemus frowned again, looking to Clay for some type of explanation. And Michael provided it. "I can help you see them. If you will close your eyes and bow your heads, I'll pray for God to grant you the eyes you need. You have to believe he will, or he won't give them to you. After I've prayed, don't open them until I say."

Janis couldn't help herself, she had to ask. "So, Michael, you talk to God too?"

Michael nodded nonchalantly. "Sure. Anybody can."

Janis rubbed her face with her hands, thinking, *I don't believe this kid!*

Michael added. "If God opens your eyes, what you will see is going to scare you, but they are not here to hurt us. They've come only to show you they are here. I don't know why they've come; only that it's important you see them."

Clayton Cooper's heart felt heavy. He hated that his son was in the middle of all this, but they had not been left any choice. He hoped he and Nancy had been correct in telling him the truth.

Following one final glance into each other's eyes, the group bowed their heads and young Michael began to pray; "*Father God, these evil things that have come into our house are here because you have allowed them. Why, we do not know. But we know that all you choose to do is always right and perfect. So, I pray you open the spiritual eyes of my Dad and Mom and their friends, that they can see what I see. And once they've seen, I pray you order these evil things to go away. Amen.*"

Michael lifted his head. "Okay everyone, open your eyes".

CHAPTER 18

In the house across the street from the Coopers, the lights were dim, and shades pulled. In the basement of that house, the owners, Roland and Wynona Ottis lay bound and gagged with duct tape. Friends with the Coopers; the couple had no idea their neighbors were the reason for their nightmarish predicament.

Above them in the Kitchen the Blue Eyes killer and his seven-year-old son Cain, were rummaging through the refrigerator for a snack. They decided on BLTs with a side of chips and dill pickle. Upon spotting four cans of Mountain Due, Cain cheerfully chimed, "YEAH".Beside the Due sat six cans of Coke. Looking at his son with a return smile, Blue Eyes told him, "Coke too! My favorite! Your choice of words could not have said it better little man... "YEAH."

While eating, Cain asked. "Are our Demon friends across the street going to hurt the Coopers?"

"No, Cain. They are there only as a reminder that Mr. Cooper must do as told this time. If he does not the circumstances for him will be...let us say, catastrophic".

As an afterthought Cain made a face, "I would prefer that you did not go away Father. I will miss you so terribly much."

Blue Eyes smiled warmly. "Worry not my son;" he told the boy, "You will be following in my footsteps here, and eventually joining me in Hell." And both events, I assure you, will prove exciting and worthwhile"

Blue Eyes sipped from his can of Coke. Wanting to change the subject and leave his son's thoughts on a positive note, he asked, "Now, my young apprentice. Tell me something you have learned from your Scribes?"

Cain smiled, happy for the opportunity to show his Father how much he was learning, "In my studies of the Christian Bible, I learned the road to Heaven is narrow, and the road to our Hell is wide. That tells me more people will be joining us in Hell, then joining their God in Heaven"

Blue Eyes smiled again, "Yes, doesn't it give you chills and an exquisite sense of accomplishment?"

"It does Father, especially with this world so filled with people claiming to be so religious. One would thing it to be the other way around."

Blues Eyes smiled again. "You are learning so much, Cain. Can you explain to me the difference in the two roads? Why ours is wide and heavily traveled, and the one leading to Heaven is narrow?"

"Sure Father." Cain explained. "It is because many believe that as long as they go to Church on Sunday, that is all they need to get to Heaven. When actually, their Bible clearly explains that has nothing to do with their getting into Heaven."

Blue Eyes gave a nod, "Yes indeed. Tell me more as to why that is so."

Cain took a sip of Due. "Well," he began, "to borrow from one of their Bible Scriptures it states, that he who believes and accepts Jesus Christ as their Savior becomes a new creation, that the old person is gone, and the new person has come. And when that new person arrives, they will change from living in sin to fighting to be free of sin!"

Blue Eyes squeezed his son's hand feeling proud. "Well then, my young genius of the dark way," he said, "I've but one last question. In their Bible it is pointed out that many who believe they are going to Heaven at death, will indeed NOT be going to Heaven. But instead, when they knell before Jesus for their judgment; or perhaps I should say anticipation of rewards, He will say to them; you are 'Lukewarm' get away from me, I never knew you. And thus, those souls will be sent down to us weeping and crying. Some even screaming."

Young Cain looked thoughtful a time before speaking, "Well father, just because they believe in their God, that will not save them. Even our Demons believe in His existence, and they certainly are not going there to be with Him. My Demon Scribes," Cain continued following a sip of Due, "have taught me that their preventing being 'Lukewarm' is really an easy thing for them; and that is to simply spend more time seeking a close relationship with their Savior, Jesus. But" Cain continued following another sip of Mountain Due, "lucky for us, so many of them choose instead to spend more time taking part in what we in Hell offer...the desires of their Flesh."

Blue Eyes grinned, proud of his son's growing knowledge.Little Cain took a bite of sand-which, chewed and swallowed, then continued. "I have been taught if they are serious about being a Christian and going to Heaven, they cannot just go to Church on Sunday believing that alone is sufficient, and yet knowingly continue living in sin," They need to fight against us, we the darkness, they must avoid us as much as they can. Simply Father, they will remain 'Lukewarm' without their Savior's strength. They are far too weak without it.; for we Father, are more powerful than they know. Without their Jesus, they cannot fight us and win."

Blue Eyes gave a nod of approval. "And so then, in one sentence my wondrous son, can you sum it all up?"

"Yes sir. Many who believe they are sufficiently 'religious' remain within their worldly comfort zone and do not truly have faith."

Blue Eyes whistled joyfully. "You cause me to tingle with pride, young man."

Smiling happily, Cain took another sip of his Due. "Father", he said, "I actually find it exciting being so close to the Coopers and the others, and they not knowing. It's almost like playing hide-and-seek."

"Yes, it is quite thrilling." Blue Eyes said.

"Did you always remain this close when you were doing our master's work, Father?"

"As much as possible, yes. It truthfully gives me goose bumps."

Cain smiled. "Father, I know that all the things you do have a purpose. What is ours for being here?"

"We are going to visit the Cooper house, to talk with Mrs. Cooper and her son Michael."

Cain showed excitement, "I look forward to meeting Michael. He is my age, is he not?"

"He is, yes. Perhaps you two will get to exchange thoughts and you can win him over to our god while we are there."

"But what if they do not wish to visit with us, Father?"

Blue Eyes downed the last of his Coke. "Well Cain, as you will learn. Sometimes, we simply do not give our prey a choice."

CHAPTER 19

Just as Michael had told them, they opened their eyes. Nancy screamed. Clutching her hand Clay looked on in awe, as did the others, their heads whipping in all directions; as best they could. The interior of the Cooper house had all but vanished, buried beneath things from the dark dimension.

The Coopers, Bob, Janis and Ron, had all encountered demons in Louisiana, suffered greatly because of their power, but what now sated this house went beyond what they had experienced; it surpassed comprehension. These were things never before seen by the human eye, things haunting, terrifying, things unspeakable.

Clay and all the others, each understood the vileness of demon possession, and if these were the things that entered into and took control of the human body and soul, then the horror of it was truly something to be feared.

Michael squeezed his father's hand with a firm grip. The boy's faith and belief in God was phenomenal, a spiritual gift. He possessed the strength of seasoned clerics, yet Clay could feel his son trembling; or maybe it was himself.

No one moved. They, nor the numberless creatures taking up every inch of the Cooper house, made a sound. They were everywhere, in every room of the house: halls, stairways, over sinks, filling every available inch of overhead space.

Gathered this night in the Cooper home were minacious Legions of half-human and half-demon Bat-Like things. They were near human size and hanging upside down from the ceilings by Falcon-Like feet. From the three huge toes of each foot extended a long, thick curved Black Talon; Clay guessed them at least 8 inches in length and approximately 3 inches in diameter - obviously feet of Prey. Their faces were human but with vertically positioned eye lids, the lids were closed. In the crowded living room, some of their faces were hanging nearly eye to eye with the face of Clay and the others.

Clay swallowed hard. From the neck to the feet their entire human shaped body lay covered with the skin of a Raptor; to include long wings wrapped tightly around them.

Suddenly Nancy screamed once again pointing a finger. Below the elongated hanging Creatures, the baseboards of the living room fell away from the walls. Up and out from the thin crack of wall and floor, began an onslaught of scurrying insects of uncountable shapes and sizes; crawling, wiggling, slithering and some taking flight buzzing their heads and attempting to land on their skin. The floor quickly vanished and a fight for room began as they continued pouring in and piling higher and higher on top of one another.

Like a flooding lake of dark, infected water they were rising. Clay and the others pulled their legs up and huddled within their chairs and on the sofa cushions. It took little logic to know that if the onslaught did not stop; this building mountain of evil arthropods would soon have them cocooned.

The entire Cooper house looked as though Michael's message had transported them to an undisclosed location in Hell itself; a location of darkness so secret, the most practiced of Biblical Scholars had no knowledge of its existence.

Fear rose to equal the rising sea of insects; whose depths had now reached the bottom of the cushions; and still climbing.

Clay felt sick, feeling responsible for all of it. He should have killed Blue Eyes when the opportunity was there seven years ago. Now once again all those he loved were in danger.

Suddenly it was as if the elite Army of Evil had been given a command by the dark imprisoned soul of Adolf Hitler himself, the hanging demons turned their heads, a smart synchronized movement ending with every vile eye opening and focusing on the human group they surrounded.

Immediately the whispering began again, and this time Clay recognized its horrid mantra: *Kill him, kill him, kill him, kill him...*

Nancy glanced at her husband. She too understood what it was they were saying. Because of their sheer numbers, the chanting demons caused the walls of the house to physically vibrate.

Clay, having reached the end of his endurance shouted...." Get Out of my House!" He and Nancy could not go through this again. The last time it had nearly destroyed their lives, and now they had Michael to consider. But Clay's demand was totally unheeded, and the chant continued: *Kill Him, Kill Him, Kill Him...*

Michael's eyes were blurring with tears, the demons were hurting his dad; they were not supposed to. The rising insects had now reached their waists and were already crawling beneath their clothing and up their bodies.

Michael yelled this time; and louder than his dad., "NO!" He jumped from the couch and into the pool of insects, their depth reaching his neck. Raising his head, the young boy shouted at the horror filling his house, "In the name of Jesus the Son of God, by His power, through His authority, I commend you leave this house."

Immediately the chanting stopped, there was silence, the insects quit moving and the Bat-Like creatures turned their eyes upon Michael. Again, he shouted, "Leave now."

Michael's God-Given authority angered the huge Demonic Bats and they screeched in protest; so loud everyone shuttered and covered their ears. But all over the house the hanging horde began to vanish. The sea of insects scrambled back into the woodwork, their depths shrinking rapidly- draining like a lake of horrors back into Hell.

Hundreds were clambering out from beneath their clothing to get away.

Clay, Nancy, Ron, Bob, Janis and Michael; even Ever, uncovered their ears and sighed with great relief. Upon the last scurrying insect disappearing back into the woodwork, the trim slammed back into its place against the wall. And finally, as if nothing had ever happened, the Cooper house looked just as it did when they had all first sat down. Starring at one another for a time, saying nothing, they one by one slid back down into their chairs and couch.

Michael remained standing. His eyes were closed and lips moving in silence. All stared at this little boy. A seven-year-old capable of commanding Demons. Finally, his eyes opened, and he broke the stillness. Looking at his mother he asked, "Mom, can I have a peanut butter and jelly sandwich?"

Nancy stared at him a few seconds then replied as she stood up. Kissing him on the top of his head she told him, "Yes sir, you can. And today you get a lot of extra jelly."

Janis watched Nancy march away than shook her head, "Michael Cooper," she said smiling as he climbed up into his dad's lap, "You are simply amazing."

Clay gave Michael a hug. "Yes, he is. And let me be the first to say it, "Thank you, Michael."

Bob Lemus added to the conversation. "I've got to ask you something Michael. And think about it before you answer, "Would you consider coming to work for the F.B.I.?"

CHAPTER 20

Across the street Blue Eyes and Cain watched the outside activity of the group leaving for Bolivia. They were loading the black sedan driven by yesterday's arriving stranger. The vehicle bore DC plates, so he was confident it was a fed car. Nancy and Michael, along with two agents the Killer remembered from seven years ago stood watching.

The morning was cold despite a picturesque sky of blue and white. Blue Eyes watched as Clay kissed his wife then held her a moment. Part of Clay was anxious to leave for the rescue of Michelle, but another felt ill at ease leaving Nancy and Michael behind.

While his confidence in Jones and Clendes was strong, Blue Eyes had proven himself a step above, and this time aiding the psycho would be Demons and Vampires. Clay closed his eyes and shook his head with worry.

Following one last squeeze, he released Nancy and squatted in front of Michael. "You take care of mom for me. You're the man of the house until I get back. I'll be home soon, I promise." Rising he winked at his wife then climbed into the car. The door slammed and they sped away with the wheels throwing up water from melting snow.

Nancy held Michael's hand as they waved. When the vehicle disappeared, they hurried into the house to the waiting warmth. Jones and Clendes did a thorough security check, inspecting every window and door, upstairs and down. After locking the door leading into the garage, they reinforced it by prying a chair beneath the handle. The front and back doors were dead-bolted.

Lastly, the agents went into the basement. Other than the door leading down from the kitchen, four small windows were the only way in or out. With permission from Nancy, they nailed boards over them. It was decided if Blue Eyes or his Vampires attacked and it appeared they might be overwhelmed, then the four would retreat to the basement and defend the entrance way, killing anyone or anything that tried coming down. Clendes and Jones understood such a move might very well sign their death warrant, but it would certainly be a last resort.

Across the street Blue Eyes and Cain made omelets for breakfast. When finished, Blue eyes positioned his son at the window to maintain observation of the Cooper house while he went to the basement.

Roland and Wynona had drifted into a restless sleep, but his footsteps startled them awake. Daylight was filtering through the window where they lay, and they could see clearly. At the couple's feet Blue Eyes squatted with a smile. "And how are my munificent hosts this morning?"

The duct-tape covering their mouth prevented any conversation, but he could see Wynona's nostrils flaring partially due to her inability to use her mouth for breathing, but mostly the result of sheer terror.

Closing his eyes Blue Eyes lifted his face into the warm ray of light penetrating the basement window. He smiled. There was a stirring in his penis; fear was such an aphrodisiac.

CHAPTER 21

The Ferret's driving was making Janis nervous. She disliked traveling at high speeds when sporadic patches of black ice spotted the highway. Staring out the window into snow-covered fields, she countered the discomfort through the recall of a pleasant memory.

Smiling, in her heart she sat beside her dad on the front porch sipping a beer. They had talked about everything that day recalling life before his illness: family vacations, her sucker-dad sweetness as a little girl, the terrible teen years, and his cherished support of her decision to become a private investigator instead of following in his footsteps as a New Orleans Police Officer.

Grinning through the window across the vast openness, she recalled the advice he had given her on the workings of a happy marriage. *Jannie,* he had said, *someday you will meet the man of your dreams. When that day comes both of you will know. And a big part of it lasting forever -at least from a man's point of view, he had grinned,*

is while he's still young let him have a fast car or a Harley, go all out for the holidays- even if he pretends it's no big deal. From time to time fix him a good home cooked meal; and most importantly...when the World Series comes round keep him filled up with chips, dip and cold beer

The car fishtailed slightly, and her smile disintegrated. She was in as big a hurry to get to Michelle as any of the others with the exception of Ron of course. But she possessed no desire to find herself pinned in a wrecked vehicle in the middle of a freezing, snow-covered field;

the Bureau Jet was waiting at the Purdue Airport and would not leave without them. The high speed was an unnecessary risk.

Following a reassuring tug on her seat-belt Janis recalled what lay ahead. The pilot would fly them to South America into Santa Cruz. From there they'd hop an aquaplane to Lake Laguna San Luis, take a boat up the San Miguel River to the town of Magdalena and finish the journey by horseback. She hadn't sat a saddle in thirty years.

Just past 10:00 am, they took off from Purdue. The pilot climbed to ten thousand feet and leveled for cruising. Ever gathered everyone for a briefing, spreading out a topical map and passing around photos of the castle they would be breaching. The fortress was surprisingly small, constructed of large block stone with a large center house and attached tower on each side. One tower was square and the other octagon, both rising a hundred feet in height with a parapet. Guards were always posted.

Because the castle stood nestled in the middle of jungle terrain, cover would be to their advantage, as well as the dark of night. Ever pointed to the octagon tower, "This is the tower in which she is most likely being held. However, because our information is not irrefutable, we will pair up. Mr. Cooper and Bob will take the square tower, Mr. Parks and I the Octagon. We will enter them from inside the main house. Once we've made entry Janis will remain below in the house as backup. We will all have wrist-communicators, so Janis will keep us informed of any traffic moving up the tower stairway behind us."

Ever searched their faces for acknowledgment then looked back to the map. His finger traced along a section of jungle, "Here there lays a trail wide enough for our horses. It leads into the forest three miles to the castle. We will stop short and cover the rest of the way on foot. I have a gear bag on board for each of you. Fitted for your size, you will find inside a black Kevlar helmet and tactical hood, which covers all but the open face area. Also, protective gloved sleeves; if bitten it will hurt, but the sleeves will provide protection not only from bite attempts but from knife wounds as well."

None of them remarked, but each felt better knowing such equipment would be available. "You will also be wearing an advanced Kevlar upper body protection system; it will help against hard blows. Vampires are quite strong. You will also find a pair of black Kevlar pants with shin guards and safety toe Zipper ETC tactical boots. Each of us will be wearing head mount infrared illumination. And of course, we will carry the weapons issued at the Cooper house. I estimate the trip by horseback from Magdalena to the castle will take just under two hours. We will go in just before dawn."

Janis remarked. "Dawn means daylight. I assume they will cease pursuing us when the sun comes up?"

Ever shook his head. "You have assumed incorrectly. As with me, light will not have any effect. The daylight will help only because it will be easier for us to see them. As mentioned, they will be relentless. They will not retreat. For all of us it will be a simple case of kill or be killed."

"Why are they so vicious, ever?" Janis asked.

The Ferret held his eyes on Janis before replying. "It is because Castle Blasonar de Racista is to them, holy ground. Neither your government nor the Bolivian authorities go there. Since the castle's construction a century ago, three United States Agents have attempted to make an arrest at the castle; none ever returned. The Bolivian government supposedly investigated each case but turned up nothing."

"Didn't the U.S. go in and do their own investigating?" Janis asked.

"No, they did not. Bolivian authorities decline them access."

"Sweet," Janis said glancing at Bob. Again, she looked at Ever. "Castle Blasonar de Racista. It's Spanish. What does it mean?"

"It means to boast of racism. Vampires think of themselves as a superior race," Ever shrugged, "and in many ways they are, as you will soon see."

CHAPTER 22

The madman who had bound Roland and Wynona Otis now knelled at the frightened woman's side. "Let's play a game of mime, shell we." he told her musingly. On her back, Wynona's eyes stared fearfully into his.

Stroking her hair Blue Eyes marveled over her beauty. She was virtually flawless: mid-thirties, soft auburn hair, magnificently shaped derriere, scrumptious breasts and eyes of hazel. Eight hundred years ago as a Sultan within the Ottoman Empire, he'd have most assuredly made her a cherished concubine.

The back of his hand drifted to her cheek, *so soft, the feel of silk*. Wynona closed her eyes; they were beginning to tear. She wanted so much to pull away, to scream, but the gray duct tape covering her mouth made that impossible.

"Please open your eyes, Wynona," he asked softly. Not wanting to but fearing the consequence of disobedience, she opened them blinking at the wetness. Wynona was tall and her neck seemed as if it stretched incessant; and this madman, this sociopath's fingertips were dancing upon its softness.

Blue Eyes tilted his head to the side, mesmerized. This woman took his breath away. She lay before him a work of art, a masterpiece of perfected femininity. And as his fingertips played upon the soft erotic vulnerability of her neck, his inimitable blue eyes stared longingly into hers.

Strangely a feeling of calm was replacing the fear rushing through her body; an odd sense that all would be okay, that he wasn't going to hurt them, that in the end this would all be over and feel as it had been little more than a dream.

Within a second, however, his big hand had slipped around her throat and began to squeeze. Wynona's eyes widened, the pain instantaneous.

Oh, how he loved the sight of fear on the faces of those about to die. Wynona sucked frantically through her nostrils fighting for oxygen; her larynx was beginning to crush, her face turning blue. Roland struggled to free himself, mumbling hysterically behind the tape covering his mouth.

Then the madman released his grip. Wynona's nostrils opened and closed like overworked valves. Blue Eyes continued to watch, amused. After several seconds, when panic had lessened, he leaned close to Wynona's ear and whispered, "When your time comes to do my bidding, do not cross me. So, behold, and observe as I reinforce the gravity of my warning."

Reaching into his pocket he came away with a blue-handled, straight razor. His wrist flicked and the blade flung open. Its sharp-edged steel glistened within the ray of sunlight pouring through the basement window

Both victims climbed to a new level of terror. Again, they struggled to free themselves, wiggling like impaled worms on a fisherman's hook; but there was no escaping, this crazed man controlled their fate. Fear, like water cascading a dam, flushed away any remaining thread of control, their hearts pounded, tears cascaded their cheeks; neither wanted to die...not this way, not by the sharp sting of a blade.

Turning to Roland, Blue Eyes smiled. "Okay my endearing friend, lct's show your lovely wife how serious it is to take my commands to heart"."

With one slash, he cut the tape binding Roland's ankles and pulled him to his knees. Roland's hands remained duct taped behind his back, so his head lay against the cold cement floor and his buttocks raised.

"Now Roland," Blue Eyes told him soft spoken, "Please do not move. I really do not wish to cut you." Beginning at the right cuff of Roland's blue jeans, he sliced up the seam and through his leather belt. Then piece by piece he slashed and tossed aside every stitch of clothing until Roland was naked. Wynona lay on her back watching. She was crying again, empathy for her husband. The entire time Roland had been mumbling beneath the tape, begging his captor to not do this.

With the last piece of material on the floor, Blue Eyes pulled back to admire his work. "Now Wynona," he said turning to look at her, "I want you to understand, what I am about to do to your husband, I do it for you. Why you ask? To illustrate the seriousness of the task I will soon be calling on you to perform. I am not going to kill Roland, not so long as you cooperate. Trust me; there will be no room for error when your time for service comes."

Setting the razor on the floor beside him, Blue Eyes rose to his feet and began removing his own clothing. When totally nude, he knelled again - close behind Roland's rear. For a time, he playfully kneaded Roland's buttocks, running his hands up and down the cheeks admiringly; he liked what he saw: firm, rounded, virgin. Softly his hand slid between Roland's thighs and cupped his hanging genitals - gently, careful not to cause him pain, he worked them in his hands.

The insane man closed his eyes and breathed deeply, feeling himself beginning to stir. Continuing to cry, Wynona wanted to help her husband, to do something. Never before had she considered herself capable, but if it were possible now, she'd pick up the lying razor and kill this evil monstrosity; hack him into a hundred tiny pieces, and when he lay dead…

Blue Eyes snapped his head toward Wynona and opened his eyes. Her thoughts disintegrated, exploding into a million non-sensible fragments. The man fondling her husband had…changed, altered. His once bright blue eyes were gone, having turned black as a starless sky. Behind the tape Wynona screamed, playing her part well in this deranged game of Mime.

Roland's face was lying in a pool of his own tears. He could not see the strange metamorphosis, but as he cried, he wondered what he had done to deserve such humiliation, and in front of his wife. Why them? Why their house?Of all the other homes in Brooke, why had this… evil, come here?

Wynona's eyes suddenly widened. She shouted her husband's name, but it was lost to silence. Roland's body began lurching forward, rocking faster and faster, his face scraping against the cement floor. His screams beneath the duct tape were loud in his heart and mind but mumbled to the world. Never, never ever had he experienced such pain. It felt as if he were being ripped in two.

CHAPTER 23

When Lemus and the others landed in Santa Cruz, they found the weather a sweltering 98 degrees; 111 with heat index. Wasting no time, they tossed their gear into a small motorboat that skipped them across the water to the precarious aquaplane rocking gently from the boat-made waves. Less than ten minutes found them loaded and in flight. Quietly, each stared wonderingly at the Tropical Forest a thousand feet below.

It was Janis that broke the somber silence.Sitting directly behind Ever, she pulled her eyes from the window staring at the back of the Ferret's head. "Why here, Ever," she asked, "why build a castle in the heart of a jungle, why not a metropolis with lots of people and an endless supply of blood?"

Sharpening a K-bar he made no effort to turn around. Speaking as he continued sliding the knife's blade methodically up and down the wet stone, he told her, "Bolivia, Janis," he said, "is one of the poorest countries in South America. Three times the size of Colorado it is covered largely by Rainforest. Here there is little work and few governments assisted programs to help its citizens. In Bolivia people will do anything for money to feed their families; including selling their blood…in any way requested. And sadly, when a man, woman or child disappears here, the world nor local government pays no attention."

Janis felt no need to reply. Turning back to the window she looked once again at the jungle skirting beneath. Oblivious to the warm sun on her face she shook her head; *what kind of fucked up world have we turned ourselves into?*

Just under two hours they were splashing down on Lake Laguna San Luis.

The boat that carried them up the river to the town of Magdalena was an old, fourteen-foot pontoon, powered by an outboard mercury engine looking as if it had been stolen from a museum. The sweat-drenching ride took forty-two minutes ending in North Magdalena.

Killing the engine, the dark wrinkled-skin operator waited patiently for the boat to bump against a dilapidated Wooden Dock. Jumping free he fastened the ropes then assisted with the disembarking. Once unloaded he and Ever began a conversation in a dialect sounding Spanish, yet dissimilar.

Along the river's edge women dipped clothes in the muddy water, then beat them over the dark stones casing the shore. Janis watched in silent awe. In her home state of Louisiana, there existed a fair share of underprivileged people, yet, even in the desolate out-reaches of the Bayou, it was nothing like this.

After shaking hands with the old helmsman, Ever steadied the craft as he climbed back aboard, then untied the lines and tossed them onto the boat floor. The motor started and the pontoon pulled away. Ever turned to the others speaking abruptly, "Follow me."

Grabbing their gear, they trudged single file up a grassy knoll and into town.

This section of Magdalena resembled something out of the old American West, made up of worn wood buildings, horses and donkeys tethered to hitching posts, and free roaming Oxen sharing the dirt streets with barking dogs and clucking chickens. People were reserved watching Ever and the others with suspicion.

Ever lead the way down main street to an old hovel serving as an open-air bar and restaurant. The three-room shack was void of patrons so locating a table was no problem. Thankfully the shade did offer some relief from the heat.

An old woman limped over to take orders. She could not speak English so Ever interpreted. No one was hungry but everyone, except Ever, ordered a bottle of water; he requested a Jim Beam on the rocks.

When the drinks arrived Bob Lemus glanced at his watch then grinned at Ever, "Its 12:03 Ferret-man. Barely past noon."

Ever raised his glass returning the grin; "true, my friend," he said, "but all is fair game when the sun *is* past the yardarm."

Raising his bottle of water and with a nod, Lemus returned the toast, "Rightly so indeed.For many of us some things should never change."

Ever downed the contents and set the glass on the table. Following a glance about the room he spoke quietly, "Kepi, our boat driver, will meet us here in the morning at 2:30. He will have our horses with him. When he arrives..."

Ron interrupted, "Ever, I'm sorry but why in the hell are we waiting? Let's just go in as soon as it's dark?"

Although he disliked being questioned, Ever was empathetic. "Even Vampires sleep, Mr. Parks. Like humans, very few are up and about at the wee hours. Trust me, we will need every advantage, and there is not one better than the element of surprise."

Janis reached out and squeezed Ron's hand. "It's okay Ron. We'll get her back. We just need to do it the right way."

Ron stared at her a moment, started to say something, paused, then sighed and looked away. The others felt Ron's pain but knew that listening to the Ferret would be the best chance Michelle had.

Within the hour, they were checked into a single-story motel; this building too, like the restaurant revealed its age. Ever advised everyone to ready their equipment, then get some sleep, 2:30 would come quickly.

Janis and Bob took a room and Ron and Clay shared another; Ever threw in with them and stretched out on the floor. Both rooms were fitted with window air conditioners, and it was a great relief.

Taking Ever's advice they readied their armor, fitting it to their bodies, adjusting straps, moving around in it getting the feel of it. Each understood that in a very short time this gear could mean the difference between life and death.

By 7:00pm each lay in bed waiting for sleep to come. Clay stared into the ceiling thinking; *Vampires! Unlike Hollywood, these beings actually existed. Killers unlike no other: possessing incredible strength and the ability to regenerate in minutes; biters, discrete hunters of the human race, Sighing,* he continued his distraught reasoning, *"UFO's, Area 51, the Bermuda triangle! What other perilous secrets were governments hiding from the world? Sighing again, he shook his head. It seemed the older he grew the more he learned, and the more he learned the more he realized the less he knew.*

And his family? Blue Eyes had nearly destroyed them seven years ago? Where was this maniac now, what was he doing? Was he planning to harm his wife again, and now, his son too? Would staying home have been the wiser choice? Yes, Jones and Clendes were there with them, and they were the agencies best, handpicked by Bob Lemus himself. And he trusted them both. Yet, the Blue Eyes killer was unquestioningly criminal perfection, a genius, and near flawless in all he chose to do!

In the bed beside Clay, Ron Parks lay on his left side asleep: dreaming and twitching from a torturous nightmare;*Michelle lay trapped, entangled within a vast stock-pile of dead bodies, all bloodless and pale, eyes staring blankly with mouths agape from having died screaming.*

Her chest now collapsed, Michelle's outcry for Ron to help her had faded. Crying, he struggled steadily through the muddle of enmeshed arms and legs to reach her. There had been no time to remove bodies and lighten the load crushing her, for the pallid corpses proved far to many in number. To Ron Parks it felt as if he were moving in fragments of seconds, but finally, after all the clambering through the tangle of pallid limbs he at last grasped his beloved's hand; and upon contact Ron screamed! Her touch was cold as winter ice, void of any warmth, and here open eyes stared out through the dull film of death, dilated and fixed. He was too late; they had killed his Michelle. " BASTARDS," he screamed, "DIRTY FILTHY VAMPIRE BASTARDS!" His screaming echoed loud through the dark regions of his subconscious. His nightmarish twitching stopped; for there, in his dream, he too had died, and not from the draining of his blood; but for the heartbreaking loss of his reason for living!

Stretched out on the floor at the foot of the bed, Ever rolled onto his side. Awake, his dark eyes watched a cockroach scurry across the floor. In an eccentric sense, he felt kin to the insect. Like himself, the cockroach was constantly evolving, redefining itself, utilizing evolution as a means of survival.

Ever disliked what he was, what he had become. His living with the need for human Blood to survive had grown both tiresome and repulsive. It was for this reason he had chosen to become a hunter, a killer of his own kind. Yet in retrospect, he liked to think his discontent was more a matter of morality than disgust; and that helped him feel more human than Vampire. And it helped strengthen his resistance from turning back to what he once was.

Morality aside, as much as he hated himself for it, there were occasions when instinct, like a dark whisper, aroused his desire to do that which felt natural, to hunt humans, to kill and feed.

Except for a time in his early teens, he had always been able to resist the urge, yet he feared one day it may return. And for that reason, he clung optimistically to his one great hope; that science would one day find a way to end their need for blood.

In the room next door, Janis lay nestled in the arms of the man she treasured. The couple had just made love and now contentment was sanctioning Janis with the blessing of sleep. Despite her underlying worries, she had slowly drifted away.

Bob however, lay awake smoking a cigarette. He understood to well what they would be going up against in just a few hours. The odds were significantly stacked against them. He had grown close to everyone in the group and feared for them all. But Janis, his sweet piece of candy, his beloved sliver of white chocolate; it was her he feared for most.

CHAPTER 24

Michael was helping his mom clean the house, having chosen vacuuming over laundry. Despite the roar of the motor, he heard the doorbell and shut the cleaner down, shouting, "I'll get it." But agent Clendes rushed past beating him to the door.

"That's alright Michael," he said, "I'll answer it." Removing his weapon and holding it at his side, Clendes peered through the window left of the door. A male, late sixties or there about, wearing a brown-tweed sport coat, silver hair and a look of sincere patience stood waiting. He was gripping a brown briefcase.

Jones appeared suddenly at the kitchen entrance and Clendes nodded his recognition. Turning then, Clendes opened the door. Taken aback, the elderly man offered a bewildered look. "Hello. Are Nancy or Clay at home?"

Michael stepped within the visitors view and smiled with exuberance. "High, Pastor Hart."

Recognizing a relationship, Clendes stepped aside allowing Hart to enter. Following one last look outside, he closed the door and holstered his weapon.

Michael gave the older man a hug, "Right on time as always!" he said.

Hart smiled, "Of course. When God twists your arm, you can't say no."

Michael smiled wider looking up. "Yeah right, twist your arm!"

Nancy came down the stairs face aglow. "I thought that would be you." She chimed. "Michael's been waiting anxiously for his fix."

Clendes glanced at Jones, quizzically. Nancy caught it and realized she'd left them in the dark. "Agent Clendes and agent Jones I'd like you to meet Pastor Phillip Hart. I'm sorry I forgot to tell you about him. He comes once a week to work with Michael. Since we home school our little angel," she hugged Michael and he blushed, "we've included religious studies in his curriculum. Pastor Hart is his tutor."

The three men shook hands then Nancy, Michael and Hart went into Clay's den. The pastor sat behind the desk as always, setting his briefcase beside him on the floor. Michael carried a folding chair around beside him and sat. Nancy settled into the blue loveseat left of the desk.

Clay's den looked as much a psychologist's office as a study, and they had jokingly come to call it Doctor Hart's Room. "So," Pastor Hart asked. "Is something going on here?"

Nancy sighed stretching out on the loveseat, throwing her legs over the arm and folding her hands in her lap. "Well Doctor," she said, attempting to lighten the moment, "it's a long story, but the best answer is, what isn't going on?"

"Do you want to talk about it?" Hart asked.

Nancy frowned. "Yes, if you don't mind." She explained everything, beginning with the fact Blue Eyes had escaped, that Clay and the others were in route to Bolivia to rescue Michelle, and that there were really Vampires. And worst of all, Blue Eyes had once again opened the doorway to Hell letting everything out to come after Clay.

Pastor Hart sat back in the chair ignoring the soft squeak. Folding his arms, he stared at the desktop a moment then glanced at Michael, realizing he had obviously been included in all of it. Following a nod, he moved his eyes to Nancy, "Well," he told her, "The Vampire thing is new, but we've gotten through the other before, and we'll do it again. Remember, we've got the Big Guy up above on our side; and if God be for you, who can be against you?"

Nancy had wanted so much to hear his encouragement. The Pastor had been instrumental in helping her and Clay get through the last horrible ordeal, and now he stood with them once again. She considered him an inimitable blessing, already the burden felt lessened, and the enlightenment caused Nancy to begin to cry.

Leaving his chair Michael moved to where she lay and sat beside her. Placing his little hand on hers he told her, "Don't worry mom, God will help us get through this, I promise."

Hart grinned warmly from behind the desk, "That's right Nancy," he said in agreement, "Listen to Pastor Michael."

Nancy sniffled with a bit of laughter. Sitting up she took her son in her arms while kissing his cheek. She then threw Pastor Hart a teary smile.

CHAPTER 25

In the Bolivian motel Clay's eyes opened suddenly…he didn't move, something had brushed his neck. Peripherally he could see the motel door standing ajar; *the door he himself had personally closed and locked.*Moonlight poured in through the breach casting a distorted shadow across the plaster-cracked ceiling above him. Someone or something was standing beside the bed.

He lay motionless, weighing on the side of instinct: *don't move, assess.* His heart was racing, pounding through his carotid arteries… *great move Clay,* **he thought to himself,** *a personal invite to a fast-food dinner.* Whatever was there, they were to his back, and it touched his neck again, this time briskly. The touch was cold.

The semi-automatic with vampire killing rounds lay on the bed stand just an arm's length away; but it lay to his back and right next to who or whatever was standing behind him. Until meeting Ever, he had never seen a Vampire, or understood their workings; and what he did know now, he feared. These things were fast, deadly, and liked to play. And when playtime was over…

Through the tense silence came a voice. "Wake up Mr. Cooper, it's time to go." Ever's fingers again tapped the side of Clay's neck. Realizing now what was happening Clay pulled himself into a sitting position shouting, "Ever what the hell do you think you're doing?"

The Ferret expressed surprise "I'm waking you. It is time to go."

"You scared the shit out of me. It ever dawn on you to wake someone by shaking their shoulder…especially here?"

Shrugging, Ever frowned. "Sorry. That is how we wake one another in our society. Habit, I guess."

Shaking his head Clay pressed the illumination button on his watch: 2:36 am. With a sigh he wiped sleep from his eyes and realized Bob and Janis were also in the room watching it all. Both were dressed, armed, and ready. Bob was smiling, his teeth gleaming in the moonlight.

Swinging his feet to the floor Clay looked directly into Lemus' shadowy face. "What are you grinning at? You think a man being scared to death is funny?"

Lemus shook his head trying to make the smile go away. "No Clay, I don't."

Night in Bolivia took on a disengaging allure. Peaceful and calm, the full moon burnished the land with vivid silver light while clusters of stars sparkled amid a soft velvety backdrop. Orion, the big and little dipper, Pegasus and other constellations seemed to standout as if in 3D splendor. Visibility was prodigious. Perfect, Clay thought, for what was to come.

The man named Kepi and a young woman stood waiting, holding five saddled animals by the reins. Once again, Ever and the old man spoke in the odd Spanish dialogue. After several minutes, they each gave a nod and the couple hurried away, vanishing quickly into the darkness.

Of the five mounts, Ever had been supplied a Black Stallion, Clay a well-defined Palomino, Ron an anxious Paint, and Bob and Janis had each been issued a mule; Kepi apologized for the two subordinate castes, but it had been the best he could do.

When saddled, they rode north following the river. Just under five kilometers they turned west, entering into a narrow trail cutting through the jungle. The moonlight diminished considerably beneath the thick leafy canopy, but enough light remained to make out the dark form of the rider ahead. Bob had adjusted the stirrups for Janis, and it made her ride easier, but she still clung tight to the saddle horn rocking to the animal's gait.

Ever had timed their ride to insure they did not run the animals, fearing the pounding of hoofs might alert those they hoped to surprise. And, if luck did prevail, he wanted the animals fresh for a hard and fast ride back.

The forest was alive with unsettling sounds, things constantly scrambled through the heavy foliage. Out of the darkened distance came occasional howls and screams, but most nerve-shattering of all was the expectation that at any moment Vampires would leap from the darkness pulling them free from the saddle.

Because the trail was little wider than the animals they rode, undergrowth persistently mauled their face and body. There was no breeze and sweat saturated the clothing beneath their armor.

All rode in somber silence, their thoughts all in one accord. In a short time, if awakened, the altered humans would engage them in a fight to the death, a fight they feared, but would face with honor.

And too, though they had no idea, a different enemy was round and about; to their front, sides and rear marched a great army of Demons; their evil expectations running high, all anxious for the bloody slaughter soon to come.

And though this enemy marched not to join in the fight, their presence was not without purpose. In the aftermath of battle, they would claim those souls not worthy of God's inheritance; bind them and drag them fighting and screaming into the darkness of Hell. And it mattered not if they be Human or Vampire.

Twenty-two minutes from the time they turned onto the path, Ever reined his horse to a stop and dismounted. The others followed. Upon securing the animals they huddled in the darkness.

"Activate your night vision." Ever whispered.

Removing their helmets each slipped the infra-red goggles over their eyes and adjusted the strapping. The jungle transformed into a green, hazy-clear world. "We are one hundred yards from the castle." Ever explained, "It lies at the end of this path. There will be two guards, one at the top of each tower. I am the only one with a silencer so I will enter and take them out. When you see them drop, run quickly to the center building between the towers. I will meet you there. As I stated earlier, Mr. Parks and I will take the Octagon tower to the right, Mr. Cooper and Bob the square tower to the left. Janis will position herself inside the main building, hidden, informing us of any approaching traffic. Is this clear?" Each whispered a positive response.

"Please test your wrist communicators." Securing their earpieces, they spoke softly into the tiny screens, verifying effectiveness. "When we've taken possession of Mrs. Parks," Ever went on, "she will be brought down to the main floor. No one, *no one*, is to leave until all are together again and we move out as a group. Under no circumstances does anyone go out on their own, understood?"

Again, they whispered recognition.

Ever in the lead, automatic weapons in their hands, they moved out, remaining close to the jungle's edge for cover. Slowly, crouched and silent, they made their way to within view of the castle. Lying prone, concealed by foliage they observed the hundred-foot cleared perimeter circling the complex. The place clearly matched the photo: two towers connected to a middle stone building. The center structure resembled a large, two-story open atrium Block Church, minus the cross. Two arched glass-stained windows and a huge clear-glass arched door made up the front.

Just as Ever had said; barely visible, behind Parapet walls, a guard atop each tower walked the darkness, fading in an out of sight. Ever screwed his silencer to the barrel of his weapon; a soft metallic sound brushed their ears. "I must enter the building and climb the towers; the guards are too far away to risk a shot. Everyone stay put until I reappear at the door and signal for you. When I do come running. If I have not shown after fifteen minutes from the time I enter, then something has gone wrong, and they know. Should that happen, rush the building yelling. Wake them and fight. It will do no good to try and reach the horses and run. They will catch you. Your only chance will be to fight as a group."

Ever looked toward the towers. At a point when both guards turned away, he scrambled to his feet and dashed silent across the clearing. At the door he stopped and knelled, trying the handle; the door did not budge. Pulling a pick lock carapace from his vest, he began working the keyhole.

The others watched nervously though the green hued world of night vision. The clock was ticking with daylight fast approaching. Around them, the strange night noises continued, and although there was no indication whatsoever, each felt as if they were being watched.

The door finally jarred. Ever rose and glanced quickly back at them. He then disappeared inside.

CHAPTER 26

Pastor Hart possessed a deep admiration for seven-year-old Michael Cooper; actually, it was one of profound wonderment. The boy had grown far beyond the expectations of any Vicar. While there was little known of the childhood of Jesus Christ, Pastor Phillip Hart believed Michael's formative years might possibly parallel that of the Savior himself. Of course, the boy had not, to date, walked on water, fed a multitude of thousands with two loaves of bread and five fishes, nor raised anyone from the dead. But he did, by grace, possess a virtuous connection with God that surpassed even his own, or any other known clergy for that matter.

The two talked and shared scripture for over an hour. Michael as always, held his own in biblical understanding and at the end of their class time, completed the session with prayer, giving special thanks to Jesus for allowing Pastor Hart to be not only his teacher, but a dear personal friend as well.

Hart had left homework for the young boy, jotting down a scripture verse Michael was to read, to think about, and be ready to discuss at their next session. Following the Pastor's departure Michael moved around behind his father's desk and sat. Bowing his head, he said a quiet prayer then opened his Modern English Version Bible to the Book of Proverbs.

CHAPTER 27

Just inside the main building of the Castle, Ever heard the door click behind him, re-locking. Kneeling on one knee, he remained quiet and motionless, listening. Cloaked in soft wavering shadows, he found himself inside a small foyer made up of iron bars. Not unlike a prison cubicle, a cell door stood directly in front of him. Beyond the foyer, angled out from the walls of a large open room, flickering torches draped the room in plots of shadows and darkness. He removed his night-vision headgear.

Glancing back over his shoulder he studied the glass door through which he had just come. The place a handle should be, was now an iron plate; *no handle; and no lock with which to pick his way out.*

Climbing to his feet, he walked to the barred door; no lock there either. Frowning at his idiocy he unscrewed the silencer from his weapon, placed it in a vest pocket then holstered the piece. *Electronic doors run by generator!*

Across the room arose the sudden tap of footsteps moving slow and deliberate. They echoed through the shadowy expanse, moving in his direction. Ever looked at his watch; seven of the fifteen minutes remained.

A tall form stepped from the shadows, followed by two men with shotguns. "Hello Ever." The tall man said.

Staring through the bars, the Ferret gave a silent nod, studying the powerful six foot four-inch man standing in front of him. Wearing clogs, black shorts, white tee-shirt and long black hair falling to his shoulders, Ever's visitor looked unceremoniously tropical and at ease; actually, Ever knew it to be arrogance. "As you can see Ever," the tall man began again, "we've made some modifications since you were here last."

Ever glanced casually about the barred foyer surrounding him, "Yes, so I see." He said coolly.

"Like them?"

Ever shrugged, glancing around once again. "You might add curtains; bring in a recliner and small side table; dress the table with a bucket of ice, a tall, frosted glass, and 64 ounce bottle of Jim Beam. I might find it likable then?"

The tall man grinned. "It appears you still enjoy the sauce."

"Keeps the joints oiled."

"Blood use to do that for you."

"Things change."

"Like turning on your own kind?"

Ever never raised his voice, "No Aluka," he said, "I'm still a bloodsucker; I just specialize in eliminating cocksuckers."

The man called Aluka folded his arms ignoring the remark. "So, what shall we do with your friends outside?"

"Let them go," Ever said, "then open the door. I'm beside myself with the want to bite a three-inch section of airway out of your windpipe."

Aluka grinned again. "Ever, look at me. I'm young and strong. Look at you, you're old and slow. I'd kill you in the time it takes to bleed out a small child."

"You've always been arrogant, Aluka. That's your weakness."

"I have no weaknesses. I can hunt and kill faster…or slower, than anyone. If injured, I recover faster than Vamps ten years my junior, and when it comes to women, I can make them climax so much they're too tired to stop smiling." He glanced over his shoulders and spoke into the shadows. "Give us light."

Somewhere the throwing of a switch echoed through the openness and sudden bright light chased away the torch-shadows. The cell door clicked. Ever pushed it open and stepped into the large, now lighted room.

"Please." Aluka said motioning with his hand. "Lay your armor and weapons there in the corner. They will do you no good now."

Ever did as he was told, stacking everything neatly. There was no other choice; at least for now. Aluka, the Vampire men feared, women desired, and he hated; held the trump card…Michelle Parks.

CHAPTER 28

At the Book of Proverbs Michael turned to Chapter 11 pulling his finger down the page to verses 5 thru 7. He read aloud to himself, *(5) The righteousness of the upright will direct his way, but the wicked will fall by his own wickedness. (6) The righteousness of the upright will deliver them, but transgressors will be taken by their schemes. (7) When a wicked man dies, his expectation will perish, and the hope of unjust men perishes.*

Michael let the bible lay open and sat back in the chair. It was time for thought. Lacing his fingers behind his head he lifted his feet atop the desk and closed his eyes. When his dad needed to think this was the way he sat. And if it was good enough for dad, it was good enough for him.

CHPATER 29

With the open room lighted now, Ever could see clearly. The shadowy boroughs born from the torchlight gave up the things hidden within them. A dozen Vampires sat huddled in pairs around six chaise sofas: feeding. Bolivian citizens lay stretched upon the furniture, awake, all naked, dazed, and stippled with blood where they'd been bitten.

Aluka smiled. "Hungry?"

Ever stared coldly into his eyes. "Yes, for your blood."

"My blood! Wouldn't you prefer something a bit more… succulent?Say for example, that which lies upon the chaise at the far end."

Ever's eyes moved there and stared.

A young teen girl lay motionless, staring blankly into the ceiling. Two male Vampires, one at the brachial artery of her right arm and the other at the left femoral artery, where knelled feeding. Blood dribbled but little was being lost. On the remaining lounges lay four other women and a male.

Ever looked once again into Aluka's eyes; "You're a disgrace to our kind. The government supplies you with all the blood you need, they do not hunt you, and they leave you alone. Yet you lead others into this."

Aluka cupped his hands behind his back his voice remaining calm. "We are our own people and in need of no one's handouts. The world is filled with billions of what we need – every one of them there for the taking…and personal liking. Many of us have grown disenchanted with the government's paper decree. Recall your American History Ever, for land this so-called government poisoned, butchered, and diseased the American Indian, did the same to the Mexicans, and even now continue fighting a war far across the world in the Arabian sand, and for what… humanitarianism? Please! You know and I know they have kept us secret because they cannot destroy us. And if the world discovered our existence, they would demand we be eliminated. And that, my dear Ever, would become a new age war."

Aluka spun on his heels and marched into the cell cubicle. Approaching the outer door, he stood at its threshold until it made a clicking sound. Immediately he pushed it open and stepped out into the tropical warmth. Holding the door open with his shoulder he gazed where the others lay, "My name is Aluka", he said loudly, "please; all of you put down your weapons and come in. Consider yourselves guests."

Clay and the others lay stunned. Obviously Ever had been caught. Aluka spoke again. "You hesitate, yet I am a fair man, so I shall offer you an option. I will give you Mrs. Parks, in exchange for Janis Barr-Lemus. Following the exchange, the rest of you may return to your horses and ride away. I give you my word we will not interfere."

Several moments passed with no response. Aluka, leaning comfortably against the door glanced inside, "Bring her to me."

Down the stairway leading from the octagon tower, two men descended, one carrying a high-powered rifle, and the other with Michelle Parks draped over his shoulder clad in bra and panties; Ever heard her moan as they passed. Though she was far too weak to resist, she was at least alive; a promising revelation considering the multitude of bites covering her body. Ever wanted to make a move but the two Vamps with the shotguns remained too far out of reach.

At the door, Michelle was lowered to her feet, the carrier standing behind her for support. Ron cried out from where he lay. "Michelle!"

Aluka spoke again. "Now which will it be? Put down your weapons and come in, or we make the exchange, and you go free? Trust me you do not want to make a fight of it." He stuck his hands into his pockets, "I will count to ten. Have your answer ready," He began: "One. Two…"

Janis removed her helmet and pulled the night goggles from her face. She looked at Clay, then Ron and lastly, Bob, holding his stare. "I'm going in." Bob Lemus remained silent. Janis pulled her eyes back to Ron. "Come on, let's go get Michelle." Rising to their feet, they began removing weapons.

Aluka's count continued, "Six, seven…"

Clay started to get up, but Bob Lemus grabbed his arm. "No. There's no other way."

Clay glanced at Bob's hand then glared into his eyes, "What the hell are you talking about?" Just shoot the son of a bitch and we'll go get her."

"Look Clay," Bob was talking quickly, "if we challenge them now, we'll definitely have to fight. We have weapons yes, but long before the fight is over, they'll see to it Michelle is dead anyway…and probably us too. It just has to be this way."

"You ass, Lemus," Clay sputtered, "we're just trading fresh blood for old blood. Let's fight these freaky bastards, take our chances. Think about Janis, what they will do to her."

Bob Lemus understood all Clay was saying. Looking up he met Janis's eyes, "You sure you're okay with this?"

She nodded. "I'm sure. Just keep the glass half-full."

Aluka finished, "Nine…Ten."

Lemus looked back to the castle. The retired agent also hated the man called Aluka. Knew who he was, had dealt with him in the past. In their covert world, Aluka was to the Vampire, what Osama Bin Ladin was to terrorism. Officials feared him, understanding the chaotic potential he possessed. And had Clay known he would have agreed.

Turning, Lemus shouted across the open yard, "Okay, they'll meet you halfway."

Aluka shook his head. "No, I'm afraid not. Have them come here to us. I give you my word, agent Lemus, we will make the exchange, no tricks."

Lemus whispered under his breath. "Fuck!" Quickly he looked to Clay. "Okay, put your sights on the one holding Michelle, I'll take Aluka. If the exchange takes place without a glitch, let it be. If not, don't miss." Lemus looked up at Ron and Janis. "When you reach them stay out of the line of fire." The two nodded solemnly then turned and began their walk across the open yard.

Clay and Bob, arms stretched, took careful aim and waited. The jungle remained muggy, its anomalous sounds sharpening. All had removed their night vision equipment. Sun light was now shimmering through the jungle canopy.

Eyes on his wife, Ron spoke softly to the courageous little woman matching his every step. "You realize you're not going in there, right? When we reach them, I'll take the big shit doing all the talking. You get to Michelle."

Janis stared up at Ron. "No. You take Michelle and get her out of here. She needs a hospital and needs it right now. Trust me, you can bet your tight puckered sphincter muscle, I'll think of something. Besides, I'm a Cajun. The minute they bite me my blood will melt their teeth."

Ron smiled warmly. "I'll never forget this, Janis."

"Hey, you're not going to cry on me, are you?"

"I could."

"Well don't. Just grab Michelle and go home."

CHAPTER 30

Michael Cooper slipped into his pajamas, the ones decorated with his all-time favorite action hero, Superman. He brushed his teeth then climbed into bed. The superman lamp beside him furnished the perfect lighting by which to read - his most favorite thing to do. Superman bookends - the action hero with arm forward, fist closed, and flying straight toward the sky - held six books; Michael grabbed the one cuddled in the middle: Harry Potter and the Cradle of Stone. He possessed the entire series and owned every available DVD.

Snuggling down he opened to his bookmark and began reading.

Below, in the living room Clendes and Jones were watching TV.Nancy lay asleep in her recliner, reading glasses resting low on her nose. She had drifted slowly away while reading the paper.

Wind moaned at the doors and snow fell relentless. Already nearly a foot deep, it covered everything. Nothing moved in the streets. The citizens of Brooke were locked warmly away in their homes, accepting the winter's entrapment.Around 9 o'clock houses began to darken as families called it a night.

11:30 Nancy's eyes opened, the house was quiet and she yawned pulling the glasses from her face. Clendes and Jones lay asleep, their heads resting on the back of the couch. Jones was snoring.

Quietly she lowered her footrest and rose, setting the paper noiselessly in the seat of the recliner. She went upstairs and found Michael still reading. He smiled when she came in but knew it was coming, "I know," he said, "turn out the light it's late, I need my sleep."

Nancy reached the bed smiling back. "That is correct young man. You know ten o'clock and it's lights-out." She paused briefly, "You must really enjoy that book, you've read it more than twice I know?"

"It's the greatest. Aside from Superman, I'd love to be Harry Potter mom, he's so cool."

Nancy lifted the book from his hands and placed it back into the bookends. Pulling the covers up she leaned and kissed his forehead saying, "Well let me tell you something my precious young man, "to me you are Harry Potter, my personal, very own Harry Potter. And you don't need a wand to make you special." Throwing him a wink, she clicked off the lamp, "now go to sleep."

Downstairs she woke Clendes and Jones and told them to go to bed as well. Clendes declined, remaining awake to stand watch. He and Jones decided on taking four-hour guard through the night. Smiling her appreciation Nancy went upstairs and readied for bed.

This time she chose not to read before turning out the light. Now she lay awake in the darkness thinking of Clay and the others. Her heart ached for the want of him lying beside her. So much had happened in such a short time. And that blue eyed monster, that…bastard, he was beyond the evil of Hell.

She could not shake the anxiety of feeling he was near, somewhere close, perhaps even now standing in the darkness at the foot of her bed watching, smiling.

Instinctively she sat up quickly turning on the bedside lamp. Nothing was there. Falling back against her pillow, she began to cry. Grabbing a tissue from the bed stand and wiping at her eyes she mumbled into the stillness of the room, *"may God damn your soul."*

It wasn't quite 1:02 am that her troubled mind finally quieted, and she was able to shut out her light. It was a welcomed relief to close her eyes. However, in the next room little Michael opened his.

Lying on his back, he did not move, did not have to, something was in his room, and he could see its dark form moving slowly through the shadows at the foot of his bed.It was a man, or something that had taken the shape of a man; yet it could not be a man, for this person was strolling easily across the ceiling upside down, as if weightless.

Michael watched as it turned and began moving toward him. His little heart was pounding beneath his Superman pajamas. How he wished he were Superman right now. He wanted to scream for his mom, but remained silent instead, fearing whatever it was might hurt her. Tears were filling his eyes.

His voice soft as the wings of a hummingbird; Michael began to pray.

CHAPTER 31

Ron and Janis had reached the Castle door. Morning light glared atop the jungle foliage but remained too weak to penetrate the dense jungle growth. In the openness of the castle yard, however, it shined with appreciative generosity.

Ron grabbed Janis's arm and the two stopped in front of Michelle and the man supporting her. This left a clear shot open for Lemus.

Lying still, maintaining steady aim, Lemus considered Clay's words spoken only minutes earlier: that they were trading fresh blood for old blood. The idea of it made his stomach churn. "Screw this." He said barely audible.

Clay looked at him, staring a moment, then grinned, "Yeah," he said, "that's what I'm talking about. Welcome back Bob Lemus."

Ignoring the remark Lemus told him. "The moment Aluka drops, charge the door, but watch the guys in the tower. I'll cover you as best I can." His right eye closed as he stared down the barrel of his weapon focused on Aluka's chest. Taking a long, deep breath he held it. Easy, slowly, he pulled tension on the trigger; but Aluka suddenly changed positions stepping in front of Janis. Gritting his teeth Bob lowered his weapon, "Fuck a stuck Duck." Although a foot taller than Janis, Aluka's move had made the shot too risky to take with a handgun.

Aluka leaned over Janis. Nearly touching her hair, he breathed deeply with a sniff. Following a grin, he straightened and told her with a voice carrying across the open yard, "Well, Mrs. Barr-Lemus, my senses tell me you had an active night and did not shower this morning. Was it as good for you as it was for Bob? He had a cigarette afterward too, didn't he?"

Janis held Aluka's eyes as she spoke. "It's like the song Elvis Presley sang, 'Oh, such a night.' In fact, it was fantastic. I begged him not to stop. Hell, I'm still bull-legged; you should have noticed that while I was coming; no pun intended."

Aluka grinned. "I can assure you, compared to how shamelessly wanting I can make you feel, your husband's moves last night will be likened to those of a bungling Teen-Ager. Lemus looked at Clay, "That asshole."

Aluka held Janis's eyes for several seconds before turning to Ron, "Your wife has been a most hospitable guest, take her now and go. Tell agent Lemus I will personally look after his wife. As for Mr. Cooper, inform him that we here at Castle Blasonar de Rasista are not his problem, there are far worse fish he must out swim than us. Now take your wife and go. Remember, we will hunt and kill anyone who assists Mr. Cooper."

Janis looked at Ron, her voice stern. "Go Ron, take Michelle and get out of here."

Ron stared into her eyes, began to speak but stopped. Quickly he moved around her and swept Michelle into his arms. Saying nothing, he stormed across the clearing. Although weak, Michelle managed a hoarse whisper, "I knew you'd come."

CHAPTER 32

Michael Cooper stared terrified at the dark apparition moving toward him. The Bible told of God on occasion sending Angels to earth disguised as people: It took little understanding that if God sent Angles in human form, so would Satin.

The boy's crying had stopped but his nose was running; he wiped it with the sleeve of his pajamas thankful his mom was not there to see it. Michael wanted to pull the covers over his head and hide, but that was not what he was supposed to do. What was happening had a purpose.

In the exact moment of that thought, the silent, shadowy figure spoke, its voice deep and hoarse. "Child, I have come to speak with you concerning your father. My master has ordered me to take this form and not hurt you. So be not alarmed. Yet, I will not mislead you. If permitted, I would crawl inside you and take possession of your body. I would seal your mouth and watch as you starved. I would take great delight in your pain as the skin on your body began to rot and the intolerable stench rose to your Master," Michael swallowed as the apparition continued, "but I know of your power, so this cannot be," the demon shrugged, "hence, there is no need of you further crying or being afraid."

The demon stopped as Michael pulled himself into a sitting position. Now directly in front of him hanging low enough to be face to face, the transformed figure continued. "Young one, you know the truth of Cain and Abel. When the brothers were in the field they argued, and out of jealousy and anger Cain did slay his brother. The mark which your God put upon Cain has both haunted and brought him pleasure, but for him, the time has come for he and Abel to reunite for his retribution and new life."

"New life," Michael asked, "are you saying Cain has been born again?"

The demon laughed, sounding almost as if it had growled, "Born again? Oh yes, again and again to this plane, as flesh and blood; but not as you think, not spiritually in Him who you serve; Cain's master is another. With each of Cain's returns, he has been granted increasing power from his master, much the way you receive power from yours. This very day Cain walks among us, as does his brother Abel. Know this, that just as Abel died by the hand of Cain in that field so long ago, now, in this life, Cain must die by the hand of Abel."

Michael had become so intent on what the demon was saying he had forgotten he was frightened. "Wait," he said, "Your saying Cain and Abel are here today? Are you talking about reincarnation?

"Yes, many times both have returned. But at each rebirth, your God's Angels have managed to prevent their contact, but not this time. That is why I have been sent to you. Soon, Cain will come to visit that you will know him. As for his brother Able, he you already know; Abel is your father."

Michael sat a moment sorting it all out, staring into the face of the apparition. When his mind made sense of what the apparition was saying, he practically shouted it out, "That's Crap!" Glancing up he said, "Sorry God." His eyes quickly snapped back, "My dad is not Abel, he's dad. What you say can't be true; reincarnation is not part of the Christian faith. You're just trying to deceive me, just as satin did Eve."

The apparition continued to stare, "I will not waste my time with you, child. You know your God encourages the search for truth, you must —

The door opened suddenly and light from the hallway poured in. Clenching the door handle with one hand and the jam with the other, Nancy's eyes scanned the room. "Michael, are you alright?" she asked, "I heard voices."

The apparition raised a finger to his lips for silence.

Twisting to see around him, Michael realized from the expression on her face, his mom could see nothing out of the ordinary. He asked, "Mom, do you see anyone?"

Nancy glanced around once more. The apparition waited patiently; arms folded across his chest. She shook her head. "No."

"Think maybe it was me talking in my sleep?"

Following a deep sigh Nancy frowned, "Apparently so. Are you okay?"

"Yes." Michael told her. "Okay" she said. Go back to sleep." The door closed and she was gone. The apparition spoke its final words in a whisper. "Convince your father he must kill Cain. There are no choices. I am to leave you with one simple thought. Imagine life without your mother and father?"

CHAPTER 33

Clay lifted himself from the ground. There was anger in his voice. "That's it. It ends here. It ends now!"

With Michelle still cradled in his arms Ron had just reached Clay's side, "What are you doing?"

Lemus climbed to his feet as Clay gave the answer, "I'm walking across this yard and have a one on one with the asshole in the shorts."

Placing a hand on Ron's shoulder, Lemus told him quickly, "Get Michelle to the horses and ride hard back to Magdelene. Find Kepi and tell him to take the two of you down river and hide you there until we've finished."

Clay nodded his approval as Lemus added, "if we're not back in 24 hours have him take you to the plane. Get Michelle back to the states and checked into the best damn Hospital in the country. Call the FBI; tell them I want guards on her 24/7. Tell them why."

Ron began to protest but Clay stopped him. "Just do it, man. We got it here. Go!"

Michelle moaned, and Ron's face showed the pulling of his heart. But he nodded and started down the trail to the horses.

"Bob Lemus looked at Clay. "Got a plan?"

"No. But stay here and wait for my lead - what the hell ever that might be?"

Bob stood forlorn staring as Clay started across the open yard."

It was daylight now and the night noises had been replaced with a loud chatter of birds.

At the castle door Aluka grabbed Janis by the arm and turned to go in. Clay shouted after him, "Hey, Hollywood!"

Pausing, Aluka looked back. He grinned. "You need something Mr. Cooper?"

"Yeah; Janis and Ever. You give them to me now and I won't kill you."

Aluka was amused. "That can not be done."

"Can and will. Let them go."

Clay was within thirty feet when Aluka spoke. "One more step Mr. Cooper and I kill her now." Aluka pulled Janis in front like a shield, grabbing her hair and jerking her head to the side exposing her neck, he lowered his head to her shoulder staring at Clay. White fangs descended immediately from his mouth; his eyes changed color while glistening beneath the warm tropical sun.

Stopping, Clay gave Aluka a grin. Pulling his weapon, he placed the barrel to his own temple. "I have just two simple questions, Aluka," he said, "one, do you have even the slightest idea of the power I hold over you?" Aluka remained poised, listening, "I am the only person alive," Clay went on, "who can send Blue Eyes to Hell…the-only-fucking-one! If I die here, no matter how, he'll blame you personally. And I promise you, the last thing you want are the gates of Hell opened and everything down there coming after you. You may be superior to my kind, but rest assured, you are just a dribble of shit against things that are already dead."

Aluka's teeth quickly receded, his eyes returned to normal, and he slowly lifted his head, yet kept Janis held ready to bite. "You are bluffing, Mr. Cooper." He replied.

"Sure I am. Just bring those pearly whites right back out and bite her. Sink em deep and savior the flavor. But she'll be the last female you ever taste, because if I don't kill you here and now, Blue Eyes will; real soon."

Aluka paused, staring calculatingly into Clay's eyes. Nothing moved, even the birds ceased their chatter. A light breeze tickled the trees.

Clay shrugged, "tell you what, I'll count to ten this time. If, before I reach the end you've not sent Ever out to us and turned Janis loose, I pull the trigger. Because right now I have nothing to lose, the gates have been opened and everything is already crawling out after me."I pull this trigger, its over for me and just the beginning for you. You think I'm bluffing…you decide. One…Two…Three…"

Aluka stared hard at Clayton Cooper, feeling the stress. Clay continued his count…six…seven…" Aluka gritted his teeth, breathed deeply, Cooper was just impossible to read.

Eight…Nine…"

"Okay," Aluka said, "perhaps you are not bluffing. But rest assured there will be another time."His eyes never moving from Cooper's he shouted, "Send out Ever."

Inside, Ever picked up his gear and walked out, grinning for Aluka as he passed. Aluka began backing to the door maintaining his grip on Janis for cover. Clay redirected his weapon toward Aluka's head.

"One more thing," Clay said as he re-positioned, "order the tower guards to throw their weapons over the side. Aluka shouted the order and the rifles rattled as they struck the ground.

When just inside the door Aluka stopped and asked, "before I turn Bob's little piece of tail loose, you said there were two questions Mr. Cooper. Please do tell. What was the second?"

"Turn her lose first. You'll just have to trust me. I will not shoot anyone in cold blood, not even you."

Aluka's eyes glanced at the barrel of Clay's gun than into his eyes. "I am very much aware of the rounds in that weapon, yet I believe you." He turned Janis loose, and she moved to Clay's side working her neck and shoulders. Ever quickly re-donned his gear.

"Now Mr. Cooper," Aluka said, "the second question?"

Clay began a slow pace backward, his weapon still pointed, and Janis and Ever moving right behind him. "It's a simple question, really," Clay said holding his aim, "but I will tell you, it's personal."

Aluka shrugged. "Please, feel free."

"Okay, here goes. It's your teeth. They're so white. What brand of paste do you use?"

Aluka smiled. "My, that is indeed personal. Perhaps the next time we meet I will share that with you."

Clay returned the smile. "No need to meet. Just e-mail me."

CHAPTER 34

Back at the horses, they mounted quickly, reining hard and heeling the animals into a fast brutal ride. Janis clung to the saddle horn bouncing as if she possessed no skeletal frame.

Bob rode directly behind as the last rider. An excellent equestrian he turned frequently watching the trail behind them. No one was following, but just shy of breaking free of the jungle the group reined to a clamorous halt with the animals heehawing and whinnying from the pain of crushing bits.

Just inside the mouth of the exit, sitting upright on their hind quarters, a pack of what appeared to be dogs sat in a plot of light stabbing through the jungle growth. Their presence was obviously a deliberate assemblage.

Hands resting on the saddle horn, Ever stared fixedly. The others reined in as close as the narrow path would allow and looked from the strange rabble to him; it was Clay who asked, "what the hell are they?"

The things impeding their exit were not exactly dogs, couldn't have been, if so, then they had been genetically altered. While possessing the general shape of a canine and looking to be the size of a German Sheppard, there were observable differences. Their paws were much larger with three long hook-shaped claws projecting from both front and back pads. Down their back, a single line of thick tapering quills protruded from their spine, and they possessed no fur, only bare skin resembling the thick composition of ancient Dinosaurs. The shape of their head followed that of a dog, but from beneath their lips, two narrow, elongated teeth protruded. Their eyes were the strangest, elliptical and red.

Janis reiterated the question. "Come on Ever, tell us. What are they?"

"They are Chupacabra," he said not breaking his stare.

Clay and Janis said it at the same time. "Chuba what?"

"El Chupacabra, actually," He said, "It means Goat Suckers."

Janis turned to her husband, "Let me guess Bob, they're some kind of vampire dog right, another freaky Nasif secret?"

Bob nodded, "Afraid so sweetie." Looking pathetically pessimistic, he added, "but how about we see it as the glass being half-full."

"Okay," she said, "I'll bite, no pun intended. How can we look at those freaky things and see the glass as half-full?"

Bob forced a smile, "Because they haven't killed us yet."

As if keyed by Lemus's statement, the lead Chupacabra gave a guttural growl; the others did the same. The pack rose to all fours and hunched. Janis asked although certain all were seeing it, "are those things on their back quivering?" There was no time for anyone to reply. The Chupacabra charged, traversing the distance in seconds.

Clay's horse reared and whinnied while the others struggled to untangle and run, but there was no time. Five of the Chupacabra targeted the frightened mounts, leaping through the air and clinging to their chest and neck with their hooked claws digging into the muscle and flesh. The animals were still crying out when the dog-beasts impaled their jugglers. Chaotic, there was no room to maneuver, the horses and mules clashed, their heavy torsos slamming one another trying to shake lose the things draining them of blood. Soon, having gown weak, their legs buckled, and they fell, throwing their riders to the ground.

The Chupacabra clinging to them remained through the fall, slurping wildly, ravenous, ignoring both the thrown riders and fellow Goat Suckers attending to their own undertaking.

Ever and the others had rose to their feet, but slowly. A Chupacabra stood in front of each, hunched and snarling; a warning not to move.

Smiling, Aluka stepped out of the jungle and onto the narrow path. Ambling to Ever he stared into the Ferret's eyes. Saying nothing, he shook his head then walked to Lemus, "Well now," he said flippantly, "it would appear once again the FBI has dared approach Castle Balasar de Rosista determined to deliver justice…and failed."

Clay eased his hand to his weapon, slowly. Following the movement with its scarlet eyes, the Chupacabra heightened its growl, "I would not do that Mr. Cooper," Aluka said turning and moving to his side, "he may not kill you, but your friends will be dead in seconds." Clay eased his hand away. Eye to eye now Alka told him, "Since this is our *next* time to meet, and I am a man of my word, allow me to answer your periodontal inquiry. I use an undisclosed blend of three different toothpastes with a pinch of baking soda, a soft bristled brush for each new day, and once a week I gargle morning and night with the blood of a toddler."

Clay held Aluka's stare, "I don't like you."

Ignoring the remark Aluka simply said nothing and walked to Janis.

"Janis Barr-Lemus." He said sweeping her with his eyes, "It has been some time since meeting a woman of your spirited ostentation. I don't suppose you'd consider leaving Bobby to become my lover?"

Janis forged a smile. "I'd sooner screw one of your Goat Suckers."

Aluka grinned. "Yes, I expected as much. But give the idea some thought, I may make the offer again in the near future." Aluka glanced back at Lemus, "Then again, maybe I won't have to."

Laughing lightly, he strolled to the edge of the jungle then paused. Hands in his pockets he glanced back, "Mr. Cooper, I suggest you convince your friends to stay out of your affair with Blue Eyes. As for the rest of you, do not come back. Next time you will be joining us for dinner."

He then yelled out in Spanish, "y mucho menos". Immediately the Chupacabra broke rank racing to his side. Together they disappeared into the foliage.

A moment of silence passed as the five stared disheartened at the dead animals. Their demise left a sadness in all of them. It also meant a long walk back to Magdelene in the Bolivian heat.

Bob tried to cheer them up; "Hey you guys, look on the bright side," each turned wearing a frown and Bob quickly added, "let's try and see this as the glass being half-full." They didn't exactly chime in harmony, but all yelled out the same word...HOW?"

"Well, "Bob said, ' The horses and mules, bless their mammal family hearts, will provide a tasty dessert for many of the jungle's population. And we...are not going to be the entree."

CHAPTER 35

The winter storm over Brooke had begun a steady light drizzle before turning into snow. Lasting well into early morning its unrelenting bombardment had left nearly ten inches in its wake. And now, because the temperatures had dropped into the single digits, the small town looked as if it were buried beneath a thick layer of ice.

At the Ottis house Blue Eyes and his young son Cain clambered down the basement steps where Roland and Wynona lay asleep. Although the basement housed the furnace, the room in which the couple lay remained chilly. Roland, still bound and naked, lay shivering in an ever-deepening state of shock.

When Blue Eyes switched on the light, the couple did not move. The horrible run of events had taken its toll, leaving them mentally shattered and physically exhausted.

At their feet, Blue Eyes tapped them with his toe startling them awake. They opened their eyes and behind the redness and dark circles, he saw the instant rekindle of fear. A tingling of delight surged through his body.

That delight was heightened by his having awarded his son responsibility of creating a plan for gaining access to the Cooper house. He had offered no assistance in its conception and now the young boy was ready.

Standing beside his father in the cold basement, Cain quietly observed the bound couple, especially Mr. Ottis. Staring at his naked shivering body a few moments, he glanced up, "Father, before we begin may I cover up Mr. Ottis? He is shivering terribly?"

Blue Eyes nodded. "Of course, you may."

Leaving the bound couple, the boy searched the basement and found two sleeping bags on a shelf among several other camping items. One bag was red the other pink. Retrieving the red one he returned with it. Opening it up he covered the shivering, naked man. With youthful benevolence he said, "There we go Mr. Ottis. You will be warming up soon."

Roland nodded his appreciation.

Moving to their side Cain took a deep breath; "Well," he said taking time to position himself Indian Style on the floor, while behind him his Father did the same establishing his lesser role in this great chapter of his son's life.

Positioned Cain continued his conversation,' "the time has finally come Mrs. Ottis." Her eyes moved to the kind little boy who had helped her husband.

Cain laced his fingers resting his hands on his lap, "My father and I want to invite Mrs. Cooper and her son over for a visit, but they have company. That company is not invited. So your responsibility is this; you will go across the street to Mrs. Cooper and tell her you and Mr. Ottis are having a very bad fight, and you needed to get away. After you have pretended to cry and feel bad, ask if you could lie down for a few minutes where it is quiet. I believe Mrs. Cooper will take you to a bedroom and leave you there alone to rest. When she does, you will unlock the window so my father can enter. Once he is in you get up and tell Mrs. Cooper you feel much better, thank her, and return here to me and your husband."

Cain paused before beginning again, "As my father has taught me, every good plan should have a backup. "So, should Mrs. Cooper not place you upstairs, then tell her you apologize for bothering her, and ask...no insist, she walk you home to insure everything is okay between you Mr. Ottis. That is all you have to do."

Wynona's tired, puffy eyes studied the boy. She was amazed by the child's maturity; and thankful for the kindness he had shown to her husband; there was a good side to this child, and that would be her and Roland's salvation.

The plan contained a loophole; not only was he a nice boy, but he was also a *small* boy; easy to overpower if need be. She would go to Nancy Cooper's and do as told. The moment she let the monster in, she would return and while ignoring the boy, she and her husband will rush out the back door to another neighbor and call 911.

"Well, Mrs. Ottis," Cain asked, interrupting her thoughts, "are you up to it?"

She nodded. The boy looked back at his father and climbed to his feet. Moving to Wynona's head he apologized for the pain he was about to cause her, then ripped the strip of duct-tape from her mouth. The sound of it tearing free was followed by a whimper, then a deep breath of air.

Blue Eyes handed his straight razor to Cain, "Take caution you do not cut yourself, or Mrs Ottis."

The boy took the razor and sliced the tape holding her. Immediately she sat up, pulled free all remaining pieces of the gray tape, then rubbed her wrists. Cain continued explaining his plan. "At 4:00 o'clock you will leave here, wearing just what you have on. You may grab your coat-then run across the street to Mrs. Cooper. Tell her exactly as I said. Your husband will remain here with me. The moment you unlock the window and Father is in, return here. If you stay, you may not like what you see happen there, and equally dislike what you find when you return here. You must come straight back from the Cooper house. Okay?"

Wynona felt a surge of hope. The youngster was playing it just the way she wanted. She nodded her agreement. As to what was going to happen across the street, she did not know, she did believe, however, that this madman was capable of anything. She and Roland thought very highly of the Coopers, the four of them had been friends for several years, but now, it had become a matter of self-survival. The Cooper's fate, however horrific it might be, was at this point little more than a warm concern. She would pray the 911 call would get help to them before it was too late…but there was simply nothing else she could do.

Just a little before 4:00, Wynona embraced her husband, tears filled her eyes. She kissed his cheek not wanting to let go. Her heart ached to tell him she had a plan now, and soon they would be free. But Blue Eyes pulled her away and took her upstairs.

At the door, one minute before she was to leave, Blue Eyes leaned close to her ear. "You do one thing wrong, and my son will cut off your husbands testicle and watch him bleed all over the basement floor. Then I will personally deal with you"

Wynona had no intention of doing anything that might ruin their only change of staying alive. Besides, if something did go awry - regardless of what this monster thought or expected from his son - no little boy was capable of doing such a thing.

She was actually anxious to get going and do everything right. She wanted it over and this maniac out of their lives. Dressed in blue jeans, sneakers and a red tee, she moved to the door and grabbed her coat from the tall rack standing to the right. When she turned to slip her arm through, Blue Eyes punched her hard in the face; she slammed backward against the door sliding to the floor. Blood was running from her nose. The pain was excruciating and immediately she felt swelling.

Blues Eyes squatted beside her, "Just a touch of realism. Go into the bathroom and get a wet washcloth. You can tell Mrs. Cooper Roland just struck you. Tell her you do not want the police called, not yet anyway. Not until you've stayed away a bit, and at least tried talking to him one more time."

Wynona rose holding both hands over her nose, blood seeped between her fingers. Hurrying, she staggered to the bathroom.

Cain looked questioning at his father. "Why did you strike her, Father?"

Blue Eyes stood and placed a hand on his son's shoulder, "Next door, Cain, are two very experienced FBI agents, little slips past them. Remember, they are already on guard and suspicious. Think of Mrs.

Ottis's injury as a movie prop, like Hollywood makeup; remember, it's the realism that grabs the audience," Blue Eyes smiled, "it's as if we are making a movie and you are the director."

Cain pondered his father's words, glanced at the open bathroom door where Mrs. Ottis had gone, then looked back at his father. Slowly he cracked a smile.

CHAPTER 36

The Bolivian sun had climbed straight overhead holding back none of its burning heat. Now free of the jungle and following along the river, Clay and the others trotted wearily along coated in sweat. Magdalena was finally coming in sight but remained a tiny speck in the distance. The last five miles had been cruelly challenging.

Michelle was growing worse, totally unable to walk even with assistance. She was dangerously anemic and in dire need of medical attention. The Vamps had drained her of far too much blood. Hypoglycemic shock was closing in. Clay and Bob were taking turns with Ron carrying her.

Janis shaded her eyes and gazed out across the dark water. Something large had jumped and she barely caught it. With the spot still rippling she pulled her eyes away and looked up at her husband and asked, "Bob, those goat suckers" -

"The Chupacabra?" He replied.

"Yes. How long has the government known about them?"

"A few years." He glanced at her then back ahead. "We don't believe their numbers are that many, but they are spreading. We've killed half a dozen in various South American Countries, managing to keep it quiet, blaming it on wild dogs and such. Some civilians who've actually seen them claim they're aliens. We let that spread, it lessons credibility."

"Are they in the United States?"

"We have one incident that took place in Miami a few years back. But that's been the extent of it.Most cases are reported here in South America."

"As I'm sure you guessed, Janis," Ever chimed in, "Vampires tame the Chupacabra as pets. Of course, they are forbidden to do so, but it is difficult to prevent."

Janis wiped a run of sweat from her eyes, "Well as far as I'm convinced, there's one way to help stop it, nuke the freaking castle and everything in it."

CHAPTER 37

Wynona pounded frantically on the Cooper's front door. When Clendes answered it, his eyes scanned her quickly- she was dressed only in jeans, sneakers caked with snow, and a red Tee. She was holding a yellow washcloth covered with blood over her nose.

Gun drawn and at his side, he let her in, scanning the back of her and noting nothing unusual.

Nancy came in startled. "Wynona, my God what happened?"

Wynona pulled the cloth from her face. Already it was greatly swollen. Rushing to her side Nancy sat her on the couch. "What happened?"

Wynona played her part well. "It's Roland, we've been fighting for two days. A few minutes ago, he hit me."

Nancy frowned, "That doesn't sound like Roland at all. Do you want me to call Carl?"

"No! I just need to sit a moment, pull myself together. If I can rest a bit, I'll go back and try talking with him," She looked woefully into Nancy's eyes, "please, if I could just lie down for a while, where it's quiet."

"Of course," Nancy said in agreement. She assisted Wynona to her feet, "Let's go upstairs. You can lie down on my bed for a time." On the way Nancy ordered Michael to put ice in a sandwich bag and bring it upstairs.

As Michael headed to the kitchen, Clendes and Jones watched the two women slowly climb the stairs.

Once Nancy had Wynona settled on the bed and covered with a warm chenille throw, Michael arrived, and she placed the small icepack tenderly on her nose. Smiling as best she could she reassured her long-time neighbor, "We'll get all this worked out; don't you worry." She and Michael slipped out quietly closing the door.

Immediately Wynona threw off the chenille and scrambled off the bed. At the window, she pulled back the curtains. The maniac was not there. Twisting her head, she looked out from every angle; where was he? Another window. He would have to check all of them, there was no way of knowing in which room Nancy would place her. She would just have to wait, be patient.

Hurrying across the floor, she cracked open the bedroom door and peered out. Everyone was done stairs. The tap startled her. He was there! Hurrying to the window, she opened it and he slipped in, closing and locking it behind him. "Okay," he whispered, "we'll wait fifteen minutes, then you'll go back downstairs and tell them you can't sleep, that you're going home to try and talk with Roland."

That's not what Wynona wanted; she was supposed to return immediately, but what choice did she have. From the small of his back, Blue Eyes pulled a semi-automatic pistol. He slid the slide, then moved to the hinged side of the door. After listening a few seconds, he motioned with his finger for Wynona. Reluctantly she moved to him. Wrapping his gun arm around her neck he pulled her close and whispered, "Take off your clothes, everything." Wynona's face expressed her disbelief. "Do it." He demanded.

Wynona hesitated. Blue Eyes whispered again. "Take them off now and get down on your knees in front of me. Do it or I'll shoot you in the head, then go downstairs and kill the others…saving your husband for last."

Realizing she was left with no alternative, she pulled her red Tee over her head, unlaced her wet sneakers and pulled them off slowly, first one than the other, then her socks. She unzipped her jeans and removed them. Lastly, she removed her bra and bent peeling off her panties.

Slowly, with cold reluctance she knelled in front of him. He whispered again. "Unzip me and take me into your hands." Beginning to quietly cry, she did as she was told. He grew hard rapidly. She marveled over his size, realizing how incredible painful it must have been for her husband. "Now lick, suck and stroke like you're enjoying it," he said, "if I do not cum in twelve minutes or less, I will kill you right here."

Wynona worked him, stroking his shaft using both hands, covering his huge head with saliva, taking him into her mouth as much as possible. Blue Eyes closed his eyes, the sensation was a utopia matched by few other worldly pleasures. Wynona slaved at her task, watching the pleasurable expression on his face. She wanted him to climax, to get it over with, she wanted these insufferable minutes to fly past; she wanted to get back to her husband.

Behind the door, drifting up from downstairs they could hear the drone of conversation. Outside it was still light but dark would soon arrive. Blue Eyes suddenly climaxed. Like hot liquid shot from a cannon it streamed, powerful; seemingly endless, surge after surge. Wynona stroked hard, ensuring every drop exited and not a moment of his pleasure was lost…. lives depended on it.

Sighing, Blue Eyes opened his eyes and looked down. Smiling, he whispered, "look at you, you're a mess." Moving to the bedroom closet he soundlessly slid the door open, gazed over the hanging clothes and pulled a silk blouse from one of Nancy's hangers. "Here," he said softly returning to Wynona's side, "stand and close your eyes, I'll clean you up." He wiped her face and chest than whispered for her to get dressed.

After wiping himself clean, he returned to the closet and re-hung the silk blouse. "There," he whispered when he returned to Wynona's side, "Nancy will never know," he winked, "it will be our secret."

When Wynona was dressed, Blue Eyes whispered his final orders. "Remember, tell them you can't sleep, you're going back over to go talk with Roland."

She nodded and slipped out the door. All were sitting in the living room when she descended; they looked up at her. Nancy rose crossing the room to greet her. At the foot of the stairs, she slipped an arm around her, "what's the matter Wynona, can't sleep?"

Wynona flashed a sort-lived smile. "No, I can't. I'm just going to go back over and talk with Roland." Nancy glanced with concern toward Clendes and Jones then back to Wynona.

"Are you sure that's a good idea?"

Wynona nodded. "Yes, he's calmed down by now and is probably crying, although never tell him I told you that."

Looking once again at Clendes and Jones Nancy shrugged. "Okay, if that's what you want to do."

Moving to the door, Wynona forced another smile, "thank you, for everything." Hurrying across the street, she disappeared into her house.

CHAPTER 38

Upstairs Blue Eyes slipped quickly from Nancy's bedroom into the hallway. He made his way to the edge of the landing and peered around the corner. Clendes, Nancy and Michael had returned to their chairs and were discussing the potential danger Wynona was putting herself in. Jones was missing!

Blue Eyes leaned back against the wall and gave the situation thought. Where would Jones be: in the bathroom, or in the kitchen maybe? No one had come up the stairs since she went down them. The agent had to be down there, somewhere. The conversation he had just heard made no indication anyone had gone with her back to the house.

This was all so exciting; it had been seven years since his Adrenalin had flowed like this. He wished Cain were there beside him sharing the rush.

Slowly, he slid down the wall into a sitting position, then quietly stretched out onto his stomach and inched his way to the corner. Careful to not be spotted, he positioned the automatic, so its barrel pointed downstairs at Clendes chest. He then heard Jones yell from the kitchen, "Anyone like a sandwich, or chips; something to drink?"

Michael yelled out. "I'll take a coke please." Nancy looked at him "Hey, you're quite capable of getting up and helping yourself, young man."

"Mom," he said, "Mr. Jones asked!"

"Go see if he needs any help." She told him.

"Okay." Michael said, hopping out of his chair and jogging to the kitchen.

Nancy followed him with her eyes grinning, then looked back to Clendes changing the subject. "Do you think I should go next door, I'm really worried."

Clendes appreciated her concern. In his career, he had seen more than his share of wife battering. "Why don't you give her a call?" he recommended, "truthfully, I'd rather none of us leave this house. But, if she doesn't answer, or you're led to believe the situation has worsened, then I'll go over myself and have a look."

Nancy smiled. "Thanks. I'll go upstairs and call, just in case she wants to talk." Moving to the stairs she started up, glancing back at Clendes, "thanks again. She really is a good friend."

Topping the stairs Nancy made a left, passed the open bathroom door then hurried down the hall and turned into her bedroom. At the door she stopped abruptly, puzzled. "I must have a brain tumor," she told herself out loud, "I smell…" she sniffed deeply… "sex." Glancing about, she saw nothing unusual and shrugged, talking to herself again, "Clay, you better hurry home and take care of me." She walked to the telephone and tapped in Wynona's number.

Blue Eyes stepped out of the bathroom shower and reentered the hallway. He positioned himself once again prone on the floor at the stairway landing. Michael and Jones were still in the Kitchen.

Time was now a limited commodity. Nancy could come out of her room at any time; of course, if she did, he would just turn quickly and shoot her. Then charge the others and shoot them."

Jones and Michael exited the Kitchen moving back to the living room. Jones held a plate with a sandwich and chips in one hand, a can of Pepsi in the other. Michael held only his drink. They were laughing. Jones joined Clendes on the couch that partially faced the stairway, Michael returned to his chair opposite. Blue Eyes could see just the very top of the boys head.

Clendes was reading the paper. Jones was focused on his eating. Carefully, Blue Eyes took aim on Clendes; he would take him out first,

Jones second. There was nothing between he and them, just wide-open area, a no-brainer turkey shoot.

He took in a breath, aimed and fired. The dart from the semi-auto tore through the paper and buried deep into Clendes's chest, just to the right of his breastbone. He lowered the paper, looked at the feathery dart, then slumped into unconsciousness. Immediately Blue Eyes shot Jones, who had begun to stand, but his knees buckled, and he fell face first to the floor in front of the couch. The plate and drink fell with him, the Pepsi pouring out over the carpet.

By the time Michael recovered from the shock of what had just happened, and left his chair, Blue Eyes was right behind him, circling to his front, the semi-auto pointed at his little chest. Blue Eyes was smiling, "Hello Michael," Michael stared saying nothing as Blue Eyes continued, "my name is Quinten Christenson. I'm an acquaintance of your parents. They call me Blue Eyes. Have they told you about me?"

"Yes." Michael replied, both frightened and bewildered.

Blue Eyes pulled his gaze from Michael. Nancy was now standing at the top of the stairs, the red dot from her Lady Lazor .25 caliber centered on the killer's forehead.Michael looked over his shoulder..." MOM!"

Slowly Nancy descended the stairs, her face composed, the red dot holding its place. Inside she felt shaky as a lone strand of hair in the eye of a tornado.

Blue Eyes grinned. "Still that beautiful, tenacious creature I remember."

"Take that gun off my son, because I will kill you right now."

"How about this," Blue Eyes replied, "I drop my gun, you drop yours."

"Mine doesn't move, this clip holds five hollow-point rounds, small but deadly at this close range. I will, and I swear it, put four of them into your head and the last one in your heart."

Blue Eyes widened his smile. "How about this, your gun drops and mine doesn't. You see, Nancy, my weapon holds four remaining heavily dosed tranquilizer darts. Each holding the amount of chemical needed to take down a large sized adult, unfortunately it will not work on children, their bodies are too small; it kills them. If I fire, Michael will be dead shortly after hitting the floor."

Nancy knew he meant it. Slowly her arm sank to her side, the .25 falling from her hand and landing on the last step of the stairs. She walked to Michael's side and embraced him. Blue Eyes placed the tranquilizer gun back into his belt stepping over Jones and sitting comfortably on the couch beside the unconscious Clendes. Nancy lowered herself into a recliner pulling Michael onto her lap.

For a time, they stared: he is admiring her beauty, the striking natural blond hair, luscious full lips so perfect for pleasuring a man, the bedroom eyes, breasts perky and round, and although it had been seven years it felt as if only yesterday, he had fondled that most perfect heart-shaped derriere a woman could possess; a work of art with the promise of explosive visual pleasure when making love Dogie Style.

Nancy was staring at an animal, flesh and blood, yes, but a beast with a twisted, deranged sense of compassion, capable of doing anything. He was a murderer, rapist, kidnapper, thief, and no doubt demon possessed.

Looking from his mom to Blue Eyes Michael broke the staring, "I know who you are, who you think you are. My dad is not Abel and you are not Cain. The man-looking demon who came to my room was only trying to deceive me."

Blue Eyes looked at Michael and smiled. "Deceive! Indeed, I am impressed. A most adult word, yet you apparently understand its meaning. However, Michael, I assure you, everything he told you is true. I am Cain and your father is in fact, my brother, Able. And I will assuredly die by his hand, and his hand alone. Seven years ago, that very event should have taken place, but it did not, and why, because your father, if I may use a less…erudite word than yours…fucked it up!

He folded his arms. "I am here today to assure you Michael, this time he will not. If, this time, he does not kill me as I have asked, many people you know will start dying; each in a horrible and gruesome way."

Nancy nearly shouted it, "That's enough."

Blue Eyes shifted his eyes to hers. "Nancy, you require no convincing. As you can see," he gestured toward Jones and Clendes, "just as it was seven years ago, I am in control, and can do just as I wish. No one is safe unless Clay does as I demand. You and Michael are at my mercy. However, I have chosen not to harm you. So be sure to tell my brother this is the one and only good deed he will receive...and this time, I expect the same courtesy from him."

Getting up from the sofa he added, "So as not to offend our mutual friend Bob, I feel it only right I leave something special for him." Blue Eyes reached into his pocket; Nancy caught her breath, her grip tightening around her son.She feared for the unconscious agents; whatever he chose to do to them, she knew she could not stop him, and it would be done in front of her son.

Blue Eyes pulled his hand free from his pocket. In it he held a permanent black-ink marker. Leaning in front of Clendes' slumped figure, he drew a mustache beneath his nose, then a small go-tee on his chin. Happy with his masterpiece, he knelled beside Jones. The agent lay face down, so he grabbed a fist of hair and pulled up his head drawing a near-perfect handle-bar mustache. When finished he stood and recapped the marker. Sticking it back into his pocket he walked to the door.

"Clay and the others," he said looking one last time at Nancy and Michael, "will be here within twenty-four hours, tell my brother this, if I visit his family again, things will be much different. Tell him I'll be calling. And lastly, as you have probably guessed by now, my son and I are visiting with Roland and Wynona across the street. They have been most entertaining, although I must confess, I think they are in a hurry for us to leave."

He sighed, "Remember this, so long as you do not call the authorities, or permit Laurel and Hardy to come over and try rescuing them, you have my word I will not kill them." He looked specifically at Michael, "I want you to come over at noon and have lunch with my son, Cain. I'd like very much for you two too meet." He glanced at Nancy, "he's to come alone."

Nancy shook her head, "Absolutely not. I come with him, or not at all."

"There is no option, here. It will be alone. I promise you Nancy, and you can believe me, we will not hurt him in anyway. He will return home safely. If you do not consent, you will be responsible for Roland and Wynona's demise. He opened the door and left.

Hastily Nancy removed Michael from her lap and checked Clendes and Jones. Both were breathing, their pulse slow and steady. She stretched Clendes long ways on the couch and put a pillow beneath his head. Jones, she rolled onto his back and placed a pillow beneath him as well, then cleaned up the spilled food and drink. Under normal circumstances, the black mustaches would have been humorous, but right now there was no room in her heart for joy.

In the Kitchen she poured a cup of coffee and returned to the living room to her chair. She wanted to keep an eye on the agents. Michael, still shaken by what had happened sat in his Dad's recliner beside her. Nancy reached out and took his hand. She smiled, "A heck of a day, hey?"

Michael looked at her. "Does anybody around here realize I'm just a kid?"

Nancy squeezed his hand. "Of course, we do. But sadly, what's happening involves all of us, including you. Believe me, Michael, your dad and I want nothing more than to keep you out of it, to protect you, but even at your age you know what we are dealing with."

He nodded. "I know mom. And I want to help Dad so much. It's just that," he paused, "the man Blue Eyes scares me."

Nancy's heart felt like an anvil dropping into her stomach. "I know he does, sweetie. He scares me too."

"I really don't want to go over there." Michael told her.

"You don't have too, Michael. Now that we know he's there, we'll just stay here with the doors and windows locked; ready if he comes back."

Michael's eyes were filling with tears, "I know mom, but he will hurt Mr. and Mrs. Ottis if I don't go."

Nancy moved to his recliner and pulled him onto her lap. "I know my little man," she said squeezing him tenderly, "but he might hurt them anyway." She followed with a soft peck on the cheek.

Michael wiped at his tears, "We have to trust God he will keep his word and not do anything to them, or me. If I don't go, mom, I know he will kill them."

Nancy tightened her hug, beginning to cry herself. "Oh, my dear little man."

Her eyes glanced at the clock on the wall near the kitchen entranceway: 11:02. Although blurry, she stared at the relentless bounce of the second hand…tick, tick, tick, tick.

Oblivious to it all, Clendes, stretched out on the couch, and Jones face up on the floor, continued to sleep peacefully. They were both snoring.

CHAPTER 39

The agents were still sleeping when Nancy knelt helping Michael into his coat; she zipped it, then embraced him, her hands were shaking. What she was about to do tore agonizingly at her heart. She understands clearly that if Blue Eyes did not keep his word, then dear God, there may be no getting her son back, ever; and even worse, she would forever dwell on the horrible, unthinkable things he could have done to Michael before he… She choked back her tears.

Yet, if she did not allow him to go, the insane son of a bitch was capable of succeeding in anything he set his mind to; and in his anger of not getting his way, he would stop at nothing in stalking them until Michael were in his possession.

Nancy began to sob, trying her best to conceal it, to be brave. Nothing in this world could be worse than losing your only son to someone like him, losing him to the truest form of horror and evil. As if a revelation, Nancy paused at the thought. For the first time in her life she understood, truly understood, the impact of a Bible verse she had learned long ago. She could not recall the book, the chapter or verse number in which it lay, but the words poured from her lips as she began sobbing aloud; *for God so loved the world, he gave his only begotten son, that who so ever believes in Him, shall not parish, but have ever lasting life.*

Pulling away, wiping at her nose, Nancy brought her sobbing under control and smiled for Michael. Michael smiled back wiping her tears with his little hands. "It's okay Mom," he said, "I've prayed, God will be with me. Now you've got to let me go."

Nancy released him. Standing, she sniffled, "You be careful over there, I'll be right here. Anything happens and you need me, get my attention somehow, throw something through the window and I'll come running."

Michael smiled again and opened the door. The sun was out, and the air felt warm. The ice covering the town was melting rapidly. To help keep his feet dry, Michael tried stepping into the tracks already made by Mrs. Ottis. With each long step taken, he repeated to himself… "I trust you God, I trust you God, I trust you God."

CHAPTER 40

At the front door of the Ottis house, Michael started to push the bell, but the door opened before he touched it. It startled him. A kid like himself, stood beside it smiling. He was Michael's height, blond hair, and a pair of blue eyes that matched the warm, clear sky.

"Hi, Michael," he said cheerfully, "I'm Cain. It is nice that you could make it. Cain stuck out his hand and Michael took it. They shook and Cain asked him to come in.

Michael had been in the Ottis house several times over the years. A quick glance around told him things looked pretty normal so far.

"You can put your coat on the floor there by the door," Cain said. Michael unzipped it and laid it down. "I told Father I was very excited about you coming over. I haven't played with another boy in a very long time." Walking away, he continued speaking over his shoulder, "I have pizza ready here in the kitchen. "Michael followed him into the room, still looking around. The pizza lay on the table fresh out of the oven, Pepperoni and Mushroom. He loved pepperoni and mushroom. "What would you like to drink; we have Coke, Diet-Coke, Pepsi, Milk, Mountain Due, ice-water, and Coffee…big yuck on the coffee as far as I'm concerned."

"Mountain Due," Michael said, "my mom rarely allows me to have it."

Cain grinned, "My mom too, she says all the sugar turns me into a monster. So, since we're a couple of UN-parented men today, we'll both have Mountain Due."

The Due sat on the sink counter in a 2-liter bottle. Cain noisily filled two glasses from the icemaker and poured the drinks. Michael sat at the table and waited. When Cain finished, he moved to the table with the drinks and sat down to the left of Michael.

"You mind if I pray," Michael asked.

Cain shrugged, "Sure, if you want. Our religions are much different you know. You believe in God, and I don't, I mean I know he's real, I just don't like him. I believe in Demons, that's who I pray too. But please, go ahead."

Michael bowed his head. "Dear God, I thank you for the food Cain has made for us, send it to our bodies and make us strong. I love and trust you. Amen.

"Now I'll pray." Cain said bowing his head. "Dear Lucifer, I thank you for the food I've made and ask that you send it to our bodies and make us strong as well. And thank you for allowing Michael to come over. Amen.

Michael took a drink of his mountain dew. "Your prayers to Satin sound a lot like the way I pray to God."

Cain shrugged. "Yes, and it makes sense. We are simply praying to two different Holy-Beings."

"Satin isn't a Holy-Being." Michael said.

"He is to me, Michael."

"Yeah, okay. But do you realize what the difference will be between your Holy-Being and my Holy-Being when the end of the world comes?"

Cain pondered a moment. "I do, but it's a difference of opinion." Cain took another sip of his Due. "This stuff is sooooooo, good. "he said.Michael took a sip too and nodded. They set their glasses down almost at the same time and Cain added. "Michael, you and I have each been blessed; you by your God and I from mine; so, both of us know that my Angles, the dark Angels, are constantly fighting with your Angels, the Angels of light. I believe that in the end, my Angels will win against your Angels, and we will overthrow God, then we will rule."

"You mean the way Fidel Castro took over Cuba?"

Cain took another sip, "Yes, that is a good analogy."

"Well," Michael said, "I am confident my Angels will win, and Satin and all of his fallen Angels will be chained in Hell for ever and ever. Then my God will continue to rule. And everyone will know only happiness for all eternity."

They each took a bite of pizza. Following with a swallow of due, Michael shrugged, "when the time comes, I guess how the fight of good and evil will end, will always be as you said, a personal opinion."

Cain nodded his agreement.

Michael took another bite and swallowed. "Cain," he said, "I think way down deep in your heart you think like me. You realize that the end is very near. That your dark angles have already lost. I like you Cain, but I fear if you do not ask Jesus to come into your life, you'll lose with them, and be chained up too."

Cain rose from his chair knocking it over, anger flashing, "Michael I think that's a bunch of your holy shit," his arm swept everything from the table as his anger raged: glasses crashed to the floor shattering across tile, ice slid in all directions, Mountain Dew splattered, and slices of pizza left an aftermath resembling blood and pieces of flesh.

Michael was frightened and speechless, but what he saw happening to Cain's blue eyes, made the hair on the back of his neck stand up. Their beautiful blue had vanished, replaced with a darkness he knew came from hell.

Rising slowly from his own chair, Michael backed carefully from the table, his heart pounding. Pastor heart had taught him about demon possession, their power, their goals and limitations. He had explained the horror of being possessed by them, but this; this was something he could never have imagined. It went beyond possession. Michael backed into the kitchen wall, he stood frozen, unable to move.

Cain stared coldly at him, saying nothing. Michael knew the demons inside of him were very capable of convincing him to kill. In his head Michael was praying. He was frightened, more than he had ever been.

Cain did not move but continued to stare. Back pressed to the wall, Michael began inching toward the doorway leading to the living room and outside. Cain closed his eyes. Michael was counting to three, on three he would run. It was on two Cain reopened his eyes.

The beautiful blue was back. To Michael's surprise, Cain began to cry pleading as he sobbed, "I am so sorry, Michael, I did not mean to frighten you. It seems I always scare my friends away. Please don't let what happened frighten you away too, please stay and visit. Cain wiped at his tears and forced a smile. I promise I will not do it again."

Blue Eyes walked into the kitchen and both boys turned in silence watching his approach. His eyes scanned the floor while biting thoughtfully at his lip. Stepping over the mess, he moved to Cain's side. "Well Michael," he said, "I see by the looks of things it's time for my son and I to go."Cain looked up at his father. "Please Father, let us spend a little more time together?"

"I'm afraid not," Blue Eyes said while continuing to stare at Michael, "I am afraid we just have too many things needing done." Cain's father smiled, "Michael you are free to return home. First, however, you will want to go into the basement; you have people waiting for you. As I promised, Mr. and Mrs. Ottis are very much alive."

Taking Cain's hand he added, "Tell your mother, and the Lemus's clowns to not bother calling the authorities, it would only make me angry. It was very nice meeting you; now, off to the basement with you and greet your friends."

Michael hesitated, unsure of what he should do. He looked at Cain, "I guess I'll see ya."

Cain acknowledged, "Thanks for coming over. I hope we get to do it again."

Blue Eyes lead Cain away glancing over his shoulder, "In case you don't know, the basement is the second door down the hallway."

CHAPTER 41

Michael charged down the basement steps cheerful, thankful Cain's father had kept his word. At the bottom he turned right and there they were. Mrs. Ottis was sitting on the cement floor beside her husband who was lying on his side covered with a sleeping bag. Wynona recognized Michael immediately. She said nothing but her eyes told him to go, to get out of there. Michael approached her slowly. "Mrs. Ottis, I've come to take you and Mr. Ottis to my house. Mom will be waiting."

She shook her head, "no, Michael, run, get out of here now."

"It is safe Mrs. Ottis, Cain's dad promised he wouldn't hurt you anymore. Mom is waiting to help you." It's okay, you're safe now.

Wynona shook her head and looked past Michael. He heard nothing, but knew she was staring at something there. Whatever it was, it terrified her beyond what she had already experienced. Michael did not want to look, but he turned anyway, glancing slowly over his shoulder.

There were six people standing in a group, one of them a woman. Two of the men looked older, his grandfather's age, they were dressed in slacks, sweaters and dress shoes, two of the other men looked the age of his parents, the remaining two were teenagers, sixteen or so, no older. They wore blue jeans, shirts and sneakers. All had removed their winter coats; looking as if they had made themselves at home, waiting.

The oldest of them, spoke. "We have been waiting for you. You are young Michael Cooper?"

Michael nodded in silence.

"We have been told to bleed your friends. But instructed to wait for you, you are to watch."

Michael shook his head. "No, you don't understand, Mr. Blue Eyes promised he would not take their life if I came over."

"We were told you would hold him to his word. So, I have been instructed to tell you, it is a matter of semantics; he himself is not going to kill them; we are. He has kept his word. He is not even in the house any longer. It is us who will be bleeding them."

Michael grew angry. "No! You will not hurt them, In the name of Jesus I command you to leave, by His authority I order you to get out of this house."

The man he was speaking too glanced back at the others and they all chuckled. "We are not demons, Michael," he said turning back, "we are flesh and blood like you…somewhat, anyway; we do not live in the spiritual realm. You have no power over us." He waved with his hand and one of the teenagers approached Michael and wrapped his arms around him to hold him. The remaining five advanced on Roland and Wynona. Again, the older man spoke, "What you witness here now is a reminder; convince your father he must kill his brother."

Michael watched in awe and fear as the five visitors opened their mouths and hissed. Sharp, narrow pointed teeth began growing downward out of their gums. Michael began crying, knowing what these people were, understanding what they were about to do.

"NO, please, don't hurt them," he begged, but it was an empty plead. The group converged like hungry dogs on their victims, plunging their sharp teeth, sucking and slurping at the blood surging up from the multiple arterial bites. Wynona screamed at the initial pain, but quickly fell silent.

Michael closed his eyes still crying. Pastor Hart had taught the importance of loving your enemies. But at this very moment, that made no sense, it was impossible. Here and now, he hated Blue Eyes; despised him with all of his heart. And had he possessed the power, he'd have used that power to order Blue Eyes' body to explode, be torn apart into a hundred-thousand pieces.

The Vampires feeding took only a few minutes. When finished, they stood. The one holding Michael's arms released him. The older man, his face swathed with blood, moved to Michael and knelled in front of him, his long teeth now retracted, "this will be the fate of you, your family, and all of your friends if your father does not cooperate. Tell him he failed seven years ago, that will not happen again. Now go home!"

Michael couldn't help himself. He stood frozen, staring at Mr. and Mrs Ottis. They lay on their backs, eyes open, staring lifeless into the basement rafters. He remembered the times he had come over here with his mom and dad for cookouts or to borrow something, how friendly and kind they always were. Mr. Ottis would always shake his hand with a smile.

It was a shout, "GO HOME!" The older man yelled it in Michael's ear causing him to jump while those watching, laughed. Bolting away and up the stairs, through the living room and out the front door Michael never bothered to pick up his coat. Frantic, he waddled through the snow, struggling, wanting only to get home, to run into his mother's arms and be held. The door burst open, and Nancy rushed out to meet him; she stepped high to maneuver more quickly through the white mass.

Running straight into her arms, Michael was crying. Sweeping him up she rushed him into the house and straight upstairs. There she laid him on his bed, pulled off his sneakers and covered him with a throw. Then laid beside him holding him tight as he wept.

For some time, the tears fell. And when he finally quieted and was able to talk, he explained the horrible things he had witnessed. The sight of it had taken a great toll on him. Following a long squeeze, Nancy kissed his forehead and got up from the bed. "Well, you're home and safe now little man" she told him, "So try and get some rest. Dad will be here soon, and we'll get this all straightened out once and for all." Throwing him a reassuring wink, she left the room, closing the door quietly behind her.

On her way down the stairs, she was mumbling… *"you evil son of a bitch, I'll kill you before Clay does."*

CHAPTER 42

Upon their return, it was like a family reunion at the Cooper house. When told how the artwork got drawn on Clendes and Jones' face, Lemus had to have a cigarette and shake his head.

While all were saddened by the deaths of Roland and Wynona Ottis, they were thankful Blue Eyes had, for whatever reason, spared everyone else.

Nancy cheerfully took on the task of nourishing Michelle back to health; feeding the poor woman so much she covertly had to beg her husband to help her eat it each time Nancy would leave the room.

On the third night of their return, they invited Pastor Hart to dinner and after eating, gathered in the living room to sort things out. Seven years ago, Blue Eyes had stopped at nothing to force Clay into the satanic ritual of killing him. Although with much personal suffering, they had managed to avoid it and place the lunatic on death row instead. This time however, that would prove much more difficult; if even possible. Having employed renegade vamps to reinforce the powers of darkness; that perilously increased the risks of everyone's safety.

For the meeting Nancy had brewed a pot of fresh coffee. Following much discussion Clay sipped from his cup and stared into the face of everyone sitting around him. Each understood the risks. Each realized they would be putting their life on the line; and this time, one or more were likely to lose it.

Clay wiped at his face with his spare hand, frustrated, he told them, "Bottom line, we really have no choices here. The risks are too high. When Blue Eyes makes contact, I'll agree to meet him and do as he ask, I will kill him."

It sounded cold, but all agreed, all except Pastor Hart. He cleared his throat. "Please if I may; allow me to interject here." Willing to listen to any possible alternative, they shifted their attention. "While sometimes killing has to be the answer," he went on, "and although the Bible is full of times when God used killing to accomplish righteousness, this is not one of those times. I feel it my responsibility Clay," he said looking at him, "to point out to everyone, especially you, that in killing Blue Eyes, should this brother thing in anyway be real; it creates what I call a biblical glitch."

Hart opened the Bible he had brought to the meeting, "It's important you hear this." Placing his reading glasses on his nose Hart stared over the rim at the others saying, "All of us I am sure know the story of Cain and Able, that Cain murdered Abel out of jealousy and anger."

Hart continued speaking as he thumbed through his Bible. "You all remember that God grew enraged with Cain and cursed him for what he had done. Listen if you will, to Genesis chapter four, verses 8 thru 15," Pastor Hart began to read, "*And Cain talked with Abel his brother: and it came to pass when they were in the field, that Cain rose up against Abel his brother and slew him. And the Lord said unto Cain, where is Abel thy brother? And he said, I know not: Am I my brother's keeper?And He (God) said, what has thou done? The voice of thy brother's blood crieth onto me from the ground.*"

Pastor Hart glanced up. "Now listen, here comes the glitch." He continued reading, "*And now art thou cursed from the earth, which hath opened her mouth to receive thy brother's blood from thy hand; When thou tillest the ground, it shall not henceforth yield unto thee her strength; a fugitive and a vagabond shalt thou be in the earth. And Cain said unto the Lord, my punishment is greater than I can bear. Behold, thou hast driven me out this day from the face of the earth; and from they face shall I be hid; and I shall be a fugitive and a vagabond in the earth; and it shall*" *come to pass that everyone that findeth me shall slay me. And the Lord said unto him, therefore whosoever slayeth Cain, vengeance shall be taken on him seven-fold. And the Lord set a mark upon Cain, lest any finding him should kill him."*

Hart ended the reading and looked up. Removing his glasses he directed his attention to Clay, "If this Blue Eyed Killer is correct, remember this. God is perfect and pure; he will always keep his word. If you kill Blue Eyes, and he is truly Cain; regardless if you are Abel or not, God will execute his vengeance. He must, even though He will not want too. The last thing in the world you want Clay, is for God to be against you. It is such a costly risk."

Clay sat staring at Hart then lowered his head thinking; *If in fact he and Blue Eyes were Cain and Abel, and reincarnation was the case, then Blue Eyes knew all along what the outcome of this switching the murder rolls would mean. That Abel, upon killing him, would immediately be charged with the seven-fold vengeance. God had declared it would apply to* **anyone** *who killed him. And to Cain's delight; he knew very well, not only would God have no choice but to punish Abel; but because he loved him, it would break God's Heart in two.*

How, Clay thought, could anyone want to hurt God!

Not realizing he was nodding; Clay had reached his final conclusion; even if killing the Blue Eyes Killer meant being sent to Hell right alongside of him; on the way down, he'll just say: misery loves company you evil son of a bitch.

CHAPTER 43

By the 14th of January everyone had left the Cooper house to return home: Bob and Janis to Alexandria, Louisiana, Ever to Washington, Clendes and Jones to New York, and Ron and Michelle back with their children; beginning a new life.

To date, there had been no contact with Blue Eyes; but because everyone had personnel lives to get on with, there had been no choice but go their separate ways; at least for now.

Clay greatly appreciated the involvement of his friends; each putting their lives on the line with no questions asked. And he realized too, the gravity of Bob and Ever sharing national secrets; without which, Michelle would have become just another lone corpse lost to the vast Bolivian Jungle.

With everyone gone, Clay and Nancy went about their routines; he with Marshaling duties: writing tickets, responding to traffic accidents, domestic calls, investigations, and all other less tedious tasks of small-town Law-Enforcement.

Nancy continued maintaining the house, schooling Michael and living on the PC working on her degree. And with all of it, although unspoken, it was done with angst-ridden expectation. Blue Eyes was going to call. Of that there was no question. With trepidation, they just wished he'd get on with it.

CHAPTER 44

The Boeing 747 dropped steadily through the black firmament. Three thousand feet below, the waiting airport glittered brightly: but it was no match for the scintillating sight of late-night New Orleans.

The man with beautiful blue eyes caught his smile in the shadowy oval window through which he gazed. There was joy in his dark soul, feeling as if he were coming home. The remaining two hundred and six passengers sat tense in their seats, waiting for the welcomed squeal of tires and feel of earth once again beneath their feet.

It was a perfect landing. The reversal of engines and lowering of flaps cut the aircraft's speed with noticeable shudder. When slowed, the big plane taxied to the waiting terminal.

Rising from his seat Blue Eyes retrieved his carry-on bag from the storage cabinet above and joined the cramped, single file exodus. There would be no one waiting to greet him. He was here alone to take care of personal business. Then it was back to Indiana for something special.

At baggage, he retrieved his one piece of luggage, then made his way to the Car Rental where he picked up an Apple Red Convertible Lexus. He had hoped for black, but there were not available. Although disappointed, he still managed a smile for the young raven-haired attendant staring helplessly into his bright blue eyes.

Before leaving the airport, he made a phone call, talking only briefly, then drove to the French Quarter. Locating a place to park, he locked the car and made his way to 739 Bourbon Street, once Marie

Laveau's actual residence. The building was now a tourist shop and museum. But he loved visiting here, even now, years after the Queen of Voodoo's death; her presence could still be felt.

Inside, he browsed; amused at the large amount of merchandise available to all those amateur dark-side practitioners. Suddenly the warm, soft lips of a woman touched his ear… "Mr. Christenson?"

Turning, he gave the young girl standing behind him a slow, immodest head to toe appraisal. She was young, a Creole, her skin light ebony, her eyes were brown, alive and snappy with a trace of orient. Her cheekbones were beautifully prominent, and her hair black as the sky he had just descended. An orange-patterned blouse dipped just low enough to display full rounded breasts, and a loose dark skirt hung to her ankles hiding a pair of powerful, youthful legs. Multi-colored beads circled her neck, her nose had been pierced with a small cross-shaped diamond, a string of tiny black skulls dangled from her ears, her nails were polished black, and rings covered the fingers of both hands. His eyes moved back to hers. She made a face. "Satisfied?"

Blue Eyes nodded. "You're young."

"Yes, but taught well."

"I believe it," he said, "I've utilized the talents of your great-grandmother."

"Yes, she has spoken of you from time to time."

"Oh. And what is it she said about me?"

"That you frightened her."

That amused him. "And do I frighten you?" Blue Eyes felt a stirring in his loins.

"No." the young woman said, "You do not."

He grinned, casually sticking his hands into his pant pockets. "Young Voudoun, I hope you hex better than you lie."

Ignoring his remark, she whirled on her heels. "Come," she said, her voice barely heard above the chatter coming in from the busy street. "I will not do business in this revered place."

Moving through the crowd of punters, they descended the steps of Marie Laveau's house and onto the sidewalk. Crossing to the curbside the young girl turned and faced him.

Bourbon Street was thronged with chattering people. The absorption of voices, music, lights and strong smell of alcohol created a dark chaotic inspiration. From her pocket she removed a sandwich bag containing a small amount of gray ash. She handed it to him. "As requested," she said, "there is dose enough for two. Each must inhale a breath of the ashes. Once breathed in then plant the seed; the rest will be done through powers beyond our own."

He handed her an envelope in exchange.

Taking it, she turned and began walking away, saying nothing. Above the noisy chatter, he called after her, "Voodoun." Stopping, she looked back over her shoulder. People passed sporadically between them, yet their eyes remained locked. He smiled boyishly; she had to admit, it possessed charm. The most beautiful eyes she had ever seen on a man were staring into hers, desiring her; she could feel the slow, disarming of her soul.

From the Tricou House Bar down the street, Cajun music flowed with an arcane erotic stirring. "Ten-thousand dollars if you spend the night with me?" He said through the mix of voices and endless mass of wandering people.

She stood staring, then began to smile; "I am a Voodoun Mr. Christenson," she said, "not a whore." Turning then, she disappeared into the Bourbon Street crowd.

Sticking the sandwich bag into his coat pocket, Blue Eyes grinned and walked back to the Lexus. He took Highway 10 west out of New Orleans through Baton Rouge. In Lafayette he turned north on 49. The drive time to Alexandria would take close to four hours, but he didn't mind; he was energized. The great venture awaiting Janis and Bob Lemus was well worth the time; and it would, although he felt a bit distraught in his own way, finally take them both out of the picture…permanently.

CHAPTER 45

Janis Barr was hungry. Naturally her first choice to break for an early supper was the Ragin' Cajun. Bob had been called to New York so supper would be a loner, and cooking for one just didn't sound appealing.

Pulling onto the restaurant's crushed-stone lot, she parked far to the rear so she would have to walk a good distance to the door; it was one of several little things she did regularly to stay trim and fit. She also took the stairs, sipped water each time she passed a drinking fountain, ate an Apple a day, drank a glass of red wine each night and studied Aikido three times a week.

Inside she walked to her favorite booth, located at the rear of the building and near an exit door. She sat herself on the far side, putting a wall to her back and allowing full observation of the main dining area.

When the server showed, she ordered a Diet Coke and glass of water. There was no need to look at the menu since she could practically quote it verbatim. Her choice this late afternoon was a bowl of 'Lot O' Spice Gumbo' and slice of Garlic Bread. The server finished scribbling on her note pad and smiled, "you got it darlin'."

Janis glanced first at her watch: 4:28, then around at the fellow patrons. She observed a high school couple sitting side by side in a booth near the door, a lone man in a Navy-blue three-piece suit six booths down sipping coffee and reading the paper, and lastly a family of six consisting of mom, dad, and four loud children sharing a long table in the center.

The server delivered Janis's drinks and she nodded with a smile. Tearing away the paper, she stuck her straw in the Diet Coke and sipped, realizing she was as thirsty as she was hungry.

To the right of the main entrance-way door, a huge bay window provided a clear view of the front parking lot. Placing an elbow on the table, Janis cupped her chin in her palm and stared a while. Beyond the lot, the busy highway hosted a steady stream of traffic, and beyond that, black storm clouds were approaching the city. That surprised her.

All day the weather had been perfect, the sky a beautiful blue and overflowing with droves of fluff whites. The radio had mentioned nothing of bad weather; this storm was a freak. A bright whip of lightening streaked across the progressing blackness, and she sighed telling the gloomy tempest something it already knew it was going to be a nasty.

Refocusing her attention, Janis took another sip of Diet Coke and studied the kids at the middle table. They had grown louder and were now blowing spit-wads. Watching their obnoxious behavior, she guessed at their ages: a girl six, a boy of eight or nine, another girl twelve maybe, and the oldest, a third girl of sixteen or seventeen. The parents repeatedly told them to settle down, but they may as well have been talking to their paper placemats.

When her gumbo arrived, Janis ate it slowly despite feeling famished: another of her stay healthy practices. The soup was just the way she liked it, Cajun spicy; hot enough to form little beads of sweat on the brow. She took a swallow of water then dipped another spoonful.

Her cell phone rang. When she answered it, no one was there. She started to place it back into the case when the front door opened. She glanced up. The bite of gumbo was at her lips, but she stopped dead, lowering the spoon and setting the cell phone on the table she whispered, "Crocks, Crooks and Crapola."

Blue Eyes smiled graciously for the host as he walked past, sauntering casually to where Janis's was sitting. When he passed the middle table the whole family stared, amazed at his eyes. He winked at the sixteen-year-old girl. Captivated that such a tall, handsome man with incredible eyes would find her worthy of a wink, she blushed. Her stare followed him all the way to the booth where he slid in opposite Janis.

When seated he smiled again, "Surprise."

Janis placed the spoon of gumbo into her mouth and chewed slowly while staring at him. She swallowed, followed with a casual sip of water then asked never removing her eyes from his, "Come to do your own dirty work, have you?"

The server approached their booth. "High, what will it be? If it's a long list, I get off at 7:00." Janis rolled her eyes.

"I'll have a cup of coffee, black, please. "Blue Eyes grinned.

She wrote on her pad and told him, "Beautiful eyes."

He told her thank you and when she was gone, turned back to Janis. "There is no dirty work to be done, if you stay out of it."

Janis shrugged. "Like I've already told your gang of multi-toothed wonders, Cooper is a friend. He needs help, he gets it."

"You'd rather be dead?"

"Actually, I'd rather be in the front row of the observation room watching you fry."

"Not going to happen."

"Okay than, how about this, you're tied spread eagle, bare-assed on a wooden table with a blind, drunk, sailor giving you a vasectomy; and he's using a dull, rusted knife and no anesthesia; and that's after he's injected you with a hundred and fifty milliliters of an anti-coagulant."

Blue Eyes let a grin show. "You have spunk, Janis. May I call you Janis?"

"No, you may not."

"Okay, Ms. Barr-Lemus."

"That's better, but I'd prefer you didn't talk to me at all."

"I'm just trying to be nice."

Janis took a sip of her Diet Coke. "If you really want to be nice, you crazy bastard, go find a dirty alley and commit suicide."

"Sorry, that is not going to happen either. So where is Bob, I really wanted to say hello."

"He won't be along until later. Besides, and this may surprise you, but he doesn't like you anymore than I do."

"Yes, I know, but I had something special planned for the two of you. And now, because you're alone, it becomes a question of what to do."

He drummed his fingertips thoughtfully against the table.

Janis looked at his bouncy fingers and back into his face. "Nervous?"

"Tell you what," he said ceasing the drumming, "what say you make a new friend today."

Climbing out of the booth, he reached into his pocket. Janis watched cautiously, placing a hand on her weapon. Having retrieved a small sandwich bag from his pocket, Blue Eyes opened it pouring a small pile of gray ashes into his palm. Janis watched the strange action, bemused.

"May I?" He picked up her glass of ice-water and with no warning, dumped it down the front of her. Janis gasped. Bending, he puffed his cheeks and blew the mound of ash into her open mouth. Some, although her eyes closed instinctively, had fluttered its way in clinging to the moist mucus membranes. Immediately her eyes began stinging and she rubbed.

The bitter taste of the ash caused her to gag, and she blindly felt for her Diet Coke, taking a long hard swallow. Blinking in rapid succession her vision began to clear, and she looked up. Blue Eyes was gone.

He was now at the middle table whispering into the older teen's ear. The young girl twisted to stare up at him, smiled, then glanced around him to ensure Janis was watching. She than took his hands and placed them over her breasts.

Enraged, the girl's father rose from his chair. The man foundling his daughter snapped his head and stared into his eyes. The once lively blue color had turned to black. There was a silent moment of intense staring. Then calmly, the father sat back down, picked up his fork and began eating a piece of pie as if nothing had happened. Blue Eyes turned his gaze to the mother. When that stare broke, she looked to her daughter and smiled her approval. The smaller children had been watching it all with youthful curiosity, giggling. Blue Eyes giggled with them, sharing the humor of this fun game.

Janis frowned, looking the room over. Everyone was going about their business as if nothing out of the ordinary were happening. The young couple in the booth sat chatting, the man in the business suit sipped his coffee continuing to read; and the server stood at the register exchanging pleasantries with the host.

Janis shook her head, "This is so not right." Her gaze moved back to the table, "Shit." She said it just under her breath. Blue Eyes was gone, and so was the young girl.

CHAPTER 46

It was just a glimpse. Janis saw them only seconds before the men's bathroom door closed. She shouted it this time, "Shit!"

Both restrooms sat at the front of the dining area side by side on the west wall. The men's room was closest, almost in line with the table where the young girl had been sitting. Janis scurried from her booth, fearing for the girl's safety. She estimated her time reaching the bathroom door to be less than twenty seconds; a lot of harm could be done to someone in less time than that. She was closing the distance.

Within five feet from the door, the girl's father left his chair and intercepted Janis, stepping squarely in front of her, forcing her to come to an abrupt stop. She realized he would want to help but this kind of problem was her area of expertise. And if bad turned to worse, she at least possesses a weapon.

He was a big man. In years past, he had been nicely built and ruggedly handsome. But now, after obvious neglect, his rotund belly prevented his green tweed sport coat from buttoning. Janis guessed him near six-foot.

Grinning down on her small frame, he told her. "Why don't you just leave them alone?" His tone was soft and untroubled.

Janis frowned. "What?"

"Let them be, let them…you know."

Janis shook her head, dumbfounded. "No, sir, I don't know. Get out of the way."

The big man shook his head. "Look little lady, you just go back to your booth and let it be."

Janis looked sternly into his face. "What the hell is the matter with you? Your young daughter is in there with a complete stranger. He could be murdering her for all you know."

The man with the big belly stared as if she were making no sense. When Janis moved to step around him, he placed a hand on her shoulder. That was a mistake. Stepping back, Janis quickly gripped his right hand at the pad of the thumb, lifting and twisting. Instantly her other hand came up and applied firm, steady pressure against his wrist quickly taking him effortlessly to the floor. In Aikido, the move was called Kote Gaeshi, *wrist turning throw*. To him, it was disbelief. He struck the floor with a thud.

She shouted in his ear. "Now stay there."

But when she released the pressure, the fat man began scrambling to his feet. A scream erupted from behind the closed door and Janis looked up. A second scream followed. "Oh Lord" Janis said under her breath.

The fat man had climbed to his knees shouting, "You smart-ass little bitch! I'm going to break your scrawny neck." Turning back to face him Janis caught a glimpse of his wife coming around the table snarling, obviously in defense of her husband. A third scream came from behind the door.

Janis pulled her weapon, "enough of this shit." She brought the butt down hard against the man's head and he collapsed unconscious to the floor. In the same instant, the wife tackled her, and they tumbled over his rotund body. The kids at the table were crying now, realizing it was no longer a game.

The wife grabbed for Janis's hair, but Janis caught her wrist, shouting, "I've got one for you too." The pistol came down again, and like a rag doll, the woman fell limp across her husband's legs.

Scrambling to her feet, Janis told the crying children their mom and dad would be fine, then positioned her back to the wall beside the bathroom door. She listened intently, but there was no sound.

Gun at the ready, she took hold of the door handle and turned it slowly, then pushed it open. It swung easily inward coming to rest flush against the wall. The small room was quiet, no movement and no sound. She positioned her head just enough to see in.

There were two urinals divided by a partition on the far wall and one stall with a closed door to her right. A small smoky-glassed window, shut and locked, let in a dull patch of afternoon sunlight. The room was small, ten-by-sixteen or so. No one appeared to be in the room, but Janis knew that couldn't be.

She entered cautiously. There was but one place they could be – inside the stall. Keeping her distance, she bent enough to glance beneath the opening at the bottom of the door. She saw only the foot of the stool. They had to be huddled atop the seat.

Glancing over her shoulder, Janis looked back at the window. It was locked from the inside and far too small for a man to fit through. They had to be on the stool. Stepping back to a safe distance, Janis leveled her weapon and said, "Alright, I know you're in there, come on out."

There was no reply. She shook her head, increasing the tempo of her persuasion, "I'm going to count to three. If you don't come out, I'm coming in and I'm gona' be pissed. And you don't even want to think about that."

Nothing happened. Displeased, Janis inched her way to the stall door.

In the other room, the children had huddled around their unconscious parents trying to wake them. Beyond the children, the young couple in the booth continued to talk as if nothing were going on. Janis was sure the others were doing the same. Outside, the sky was suddenly dark, and the city of Alexandria lay shrouded in a strange drifting blackness – not clouds and not a fog, it was something else. She could not explain what it was, only that it was neither; nor somehow it looked alive, creeping its way up the side of the building. Whatever it was, it had already reached the windows and begun to blacken them.

Janis was now at the stall door. Standing to the side with gun pointed, she jerked it open. Blue Eyes was not there, but the girl was.

She was sitting on the tank of the commode, feet in the water. She was naked and not moving, her head lay resting against the wall. A piece of brown paper toweling had been partially stuffed into her vagina. The young girl looked dead, but Janis couldn't be sure. Moving to her side, she checked her carotid pulse; it was there, and she sighed. Janis could see writing on part of the protruding paper and knew it was a note. Pulling it free she read its contents:

Do not assist Cooper

B.E.

Crumbling the note Janis tossed it to the floor and mumbled, "Fuck you B. E." Carefully she removed the girl from the stall and laid her on the floor in the middle of the room. The teen began to awaken and although startled at first, quickly realized Janis was not the man who had accosted her.

When she was awake, Janis helped the girl to her feet and at the same time swept the room with her eyes. *Where had Blue Eyes gone?* She had not seen him exit and there was no room for anyone to hide behind the door resting flush against the wall. The single window was both locked and too small to climb out of. The floor and walls were tiled; the ceiling was painted drywall with no breaks anywhere. Frowning, she shrugged. Maybe he had managed to slip out during her struggle with the girl's parents.

Janis turned to the teen. "Are you alright, sweetheart?"

"Yes." The girl pointed to the commode, "He threw my dress and under-things into the toilet." Janis retrieved them and the girl redressed into the wet garments.

"Did he harm you in anyway?" Janis asked.

The girl shook her head, "No, not really. It was just his eyes. I screamed and he grabbed my hair, forcing me to look into them.

They…" she shuddered, "they turned black right there in front of me. It was so freaking creepy. I guess I fainted."

Janis put an arm around her and squeezed. "It's okay now. Come on let's get you back to your family."

When they turned, Blue Eyes was standing in the doorway entrance.

Janis's gun was still in her hand, and she raised it, targeting his heart. Blue Eyes stood leaned against the door-jam; arms folded casually. "You wouldn't shoot me in cold blood, would you…Mrs. Barr-Lemus?"

Janis pulled back the hammer. "I'll empty this clip in less time than it takes your heart to make a beat. Now back away from the door and raise your arms above your head. And if I even see your eyes begin to change color, I'll kill you instantly."

Not moving, Blue Eyes smiled. "Tell me Mrs. Barr-Lemus, do you like to travel?"

Janis puzzled over the question only a second. "No, now back up like I said."

He smiled wider. "That's unfortunate, because I'm going to send you and your new little friend on the adventure of a lifetime. It was supposed to be you and Bob, but hey, he can learn to live without you." Blue Eyes shrugged than, "In any event," he went on, "before you leave, I am obligated to tell you this, so listen: In Frenier, if you slip, it's a one-way trip. And Blue is your only clue."

Janis moved toward the door, finger on the trigger, "The only trip to be taken is you going back to prison."

Blue Eyes stepped back clearing the doorway. His eyes began fading to black but before Janis could fire, the bathroom door slammed closed between them.

"Son of a bitch," Janis shouted, rushing to the door and shaking the handle. The door would not budge. She and the young girl were locked in. Following a deep breath, Janis whirled around and walked to the center of the room, placing her weapon back in its holster. She looked about while talking to herself, "Well, Janis, what to do? You can't crawl out the window, too small. You can't get the door open, locked. You can't call for help because no one realizes anything is going on. There is no fire alarm to pull, no sprinkler head to set off, and no Axe to chop down a wall. And you left your cell phone on the damn table."

The young girl waited until Janis quit talking to herself then asked, "What's Frenier?"

Janis looked at her, breaking her concentration. "What?"

"Frenier, what is it. He said something about slipping in Frenier."

Janis moved to the window and pulled her weapon. "Get back, I'm going to bust out the glass." She slammed her pistol butt against it, but it would not break. "Damn it," Sighing, Janis looked at the girl. "Frenier was a small Cajun Village just outside New Orleans. It's gone now."

With her pistol still gripped in her hand, Janis walked quickly to the door and shouted, "Can anyone out there hear me?" She waited but no one responded. "Okay," she shouted, "if anybody is there, back away. I'm going to shoot through the door." Angling the barrel downward while holding it close to the door handle, Janis fired.

The clip held fifteen rounds; she fired five in a circular pattern around the handle, leaving ten available to be used elsewhere. The noise rocked the small bathroom. Stepping back, she kicked the door handle and the knob fell out on the far side; the door jarred free. Quickly she pulled it open and looked out into the restaurant.

"What the…"

The young girl moved beside her to see, "What is that?"

Janis shook her head. "I think its Frenier."

CHAPTER 47

The restaurant was gone, the tables, silverware, napkins and people – all of it gone, vanished. In its place existed another world, a small town of dirt streets and old shacks surrounded by swamp and woods? Was this Frenier? That was the name Blue Eyes had said. But Frenier was near New Orleans, over three hours away, and more importantly, the town of Frenier no longer existed; it had been totally destroyed over 90 years ago. "Wait," Janis told herself, "This has to be a dream. An allusion."

The young girl grasped Janis's arm, gripping tightly. "What's going on? Where is the restaurant?"

Janis shook her head. "Girl, I haven't a clue."

"Well, how did that place get here?"

Again, Janis shook her head. "Sweetheart, I don't know that either."

Above the town, storm clouds resembling the black smoke-like substance that had enveloped the restaurant earlier, swirled and rolled, and it appeared to be accumulating. Somewhere in the middle of its dark amorphousness, a flash of lightening lit the strange blackness. Thunder exploded and the young girl jumped.

Janis ran a hand through her strawberry blond hair; there was no way of making sense of this. Was it Voodoo, the result of a dark spell? This was Louisiana after all, and she had seen more than her share of unexplained things here. If it turned out to be nothing more than a bad dream, then all she had to do was ride it out and wake up. But what if she wasn't dreaming? What if…THE ASH! The gray ashes Blue

Eyes had blown into her face. "Son of a bitch," she said aloud, *there's no waking up here, only finding a way out, that is if one even exists.* They had been cursed, Voodoo. A large number of people, especially religious leaders refused to believe in its power, denying it even existed, but it was true, and she knew it, she had witnessed to many cases. There was power in it, very dark power.

Janis looked into the face of the young girl clutching her arm. "Sweetheart, do you think you might ease up on the grip? You're cutting off circulation to my arm."

Realizing what she was doing, the girl let go. "Sorry."

"You know," Janis said kneading away the fingerprints left on her skin, "I don't even know your name."

"Jody Jean Jamason." The young girl said.

"I'm Janis, Jody Jean Jamason." Janis frowned, "Wow, try saying that fast five time without laughing."

The girl's expression remained blank! "Little sense of humor I see," Janis said, "you might want to work on that. Humor makes the world go round."

Jody ignored it. Her big eyes were locked on the anomaly beyond the door. Janis did not like it either, but knew right or wrong, good or bad, it had to be faced. Soberly she nodded toward the waiting town. "It appears we have no choice, Jody Jean. We have to go out there. It's our only way back."

The girl pulled her eyes away and looked at Janis, her face white. "I can't."

"You have to sweetheart. I can't leave you here and I don't think we're going to wake up."

Jody grabbed Janis's arm again. "What do you mean, wake up?"

Janis patted her hand. "I don't mean to scare you, but this is no dream."

"Oh God," the girl exclaimed, "then what is it?" She began to cry.

"You're not going to like it, but I believe it's a game designed by Hell, and you and I are the key players."

Janis closed her eyes and said a brief prayer, then crossed herself and looked up. Following a deep breath, she took the young girl's hand, "Common sweetie," she said, starring into the mysterious malformation. "Let's do this."

Together they stepped through the doorway and into the waiting unknown.

CHAPTER 48

Clay's eyes opened and he blinked several times. It was dark. The phone ringing had startled him awake, but he knew where he was. Reaching for the receiver he knocked over a glass of water on the nightstand and cursed quietly, then snapped his frustration into the receiver, "Cooper."

Silence!

Clay's tone tightened. "Hello!" From the other end came the sound of someone breathing. "If this is an obscene phone call," he said irritably, "redial, you want somebody with a hard-on." Stretching to re-cradle the phone, a deep, raspy voice hissed a single word.

"Coooooopeeer."

Clay sat up abruptly. "What did you say?" Throwing back the covers, he hurried out of bed and onto his feet. The floor was cold. Nancy rose to an elbow. "Clay what is it?"

"Who is this?" Clay demanded, ignoring her question. He crossed the room to the window and pulled back the curtain: nothing but a sleeping town buried in white.

Letting the curtain fall, Clay turned back to the room. Again, the voice spoke. "Cooooopeeeer, lissssssssteeeeeen."

A scream pierced through the receiver, then another and a third. Whoever it was, they were experiencing excruciating pain as if being tortured. There came two more screams followed by distressful sobbing, and in broken words, whoever it was managed to speak, "It hurts Clay, help...oh please help me..." Clay recognized the voice and shouted into the room with fear and despair, "Fuck!"

There was another scream and the phone pulled away; the raspy voice returned, "Coooopeeeer, elevaaaatoooooor." A click followed and the dial tone played in Clay's ear.

Nancy scrambled out of bed and snapped on the lamp. Moving to Clay's side she gripped his arm, "What is it. Who was that?"

Clay looked into her face; he was crying. She went pale. Oh my God Clay, what now?

Clayton Cooper hugged his wife. He cried a moment longer and broke away. "I got to go, right now."

"Go where?"

"To the old elevator, it's Carl. He needs help."

"Help? What's wrong?"

Saying nothing more, Clay hurriedly dressed into blue jeans, T shirt and black sweater. He strapped on black combat boots and slipped a knife into the high neck. He clipped his nine-millimeter to his belt than pulled the weapon and slid the slide. Clay never did that; he never loaded his weapon until he was out of the house.

Nancy followed him down the stairs and to the garage door. "Will you please tell me what the hell is going on?"

Clay flipped on the garage light and paused long enough to stare hard into her eyes.

"Someone is torturing Carl, murdering him. And it's that fucking monster."

Nancy stared at him, "Blue Eyes?"

Walking around his 1972 red Willies Jeep, Clay pulled open the door, pausing, "No," he said, "it's that thing that came out of the cornfield that night seven years ago. That thing from Hell that chased my truck and caused me to wreck; the same monster who pulled you and Michelle from Ron's shoulder at the Baton Rouge plantation. It's back Nancy. It's come back. And now it's torturing Carl Brown to death."

CHAPTER 49

Except for the chirping and chatter of sounds coming from the swamp, the town Janis believed to be Frenier, was quiet and appeared deserted. Again, lightening flashed illuminating the strange blackness.

Janis shouted into the empty settlement, "Anybody here?" There was no reply and with the young girl clinging to her arm, Janis led them down what she believed to be the main street.

Old wooden shacks resting on elevated foundations lined both sides of the dirt path. The buildings were early Cajun, constructed of rough hewed boards and wood-singled roofs. Most windows were dark gaping holes void of glass and bordered by wooden shutters. Much to Janis's dislike, a light fog drifted in from the swamp and hovered just above the ground. It hid their feet, giving her the willies; she disliked not being able to see what might be crossing their path and slithering between her legs.

"So where are we?" The young girl asked.

"I have no idea how we got here, but I think we're in the Manchac Swamp."

"Is this that town, Frenier?"

"I think so."

"But how can that be? We were just in the restaurant?"

Janis took a deep breath. "I know, and it doesn't make sense, but like they say: what it is, is what it is. And like it or not, here we are, and this is what it is."

Janis turned off the main street and onto another. There were no street signs, no light poles, nothing but empty hovels. Where were the people? Above their heads, the dark sky continued to roll and churn, thickening to the point it was beginning to drop down around them. Janis halted; her forehead furrowed. It frightened the young girl. "What? What's wrong?"

Janis raised a hand for silence. The things in the swamp continued making their noises, but there was something else now. It was quiet, but Janis could hear it. She looked at the girl, "do you hear that?"

Frightened, Jody asked. "Hear what?"

"Close your eyes and really listen." Janis said.

Jody Jean did just that. Her eyes closed and she focused on the sounds coming from the swamp. Taking a deep breath, she held it, straining to hear. Soon her head began to nod. "Yes, I hear it now. It sounds like…someone singing."

"Exactly," Janis acknowledged, "it's coming from the next street over. It could be our ticket out of here." She flashed Jody Jean a smile, although she herself wasn't totally convinced. "Common, let's have a look-see."

Janis pulled her weapon and held it hanging at her side. They returned to the main street, walked one block down and turned left. This street was like the others: old shacks on both sides with a dirt walkway covered by fog. On the right, four houses down, they located the source; an old black woman sat in a rocker on the porch, strumming a guitar and singing softly.

With Jody Jean clinging, Janis cautiously advanced until they stood nearly touching the aged porch. The old woman stopped what she was doing and looked up. She smiled, speaking in a voice softened with age. "I been waitin' fer ya' all. He told me you'd be a comin'." I don't reckon either of ya would have a cigarette?" Both shook their head no. "Didn't think so," the old woman said, "I ain't had one fer over eighty years now. Course, when I finish telling ya' what I got to say, I ain't never goin' to have a chance for one ever again."

Janis re-holstered her weapon. "Ma'am, is this the town of Frenier?"

The old lady nodded, "Yep, sho is.'

"You wouldn't be Julia Brown, would you?"

"Yep," she nodded again, "I sho is."

Janis stared a moment, "But I thought you-"

"You are correct in your thinkin' honey," she interrupted, "I been gone a long time now, as is this place around us. And as ya' all have probably guessed by now, bein' here with me, you ain't in your world no more."

Janis asked. "How, I mean, we were just standing in a restaurant in Alexandria and -"

"And all of a sudden you were here?" Julia Brown interrupted again, leaning forward in her rocker, "I know child. This is my curse. Every so often, they send someone here fer one reason or another: somebody havin' a bad dream, or hallucinatin' while dyin' from some nasty drug, a chance fer repentance, or sometimes, like in ya all's case, them that have the power just want to be downright mean. Of course," she sighed, "he intends fer ya' to die here, ain't supposed to be no goin' back fer you two." Julia sat back in her chair, "Yes sa' he's mean, that one."

"You're referring to the man with the blue eyes?" Janis asked.

"Yep, that's him. He's right pretty, but he's evil."

"Ms. Brown, is the man with the Blue Eyes the Devil?" Janis needed to know.

Julia Brown laughed. "Oh, lordy no, he's a man just like any other, he's just been givin' power."

"You mean power from the Devil?"

"Well, not the Devil himself exactly, but from one of them other powerful, mean ones down there with him."

Janis nodded her understanding and began to ask. "Ms. Brown-"

The old woman laughed. "Child, I ain't your school maam, call me Julia."

"Julia, just before he sent us here, he said two things I don't understand. He said something to the effect of: if you slip, it's a one-way trip, and blue is our clue. What do these things mean?"

Julie Brown began rocking slowly in her chair, it squeaked as she moved. "Well, there's a rule in dis place. It says they can't send no one here less they be given a clue how to get back. Course, none ever figure it out." "In about twenty minutes or so, this town is goin' to flood just like it done all of them years ago, just the way it does every time they send somebody here."

Jody Jean looked questioningly at Janis, "Flood?"

Janis made a face and explained. "Ninety years ago," Pausing Janis glanced at the old woman, "I mean no disrespect Julia." The old woman nodded, and Janis continued. "Ninety years ago, Julia put a curse on this town, told them on the day she died she was taking them all with her to the grave. When that day came, and Julia did die, a terrible storm came up while they were carrying her coffin to the gravesite. It was a hurricane, actually. The winds were fierce, turning the lake into a giant mountain of water. It came crashing in, flooding the town and burying it far below the surface. Nearly everyone drowned. In fact, so many died that day, that after gathering all the bodies from the swamp where they'd been washed away, they were placed in one big, massive grave not far from here.

Julia cut in again, "Ya see, girl," she told Jody Jean, "Most of them folks treated me mean, feared me, believing me to be an evil Voodoun."

"Where you, I mean are you?" Jody Jean asked.

Julia Brown smiled, "You gots to decide that fer your own self. Now let me tell ya what them things mean fer it gets any later. As I was sayin', you got just a few minutes before the water starts comin' and believe you me, that water gonna' come a crashin.' When it hits there ain't but one place within runnin' distance ya'll can get too and hope to be safe. My old back is facin' north. That is wear da water is gonna' be common from. If ya' go east to the end of town, just a hundred feet into the swamp water, there stands an old moss-covered Cypress. She's the tallest of them all and got three stumps right in front of her that come to sharp points. If ya' get to that tree and climb clear to the top and hold on tight, and don't get washed away when the water hits, then when it settles down, the top of the lake will be resting just a few feet below ya'. Everything else will be deep under the water."

Julia's chair continued to creak as she rocked. "When ya' start climbin' don't look back, and whatever ya' do, don't slip. Ain't gona' be no time fer a second chance. Now," she said with a long sigh, "that's half of what he done told ya'." Julia laughed lightly, "I sure wish I had me a cigarette. Anyways, if ya' make it and you're sittin' there on top of that tree, grab the first log what comes along and latch onto it, cause their ain't gona' be no one comin' to rescue ya'. While you're floatin' around keep watch fer a small blue light movin' about in the air. When ya' see it, paddle your backsides off and follow it. It'll show ya' the way back home. Wherever it goes, don't lose sight of it."

Julia looked up into the dark sky, then back to them. "I never told no body what them clues mean, and I hope it puts me in proper standin' with the good Lord. Cause I don't want to stay here no more, I'm askin' fer His forgiveness. Askin' He please carry my weary soul on home." She smiled warmly. "Now ya' all best head fer that tree. There ain't no more time."

Janis reached over the rail and squeezed her hand. "Thanks, Julia. We'll put you in our prayers."

A gust of wind came up suddenly blowing with fierce intensity. It pushed them back, away from the old woman. Grabbing Jody Jean's hand, Janis turned east, and together they ran for their lives. The old woman shouted after them, "Ya' all hang on tight now. And make sure ya' follow the light."

CHAPTER 50

The edge of the swamp lay a quarter mile ahead and the lake a half mile on the far side of town. Janis and Jodie Jean were running full out. Just before reaching the edge of the swamp, it began to rain, turning rapidly into a torrential downpour. It hammered hard and lightening illuminated the odd darkness now so thick it hovered only inches above their heads and still dropping.

Side by side, they plunged into the swamp water. It was waist-high and slowed them down considerably. Somewhere in the distance behind, they heard a roaring sound. Janis knew what it was: a monstrous wall of rushing water. The wind swept the swamp water with a fierce vengeance; it was all they could do to remain on their feet.

Janis's heart pounded, part because of their hard running, but mostly because the darkened sky prevented them from seeing the treetops. The tall cypress Julia had spoken of would be impossible to identify and the three stumps, were now hidden beneath the rising water.

Jody Jean yelled above the wind and thrashing rain, "Where is the tree? Which one is it?"

Janis wiped at the water hammering her eyes, shouting, "Feel for the three sharp stumps Julia talked about and pray we haven't passed them already."

The water in the swamp was rapidly rising, now nearly chest high. The roar from the wall of rushing water behind them was screaming. Although Janis couldn't see the treetops, she knew they were swaying helplessly. She guessed the gusts of wind nearing a hundred miles per hour.

Suddenly Jody Jean slipped and disappeared under the water. Janis shouted her name and immediately went under to grab her. She felt her arm and pulled her to the surface. The young girl came up coughing and sputtering, but there was no time to stop.

CHAPTER 51

When Clay reached the old grain elevator it was nearly four am. The trip was quick and the windshield had just begun to defrost. The interior of the Willie had warmed, but his thoughts were far from the want of comfort. *What had they done to Carl?*

Snow crunched beneath the jeep tires as he slowed to a stop at the elevator's south door.In the vehicle's headlights, the place looked just the way it had those seven long years ago when he had met the Blue Eye's Killer here for the first time.

Beyond the windshield lay the same rotted heap of wood and rusted iron track; now frozen beneath a blanket of snow. The dark gaping entrance lay open like the mouth of a hungry monster digesting the remains of his deputy and friend.

Clay opened the jeep door and stepped out; the air was bitter. Cold wind howled, warning him, pushing against his coat and sock-cap. In the headlight beams a small swirl of snow danced atop the concealed pile of wood and iron.

Standing motionless, Clay switched on the flashlight he held in his hand and scanned the area seeing nothing. There was no sound, no sign of life, only wind; he pulled up the collar of his coat.

Turning off the vehicle and killing the headlights, he moved to the entrance and into the dark interior of the building. The old elevator was large with multiple rooms and scattered outreach buildings; but there would be no need to search any of them. He knew where to look. Where he'd find Carl. His friend would be deep inside the belly of this cold lonely Structure.

CHAPTER 52

The water had swollen to nearly neck level now and the brutal wind hurled it harshly into the desperate faces of Janis and Jody Jean. Close behind, the mountain of rushing water reached Frenier. It tore into the town with relentless impact. The old shacks explode as if they had been made of paper-mâché.

Janis literally bumped into the stumps. She groped them with frantic hands to be sure. There were three, all pointed. "It's them, Jody Jean," she shouted, almost screaming to be heard, "If God were here right now, I'd kiss Him on the lips."

Feeling their way, both climbed atop the pointy stumps and blindly felt through the darkness above for limbs to grab. There were none to be found.

"Damn it," Janis shouted, sputtering water. Quickly removing her shoulder rig, she stuck the pistol into her waistband and began swiping the harness high above her head in hopes of striking a branch…she did.

Working against the handicap of the pitch-blackness surrounding them, Jodie Jean balanced herself on the pointed stumps, leaned into the tree and cupped her hands. Janis stepped into them and climbed awkwardly onto the branch, then felt through the darkness for Jodie Jean's hand and pulled her up.

The rain was torrential, making everything slick. Laboring against the wind's fierce velocity made climbing both dangerous and tedious, yet they had no choice but to hurry. Their hearts pounded; both knew the wall of water was rushing with deadly force toward them; just minutes away.

Again and again, they felt for the next limb, pulling themselves up as quickly as conditions allowed. Janis understood that should one of them slip and fall, there would be no rescue; it would be as Blue Eyes had said, the slip to cause a one-way trip.

Then time ran out, they had climbed as far as they dared. Both prayed fervently they had gone far enough. The town continued exploding into splinters beneath the power of the monstrous wave, its destruction deafening even against the riotous wind.

Janis had stopped them where two large limbs grew close together, one over the other and spaced about three feet apart. Straddling the lower limb, they locked their feet beneath. Janis threw the leather strapping of the shoulder rig over the limb above and groped for the young girls hands wrapping one end of the leather strapping around her wrists; Jody Jean gripped it tightly. Janis then twisted the other end snugly about hers while shouting, "Hang on with all you got."

Then it hit, the impact knocked them free of the limb on which they had locked their feet. Tons of rushing water pounded against them, pushing their bodies diagonally outward, as though they were flags on a pole snapping in a harsh wind. Desperately they clung to the leather strapping.

The water rumbled with the rage of Niagara Falls. Their bodies slammed one against the other. Breathing was impossible. Tucking their heads they prayed, mouths and eyes squeezed tight. Boards, broken furniture, kitchen utensils, articles of clothing, toys, nails, screws and other unidentifiable items flew past; some crashing into them creating cuts and bruises. Their lungs began screaming for oxygen, their chests burned.

The new forming lake rose steadily above their heads, but for them time had stopped. The seconds had gone well beyond the time to breath; but both knew only dark water waited to fill their desperate lungs; that drowning was inevitable. There in the wet darkness, behind her closed eyes, Janis saw Bob's face. She thought of the love they shared, the happiness he had brought into her life, and she worried for him. He would be alone now; they would never have the daughter…

The great force of water, give one last push and seemed to subside almost instantly, as though it had suddenly died. Their bodies eased downward hanging at the end of the leather strapping like fish on a stringer. In desperation Janis felt for the limb above and hooked a leg, maneuvering to the top of it; she then pulled Jody Jean up.

Frantically, lungs demanding a breath, she freed the girl's wrist and grabbed her thumb, motioning it upward. Jody Jean understood. Together they sprang from the limb, swimming upward, floundering through the dark abyss. Their only hope was that the surface lay close; if it didn't, death lay one deep watery breath away.

CHAPTER 53

Clay had drawn his weapon. The thing that had chased his truck and caused him to wreck seven years ago was not human; he knew a bullet would not kill it. But if something else was in here, it might them; and even if that wasn't the case, the feel of a gun in his hand improved the mood.

The inside of the elevator felt warmer without the wind, yet without proper clothing a man would freeze to death in a short time. Thoughts shifted to Carl; had they, or it, or whatever was in here, stripped him, exposing him to the deadly temperature?

In the beam of light, Clay could see his breath. There was no heat anywhere, so even if in winter attire, Carl would die from hypothermia if unable to move about. A sense of guilt and helplessness bit cruelly at Clay's mind. Carl was more than a good deputy; he was a friend; had been since grade school.And Clay couldn't help but blame himself for all of this. Everything that had happened in the past and all that was happening now was clearly no one's fault but his own. Because of himself alone, several had been tortured and murdered so heinously.

The time had come for this Blue Eyes thing to end. As far as he was concerned Blue Eyes had taken his final crap on this earth, and he was not going to step in his shit anymore. 'No more," he told himself calmly, "no fucking more." It was time to clean his shoes.

CHAPTER 54

Julia Brown had told the truth. The top of the Cypress towered above the surface of the new formed lake. Breaking through the water surface Janis and Jodie Jean gasped hoarsely, filling their lungs with deep wonderful breaths.

A warm velvety sky gleamed with stars and the light of a happy moon glittered across the water.Swimming to a limb strong enough to support their weight, they climbed up and sat, feeling exhausted but thankful. Smiling at one another through the shadowy night, they began to laugh; it was a good laugh, a long-lasting laugh; one that told the stars, and moon and glimmering water that it was good to be alive.

Ringing water from her hair, Jodie Jean looked up into the stars and paused, "is it my imagination, or is the sky moving around us?"

Janis nodded while glancing in all directions. Well, it's definitely not your imagination. It's rotating, moving in a circle."

Stars, constellations, the moon; all of it, were moving slowly in a clockwise circular pattern. In the far distance, some sort of lighted vortex swirled; the strange anomaly reminded Janis of a dark hole in space. Studying its orange and white lighted center, she realized it was pulling everything into it. "Well," Janis said under her breath, "it's a light hole."

Jodie Jean looked across the now semi-darkness at Janis, "dear God, its sucking everything into it, and coming toward us.

Janis watched it saying nothing, remaining focused. Slowly she began to smile. As the strange anomaly digested the night, it was releasing daylight out its other end. Again, Janis spoke under her breath; "now that's the kind of poop I like to see...if I have to see poop."

Despite its observable power, it was not disturbing the water, leaving Janis with the confidence they would remain safe.

Just over a half-hour's time, the spinning abnormality had swallowed the entire night sky and then, astonishingly consumed itself and vanished, leaving behind a warm, beautiful morning.

Sitting atop the Cypress, they remained silent for some time. The past hours had been the strangest thing they had ever seen. Janis slipped into her shoulder rig and slid her weapon back into the holster. She was surprised and pleased she hadn't lost the weapon during their turbulent underwater struggle. The nine-millimeter had saved her life more than once and held a special meaning. This time however, it wasn't the weapon that had saved her, it was the rig. Patting the holster, she smiled. *When we get home, you get a first-rate, hot-oil rub.*

Stranded atop the Cypress, they waited for the floating log Julia had told them to watch for. In the distance, they could see the outline of swampland, but dared not move for fear of missing the blue light they had been warned to follow.

Out of boredom, they began taking turns identifying pieces of debris floating past. Most things were recognizable, but some, because they came out of the past of 1915, the year Frenier had been destroyed, they passed unbranded. The cascade seemed endless, and they were appreciative of the time-filler.

In early afternoon, an item floated up to the tree that caused surprise; Janis plucked it from the water with a smile, "Julia Brown's guitar." Moving it around in her hands, she shook her head, "look at this. Unharmed after having gone through that fierce flood."

Minutes later, a section of tree came floating past. Looking at it Jodie Jean felt a warmth and told Janis, "First the old woman sent us her guitar, now she's sending us our ride."

Janis glanced at her and smiled, "You're starting to think like a true Cajun." Nestling the guitar into the branches of the Cypress that had saved their lives, Janis and Jodie Jean dove into the water and swam to the log, climbing atop. They drifted for some time but drifted sharing a satisfying hope.

"The blue light we're looking for," Jody Jean asked eventually, "what is it?"

Feet dangling in the water with legs straddling the log, Janis told her, "There's a legend that the swamp around Frenier was a place where pirates often came to bury treasure. When they did, so it's said, the Captain would always kill one of the crew and toss the body into the hole with the bootee. That dead man's soul, was said to rise from the grave as a blue light, floating about watching over the treasure."

"Do you believe that?" Jodie Jean asked.

Janis shrugged. "Over the centuries, and even today, tourists or local fishermen sometimes spot a strange blue light just floating about in the air; no logical explanation for it."

"Do you think that's what it is, a Pirate's soul?"

Janis made a face. "I don't know. This *is* Louisiana, if something out of the ordinary is going to happen, it's going to happen here."

"So, if the light is a Pirate, why would he want to help us? Pirates were bad." Jody Jean said.

Again, Janis shrugged. "Why would God take a Voodoun who cursed an entire town to their death, into Heaven?"

Jody Jean pressed her lips, "For doing something good, maybe?"

Janis smiled, "Sounds logical to me."

The current moved them steadily toward the far edge of the swamp, the sun was warm, but a light breeze cooled their skin. Time crept past. Janis was in the middle of a yawn when Jody Jean yelled out pointing, "Look!"

Janis followed the direction of her finger and whispered softly, "I'll be."

The blue light was the size of a softball; it hovered several feet away as if waiting to ensure they saw it. Quickly it zipped off several feet and waited again. Janis understood it wanted them to follow. They began to paddle with their hands. It was tedious and tiresome, but just over an hour they were gliding into a small alcove where the tree trunk bumped gently into a weed-covered bank. Carefully, Janis climbed onto shore then helped Jodie Jean.

The light hovered, waiting. When ready, it led them through the swamp beneath Cypress trees massed with Spanish Moss and towering Oaks and Sycamores. The mosquitoes were thick and the two slapped at them relentlessly.

At dusk, the blue light had brought them to their obvious destination: a small, isolated wood shack. The orb flew to its open door and lingered. When they cautiously stepped onto the shed's deteriorating porch, the light bounced twice and flew away vanishing into the swamp. Janis followed it with her eyes and whispered, "Thank you!" Turning, she stepped into the shack and Jodie Jean followed.

The interior lay steeped in shadows. Janis began to speak when the open door behind them suddenly slammed, causing them both to jump.

When the pounding of her heart eased, Janis whispered, "moment of truth Jodie Jean. Taking her hand, they moved through the darkness to the closed door. Janis took a deep breath and pulled it open.

Shoulder to shoulder they stood staring out. Jody Jean's family sat at the long table, children misbehaving as usual. The young couple in the booth were still sipping Coke from the same glass and the man in the business suit still reading his paper. There was no Blue Eyes.

Spotting Janis and the young girl standing inside the doorway of the men's bathroom, the server sauntered over. "What pray tell," she asked, "are you two doin' in the gentleman's room?" Glancing around them looking in she saw nothing out of the ordinary. So, shaking her head she looked them up and down adding, "and Good Lord knows I got to ask, why is it ya' all look like ya been pulled through Momma's wash ringer?"

Janis glanced at Jodie Jean, and they smiled. "Well," Janis told the inquisitive woman, "You wouldn't believe it if we told you, so let me just say this; a man's bathroom can be a might frightful to a couple of young ladies."

CHAPTER 55

Clay stepped into the dark cold stairway; the one that would lead him down into that horrid black abyss of memories; that's where Carl was waiting. He could feel the hair bristling on the back of his neck. Nervous hands gripped the butt of his nine-millimeter.

Ignoring the fear and dread causing his heart to pound, he began the unwanted descent. One by one, the frost-covered steps creaked beneath his weight. He hadn't come anywhere near this stairway for seven long years; had planned never again to walk down them; now here he was!

He wanted to hurry, to rush, to charge into the blackness and face what awaited to get it over with, but there were many things to consider: like who or what was waiting, was this journey a gauntlet, a challenge of staying alive and fighting his way to Carl or was no one even here…maybe not even Carl himself.

Blue Eyes was the master of creating stress and delusion. Minutes could mean the difference between saving Carl or causing his death. If he had learned nothing else from his experiences seven years ago, he had come to understand that the Blue Eyes Killer was genius, impeccable in his timing, an expert in the art of murdering.

Clay heard no noise. Eight minutes ago, Carl had been crying out in excruciating pain over the phone, now silence. Nearing the bottom of the steps Clay began sensing a terrible odor, pungent, harsh like the smell of sulfur. A memory, long locked away, quickly surfaced once again evoking its recognition: the smell of Hell.

He thought of Carl begging for his help only minutes ago. Carl had been part of his life for so long. They had grown up together.

Clay reached the last step, it squeaked, and he paused, listening... again nothing. The sulfur smell had grown to near intolerable. In the distance, a hint of light was radiating from the third room. Weapon raised Clay laid his wrist over the other, shining the flashlight beam down the barrel. He stepped onto the old plank floor and as if it had triggered some sort of on-button, out of the darkness there arose an immediate murmuring of conversations.

Clay swept his light quickly over the room. Nothing was there - nothing he could see.But he knew what it was, there were hundreds of them here, a demonic throng of beings, creatures of unimaginable sizes and shapes, pressed together with excitement, assembled for this auspicious occasion, all joyous, eager, anticipating the entertainment of watching his despair. Clay feared they had already celebrated Carl's horrible long-suffering and death.

Ignoring the evil furor around him, he moved into the second room; he wanted so much to not have to enter the third, but the second room was small, and suddenly he was there.

The interior twinkled with candlelight, just the way it had seven years ago. Only this time, the old, rusted metal table was not covered with a white sheet, prepped for a ritual slaying; now it was turned upright on its end and Carl, stripped, was tied to it. There was no movement. The mumbling horde fell silent.

Clay had promised himself he would not give them the finish they were waiting for - no matter what he saw. That proved impossible. His yell echoed through the elevator like the cry of a lone hawk in a valley. Wetness filled his eyes, his legs buckled, and he dropped to his knees. He began to sob aloud, ignoring the riotous roar of laughter that rose from the darkness surrounding him.

What they had done to Carl was appalling. The man was innocent, had harmed none of them. Clay wiped at his eyes. It was near impossible to believe such evil existed, that it lived every second, every minute in the invisible darkness around us, that these beings remained at our side day and night as vile opportunists, eager to twist mistakes, misunderstandings and human frailties into tragedies, and to succeed in their most fetid goal of all; to separate man from God.

When the tears dried up and sobbing subsided, Clay stared compassionately into Carl's face; it was staring blankly toward the open doorway, as if waiting on the arrival of someone. Clay knew that someone was to have been him. Carl had hoped, amid the torture, pain, and fear that his friend would arrive in time and save him. Clay wiped at a single tear streaking his face; but that friend didn't make it.

The demons, or who ever had done this hideous work, had painstakingly cut his skin into strips and meticulously tied them into neatly arranged bows; there were seven bows total; one for each of the seven passing years. It was no wonder Carl had screamed so agonizingly.

The Demons stood huddled, eager for the climatic finish - for Clay to scramble to his feet shouting and cursing, threatening them while firing his weapon aimlessly into the darkness at them; but the big prize for which they hoped, was for Cooper to lift his eyes and curse his God.

Minutes passed in near silence, no sound in the dank, candle lit room, only that of Clays' breathing. Carl's stare remained inert. Finally, beneath the myriad of demonic eyes, Clay stood and slid his weapon back into its holster. Pausing, he looked one final time at his friend, then turned and left the room speaking aloud as he walked, "God, take his soul to heaven, he was a good man and believed in you. When I get up there, he and I can resume our friendship."

Clay marched through both rooms and climbed the stairs. The past events had caused him to forget about the frigid temperatures and deep snow waiting above; but with each step he climbed, its bitter realization returned, nipping his nose and cheeks and stealing body heat. Beginning to shiver he pulled gloves from his pocket, appreciative of the warmth they would bring.

Behind him however, down there in that dark cold hole, no more was there need for warmth, Carl was gone. The Demons were still there, he could hear them. The evil horde of bastards were cursing him, calling him names; and in some peculiarly pious way, it gave Clay a sense of satisfaction.

CHAPTER 56

Carl Brown was laid to rest the 4th of February. Clay spent the afternoon lapsed in a state of melancholy, preferring to be alone. Nancy had tried to get him to eat but he refused with a curt smile, choosing instead to remain in his den sipping on rum and coke.

Slumped in his chair he spent the better part of the day staring out his window at the glittering snow. He wasn't drunk by any means, but the alcohol was helping…if only a little.

Michael knocked lightly on the den door than opened it enough to peek in, "Dad?" He said softly.

Breaking his gaze Clay glanced around his chair, "Hey little man."

"Can I come in?" Michael asked.

Pulling himself upright, Clay swiveled the chair to face across the desk. "Sure."

Michael slipped in closing the door and moving to the couch.

"What's up?" Clay asked admiringly, knowing his son had come to try and cheer him up.

Michael spoke direct, "Dad, I know Carl's death is bothering you. I think we ought to talk about it?"

Inside, Clay smiled warmly. "Michael, I'm okay, really. I just need to sort some things out; they're nothing you need to worry about, I promise."

Michael glanced at his Nike's a second before looking up, "Dad, you're going to kill Blue Eyes, aren't you?"

Clay sat silent staring at his son. It was a difficult question to answer, especially considering Michael was a seven-year-old boy. "Michael," he said following moments of unresolved quiet, "I've taken into account what Pastor Hart told us, and it's a concern. I'd rather not harm Blue Eyes, I want you to know that, but I see no other way. I have you and your mom to consider. You have seen what he is like, is capable of doing; and doing it all without remorse."

"I know Dad, but – "Michael began to cry."

Clay left the squeaky chair and sat beside him, pulling him tight in his arms. "Michael," he said softly, "you're seven years old, but often you think like your seventy. And you see far too much of the world as a grown up rather than a kid."

Michael sniffled, "Dad, I know there is life after we die; I don't want you to be separated from God like Cain will be. You're my Dad, and I love you. When I die, I want you to be in Heaven waiting for me".

Clay gave Michael a squeeze. "Little man, don't you worry, regardless of what happens, God will see to it we are all up there. You told me once that in Heaven God will grant us the desires of our heart. So, if all of us being together is a desire of your heart than there is no need to worry, right. You yourself have said it dozens of times, you just have to trust Him."

Michael sniffled again and looked up at his Dad, "That's right." Rubbing tears from his eyes he smiled, "See Dad, it was good that we talked. Now don't you feel better?"

Clay returned the smile, "very much Michael, very much."

CHAPTER 57

ob Lemus was pleased to be going home. He hurried down the Jetway to the open door of the awaiting aircraft but was halted abruptly. The long line of passengers stretched clear beyond mid-ships.

From the open doorway onward, it was slow going inch by inch, reminding him of his old Marine Corp days when lines were always long and tight, asshole to belly button, they use to call it. Every day was hurry up and wait, men urinated in smelly open troughs and crapped on a long line of open stools shoulder to shoulder, watching each other wipe their ass. Bob grinned to himself, *the only thing close to privacy in those days, was being a private.*

At his assigned seat - the emergency exit over the starboard wing - he stored his overcoat above and smiled at the elderly gentleman and oriental college girl already buckled in. Once sat down he slid his briefcase beneath his seat then buckled in himself. Following a long sigh, he sat back observing the activities.

The craft was jammed to capacity by the time the stewardess closed and secured the passenger door. Struggling with the unpleasant sensation of feeling locked in, Bob Lemus glanced out his window. Snow was cascading heavily. To ensure they lifted off before it altered their departure, the pilot was cleared to taxi immediately to the runway. There, they sat for three minutes and twenty-two seconds; the stewardesses used the lull to demo the emergency equipment and point out escape routes.

Upon completion, the two women sat and buckled in quickly. The plane rolled slowly forward made a sharp left, then stopped. The engines whined, climbing to a roar that shook the craft. Bob Lemus reminded himself he liked the Boeing 747; trusted her, she was sound and dependable with a good safety record.

Outside the window, the falling snow was now blocking all visibility. The plane lurched forward and pressed them against the seat. Bob closed his eyes as they left the ground. Washington International vanished quickly as the 747 pressed through the endless bombardment of flakes, clambering and shuddering blindly toward her assigned cruising altitude of thirty-eight thousand feet. By the time they leveled off and announced the use of electronic devices, Bob was ready to give his fingers a rest.

People immediately began chatting, opening magazines, newspapers, books and setting up electronic devices. Closing his eyes, Bob laid his head against the seat; they were all crazy he thought. Did not the lot of them understand they were locked in a machine thirty-eight thousand feet in the air and totally helpless; shouldn't they worry? Even a little? Did any of them have even the slightest inkling that a fall from this height would totally pulverize them, turn everyone into powder. And the horror of the fall, with a three- or four-minute crash time, sitting there beside their wives, husbands, children, friends, all with hearts pounding; knowing full well what was coming.

Sighing, Bob opened his eyes, rolling his head toward the window. Seeing nothing but his own reflection, he told himself, "Shut up Bob!"

CHAPTER 58

Little Cain Christenson readied himself for bed. Dressed in his pajamas; a warm flannel two piece covered with the comical depiction of little red horned devils, he brushed his teeth, rinsed then climbed into bed.

His mother and father tucked him snugly beneath his blankets and smiled. Exiting the room, they blew him a kiss goodnight and closed the door, leaving it slightly ajar.

Feeling warm and loved, Cain closed his eyes and said his prayers. *Dear Satin, my most beloved god, as I slip into sleep, I pray that you, like always, take me on a journey of learning, that I continue my education, growing knowledgeable in your ways. That I make for you a good and faithful servant, that I may be strong like my father and work to drag souls away from their God and redirect them to Hell...a gift from me to you. Amen.*

Cain rolled onto his side and smiled with merriment.

CHAPTER 59

ob Lemus hated to fly; he understood it was the safest mode of transportation to date, and by far the fastest. However, when a mistake was made, it also took grand prize for the most fatal.

The 747 sliced sharply through the black icy sky like a tarnished silver knife. Louisiana was moving closer, now less than forty-five minutes to touchdown. Although enthralled by a Tom Clancy novel, Bob was counting the minutes.

The young college girl had been reading since take off. She now closed her book and sighed, obviously bored. Smiling, she looked over at Bob, saying "So, what is it you do for a living?"

Lemus removed his eyes from the book and glanced at her. "I'm retired." He turned back to his book not wanting conversation.

"Retired from where?" The girl persisted.

Bob tried hiding his irritation, "Federal Service." He didn't bother looking up this time.

"Doing what?"

Lemus bit at his lip and looked at her again. "I was a hunter."

The oriental girl made a face, "A Hunter! Hunter of what? Were you some sort of Park Ranger, in Alaska or something?"

Bob Lemus fidgeted in his seat. "No," he said, sternly, "I hunted people and other bad things."

The girl looked thoughtful, "Other bad things?You mean like wild animals, like run away zoo animals, like Crocodiles? I've read they've been found everywhere in the country, not just Florida or Louisiana. That people have been turning them loose in lakes and creeks and ponds, all over; you know what I mean. They actually think it's some kind of funny prank."

"No," Bob told her irritated, "I didn't hunt Crocks, I hunted Vampires, and other scary things."

The girl was stunned at first, but then smiled sheepishly, "Oh, I get it. You're irritated with me for bothering you, right."

Lemus nodded. "I'm irritated yes, but don't take it personally."

The girl made another face and reopened her book, "Sorry!"

Returning to his novel, Bob glanced down at the opened page but couldn't get past two sentences. His thoughts were locked on Janis. He just wanted to get home to her. He loved her and worried for her safety. The Vamps being on a killing spree was dangerous for everyone, but especially for her, she would not hesitate getting in the middle of things if Cooper were to call. And the Vamps would kill her without a moment's hesitation.

He realized Nasif kept the damn things under control, but in reality, that control amounted to little more than a hope and a promise.

Bob gave a soft sigh. An occasional Maverick Vamp was one thing, but renegade pockets of them were another. With powerful men like Louis and Aluka stirring things up, the United States could very well plunge into civil war.

Yawning he stretched awkwardly within the tight confines of his seat. He yawned a second time as the pilot announced they were beginning their descent into Alexandria.

Although pleased, Bob remained anxious. He knew the statistics: most aircraft accidents occurred during take-off or landing. In his early career with the bureau as an NTSB investigator, he had responded to more than his share of crash sights; walking the devastation and taking pictures, making notes, setting flags and laying grid lines; many times, while trying to avoid the mass of mutilated bodies.

Lemus shifted his thoughts to something pleasant. In twenty minutes, they would be on the ground and disembarking. Janis would be there to greet him. She would be smiling, and he would take her into his arms. His thoughts shifted again. The Washington conference haunted him. Small packs of Vamps were reported breaking away on their own in several countries, not just the US, and nearly every Ferret, including Ever, had been pressed into service.

The bureau had concluded there was little to worry about, but Lemus hadn't taken it so lightly. Aluka and the others knew the consequences of their rebellion; yet they seemed little concerned. Obviously there had been covert meetings among the defectors, and with some manner of stratagem.

Lemus glanced out the window again. The night sky over Alexandria was clear. He could see the endless network of glowing lights far below the wing; and among all that glitter laid the airport; and somewhere down there, on that wonderful firmness of earth, there waited the beating heart of his beautiful sliver of white chocolate.

CHAPTER 60

Little Cain's face rested peaceful against his pillow. He lay asleep on his left side, looking as if he were smiling. A dark sleep had whisked him away to a place not far from where his sleeping body lay, but to a time decades into the past.

Dressed in his red-deviled pajamas, he was strolling casually from room to room in an older wood building with four floors. The house was filled with men and women young and old; all cheerful, their laughter and conversations loud. It was a grown-ups party, although he did see several children being used by adults. Everywhere the thick smoke of incense filled the air.

Many of the people lay naked, kissing and feeling each other's body. There was a lot of moaning and loud cries among the laughter. Cain did not fully understand what it was and why they were doing these things, but he did realize it was something obviously fun to them; he had seen his mom and dad doing similar things in the cell during their visits.

Candles and oil lamps furnished the lighting, so he knew his prayer had been answered. Satin had sent him on a journey to a different time and place. He did not know what lay in wait, but something would happen here in this big house. Something he would witness or participate in, something that would increase his knowledge and skill. His little heart was pounding with anticipation.

His father had once told him the things experienced in life were the things that made people who they are. Since that day, Cain's personal prayer was to experience everything, he wanted to touch, and feel and see it all, because that would make him like his father.

In a room on the third floor, Cain nestled his way through a circle of adults smiling at something in the center of the crowd. A boy and girl he guessed to be near his age were lying on a rug naked. They were playing with each other's private parts.

Although he found the activity fascinating, there was much more remaining to see. He was about to turn and leave when someone put a hand on his shoulder.

CHAPTER 61

The lights of the runway were growing brighter and once again Bob's fingers were gripping the arms of his seat. Through the window he watched the ground distance closing rapidly, anxiety was knotting his stomach.

The opening and closing of flaps shook the aircraft and the noise rattled through the compartment. The college girl beside him continued reading as though they were merely sharing the backseat of a New York City Cab.

Then they were down, wheels screeching against the pavement. The plane shuddered, flaps changed directions and the engines roared like angry Lions. The 747 hadn't had time to slow when the aircraft made a sudden drop to the port side jerking everyone abruptly to the left. Cries rose from the crowded passengers. Instinctively Bob glared across the isle through the port-side emergency window. The tip of the left wing was dragging the runway sending up sparks. "Oh shit"! He said it out loud knowing the stunned pilots were struggling to keep the aircraft steady.

No doubt the Port-side landing hydraulics had failed. The thought barely registered when the dragging wing snapped free spinning like a top down the runway behind them. The fuselage made a jolting pitch to the right and toppled longways across the runway. Lying on its left side with the attached right wing pointing straight toward Heaven they began a high-speed slide down the thick concrete.

Screams were frantic. The jolt of the fall had flung open overhead compartments raining down a barrage of falling paraphernalia. The free-spinning wing left behind suddenly exploded; a fireball shot high into the night sky. Distance had put the crowded fuselage clear of the shrapnel field, but the wild slide was sending up its own spectacular and deadly display of sparks the full length of the body. The disabled 747's remaining wing still towering upward looked as if it were waiting for God to grab it and bring their fateful ride to a stop.

Struggling to keep from crushing the young girl now crying hysterically, Bob clung to the right arm of his seat trying to hold himself up. He stared through his window and up the long shadowy wing. He knew his seat was not a good location; *sloshing within the wings baffled structure lay hundreds of gallons of high explosive fuel just waiting for the right spark. If, actually when, that spark struck he would be blown apart or cooked alive.*

Bob rated his chance of surviving at a scale of 1 – 10000. He didn't want to die but accepted it. What bothered him most was that Janis was watching it all from the terminal.

It was sudden, powerful; the plane tumbled again slamming onto its top and snapping free the last remaining wing. Now wingless the long battered fuselage added suffrage and more fear to those already screaming in terror; still traveling at great speed the body went into a terrifying high-intense role; rolling and rolling and rolling, first down and off the wing lying beneath them then off onto the concrete.

The spinning was nauseating and caused a great deal of vomiting. Screaming took on a new pitch. Everything big, small and lose flew about slamming endlessly time and time again into the helpless passengers. To them it was as if strapped within an elongated fast spinning dryer filled with tumbling rocks.

The rolling fuselage was but a few feet clear of the wing when this one exploded. The huge fireball sent hundreds of large and small pieces of hot searing metal ripping through the thin defenseless skin of the plane. Like a field of burning meteorites the spray battered, cut and decapitated passengers.A howling surge of wind and smoke rapidly filled the open interior.

But the plane's continual roll down the runway cleared most of the choking smoke away. The handful of light-headed and injured passengers still alert, realized the entire forward portion of the craft was gone, leaving them trapped inside a dark rolling tunnel…a black vulnerable tunnel filled with lifeless bodies, an endless bombardment of flying debris, melting plastics, the relentless swing of dangling oxygen masks and scattered seats with and without burning bodies.

But within a few seconds the remaining maze of smoke was beginning to thicken again. Vision became as impossible as breathing. The once loud screaming had now fallen to near silence. Death, the thought of loved ones, and prayer was all that filled the fast-fading minds of the few still hanging on to life.

Then came the sudden jolt of a fierce impact. Whatever it was, it sent the speeding death-tunnel high into the air where it broke into pieces. From the terminal across the runway shocked onlookers watched as bodies flew like weightless dark objects; some alone and others still strapped together in their seats.

Bob Lemus, barely conscious, bleeding profusely from a mass of cuts and broken bones, had felt the seat tare from the bolts holding them to the floor of the craft. Now suddenly they were flying free; nothing around them but open air. Still held in place by their seatbelts they spun, flying through the dark Louisiana night. Lights, earth and stars became a wild blur of colors mixed with dizziness, pain and the distant sound of wails and sirens.

Bob Lemus was sure it was only in his head, but he'd have sworn he heard Janis shout, "I love you, Bob."

In the seconds left of his life Bob understood this had been his final flight; taken with an elderly man to whom he never said hello, and a young girl who wanted only to talk. Although unable to speak, in his mind he apologized knowing that if they weren't dead already, in just a few seconds when they made impact, they would be.

Then the ground came up, there was a flash of light, and everything was gone.

CHAPTER 62

When young Cain turned to see who had touched his shoulder, he thought at first, he had been sent to the mythical city of Agrabah. A tall man dressed like Aladdin stood staring down at him. "Hello young Cain," the strangely dressed man said, his voice familiar but not one the boy could immediately place. "I am, was once, a friend of your fathers. I was told you would be coming tonight. Welcome to my place of abode."

"Thank you," Cain replied, "Is this Agrabah?"

The stranger smiled. "No, I am afraid not. You are in the city of New Orleans on Dauphine Street, in the French Quarter."

"I've been sent here to learn something," Cain said with a trace of eagerness, "do you know what that's going to be?"

The stranger eyed him thoughtfully. "Yes, I do, and your lesson is about to begin. So, if you will, please join me downstairs." Smiling, he offered the young boy his hand. Cain took it returning the smile, then descended the stairs. A busy parade of men and women passed them coming and going, all boisterous and dizzy with the warmth of wine and drugs.

From the corner of his eye, Cain studied the man holding his hand. This friend of his father was wearing a white Turban. He had a neatly trimmed black beard and mustache that stood out against skin darker than his own and wore a shirt that looked like a short bathrobe hanging open; but there was no hair on his chest like a lot of grown men. Rings covered his fingers, and a long shimmering necklace held a large gold medallion. His clothes were bright in color; especially his orange silk pants whose legs puffed out like balloons than narrowed again at his ankles. On his feet he wore a black pair of slippers that curled up at the toes.

Cain, hoping not to sound rude, asked, "Is it Halloween here?"

"No, I do not believe it is." The new friend replied, "Why do you ask?"

"The way you're dressed. It looks like a Halloween costume. I like it though, it's really with it?"

"What do you mean, really with it?"

"Cain shrugged. "Really with it, it means, cool, neat, great, you know, makes people wish to take another look at you."

His friend glanced down the front of himself, "Thank you, I think! Am I safe in assuming than that you approve of my fashion choice?"

Cain nodded. "Yes, that's exactly what I mean. But if it's not Halloween, then why is it you're dressed like that?"

"I am dressed this way because this is how Sultans dress in my country."

"Wow." Cain said excited, "a Sultan. So, you're some kind of Prince, or King?"

"Yes," he said with a shrug, "you could say that."

As their descent ended and they stepped onto the first floor, Cain suddenly realized why he had taken an instant liking to this man, recognizing now the familiarity of his voice; he sounded just like the Grentch. *The Grentch Who Stole Christmas*: his all-time favorite video in the whole world.

Crossing the floor through a chattering crowd, they stopped at a spot just to the right of the main door entrance. "Now, young Cain, watch closely, it all begins here. There will be a knock on the door and one of my eunuchs will answer it."

Cain looked up again. "What is a eunuch?"

The Sultan smiled. "Eunuchs are my special guards."

Cain nodded just as his eye caught something that startled him; the man standing beside him holding his hand, wearing the white turban and funny pants and shoes, walked into the room opposite to where they were standing, strolled past only inches away, and exited down a hallway.

Cain's brow wrinkled, confused. Looking up puzzled, his Sultan friend grinned speaking before he had the chance to ask. "Remember, young Cain, we are in a dream. We are only watching what happens, not taking part in it."

"But how can you be here twice at the same time? That was you who just walked by you, was it not?"

"Yes, that was me a hundred and fifty years ago, when I was flesh and blood. This building we are in," he spread out his hands in gesture, "while it still stands in the city of New Orleans today, it too is in the past a hundred and fifty years. What is about to happen here, took place that long ago. You are about to witness the closing story of two brothers; one who cheated and stole from the other, and the wronged one's revenge."

Cain thought a moment, "So you're one of those brothers, right?"

The Sultan cupped his hands behind his back. "Yes."

"Which one," Cain asked.

"I am the one who stole."

Cain pressed his lips thoughtfully. "I think I understand. You're going to be murdered here tonight, aren't you?"

"Yes, young Cain, that is correct. You are a quick study."

"So," Cain asked, "are you now a Demon?"

The Sultan smiled lightly. "No, I am not. I am an apparition, a ghost. I haunt this building," he paused a moment, "it is my punishment."

Someone from the outside knocked hard on the door. To Cain, it sounded as if a series of angry pounding. The Sultan placed a hand on Cain's shoulder speaking quickly, "After you have witnessed what happens here tonight, it will be your task to tell me what you have learned."

Saying nothing, Cain smiled with exhilaration.

CHAPTER 63

The Aircraft Crash Rescue Trucks moved through the wreckage slow and deliberate; their whirling lights flooding the area with reds and blues and oranges. Powerful spotlights streaked in all directions, bright beams crisscrossing, each searching high and low with diligence. Wreckage, debris and bodies lay everywhere.

Truck turrets and hand lines laid down blankets of foam extinguishing scattered spot fires, muffled radio traffic crackled from vehicles, officers shouted orders to EMS and Firefighting personnel checking bodies and foraging through wreckage.

While the Louisiana night was cold, it was thankfully warm enough for any potential survivors.

On the runway a quarter mile upwind from the crash site, arriving Fire trucks, Ambulances, Police and other personnel were staged and dispersed when requested.

Despite their hopelessness, pain and tears, the onlookers observing from the terminal windows, felt the distant crisis appeared well organized and professionally performed. However, to the trained professionals working the appalling disaster, as always, quickly it was over, getting the job done would be a crazy, tangled, seemingly unorganized chaotic FUBAR.

A young female EMS worker walking the internal field along the east side of the runway came upon a section of seating holding three people. It lay turned up with the passengers lying on their backs as if comfortably gazing up at the stars.

Setting her tech bag on the ground, hopeful fingers began checking pulses. An older man with gray hair was first; he was dead, probably a broken neck. A young girl in the middle, face covered with blood and a large laceration on the right cheek, had a pulse…she was alive! The EMS worker looked up into the sky and whispered, "thank you." Twisting toward the main body of searchers she shouted, "Got a live one, need a backboard."

Facing back, she checked the final pulse, a black man, balding with horseshoe hair. Her fingers located the Adams-apple and slid to the side of the neck; nothing. She moved her fingers slightly lower and pressed a little harder; a smile creased her lips. "YES", she shouted gleefully. Twisting she shouted into the crowd again, "Make those two backboards, pronto."

CHAPTER 64

With aggravation the Sultan's guard opened the door. He stood staring only a second before the long-bladed knife pierced through his throat. When pulled free his body toppled to the floor, blood pooling. Eighteen men rushed inside stepping over his gasping form. None of the partying guests seemed to notice. The last man through the door closed, locked and stood guard in front of it.

What ensued was like nothing young Cain expected. It was cold blooded butchery. Swords, axes and knives held by the gang of men, began slicing and hacking everyone within reach. Heads, arms and legs were severed from bodies; blood flowed like a thin covering of red water over the floors. Within seconds the realization dawned and screaming began. Men, women and the hand full of young children darted chaotic, seeking a place to hide, but there was nowhere to go, no way out. Two years prior, the Sultan had secured all windows and doors with decorative ironwork for security; ensuring no one entered in or left without his approval. That act had sealed their fate.

The killers moved from floor to floor ignoring the cries for mercy as they hacked and sliced to the point of sweat and near exhaustion. It was a cold-blooded human slaughter and Cain watched the carnage with fascination. A strange tingling raced through his veins. It felt as if he were strolling through a 3D movie with the ear-splitting thunderous vibration of Dolby Surround Sound; it was like being on the set of an old-time version of The Chain Saw Massacre.

The assassins were merciless, leaving no one alive except for the Sultan. Heads, arms and legs, hands and feet were dismembered from everybody and kicked this way and that, creating a mix-match of human body parts strewed throughout the house on every floor.

Following mutilation of the last victim the Sultan was dragged struggling into the backyard, a grave was dug, and he was buried alive while pleading for his life. When the last shovel of dirt was thrown, the band of butchers, all sopped in blood and sweat, vanished into the darkened streets of the French Quarter.

Beneath the pile of fresh dirt came no sound; but above it seven-year-old Cain stood with eyes closed, his body still tingling. He could sense the Sultan's terror beneath the crushing weight of the earth, envision him struggling with desperation to move but unable, pictured him gasping for breaths but lungs filling only with cold, black dirt.

From the star-filled Louisiana night sky, a sullen moon draped New Orleans in gray muted light; wind swept through the narrow streets and somewhere far away a lone dog barked at something unnatural.

The Sultan's apparition cupped his hands behind his back. "So young Cain," he said, his eyes staring at the fresh mound of dirt, "what is the lesson you've learned while witnessing my terrible ordeal?"

Cain glanced up at him, pondered, then turned back to the grave. "It's quite simple actually; he said, "but there are two lessons. First, I've learned that humans are so very imperceptive, believing themselves to be spiritually strong and safe, when actually they are weak and easily manipulated by the demons of my god…all because they fail to wholeheartedly listen to theirs." The Sultan raised his eyebrows thoughtfully, "Interestingly expressed", he said, "and the second", he asked.

"Secondly," Cain said smiling up at the Sultan, "As usual, my father is correct; the price of fun and enjoyment is quite often worth the cost."

CHAPTER 65

When Bob Lemus awoke, he blinked robustly to clear his vision. A large bore IV flowed into his left arm, EKG wires ran out to a monitor, and a tall stainless-steel IV pole held two 1000 cc, and one 250cc bags of fluid. He made an irritated face; all that flowing liquid alerted him to the catheter line running into his penis. It was good they had put it in while he was under; otherwise, they'd have met with great objection.

He was wearing a cast the full length of his left leg; it was elevated at a forty-five-degree angle by a series of polys. Two fingers on his left hand were taped together against a thin wood splint. Mild pain surged through his neck and a soft-foam neck brace reminded him to limit his movement. A Nasal Cannula fed him a low flow of oxygen.

Following a deep breath he relaxed, focusing on the ceiling above. Surprised he was even alive, he sighed aloud repeating what was said to have been the last words of the famous Doc Holliday when in his Hospital Bed and he glanced down at his bare feet... "I'll be damned."

Nearly asleep Janis heard his voice for the first time in two days. Rising so quickly from the chair it scraped loudly across the floor. Tearing up, she looked down at her awakened love and smiled. "Hi!"

Bob gave her a smile back. "I'm alive?"

"Yes," Janis said, "you're still alive you Jackass." Bending she took his hand and kissed his lips gently.

Bob liked the feel of her hand in his and squeezed lightly. "Pinch me will you." He said, "I can't believe I'm still here. How many broken bones?"

"Doctors called it a miracle, but only one. Your leg."

"Well then, I have only one more question. Why am I a Jackass?"

Janis used the back of a crooked finger to wipe at a tear, "because you took ten years off my life."

Bob widened his smile. "You can't be mad at me for that," he mused, "as beautiful as you are, you could have afforded fifteen years."

Janis broke into tears.

CHAPTER 66

Clay opened his eyes. Still in bed lying on his side, he gazed into a patch of morning sunlight piercing the bedroom window; dust particles were floating inside the filmy beam, and he thought, *Streaming Sunbeams, The Final Frontier*. He imagined the drifting particles a field of Meteorites and himself as Captain Jon-Luc Picard aboard the USS Enterprise. He was warping through space... his mission: to go where no Indiana Town Marshal had ever gone before. Clay smiled at himself; "*you idiot.*"

A yawn crept up and he rolled onto his back stretching. It felt good. When finished, he laced his fingers behind his head and breathed deeply. Clay loved mornings: the sun, the warmth, the new beginning. His stomach growled and he freed a hand to pat it; he could smell bacon frying downstairs; "*What a woman*". *He told himself softly.*

Following a hurried shower he dressed in uniform, clipped his holstered weapon to his belt and clambered downstairs to the kitchen. Nancy was dressed too, wearing the red apron with the embroidered Lobster across the front; the one he had brought her last summer while they were vacationing in Boston.

In addition to the Bacon, she had cooked Pancakes, Scrambled Eggs, Sausage and brewed a pot of Coffee. Clay kissed her cheek and told her she had him salivating. Pouring himself a cup he stood silent to the side sipping while watching her work.

She placed everything on the table, pulled a carton of orange juice from the refrigerator then walked to the kitchen door and yelled up for Michael. "Breakfast, Angel Boy."

"Be right down," Michael yelled.

Clay took another sip. "What say right after breakfast we let Michael watch Superman Returns while you and I go upstairs, and I become Superman?"

Nancy set the carton of orange juice on the table and sauntered over to her husband, "because," she whispered sultry in his ear, "you played man of steel last night and I'm cleaning house today; and as for you, you're going to work." Clay frowned as Michael came bounding down the stairs.

"Morning Mom and Dad," he said charging to the table. Pulling out a chair he sat, "man mom," he told her smiling, "This looks and smells too good to eat," his eyes were primarily focused on the stack of pancakes.

Winking at Clay Nancy turned and smiled at her son. "Well young man," she said, "I'm glad you like it, because you and I are cleaning house today and you'll need all the energy you can muster."

Michael looked up, "Cleaning again?"

"Again," she told him, "Cleanliness is next to Godliness."

"I'll be honest with you Mom," he said as she and Clay sat, "I hope God doesn't put you in charge of keeping Heaven clean when we get up there. You'll have the Angles going on strike."

"Well, if He does put me in charge," she said pulling her chair to the table, "I'm making you, my foreman. Now let's pray. I hear the vacuum cleaner calling your name."

When Clay arrived at work, Gertrude was already in the office. He stuck his head in to say good morning and she smiled, "Coffee's made." Despite her early morning cheer, like Clay, Gertrude was also having a difficult time dealing with the loss of Carl. She too had known him a lot of years.

Making his way to the Kitchenette Clay filled his favorite cup stopping at three quarters; not wanting the crack along the handle allowing the liquid to leak down the front of his shirt. Following a sip, he ambled back to his office thinking about Michael; someday the old eyesore, if it survived, would be passed on to him. He wondered if it would mean anything. Sentimentally he hoped so. Although beat up and worn, the old piece of porcelain, at least to him, had personality.

At his desk, he took another sip and sat. Leaning back, he cocked his feet on the desk resting the old well-worn cup on his abdomen, he studied it. The once bright police shield was now well faded, barely noticeable. Smiling, he remembered the day Nancy had given it to him. They were so young, still newly married and in those days, Michael was but a shared dream; a dream they worked intently at achieving.

The ring of Gertrude's phone muffled through the wall dividing their offices. As always, she let it ring three times then answered. Her words barely understandable Clay often listened, unless it proved a private call.

"Clerk's office." There was a pause; then she spoke back, "Who the hell is this?" Clay pulled his feet from the desk, gently picking up the receiver of his own phone while punching the blinking line.

Gertrude spoke sternly into the receiver, "Are you the asshole who killed Carl?"

Clay recognized Blue Eye's voice and wanted to intercept but forced himself to remain quiet. "Please Gertrude" Blue Eyes told her calmly, "no need to be rude and vulgar. I am just saying, you need to convince the Marshal to meet with me and kill me, is that so difficult. I mean, after what I did to Carl wouldn't you like that?"

"What is difficult," Gertrude snapped, "is my believing your mother had any kids that lived."

"Gertrude, please." Blue Eyes went on, amused, "I am merely saying if the Marshal does not do as I am asking, he will be the death of you, literally. And for you, I have something very special planned."

Clay could no longer hold his silence. "Blue, how are you?"

"Why Clay, is that you?"

"It's me."

"Well, I have no idea how much you've heard, but I was just telling Gertrude- "

"Yes, I know. That you were going to kill her if-"

Blue Eyes cut Clay off, "If you did not kill me this time...and soon!"

Clay took a sip of coffee; it was beginning to cool. "You know, I'm wise to you Blue."

"How do you mean? And by the way, Blue, only Bobby ever called me that."

"Well," Clay said, I figured I start using the name, although by itself the word falls short."

"Short. What do mean?"

"It means Blue, that the next time I see you, I am going to kick the living shit out of you. And every inch of your body will be BLACK and BLUE! Alive or Dead."

Laughing out loud, the killer told Clay. "Cute. But don't quit you day job. Now, back to your statement. How did you put it... Oh yes, you said you were wise to me? Please be so kind as to explain."

"I mean Scripture wise. I have it figured out. If I kill you, then I bring the wrath of God down on me. Just as you did on yourself when you killed me in that field millenniums ago."

There was a pause. "Clay, where did you hear such nonsense, have you been talking with Pastor Hart?"

"That doesn't matter."

"True, really it doesn't," Blue Eyes said, "because to be honest, Hart is also on what I call The Clayton Cooper Motivation List. But trust me, Gertrude is at the top." Blue Eyes changed the subject, "So, how's the coffee this morning. Drinking it from your favorite cup, are you?"

Clay took another sip of the cooling liquid then told him, "So you know my daily routine, I'm not impressed, it's old stuff."

"Okay than, how about something not routine. Like did you know Bob was in an Aircraft Crash? It nearly killed him. He lies in intensive care as we speak. But all is well that ends well. And speaking of that, just for your information, I am arranging last minute details on our special and final meeting. I will let you know the moment I finish. If you fail to show, you'll force me to begin using the motivation list; that won't be pleasant for you; and especially for those on the list. Got to go... oh wait," he said jumping back to Gertrude, "keep an eye on the mail Gert. I'll be sending you a video of you and the bus-driver doing it last week when the husband was out on the road. If you were a few years younger, or I older, wow, I'd take a turn too."

Gertrude yelled it into the phone, "You Prick!" The phone clicked with Blue Eyes laughing.

As soon as Clay had his secretary calmed down, he called Janis. The Killer was correct, but Bob was doing well, remaining in intensive care primarily for precaution. There had been so sign of internal problems, only two broken bones and neither had been compound. So, the doctors were guessing a week most and he would be going home to recover. Janis apologized for not calling, but she had not wanted to worry them unnecessarily. They had sufficient worries as it was.

When Clay told Nancy of the accident, she wanted them to fly to Louisiana immediately to be with Janis as much as Bob. But he nixed the idea. Bob was doing well at the Hospital, and he did not want to leave Gertrude by herself.With Carl gone there would be no one to look after her or the Town. "And" Clay told her, "Don't even think about you and Michael flying there alone."

CHAPTER 67

Just one day short of a week Bob Lemus was transported from the hospital to home by way of Ambulance. The Techs rolled him into the house sitting upright on the cot. Then from there gently moved him onto the couch. He was experiencing little pain, but the leg cast was troublesome. As for the catheter, it had been removed at the Hospital; a procedure he found very uncomfortable. But when the Nurse asked if it felt better out, Bob made it clear. "Yes Mam. And oh, what a relief it is."

Once the ambulance left, Bob sighed softly as Janis covered him with a light Blanket and neatly tucked it in around him. "Hey," he said appreciating the fuss, "what would you think about fixing this pained, agonizingly, broken gentleman a toasted cheese sandwich with a side of ruffles have ridges and a Diet Coke over ice.

Janis finished and stood. Applying a strong southern accent she curtsied, "Why my dear sa', ya' all know I'd do anything in this here world for ya', that is with you bein' a gentle-man and all."

Following another curtsy, she turned heading for the kitchen. Calling after her Bob added, "And after I've eaten, my dear sweet southern Belle, there is a certain part of my anatomy that is most agonizingly painful and could use some relief."

Not stopping, Janis applied her southern draw once again speaking over her shoulder, "I am guessin' you be talkin' bout your bladda'. I indeed would be most pleased to attempt a reinsertion of your catheta' sa." She disappeared into the kitchen.

Bob called out loud enough for her to hear, "That is not the kind of insertion I had in mind."

CHAPTER 68

Ron and Michelle Parks sat snuggled on the couch drinking Pepsi and listening to Berry Manalou. With the kids in school, the house was quiet. All morning it had been snowing off and on; the sun would shine than vanish behind drifting clouds; making it dreary one minute, bright and sunny the next. But to both it didn't matter; they were together.

Ron had been granted an extra two weeks leave from the post and spent every waking moment caring for his wife, nursing her back to good health. She was recovering quickly and with their new lease on life, they felt and often acted like newlyweds.

Ron sipped from his glass listening to the ice rattle. "You know," he said thoughtfully, "we should pull the kids from school and spend a week on a Florida beach, Clear-water maybe, or Coco near Orlando and make a trip to Disney-world." He paused pecking her cheek with a kiss, "That is if you're up to it."

Michelle smiled and squeezed his hand. "I'd like that, it'd be nice getting away, and the kids would go crazy. By the time we got back I'd be all renewed and we could both get back to work."

Ron returned the squeeze on her hand, "You don't have to go back if you don't want too."

"I know," Michelle smiled with appreciation, "but it's who I am. I stayed home while the kids were all in school, and now I like having my own identity. It gives me a sense of purpose and my four years of

Communication Studies at Harvard are not wasted. Besides, I enjoy News Casting."

Ron nodded. "Then that's what I want, too." Rising from the couch, he downed the remainder of his Pepsi. "Okay then," he said, "with that settled I'll go get on the internet and make our vacation arrangements. We'll fly down to Orlando and rent a van."

Michelle stretched leisurely out on the couch, raising her arms above her head. "Before you get tied up on the internet," she said softly, "I wonder if you might do me a favor, something…personal."

Ron looked into her eyes, the slightest hint of a grin showing. "Could I do you? Is that what you just asked me?"

"A favor," Michelle said laughing lightly, "I asked if you could do me a favor."

"Oh, a favor," Ron said puffing his cheeks with disappointment, "sure, what do you need."

"I'd appreciate you refreshing my glass of Pepsi."

"Absolutely," Ron bent for her glass, and she grabbed his hand.

"Also," she said staring into his eyes, "I'd like for you to help me out of my clothes, I am suddenly so very hot." She waved her hand in front of her face like a fan. "I think the furnace might be a bit too high."

Ron couldn't help stare, amused, aroused and happy. She was beautiful and he loved her so much; he was a lucky man. "Why yes," he said finally. "I'd be happy to help you with that too... right after I get your Pepsi."

He pulled his hand free and turned with a favorable upper-handed smile.

"You know," she said watching him walk away, "From the very day you rescued me right up to now, I feel as though I've been asking far too much of you, I fill as if I've become a millstone. Just fill my glass, that will be enough. I can do without the other."

Ron stopped, slowly turning to look at her. She blew him a kiss and he caught it with his hand. "You know," he said, "I love you and there's no end to how much I'd do for you, but if you insist on it being only one thing, can I at least have a choice of which it will be: Pepsi or clothes?"

Michelle sighed as if exasperated, "Oh, I guess so."

Ron gave her a big smile. "Great. I'll be right back. You did want ice too, right?"

Michele threw a throw pillow at him.

CHAPTER 69

The Sheriff's deputy watched the dark figure shuffling in and out of the south door of the old Brooke Grain Elevator. Whoever it was, they were moving things in from the trunk of a car pulled close to the building; the trunk light had been disabled.

Although his D221 Generation2 night Binoculars cut clearly through the early morning darkness, the deputy could not make out a face. A black full-faced hood hid any chance of identity. But he knew from the clouds of warm breath exhausting from the open mouth slot, they were as cold as he was. Although a good distance from the elevator, the watchful deputy had killed the engine not wanting the sound to carry.

The night sky was dark and cloudless with a temperature of eighteen degrees. No one could be out for long and he knew who ever this person was, and whatever it was they were doing, they would be done with it as quickly as possible.

Pulling his cell from the belt holster, deputy Keen Brighton hit the call list and began scrolling down. When reaching the number, he wanted he pushed send and lifted the binoculars back to his eyes. The figure was not visible.

The cell phone rang four times before someone answered, "Hello, Cooper here."

Brighton spoke softly. "Marshal Cooper, this is sheriff's deputy Keen Brighton, I'm located two hundred yards on the south side of your old grain elevator watching someone carrying things into the building. They've been at it approximately five minutes since my arrival.

Cooper lay in bed on his side, he quickly moved to a sitting position, his bare feet coming to rest against the cold hardwood floor, but he barely noticed the discomfort. "Got a description?"

"Six feet or so, dressed in black and every bit as cold as I am."

Cooper nodded to himself. "I'm dressing now, be there in five minutes. I'll drive past on the north side. Once out of site I'll park than back track on foot. Watch for me, I'll work my way down the west side of the elevator and wave at the corner."

"Sounds good; see you in five."

"Wait, what's your cell number." Cooper asked.

Brighton gave it to him, and Clay added, "okay, put your phone on vibrate and I'll call you if need be. Listen, if he leaves, trail him, and please don't lose him. And for God sake, whatever you do, wait for me. Don't go into the elevator for any reason."

"Clear." Brighton switched to vibrate and placed the phone back into its holster, then lifted the glasses once again.

Clay dressed in a hurry and sat on the edge of the bed tying his boot strings. Nancy now awake, had snapped on the bedside lamp. "Where are you going?"

"Elevator."

"Again?" She exclaimed.

"Yeah, someone is unloading things from a car and taking them inside," Clay glanced up, "like maybe they're setting something up."

"Do you think it's him?"

"Oh yeah, it makes sense. It started here and he's decided to end it here," Clay turned back to tying his boots adding, "and believe me, this time it will indeed end here."

CHAPTER 70

Home of Janis and Bob Lemus

Bob Lemus lay sleeping on his back, snoring lightly. Because of the leg cast, this was the only position possible. Beside him, Janis rolled onto her side and the waterbed waved gently.

In the beginning, Bob hated the waterbed with its subtle constant waving each time one of them moved. However, out of his silent love-thoughtfulness, he had slowly grown accustomed to it. In fact, now after seven years of sleeping together, both he and Janis had grown habitually accustomed to the others sleeping habits. Nothing, or at least very little, interrupted their sleep.

This early morning was one of those rare exceptions. The bedroom ceiling light burst into sudden brightness, and it startled them awake. Six people were standing around the bed. Blinking sleep from his eyes, Bob recognized two of them, one from a snapshot he had seen in Washington, and the other was Aluka.

Realizing there was no chance of reaching a weapon Bob and Janis exchanged glances then pulled themselves into a sitting position. Bob spoke directly to Aluka. "What the hell is this?"

Aluka, now dressed in winter gear, shrugged. "We were in the neighborhood."

"What do you want?" Bob asked.

The vampire looked at Janis, then back, grinning. "Her." Aluka said.

Lemus glanced over at Janis then grit his teeth and made an effort at getting out of bed, but Janis grabbed his shoulder. "It's alright, Bob." Staring directly at Aluka she told him, "Look, I'm not interested in you, or anyone like you. You may think you're irresistible to women, but trust me, it's all delusional. So just gather up your pack of canine impersonators and get out."

Aluka smiled. "I will, but first I have a hunger, and you're the one to satisfy it." He waved his hand and three men pulled Bob from the bed. Two others moved to Janis's side and pulled her to her feet. Free of the bed she kicked one in the groin, and he moaned doubling over, then fluidly with lightning speed, she applied her favorite Aikido move, Kote Gaeshi, flipping the second attacker as if he were weightless. Then she stormed around the bed toward Aluka but stopped abruptly. One of the vamps had come up with a knife and was pressing it to Bob's throat.

Aluka smiled again. "Wise move. Now, if you do not cooperate, your husband's throat will be slashed, and we will feed on his blood as he gurgles into death. Are we clear?"

Janis glanced at Bob than pulled her concentration back to Aluka. "You harm him one little iota, and I'll hunt you down, cut off your dick then stuff it in your mouth like you're smoking a red Cigar. No," she added with a shrug and thoughtful look, "let's be realistic," it would be more like you're smoking a red soggy Cigarette."

"Aluka laughed, "Janis, I do appreciate your tenacity."

"It's not tenacity, its fact."

"Well then, first, I'm shaking in by boots. Secondly, and trust me on this, I will kill him and then have my way with you. You know you cannot stop me. If you want realistic, then I suggest you show some appreciation." Aluka winked with a grin. "Now, for this hunger I mentioned. It is not your blood I have come to taste."

Janis shook her head. "You really are sick. And I was right the first time I saw you. You're so ugly and stupid you have to force yourself on the women who see through you."

Aluka widened his smile strolling up to Janis. She never saw it coming, he backhanded her, sending her stumbling cross the room and slamming into the wall; her legs buckled, and she dropped to her hands and knees.

She was stunned but recovered quickly. Wiping blood from the corner of her mouth she climbed to her feet. And staring once again into Aluka's eyes, she let a smile show, "so you like it rough. What a surprise. Ya know, I'd like a minute to do a little Private Eye psychological profiling here, okay? I'm confident I can peg you to a T."

Aluka dropped his smile and folded his arms. "Okay, you have one minute."

Janis stared into his eyes a second then began, "You, Mr. Tough guy, liken yourself to some form of intergalactic Klingon Warrior: invincible, fearless and emblazoned with confidence." Janis shrugged, "Truthfully, I can see you as a Klingon, except my take of you being Klingon is this; you're nothing more than a dingle berry clinging to the Un-wiped ass of a hairy Orangutan."

Aluka cut her off, "Remove your nightgown and take off your panties, and do it now. And do it slowly, while both I and your husband watch."

Janis looked at Bob then up into Aluka's face again. "Okay," she said, "but there are two very important things you should know first. Number one, I can't take off my panties, I'm not wearing any. And number two, which by the way is a good number for describing you." Janis shrugged, but anyway, Clayton Cooper told me to pass on this little tidbit of info should you come visiting."

Aluka shifted his weight sticking his hands into his coat pockets, "Do go on, please."

Janis gave another shrug."Cooper told me to inform you that if you harm Bob or me in any way whatsoever, he will personally call the one who hired you - that being the Blue Eyes Killer. And he will make a clear, precise pact with him. That in exchange for giving the Maniac what he wants, which of course is that he die by Cooper's hand in a private Satanic Ceremony, Cooper would grant that wish without hesitation. That is, hesitation dependent upon one small, single request."

"And just what might that be? Aluka asked.

Janis grinned showing how much she enjoyed what she was about to tell him. "Well, Mr. Aluka Kling-on, I'll tell you." Janis smiled wide, "and trust me on this. You're going to love hearing what I am about to say."

Aluka glanced at the three vamps holding Bob then back to Janis.

"I've had enough already. Get to the point or I will have your husband drained here and now!"

"Okay, okay, calm down Kling! Here it is. If you cause any harm at all to Bob or me, Cooper will have Blue Eyes redirect the Army of Demons and Monsters now crawling their way out of Hell to a new focus…that focus will be you. You and every other one of your disgusting breeds. Vamps may be a superior race to humankind, but you wouldn't have a snowball's chance in Hell against the things of darkness. Now, would you like for me to put on panties so I can take them off for you, or are you smart enough to flick the head of that overzealous little dick of yours and tell it you're leaving instead?"

Aluka stared down into her eyes for some time. The interior of the house was quiet, soundless. Bob Lemus and the others watched the two staring. What would happen next none could begin to guess, but in his heart, Bob feared greatly for Janis.

It was Aluka who broke the silence. "Okay," he said, "I'll wait. But I will personally check with Blue Eyes, and if you are lying, I will come back and drain every ounce of blood from that piss-poor excuse of a man you call a husband, then lock you in chains and take you back to Bolivia.

Aluka pulled a white square envelope from his pocket and threw it on the bed. "Here, special delivery." He turned and called for the others to follow. When gone, Bob looked at Janis. "You, okay?"

"Sure. How about a cup of tea? I doubt I'll be able to sleep now."

Bob nodded, grabbing the envelope and his crutch near the bed, "Sounds great." Hobbling his way to the living room, he lowered himself on the couch and placed his casted leg upon the coffee table. Turning on the end table lamp, he tore open the envelope and read.

In the kitchen, Janis filled two cups with water and heated them in the microwave. When finished, she dropped in teabags and joined Bob. "Here you go."

Bob took the cup and Janis sat beside him, tucking her feet.

"So, what's with the envelope?" She asked, dipping her teabag.

Bob handed it to her, and she read it. When finished, she tossed it on the coffee table and looked at Bob, "A personal dinner invitation, hosted by Blue Eyes himself. Will we be attending my love?"

Bob nodded. "Yes, I think Clay would like for us to be there." Bob blew on his hot tea, remarking with a grin, "besides, I think we owe it to Clay after tonight. What a thinker that man is. He saved our asses tonight."

Janis smiled, "Kind of, sort of, yes and no."

"What?" Bob's forehead was furrowed.

"Well," Janis shrugged, "Clay didn't actually tell me those things."

"What?"

"I made it up. It just seemed like the right thing to say at the time."

Bob started to take a sip, but the water was still too hot. He repeated Janis's words. "You made that up?"

"I did."

Lemus shook his head, grinning. "You know, I have to say, you're not only mega sexy, but you're also a genius too."

"Yes, I am," she said coolly. "Got anything else to say?"

"Sure do. Are you really not wearing panties under that nightgown?"

"I am not."

Can I look?"

Janis took a careful sip from the hot cup. "Yes, you may," she said, "but not until I've finished my tea."

CHAPTER 71

At 3:21 am Clay was passing by the old elevator. A mile more where the road dipped enough to conceal his vehicle, he pulled to the side as far as the high snowbanks allowed. Killing the engine and lights he stepped out into the cold night air. A thick layer of snow blanketed the fields and even the Moonlight felt frigid.

Zipping his jacket, he placed a sock cap snugly over his head and ears then pulled on a pair of black leather gloves. Moving quickly across the field he ran to the elevator's west wall. Thankfully the snow was soft and offered up little sound.

Retrieving his weapon, he quietly pulled the slide placing a round in the chamber, then glanced around the corner. Just as Deputy Brighton had said a car was backed up to the Elevator's dark open doorway. The vehicle's trunk was open, but Clay saw no one.

He cell phoned Brighton.

The deputy's voice was a whisper. "Yeah, I see you. He just went inside."

"Okay," Clay said whispering in return, "I'm going in too, why don't you move up close to the vehicle in case he slips past me."

"You got it. Be careful."

Clay made his way along the face of the building and maneuvered carefully through the dark heap of wood and medal that was once the large sliding door. Quickly he moved into the black interior with weapon at the ready.

Once inside he stopped and listened. Nothing! Pulling his Bushnell Torch 1500 light from his coat pocket he clicked it on positioning it to shine down the barrow of his Glock 43. He liked the Bushnell 1500 light; its size and hard casing had more than once served as a handy secondary weapon.

With nothing heard or seen he moved across the large open floor to the doorway leading to the deep basement. His back against the wall, just left of the door, he quieted his breathing and listened. Still no sound! His thoughts shifted to Carl, and he quickly found himself fighting the festering anger building in his head. Why Carl, he asked himself. That Blue Eyed bastard had no reason to hurt him.

Frowning, Clay closed his eyes whispering softly into the cold icy room, "Cooper," he admonished himself, "get your head out of your sorry frigid ass and Focus!"

It would not be easy, but he had to put Carl, at least for now, out of his mind. And descending these stairs would take every ounce of strength and courage he could muster.

Breathing deeply, he let it out slowly while opening his eyes. A cloud of warm breath quickly dissipated into the frigid air. For Clay it was instant. Teeth gritted he turned quickly centering himself in the middle of the open doorway; bright light shooting down the descending rotted stairway.

The beam lighted the first few feet of steps clearly, but faded quickly, proving no match for the thick darkness beyond. Clay knew very well his ultimate destination once he reached the bottom would be the third room. After passing through the first two, it would be in that room he'd find a candle lit environment: the old iron table setting upright and draped with a white sheet, a bowl of blood sitting at its head, and all of it centered in the middle of a satanic pentagram freshly painted on the old wooden floor.

Those memories exploded in his head, and he did his best to shake them away.He wanted so much to just wait at the top of the stairs until Blue Eyes came up; but he couldn't. What if the insane son of a bitch had someone else down there, some innocent victim caught in the middle of it all, perhaps Gertrude. Clay pictured her bound and gagged, terrified; but cursing him with indistinguishable mumbles of three- and four-letter words.

Following a sigh, he began a slow cautious descent down the aged stairwell. Weapon at the ready he shined the light at his feet always aware of rotted wooden steps. He had said it in the past, and far too many times. But this one, this one was it. Tonight, it would end. Tonight, the insanity would come to a head!

In his entire law-enforcement career, Clay would never have even considered cold-bloodily killing someone. But this man, this…thing, it was so different. He wanted to kill him, couldn't wait to kill him, and do it without a conscious. And for certain, it would not be done the way the psycho demanded; a satanic ceremony in which he plunges a demonic-handled knife into his heart…that would clearly qualify as manslaughter and come with a life sentence…even though the deed would be both deserving and satisfying.

It had seemed a timeless endeavor, but Clay finally reached the bottom of the stairway. Stepping onto the frosted plank flooring; he held his weapon steady moving slowly forward. Upon crossing into the second room, he hesitated. On the far side, a small glitter of light hazed the entranceway of the third room.

As suspected the son of a bitch was in there; his elongated shadow danced on the cold damp walls as he moved about. This was it. Clay wanted to just storm in and empty the clip straight into the bastard's chest, bang, bang, bang, bang, bang, then reel with relief as he watched him fall dead on the floor.

The moving shadow stopped suddenly, its motionless figure frozen on the dirt wall; than he spoke; that voice Clay so hated and feared. 'Welcome my brother," he said, "please do come in."

Weapon raised, Clay moved forward, finger on the trigger, speaking as he advanced, "I'm not your brother, I'm the arresting officer who's putting you back behind bars. And this time I'll be sitting in the front row watching you cook like a high-stepping cockroach thrown into a hot skillet."

Clay entered the doorway, gun pointed. Blue Eyes stood staring, shadowed in candlelight. A black ski-mask covered his face, but even in the shadowy bowels of the old elevator, the brilliant blue of his eyes shined through the holes of his mask. And it was obvious he was wearing a smile. That irritated Clay.

Stepping around the sheet-draped table he knew would be there, Clay moved slowly toward this dark, evil-man and want-to-be demon, "Put your hands behind your head and turn around, keep your eyes the color of blue. The moment I see them begin to turn I'll put a round between them." Blue Eyes continued to smile but did as told. Clay moved cautiously up behind him. "Lower your hands slowly, place them behind your back."

Once their Clay placed him in cuffs and spun him around; his words pouring out with anger and hate, "You fuck, you worthless fuck." Raising his weapon, he jabbed the barrow hard against Blue Eyes' forehead. "I owe you three fucking rounds, one for Sean, Evelyn and Carl." Clay's teeth were gritted, "do you have any idea how hard it is not pulling this trigger and filling the back of that fucking mask with your foul, disgusting brains."

Blue Eyes remained silent but held his smile increasing Clay's irritation. Applying pressure to the barrel of his weapon he forcefully walked Blue Eyes backward, slamming him hard into the wall. "You asshole, wipe that smile off your face. I'm not going to kill you; do you understand that you're going back to prison and this time you're going to die. You'll be going to Hell alright, but not as a freak demonic hero. This time you're going to burn and scream in the most horrific pain you've ever known, and for all eternity."

With a fuming grip Clay grasped the mask and pulled it from his face, "You -" that was the only word Clay got out. The two stared for some time, eyes locked, neither making a sound. Finally, Clay managed to speak. "Who the hell are you?"

The man staring into Clay's face shrugged, "My name is Tag Mortison; you put me away six years ago for possession. I got out last week."

Clay shook his head, puzzled "What the hell are you doing here?"

"I got a phone call the day I got out, from some guy, offering me a hundred grand to do what I'm doing. I agreed so the guy mails me instructions, half the money, and these blue contacts I'm wearing."

Clay holstered his weapon and Mortison told him, "In my pocket there's a recorder, I was to make sure you heard it when you got here. And make sure you took it home."

Clay pulled the recorder free and placed it in his coat. "Okay, let's go." They made their way to the surface and Clay turned him over to Deputy Brighton.

On the way home Clay slammed the steering wheel repeatedly; bursts expressing his anger. At the house he put over a pot of coffee and went into the living room while it brewed. Flopping down on the couch he sighed. Nancy came in and sat beside him; "Thank God you're okay," she said, "did you get him?"

Clay looked up forcing a smile, trying to hide the disappointment still lingering, "Turned out not to be him. He left me a recording though," Clay showed her the recorder, "I was about to play it."

Nancy took his free hand and held it tightly, her stomach feeling sick. Clay pushed the play button, and the tape began: "Welcome my brother, please come in." Clay shook his head and sighed. A short run of silence followed than Blue Eyes came on again.

Clay, I do hope you're not too terribly disappointed you didn't get to see me. As you now realize, the time has not yet come for our special get together. However, it's closer than you think. As to where the grand event is going to be, well, this time I am quite sure you will find the location unsurpassed. It does appear though; you remain steadfast in your determination of not killing me. Frankly, I'm disappointed, but not surprised. I did enjoy tonight's show though; especially the stunned expression on your face when you discovered it wasn't me beneath the mask." Clay swore under his breath. *"Yes, that's right,"* the voice went on without hesitation, *"We were there too, Cain and I, watching. You walked right past us. We were within inches from you, wrapped content within the shadows. I knew you wouldn't see us; hate has a way of blinding good judgment. But then I needn't bother you with that now do I. Anyway, it appears you need a bit more motivation. So, as you will see, more is to come. See you soon!*

The tape ended and the recorder ran a second longer than clicked off. Clay looked at Nancy, "I've got to warn the others and if possible, get Gertrude to leave town for a while, some place where he can't find her." Laying his head back, Clay closed his eyes. "Nance," he said softly, "I just can't take much more of this."

Kissing his cheek she told him, "I know, sweetheart."

Releasing his hand she rose, "I'll go get us a cup of coffee, it'll help. Be right back my love." Clay could not see. But her eyes were tearing.

CHAPTER 72

The private jet lifted from the Purdue runway climbing steadily. Blue Eyes watched through the small oval window as the lights of campus disappeared. Morning was breaking and the early pinch of crimson streaking the eastern horizon looked cold.

Once in the air Blue Eyes glanced across the isle at his son, he smiled and winked. The boy smiled and winked back. Their guest passenger, still unconscious from the inhalation of chloroform, was resting peacefully, reclined in the seat.

"Father," Cain asked turning to look at the slumbering form, "what will we be doing with our guest?"

Blue eyes studied the unconscious figure rocking-flaccid in their seat. "She's been invited to a very special dinner party."

"A dinner party, how exciting Father," Cain exclaimed, "and who else will be attending?"

Blue Eyes smiled. "I've invited the Coopers, the Parks, Bob and Janis Lemus, and a few others."

Cain smiled wide. "How wonderful, I'll get to see Michael again." The boy paused, frowning thoughtfully and changing the subject, "Father, what will it be like after Marshal Cooper kills you and you become an Incubus? Will I still be able to see you, to visit with you?"

Blue Eyes unbuckled and moved to the seat next to his son. "Yes, of course," he said smiling, giving the youngster a reassuring hug. "I'll be coming back from time to time in human form to visit. I will look different, but it will be me, and I'll let you know."

Cain nodded. "I'm going to miss you father."

Blue Eyes gave his son another squeeze. "You must remember you will be taking my place here. And that will require a great deal of your time. You will go to school, attend college and work. Plus, the demons will be helping you hone your skills. You will enjoy it all, and our Master will be watching your progress. Trust me, it is a great and prestigious honor replacing me. And by your assuming this role, we add to the long running list of our family involvement. You will replace me as I replaced my father, and my father replaced his father and on and on."

Blue Eyes puffed his cheeks adding, "however, you must understand son, that our time is running out, and there are so many ignorant souls left to pilfer. The work I do as an Incubus will prepare them for you; you will prepare them for the Master."

Cain laid his head against his fathers' shoulder, "Father," he said, "I promise I will study hard and learn well. I will remain disciplined. I will become you."

CHAPTER 73

At 7:01 am Ron and Michelle Parks were frantically pounding on the front door of the Cooper house. The banging brought Clay and Nancy scurrying. When they opened the door Ron and Michelle rushed past, Ron practically shouting, "That son of a bitch took the kids." Clay looked at Nancy. Immediately she turned and dashed upstairs. "We woke up this morning," Ron raged on, "and they were gone, their beds had been slept in, but they weren't in them, the house was empty."

"Did he leave a note?" Clay asked.

"No nothing. Just empty beds."

"You didn't hear anything?"

Ron looked irritated at Clay, "Would I be here now if I had. Come on Clay, the bastard has them…or the Vamps have them." Ron placed his hands over his face shaking his head, "that son of a bitch is so fucking dead."

Placing a hand on Ron's shoulder Clay tried to calm him, "Look, I'm sure he hasn't hurt them, he took them for insurance that's all. You know how he works; he's making sure this time I do it right; and thrust me, I'm going too. We'll get the kids back."

Nancy came storming down the stairs, "he has Michael too."

Immediately Clay phoned Gertrude's office waiting for three rings, no answer. She was never late, always there at 7:00am sharp. He tried her house and received the answering machine. Gertrude's voice came through the phone: "Hi, you've reached the home of handsome Harry and gorgeous Gertrude, leave your name and number and we'll get back to you when Harry's finished…trust me it won't take long." The phone clicked and Clay hung up. He looked at the others, "No answer, he has her too."

The four sat in the living room and shared a pot of coffee. Like Clay, Ron was at his wits end, he too was a twisted compilation of worry and hate, burning with the want to kill in cold blood. The situation was bleak, but the morning sun had risen with an optimistic radiance; snow was already melting into tiny streams worming its way through the soft dirt along the edge of the streets.

Clay sat back in his chair. "I think I'm right when I say he won't harm the kids unless I refuse to cooperate. And this time I will give him exactly what he wants…and very willingly."

Nancy wanted to say something but remained silent. By killing Blue Eyes, her husband would be bringing the wrath of God upon himself; no way did he deserve that. Clay had been drawn into this an innocent man, with the key player being a delusional sick minded killer. Yet, if he didn't fulfill the killer's wish, he would be signing the death warrant for who knows how many; perhaps including all the children, especially Michael.

Nancy wanted to cry, to scream out-loud. It was all so maddening. What a snake! Such evil! There were no words to actually describe him; except that he was a progeny of Satin. She had thought of it once before, and it came to her again, Blue Eyes was undoubtedly possessed, and not by one, but by legions of demons; just the way Adolph Hitler had to have been. It made believable sense. If reincarnation did exist and souls could choose when to return, Quinten Christensen, the Blue Eyes Killer, would fit the insane, merciless, cold-blooded profile of such a man as Hitler. She closed her eyes wondering; if reincarnation did exist, perhaps this madman was *Hitler reawakened?*

Michelle sipped from her cup. She was just as worried as Nancy; she too had been through a lot and trembled over every memory of it. It just kept getting worse and worse, and now the kids were blameless pawns in the middle of it. It all churned her stomach and fueled her clad-iron determination that the moment Clay killed that foul iniquity, she would use her skills as a newscaster, and begin a relentless campaign exposing the dark-truth that demons and all their evil did in fact exist.

The sudden knock on the door caused both Nancy and Michelle to jump. Clay glanced at them with understanding, smiling lightly, "easy, it's okay." He made his way to the door silently fearing who or what may be waiting there on the other side. When he opened, he rested easier.

His Mailwoman smiled, "Morning Clay, I've got your mail. This piece was two large to stuff, so here you are."

It was a large yellow envelope. Clay took it along with four other pieces of letter-mail and smiled back. "Thanks. Enjoy the sunshine."

"I will," she assured him, "you can see I'm wearing my spring jacket."

Both smiled with a nod, and he closed the door.

The return address on the package was a New Orleans location. No one recognized it, but Nancy had a hunch. She left her chair and returned with the address book. Thumbing through it, she located Janis and Bob's number and mailing address; they matched.

Clay opened the package and pulled out two white invitation envelopes, one addressed To The Parks and the other To The Coopers. He handed the one to Ron. Paper clipped to Clay's invitation was a loose folded note. Opening it, he read aloud:

Surprise, it's not from Bob and Janis!

The time Clay has arrived, and arrangements are in motion. This time I've decided to invite everyone over for the occasion. Please see to it Mr. & Mrs. Parks get their invitation.As you've probably surmised by now, the Lemus' already have theirs.

And do come prepared to execute your task this time, no pun intended. And while it sounds brash, and I do apologize;

but for every weapon I see, one of the children will die. That is until we run out of children!

Blue.

Saying nothing the group exchanged glances and opened the envelopes. The content of each read the same:

You are cordially invited to the Celebration Dinner of my death.

LOCATION: The old Mansion in Baton Rouge. (You remember)

DATE: April 1st.

TIME: 12:00 pm

DRESS: Black Attire (Wearers choice)

Serving: Steak, salad, toasted garlic bread and red wine. Desert: Cream Fondant

Clay took a deep breath, puffed his cheeks and released it. Slumping back in his chair he told the others, "Well, no more games, now we know." Glancing at his watch he said aloud, "today is May 28th. That gives us four days to get ready, get down there, kill him, and bring our children home."

"What if the kids aren't even there," Michelle asked with panic edging her tone. Clay sighed, "Like I said, I'm sure he won't hurt them as long as I cooperate. And that is to our advantage. He brings them to us, or I refuse to kill him; and we all know that is the entire focus of this sick game he's playing." Clay gave Nancy's hand a reassuring squeeze, "We'll just have to pray and deal with it all when we get down there. Believe me, the man wants to die as much as we want our children back. He'll leave wiggle room for compromise."

"Clay's right," Ron injected, "I doubt he will harm one hair on any of their heads; for him that would be too much to risk. So here it is, we'll take my Van and head for Louisiana later this evening."

Glancing around at each other everyone agreed. Rising to their feet, Ron added, "Michelle and I will go home and pack, then come back here and pick you two up."

"Okay," Clay agreed, "we'll drive through the night."

When Ron and Michelle were gone, Clay phoned Bob Lemus and suggested a rendezvous at their house. It was agreed.

At 4:20 pm Ron's Van was pulling away from the Cooper House heading south out of Indiana. Each agreed, they would be driving faster than they should!

CHAPTER 74

Traveling 74west to 57south they made great time. The sky remained clear and sunny until north of Memphis where they picked up the final highway change onto 55south.

Evening brought with it cold and overcast, and by the time they stopped to eat in Memphis it was raining. Dashing through the cold down pour and into McDonalds, they used the restrooms than placed orders to go; and back on the road in less than twelve minutes.

Ron had driven to Memphis and now Clay took over the wheel. By the time they reached Jackson Mississippi, the women were asleep in the back seat. Ron and Clay chatted off and on; but for the most part remained silent, each lost to their own fears and implausible visions.

The rain had escalated to a noisy, distressing down poor and Clay drove to the relentless swish of wipers. The Mississippi night covered the dark ribbon of road with a thick, cold blackness, and the Van's headlights scarcely penetrated the dense wall of falling water. Understanding the wet dangerous potential, Clay had reluctantly slowed to sixty, but his irritation intensified by the steady stream of cars and trucks splashing past.

Somewhere near the turnoff for the town of Summit, Ron drifted away. Left to himself, Clay's mind slipped in and out of lingering recollections, reliving the horrors experienced in the mansion they were soon to reenter. There within the Van's dark interior, amid the noisy rain and swish of wipers, the past visualizations came alive: the site of Ron's parents, Sean and Evelyn, both dead and naked tied upright to the chairs at the mansion's dining room table; with both their hearts cut out and placed in front of them on a dinner plate. Clay squeezed his eyes hoping to chase away the vision. The memory had been haunting him for seven long years, and now new horrors were about to be born.

Far too many unspeakable things had happened there that night: Bob Lemus buried alive with a single round in his weapon, and Janis and Clendes' struggle with the demon-possessed vagabond possessing the strength of ten men.

Clay's disquiet fingers milked the steering wheel. Rain continued its vicious hammering. As if in front of him now, he stood before the human pyramid the killer had designed using Ron, Nancy and Michelle. All naked, he had balanced the girls atop Ron's shoulders with their hands tied behind their back and a noose around their necks, and to ensure no escape he had super glued Ron's feet to the floor.

Clay again squeezed his eyes attempting to rid himself of the memories. It was pointless, helplessly he recalled the uncountable number of demons filling the mansion's interior; an evil cluster watching as if guests at a dinner show. They -

The Tractor-Trailer swerved blasting the air horn. It startled Clay back to the wet, rainy world outside the Van. He had drifted across the line and the two nearly collided. Swinging back, he swore under his breath fighting the wheel as the Van fishtailed. The girls woke startled and screaming. As Clay struggled for control, Ron yelled into the dark interior, "what the hell." The van began spinning, wildly, around and around, hydroplaning atop the lake of water covering the highway; it was dizzying; they clung to whatever they could. A speeding car swerving to miss them slid off into the medium.

The steering wheel spun madly in Clay's hands as he fought for stability; the Van's spiraling interior had become a chaotic confine of darkness and flashes of light. The vehicle made one last full-spin and slid straight for twenty feet coming to an abrupt stop on the brim.

Stunned, they sat silent, the Van's headlights piercing the wall of rain. The wipers swished and the relentless sound of a million hammers clobbered away at the Van's exterior. Heartbeats beginning to slow again, they each took a deep breath.

Outside, a steady stream of traffic splashed past. The car that had slid into the medium spun free of the muddy grass and back onto the highway, laying long on the horn as they passed.

Having gathered his composure Clay apologized, "I'm so sorry guys, it won't happen again." No one replied and he felt awkward, "Okay," he added, "you don't have to speak to me, but we need to get going. Has everyone collected themselves?"

"Collect ourselves," Ron said staring, "Clay, for crying out-loud, we need to wipe ourselves."

CHAPTER 75

The old Charcloue Mansion remained unchanged: tall and stately, surrounded by six-hundred acres of isolated Louisiana woods, and despite the dulling consequence of a hard southern winter, the long oak drive still embellished the plantation's proud bravura.

Blue Eyes, leaning on the second story balcony rail, took a long draw from his cigarette. He loved this place: its quiet, undisturbed solitude. Once again, he was feeling a million miles from the world.

Blowing smoke into the warm 67-degree Baton Rouge sunshine, he looked up into the afternoon sky. Like his eyes, it was strikingly blue. Huge white clouds underscored its bright and crisp splendor. And below in the trees, birds were singing as squirrels darted playfully in and out of sight.

"It's finally going to happen my feathered and furry friends," he called out to them. Joy imbued his body, sweetening his thoughts and revving up his adrenaline. He grinned like a child waiting on the arrival of the toy of his dreams. Guests had already begun to arrive. This was going to be a grand and auspicious event.

Pulling away from the rail he stretched out his arms and swirled playfully in a circle. Light on his feet, shoes tapping with astonishing grace he began to dance; he was the great Fred Astaire, the majestic sky of blue and white his cathedral, and the proud old balcony his stage. He moved with surprising poise and elegance and imagined himself dressed in Top Hat and Long Tailed Coat with pleaded shirt, Cumber-Button and White Spats. His amazingly velvety voice hushed the birds and stopped the squirrels as he sang and danced Fred's greatest all-time hit; 'Puttin' on the Ritz'.

Below, the crowd of guests already present and walking the grounds, stopped to take in his performance. They watched entertained, amazed by his talent, elated that this long-suffering, altruistic champion would soon be receiving all that he had been hoping for. He would be honored, promoted, escalated to a position coveted by thousands over the centuries. This special person, Quinten Christenson, alias Blue Eyes Killer, had risen to great esteem as one of Hell's most admired personalities: murderer, rapist, sodomizer, and unparalleled criminal genius. Soon, he would rule over the master's abundant legions of Hell's Incubus.

The song and dance ended with Blue Eyes swirling in circles across the balcony, then bowing on a knee and throwing his hands to the sky, finishing the lyrics with a smile:

Dressed up like a million-dollar trouper

Trying hard to be like Gary Cooper

Super-Duper

Come let's mix where Rockefellers walk with sticks

and um-ber-ellas in their mitts…

Puttin' on the Ritz.

Puttin' on the Ritz.

Puttin' on the Ritz.

PUTTIN' ON THE RITZ!

The crowd below applauded. Still smiling, Blue Eyes stood and took a bow, "Thank you," he said appreciative, "thank you everyone."

Feeling as though he were floating on air, he disappeared into the mansion's upper floor, back to the numerous detailed tasks demanding his attention. The mass of Demons below also returned to their business while chatting about the man above: their beloved, blue eyed, flesh and blood luminary who, within hours, would be descending into Hell. And upon his grand arrival be hailed by all that walked, crawled, flew and slithered there.

CHAPTER 76

At 3:33 am Clay pulled the Van to a final stop. Janis and Bob's single-story stone-block house sat dark and mute in the Louisiana twilight. Clay shutdown the engine turned off the lights and yawned. The others were asleep. Following a long and comfortable stretch, he woke them, and they climbed out; the closing of the Van doors muted the noisy shrill of crickets.

On the steps, Clay rang the bell and glanced around. Alexandria lay dead asleep amid its chilling 48 degrees. The moon was full, and a million stars twinkled brightly, all thankful to be far away from that troubled world below.

The door opened and they were welcomed with hugs. Putting sleep on hold, Janis put over a pot of coffee and hot water for tea. While it brewed, she showed her guests to their rooms, then assisted with hauling in luggage.

At 4:02, they were in the living room talking.

Bob Lemus, dressed in a white terrycloth bathrobe, one house slipper and long white leg-cast with a bare foot protruding, took a sip of tea. "So," he said, "here we are, and I will admit, although it's great to see you all, it's disconcerting as hell."

"We agree," Clay said.

Bob took another sip, "You know, I was so sure the vamps were contracted to keep us apart, prevent us from joining forces. Yet Blue Eyes has invited all of us to the same party. I just wonder why?"

"Maybe the original plan turned sour," Ron suggested, "I suspect Blue Eyes never expected us to get Michelle back, so because we did, he lost confidence in the Vamps and as an alternative, took the kids."

Bob puckered his lips in thought, "Could be." The retired agent took another sip.

"Or" Janis interjected, "maybe the Vamps have yet to earn their pay, perhaps they are to ensure we do not help Clay once we're all gathered at the mansion. He just wants us there for old time sake; and get the last laugh."

"Either way," Clay interrupted, "our going there has one specific purpose; and this I tell you with the utmost assurance; I will kill the Bastard, then we walk out with our kids and it's all over... finally."

"Actually," Janis countered, "I don' believe that's entirely true." The others turned to stare. "The Vamps," she explained, "are still a part of all this, you can bet on it. Do you really think we're going to just walk out of that mansion once you've killed him?" She said turning her eyes to Clay, "do you really think Blue Eyes will give one hair on a sick rat's ass what happens to us once he's dead?"

Clay stared into her eyes for some time, then slowly shook his head, "no, I guess not."

"Damn right, not," Janis blurted, "I believe the Vamps will be there alright, and Blue Eyes conveniently failed to mention that after dinner; right after you've killed him, the Vamps will be serving us up for the last snack of the evening?"

CHAPTER 77

Charcloue Mansion
Baton Rouge

Evening, May 30th

Michael and the Parks children: Crystal Michelle, fourteen, Mat, ten, and little Ronnie, five, sat in a circle in the middle of the floor. They were talking but were doing so in whispers. None had even an inkling of where they were. They did know; however, they'd been locked in the bedroom of a big, old house.

An oil lamp atop an old dresser draped the room's interior with a mix of light and dark shadows and floating up from the lamp's dirty chimney a steady wisp of black smoke filtered into the air; it smelled terrible.

The room contained an old wooden high-back bed still made, but its pillows and blankets were, dirty, holey and smelling of mildew. There were articles of clothing still in the dresser drawers and a large trunk sat at the foot of the bed. Crystal had opened it and discovered it had belonged to a woman. It contained neatly folded dresses, under things, a thick quilt, old time pictures and a handful of dust covered books.

Of the four children little Ronnie was the most frightened; sitting close to his big sister his eyes frequently darted at sounds. The room possessed one window boarded up with a guard standing just outside on a balcony. The bedroom door was locked and beyond it they heard constant noises. Something big was going on.

Michael said nothing to the others, but he knew his parents would be coming, and based on the fact the Parks children were there too, he believed Ron and Michelle would be showing up as well.

The group that had kidnapped them were the same people who had murdered Mr. and Mrs. Ottis; Michael said nothing about them being Vampires, knowing it would only frighten the others even more, especially little Ronnie. And much to his despair, he could sense demons in the house.

The youngster was trying hard not to show it, but he too was frightened, doing his best to keep up their spirits. His efforts however were slowly weakening. It wasn't just the experience of being kidnapped, it was the accumulation of things: being locked in the old musty room like caged mice just waiting to be fed to hungry snakes. They feared never seeing their parents again and disliked the smell coming from the smoky lamp. Although given a blanket each, the nights were cold, and they shivered until the sun came up. The worse, however, was the bedrooms' dark closet. Their captors had placed a five-gallon bucket in the tiny light-less room to use as their bathroom; now after countless hours of embarrassing but necessary use, its odor was beginning to drift out into the room.

They were all in pajamas, scared and cold, but Michael worried the most; fearing this would be the place where his dad would finally face Blue Eyes. In his heart, Michael knew for their safety, his father would not hesitate killing him this time. If he did not, the Vampires would kill all of them just the way they had Mr. and Mrs. Ottis; he could think of no other reason for their being here.

Fighting back tears Michael stared at the floor. If his dad went through with the killing, and even though it set them free, his dad would face the punishment God had vowed concerning the person who killed Cain.

Climbing to his feet Michael told the others, "I've got to be alone; I have to pray." Taken by surprise, the three said nothing as they watched his small frame hurry across the room and into the closet. Looking at one another, they wrinkled their noses.

Michael moved to the corner opposite the five-gallon bucket and keeled, trying to ignore the odor. Immediately he began praying, ordering Satin out of his thoughts, out of his head, he pictured God sitting on his thrown, looking down at him; waiting, anxious to hear his request. Michael prayed hard, growing oblivious to the smells, noises and worries that had been clouding his thoughts like a dark storm. He knew, could feel that God was growing closer.

Sometime during his praying, the world disappeared, and he was alone, kneeling not in a closet, but in a holy place, an extraordinary place, where no one but he and God alone were aloud. There was conversation between them, an exchange of feelings and love and respect, and there in the presence of his God, Michael cried, sobbing, they were tears that washed his soul and strengthened his faith.

Michael cherished his prayer time and as always did not want it to end, but it did. He found himself back in the smelly, shadowy closet. Wiping at his eyes he moved into a sitting position and leaned against the wall. He sniffled glancing up toward Heaven. That's when he saw it, veiled within the dark shadows above.

CHAPTER 78

Scrambling to his feet Michael rushed out of the closet to the others. He started to speak but stopped short. Someone was inserting a key into the door lock on the other side; the door clicked, than opened.

Little Cain, towered by his father, stood at the threshold. Michael and the others stared in silence.

Cain smiled, "Hello everyone."

The others glanced at Michael wondering, who is that? "Hi Cain," Michael replied ignoring their stares.

Cain walked into the room and up to Michael, offering his hand. Michael took it and they shook. Blue Eyes, gleaming over his son's manners stared down at Michael and softly asked, "And how be you young Mr. Cooper."

Michael looked up with anger in his eyes, "You lied!" he said, "you gave me your word, you promised!"

"I promised I wouldn't kill them, and I did not."

"You deceived me and that is the same as a lie!"

Blue Eyes grinned. "There is a figure of speech I have taught my son, and so should your father have taught you...always read the fine print before you sign."

Michael sighed pulling his stare to his ambivalent friend. "Cain, what are you and all of us doing here?"

"Because Father," Cain replied with a tinge of excitement, "is throwing his going away party. And you are all our guests."

Michael knew then he was right. His dad would be coming. Fighting anger he said, "You really mean your dad's going to Hell Party!"

Cain smiled lightly, "Yes. It's all so invigorating?"

"No, it's all so sad and pitiful."

Cain stared a moment, mulling over Michael's words, then asked. "Does the thought of you going to Heaven make you sad, Michael?"

"Of course not."

"Well, to Father it is the same thing. The same kind of feeling, one of joy and excitement."

"It's not the same thing." Michael retorted.

Cain ignored his remark, not wanting to argue. "So," he asked, changing the subject, "who are your friends?"

Michael introduced them, and Cain nodded with a smile, "It's very nice to meet you." Turning back to Michael he said, "I have to go with Father right now, but I will be back later. I'll bring some games we can play," shrugging he added, "how about Monopoly?"

Michael did not reply, only stared in silence. Cain's Father put a hand on his son's shoulder, and they made their way to the door. There Cain paused and looked back. "The games will be fun for all of us. So don't go anywhere."

Michael replied with a somber tone, "Can't promise that!"

Moving his eyes to the boarded-up window then back to Michael, Cain held up the key to the door. "This tells me you will be."

The door closed and they heard the click of the lock.

CHAPTER 79

Michael counted to ten then turned to the others. With a whisper he asked, "Will you guys be okay here by yourselves?"

"What?" Crystal Michelle asked.

"I'm going to go for help."

Crystal Michelle frowned. "Yeah right, the doors locked, and the only window is covered and guarded." She smiled mockingly, "what did you do, pray for an Angel to come crashing through the boarded window and fly you away?"

Michael made a face shaking his head, "Don't be ridiculous. There's a way to the attic from the closet, a small door in the ceiling."

Crystal Michelle glanced down at little Ronnie, "Stay. I'll be right back." She hurried to the smelly room staring up into the dark ceiling, slowly her eyes focused and she saw it. A small door, more like a square lid nestled in the overhead. Returning to the others she told Michael, "I say we all go."

Michael shook his head. "No, we can't. They'd catch us. I can make it, run for help and get back with the police."

Crystal Michelle shook her head in response. "First of all, you don't even know where we are, and come on; you're only seven, it's better that I go, I'm the oldest. I can reach higher, run faster and explain things more clearly."

Mat volunteered, "I can go, I'm fast."

Crystal Michelle glanced at him, "Shut up, Mat." She looked back to Michael,

"Neither of you can go, for sure that wouldn't be safe. It's got to be me!"

"There are Demons and hit-men out there," Michael said hoping to bring Crystal Michelle to her senses, "and real Vampires too. If they catch you, they will suck out a lot of your blood before they bring you back, that is if they even decide to let you come back.

Crystal Michelle rolled her eyes, "Michael Cooper do you know how stupid that sounds. There are no such things as Vampires, and to be honest, I have my doubts about Demons." She paused, speaking more calmly, "Michael, look, I know you've got this thing about religion, you think you're this little Pope or something, but trust me, there's nothing out there but grownups. I'm fourteen; believe me, I know just a little bit more about adults than you do."

Michael grimaced; time was running out. "Crystal, honestly," he said, "if I go and they catch me, they will not hurt me, they will only bring me right straight back. I'm too valuable right now."

Crystal Michelle lost her patience "Oh please, stop being a little twerp, you're just scared like the rest of us and want to get away. Well, we all do. So, I say, it's me who goes, or we all go together."

Michael was screaming in his head, *why aren't you listening*! He knew he was right and there would be only one chance at this. He feared for her safety, knew what the Vampires would do to her. She was just so disagreeable, such a typical teenager, thinking she knows everything. Michael knew she would argue every minute until she got her own way. Even now she stood staring at him, arms folded, just waiting for him to give in.

Michael tried one more time, "Crystal Michelle, listen to me."

She shook her head, "No."

"You don't understand."

"No."

"Please, they will really hurt or kill you if you get caught."

"No

Michael put his hands over his face and shook his head. "Please."

"No," Crystal Michelle said again, "I go, or we all go."

The entire time he'd been trying to reason with Crystal Michelle, one single word kept jabbing at his thoughts. Like an angry Boxer working out on a punching bag, the word just wouldn't stop punching and punching at his brain. Finally, his patience gave out. Throwing up his hands he turned, fuming. Then turned back. The word exploded from his mouth...**Teenagers**!"

Crystal Michelle broke into a smile!

CHAPTER 80

Two roaring 22KW power generators had brought the old plantation living room and kitchen to life: their glow accentuating the kitchen's culinary activities rivaling that of a posh New Orleans Restaurant. Dishes rattled and pots and pans banged as senior Chef, Louis LaFair, along with six kitchen helpers, prepared for tomorrow evenings grand extravaganza.

All activities were iron handed by the French cook himself. Dressed in traditional long sleeve Chef Coat and tall Cap, LaFair shouted an endless string of orders; all seemingly chaotic; with the kitchen team frequently bumping into one another mumbling and making faces. Yet in reality, the preparations were falling into place with professional focus.

The TV-16 crew out of Baton Rouge had come to film it all. The Charcloues themselves had invited the two-person news team to stay at the Mansion ensuring they miss none of the festivities. The old couple had assured them that all would be newsworthy - a celebration dinner in recognition of the Mansion's 168th year anniversary.

The team: reporter Darcy Arguine and photographer Bart Smith, had arrived well equipped in a Station Van. The news crew had been informed all was to be kept under wraps until it was over; the Charcloues did not want a public fiasco.

When first approached by the charming Historian and Archaeologist, Professor Quinten Christenson, suggesting a Charcloue Mansion Documentary, the southern family, as always in the past, politely declined. However, following a look at his impressive portfolio and credentialing, and considering his very generous monetary gift, they relented.

The Charcloues had informed local authorities of the special event so there would be no need for their coming out; should the noise get a bit loud. They also informed the authorities they were leaving for Europe on vacation and in their absence, Professor Christenson would have full authority over the property.

CHAPTER 81

Struggling within the shadowy confines of the small bedroom closet, Michael dragged the five-gallon bucket across the old wood floor, positioning it in line with the attic door above. The smelly container had been partially filled with water, and now the added pee and two floating turds from Ronnie's emergency poop was swashing. Michael asked God to please keep it from splashing out.

Crystal Michelle, keeping an eye on the door, quietly maneuvered two drawers from the old dresser and carried them to Michael's side. Together they stacked one on top of the other, adding height to the stinky bucket. Then carefully, using the wall for support and assistance from Michael and Mat, she climbed her way to the flimsy top. Putting the attic hatchway easily in reach.

In a crouching position she pushed it up and slid it to the side struggling to keep her balance. The gaping hole looked dark and foreboding. But ignoring her apprehension she straightened. Her shoulders and arms were easily inside the dark room and her eyes adjusted quickly.

There were three dormers in a row on one side of the roof, allowing moonlight to filter in. It actually looked amazingly bright once her pupils adjusted. Wiggling, she pulled herself up. "Okay," she whispered," lowering her head down through the hole. "I'm in. There are windows up here and I'm going to check them out, wait right there."

She disappeared and the three below stood staring up into the dark hole. Little Ronnie was holding Michael's hand not sure what all this was about. Muffled noises continually drifted up from the downstairs area.

Michael had considered retrieving the lamp from the dresser and handing it up to Crystal, but he feared the light might be seen from below.

Little Ronnie pulled on Michael's hand. "I've got to pee."

Michael glanced down at him, "Again?" Ronnie gave a needful nod. "Okay," Michael told him, "But you have to wait until your sister gets back."

Little Ronnie grimaced and crabbed hold of himself. Crystal poked her head back through the hole. Her eye caught little Ronnie. "Gosh, you have to go pee again?" She then diverted her eyes to Michael. "It looks good. There's a window going out to the roof where a tree is close enough to grab. I'll be back with help."

Her head vanished into the darkness and the lid slid back into place. Carefully, Michael pulled the bucket back where it belonged than helped Little Ronnie go to the bathroom.

When finished, he and Mat replaced the drawers, then scoured the room for a bunch of old clothing. They piled what they gathered on the floor in the darkest corner of the room and shaped it like a person's body, then covered it with Crystal Michelle's' blanket. Anyone coming into the room would believe it was her asleep. So, they hoped.

CHAPTER 82

At 11:10 pm TV-16 reporter, Darcy Arguine called it a night and retired to her assigned downstairs bedroom. There was a skeleton-lock on her door but of course no key, so she angled an old chair snugly beneath the handle.

Their host, Professor Christenson – who had insisted she call him Quinten – had supplied the room with a small lamp powered by an extension cord run beneath the door. Snapping on the light she removed a can of *White Tea & Lily* air freshener and sprayed the room.

She unzipped her sleeping bag then stretched it full across the old bed, covered that with a thick, garden-flower quilt and changed into a pair of yellow flannel pajamas that highlighted her short pixie blond hair. After pulling a small pillow and horror novel, *Killing Blue Eyes*, from her tote, she climbed between the soft sleeping bag and warm heavy quilt. She propped up her pillow against the headboard and snuggled in.

Darcy loved reading. She had grown up the little sister of three very-boyish brothers, and along the way developed a rough-tough persona, one very few knew about; she kept that secret well concealed beneath her petite five-foot five-inch athletic build. Somewhere in her world of brother-self-defense, her reading preferences had settled primarily in the psychological, horror genre. Now, here in this old lingering mansion, in the middle of six-hundred isolated acres of moonlit Louisiana woods, she felt a twinge of erotic excitement as she opened her book.

In the room next door cameraman Bart Smith, still dressed in tee-shirt and blue jeans, minus socks and shoes lying on the floor at his feet, sat deep asleep in an old rocker. His large shoulder-held camera lay on the floor beside him.

Slightly on the pudgy side, the redheaded 32-year-old was snoring. Bart had not volunteered for the Mansion Assignment; he had made other plans with his girlfriend. His sleeping bag sat on the bed still rolled and tied. His intention was only to relax in the old chair and then make his bed; but sleep quickly crept up like a thief and stole away his consciousness. He had felt no need in locking his door.

Outside atop the mansion's wood-shingle roof, beneath a star filled heaven, fourteen-year-old Crystal Michelle was crouched and listening, her eyes drinking in all she could see. She both appreciated and cursed the giant full moon spreading its thick silvery light. The cry of a whippoorwill flushed the woods, and hidden in the grass, brush and towering trees, an ambiguous world of insects droned boisterously. She was shivering slightly; the night air was chilly.

A million things were flashing through Crystal Michelle's mind. Popping up suddenly came one of her 'never-miss' TV shows: CSI, Los Vegas. *What if*, she wondered, *Michael was right and there really were Vampires and Demons out here? What if they did hunt her down and killed her. She chewed on her lip imagining Investigators Nick and Sarah standing over her, snapping pictures of her dead body, bugs crawling in and out of her mouth and ears and nose, and while white, wiggly maggots nibbling away at her skin. Crystal Michelle gave a shiver, "God I hate television."*

From her higher elevation, she could see distant lights straight ahead beyond a thick forest. The lights stretched to the right seeming to run on forever. To her left and behind her lay only darkness. It was obvious she had no choice in which direction to go.

Glancing at the window behind her than back to the glowing lights, she sighed. She clearly knew they had all been taken from their beds and flown here by Private Jet. What she did not know was: where was *here*; and worse, she did not know what lay between *here* and those far away lights?

CHAPTER 83

Blue Eyes stood silent outside the bedroom door. Ear against it he listened but heard no sound. Slowly turning the knob, he gave an easy push. The door would not give, and he smiled to himself. Releasing the handle ever so gently, he tapped lightly waiting for a reply. Still reading, Darcy looked up from her book, "Yes, what is it?"

"Ms Arguine," Quinten said cordially, "sorry to bother you but we wondered if you wouldn't mind coming to the kitchen; you and your cameraman. We would like you to film a special event. I know it's late, but I can assure you it will be captivating."

Darcy closed her book. "Yes, I suppose we could. I am in my Pajamas give me a moment to change."

Blue Eyes injected warmly, "You know, actually, this entire project leans toward a family kind of angle, may I suggest you remain in your nighttime attire, it would add…color, to the production. And to your benefit show your boss you worked around the clock."

Darcy pondered the idea. The yellow pajamas did bring out the highlights of her hair, her figure was in no way lessened, she hadn't removed her makeup and yellow was a cheerful color; viewers preferred cheery colors. She agreed. "Okay, be there in a couple minutes."

"Thank you," Quinten said, "Meet you in the kitchen."

Darcy climbed out of bed. Pulling a hand-mirror from her bag, she straightened her hair, then placed a tab of toothpaste on a finger and ran it across her teeth to freshen her breath. She slipped into her sneakers, removed the chair and went next door.

She found Bart still asleep in the rocker. Patting his shoulder, she startled him awake with a snort. Rubbing at his eyes, he looked up. "Yeah, what's going on?"

"It's called work, Bart. Quinten wants us to film activity in the kitchen."

Bart glanced at his watch, "Damn, it's 11:28. This late?" He glanced over his shoulder, "I haven't even made my bed."

Darcy glanced at the unmade bed and made a face. "you said you wanted to be a reporter someday. Well take a really good look because this is the top rung of the ladder." Shaking his head, Bart pulled on his socks and shoes.

The kitchen was huge, a long center island stretched beneath dozens of hanging pots, pans and skillets. Old wooden shelves and glass-front cupboards dressed the walls. White-smocked workers meandered about, all watching Bart from the corner of their eyes. He was setting up his tripod just inside the kitchen's high-arched doorway; the location suggested by Professor Christenson.

Across the room, perfectly in line with the camera, a large square sheet of clear plastic lay spread on the floor, its four sides draped over a two-by-four frame; obviously designed for liquid containment. Bart snapped his camera atop the tripod and looked at Darcy. "Ever been on a cruise?"

Darcy nodded, surprised at the question "Yeah, why?" She asked.

"Twenty bucks says we're here to film the Chef chiseling away at an ice sculpture."

Darcy gave his idea thought. This was a civil war era mansion. A time when blocks of ice were commonplace. And after all, they were here to document an 1850's circa celebration in the new millennial, old meets New. Yeah, she thought, Bart could be on to something. And it would be cool to watch it all up close. Ice sculpting was an art.

Darcy bit at her lip. Being one who could never overlook the possibility of a bet, she glanced from the plastic sheet on the floor, to the thick wood beams running along the ceiling above. Some of the old timbers were still impaled by old medal hooks; one specifically located directly over the plastic.

In the days of the Civil War slaves used such hooks to hang smoked meats and butcher animals. Darcy folded her arms continuing to look about. A generator was furnishing power for the lights, two upright refrigerators and one small freezer; and she knew tomorrow night's dinner menu included Steak.

She smiled at Bart, "An ice sculpturing, hey? Well, I say no. I say there bringing in a skinned cow and hand cutting tomorrow night's steaks."

Bart grinned; "If that's a bet I'll take it."

CHAPTER 84

Crystal Michelle dropped quietly from the big Oak to the ground. Above the location of the far away lights, a particularly luminous star glittered brighter than the others; she would follow that star to the city. Now on the ground she could see only a forest of darkness.

The guard that stood outside their bedroom window had been on the other side of the building in the front, but twice, while climbing down the tree, she had spotted another walking below. He had been strolling freely, no particular pattern.

At a crouch, she darted from the tree to the far side of the Black Limousine that had carried them here. She paused, looking about. Suddenly the guard reappeared. He stopped, staring hard at the Limousine. She ducked quickly, controlling her sudden rapid breathing.

Then came her worst nightmare, footsteps. Kneeling, she glanced beneath the vehicle. Dulled by the moonlight, she could see two feet marching straight for her. Mouthing a very bad word, she slipped noiselessly beneath the vehicle.Michael was going to be pissed that she had not even made it out of the yard.

The guard walked to the back of the limo and stopped. A moment passed and he lifted the lid. She heard the soft rattle of glass bottles. A second of silence came and a small object dropped to the ground at his feet. He closed the lid quietly and walked away.

Crystal Michelle sighed. Carefully she wiggled out from beneath the vehicle and peeked cautiously over the hood. The guard was disappearing around the house taking a swig from a bottle.

Glancing up at her guiding star, she crouched again running toward a short stretch of open field between her and the woods. There were weeds and patches of brush scattered over the open area. She would use that for cover.

Always crouched, she moved swiftly among the noises of the night things, running and stopping, watching and listening, hoping and praying. It seemed forever before she had reached the woods edge. When just inside the tree line, she stopped to rest her racing heart and hard breathing.

Staring back at the dim-lighted Mansion she shook her head. What was all this about she wondered, and why had they truly been kidnapped?Turning she squinted into the darkness of the woods; wondering what manor of creatures lay in there, waiting.

Crystal Michelle glanced up at her star, then back again toward the old house across the moonlit field. Where was she? What state was this? If Indiana, then she at least had some idea of what type of creature might be lingering, waiting for its prey.Yet, if not Indiana…her gaze turned back to stare hard into this waiting world of dark thick forest; if this were not her Home-Grown State, then she had no clue what sort of creatures would be about and on the prowl hunting. Wanting to kill and eat!

CHAPTER 85

When Cain's father opened the bedroom door, Cain practically ran in. He was smiling, excited. He had not had the opportunity to play with a group of kids in a very long time, and he especially liked Michael. Beneath his arm, he carried the game of Monopoly, Chinese checkers and Battleship.

"Hello everyone." He said cheerfully.

The others pressed a finger to their lips to hush him. Quinten glanced at the lump on the floor just as Michael whispered, "Crystal Michelle is sleeping."

Cain looked at Michael disappointed. "I wanted her to play too."

"She can't," Michael told him, "She's tired. I think she might be coming down with something."

"Yeah," Mat said, "let her be."

"Yeah," little Ronnie chimed in. "It's her and she's asleep."

Cain looked at his father who tilted his head as if to say, "well."

Setting the games on the floor beside the others, Cain approached the sleeping form. Michael closed his eyes shaking his head.

At the bed, Cain pulled the blanket back and saw the pile of clothes. His head rose in rage, and he turned to the others, storming to their sides. "Where is she?"

All remained silent. He now shouted it, "Where is she?"

Blue Eyes folded his arms across his chest, proud that his son was taking charge. Cain looked at the window still boarded up. He went to the closet, no one there, crossed to the bed and looked beneath, nothing. Returning to the others, he was seething. "I want an answer, and I want it right now!"

Little Ronnie started to cry.

Cain pointed at him. "Shut up."

Mat stepped in front of Cain. "Leave him alone or I'll kick your ass."

Cain stared hard into Mat's face. Mat's jaw began to drop. The bright blue eyes of the boy he had just threatened; were changing… turning black, like, like…

Mat stopped in the middle of his thoughts. Along with Michael and Mat, little Ronnie saw it too and it scared him. He couldn't help himself, he wet his pants, the dark stain growing bigger and bigger. He looked down, embarrassed. Then as if all the strength he possessed had been instantly sucked out, he fell backwards to the floor, hitting hard and beginning to seizure.

Now it was Micheal who shouted. "Stop it Cain!"

Mat quickly knelled down by his little brother's side as Cain turned storming to the closet. There with seeming adult strength he picked up the five-gallon bucket carrying it to Little Ronnie's seizing body. Michael stepped between them, "NO!"

Cain ignored him and brushed past.

Again, Michael yelled, "Cain what are you doing? Stop it!"

At little Ronnie's body Cain dumped the contents of the bucket over the boy's face. He then threw the bucket to the side and turned to Michael, eyes still black and evil. "I will ask one last time. Where is she?"

Little Ronnie's seizure stopped and now he lay still and unconscious. Michael knew there was no stopping this rage, it would take a faith greater than his; this was a dark, overwhelming fusion of flesh and blood and demons.

"In the closet," Michael said loudly, "there's a door into the attic."

Cain hurried and looked up. Spotting it there in the shadows he went back to the others. His eyes were slowly returning to blue. Little Ronnie was beginning to rouse.

Looking up at his father Cain said, "I will start a search Father, we'll find her." Following one long silent look at Michael, Cain spun and stormed out of the room.

Blue Eyes watched his son disappear then walked to the door himself. Glancing back, he said, "Well Michael, perhaps you can find a tissue for the little kid's issue and get him cleaned up. Your parents will be here in just a few hours." He started to leave but paused looking back once again adding, "Isn't my son something so very special."

He closed the door and the lock clicked.

CHAPTER 86

Crystal Michelle moved to her feet thinking of a word her dad used often. It was to become a pinnacle in her everyday life: procrastination. Twisting to look one last time at the house imprisoning her brothers and little Michael, she panicked.

The place was now crawling with activity. People running everywhere, flashlights cutting into the darkness like Star War Laser beams. She counted one, two, three figures charging into the field in her direction; it required little doubt as to why.

Following a quick final glance at her star she charged into the woods. Immediately twigs and tree branches slapped and poked at her. Scratching and bruising, they tore incessantly at the material of her flannel pajamas. It hurt, but she could not stop, could not risk slowing down. She was young, fourteen, a cheerleader, ran track. She could outrun them. A flashlight would have been nice but…

She hit the tree head on with a thud, knocking her backward onto the forest floor. Stunned, she lay blurry eyed gazing into the starlight barely visible above the trees, she could feel the approach of unconsciousness.

Blood was running down her face. *Wonderful Crystal Michelle*, she thought to herself, *disfigured for life. Even if you get out this alive, mom and dad will keep you locked away in your room and no doubt have your name changed to Crystal Michelle Frankenstein.*

The world was fading. Sleep, or death, she wasn't sure which, had arrived and soon so would the three men be coming after her. She pictured crime scene specialists Nick and Sara standing over her dead body once again taking pictures, the flash of each snap taking second long bites out of the cold lonely darkness.

Her head was spinning, senses fading; someone lifted her from the ground and tossed her over a tree limb; no wait, a shoulder, their shoulder. She was bouncing. They were running. Unconsciousness came like a last blink of light.

CHAPTER 87

Blue Eyes walked quickly past Darcy and Bart and into the kitchen. He did glance back saying, "By the way, thank you for agreeing to film."

At the far end of the island, he stopped and clapped his hands twice, "okay everyone," he said, "show time."

Immediately the kitchen staff stopped all they were doing and moved to the left side of the room forming a single line as if preparing for inspection. The Chef took his place at the head.

Blue Eyes walked to the TV crew. "As was often the case," he explained gleefully, "here at the Charcloue Mansion prior to an important event, for the sake of freshness, an animal was brought into the kitchen and," he gestured with a hand toward the hook above the plastic, "strung from one of the meat hooks you see fashioned into the beams above. There the animal would be killed, skinned and butchered with practiced hands.

Staring up at the hook a moment he continued, "On those special occasions when ice was available, the meat would be cut and marinated according to family recipe. Tonight, we are recreating, if you will, that tradition with a couple of slight modifications; we will be killing, skinning and butchering our meat right here as usual, and marinating the choice cuts as per the old Charcloue family recipe. We will however, aside from tradition, be utilizing the use of modern appliances. IE, the Refrigerator you see to my left.According to their recipe the meat must remain immersed for precisely twenty-four hours. It will go into soak at exactly midnight tonight, then at tomorrow night's dinner, each steak will be cooked according to each guest's preference."

Blue Eyes hesitated, smiling briefly. "I do hope neither of you have a fainthearted stomach. What you are about to witness can be… mentally abrasive sort to speak."

Darcy and Bart looked at one another and shook their head. "Not me" Bart said, "I'm an avid hunter and have done more than my share of gutting and butchering. In fact, fine with me if Venison is meat of choice for tomorrow night."

"Wonderful," Blue Eyes replied "than you can appreciate what we are about to do. And you, Ms. Arquine," He said, "Will you be okay with what is about to take place?"

Darcy did not realize she had been staring into his eyes while talking to Bart; they were so blue and beautiful. And he was at all times well mannered. She simply found him sexy. If he were to knock on her door again later…"

"Ms. Arguine?"

Darcy flushed, pulling her focus back. "Sorry. I didn't mean to stare."

"Quite alright. I'm used to it."

"In answer to your question," she said, "I grew up on a farm with three older, very antagonizing brothers, and my father butchered a hog and cow every year."

Blue Eyes bowed his head in appreciation. "Wonderful," he said, "Now, at this particular time, Ms. Arquine, although you do look very eye-catching in your yellow pajamas, we have no need for further narration. I just wish for you to film and record the natural run of events. Darcy smiled her approval and he finished," "Okay than," he smiled, "it's important we begin so that we adhere with tradition. We must have the meat in marinate by midnight." He then made his way to the far end of the island and presented a nod curt to Chef LaFair.

Behind the camera Bart followed the Chef's movements. The man with the tall, white hat and long crisp smock, walked to the right of the plastic sheeting, positioning himself just within view of Bart's lens. He looked soberly at the camera, gave a nod, then turned slightly, gesturing toward a closed door on the far end of the room. He clapped his hands shouting, "qui vient."

If it was wild game, Bart wondered pressing his hunter's eye tight to the camera, what would it be: Deer, Turkey, Squirrel, Rabbit, Fish? They were all a part of the Louisiana wilderness. Maybe, he thought, hoped actually, that it would be a wild-game combo. That would be fantastic, almost worth having to give up the weekend with his girlfriend.

The door opened and Bart zoomed in. *Here we go*!

CHAPTER 88

In Alexandria, although restless, Clay, Nancy, Ron, Michelle and Janis all lay asleep. Bob Lemus sat alone in the shadowy living room smoking a cigarette. He breathed in deep and exhaled.

He was rethinking all the things that had happened seven years ago, every character, their strengths and weaknesses, the layout of the mansion, and the killer... especially the killer. Had the mad man changed in anyway; for worse or better? Seven years of isolation could affect a man, even an animal like him. Was he weaker now after so long a time alone, or had isolation somehow made him stronger?

In his gut Bob Lemus knew the answer. So many things in the mix were a given. It was without reason, Blue Eyes was more than ever determined to die, Michael and the Parks children were in grave danger, demons once again would be at the mansion, and this time, so would the Vamps with their superior attributes and thirst for blood and lust, and this time, for the sake of the children, he and the others would be without weapons.

Bob took another draw from his cigarette. And the religious thing; that whoever killed Blue Eyes would end up facing great punishment from the big guy above. Even He, Lemus thought to himself, had to realize bodies were stacking up, and soon, more would be added to the stockpile.

All of his career Lemus had been making sacrifices, Clay too for that matter. Sacrifice came with the shield. If killing the motherfucker in cold blood meant putting a stop to all the insanity, if it meant saving lives…than what the hell…he'd step forward and take God's punishment.

Bob Lemus took a final draw from his cigarette, inhaling it deep into his lungs. Clearly, one more time the Blue Eyes killer had him trapped in a corner; history was repeating itself, only this time things were a hell of a lot worse.

Crushing out his seventh and final cigarette into the ashtray, Bob Lemus smiled to himself. If he made it through tomorrow night, he would quit smoking. "You know what God?" he said speaking softly into the shadows around him, "most of my life I've been making decisions when no one else could, would or dared; well, this time is no different. I just ask that you help me make the right one."

Picking up the hacksaw beside him, he began cutting through the white plaster, beginning at the toes and working up. White particles fell to the floor in small accumulations. Finally, the cumbersome cast fell away completely. Bob wiggled his toes and smiled.

CHAPTER 89

Bart loved what he did; his camera had taken him all over the country and introduced him to some of the nation's most influential people. The pay wasn't bad and picking up extra cash on the side had always been easy. No brag, he was just good at what he did.

Now his big hand adjusted the lens to wide zoom. Two men walked out from the far doorway followed by an older woman with two more men behind her. Bert panned a close focus on each of their faces than pulled back again for more entry. However, no one else came out. One of the men behind the elderly lady closed the door behind them.

Bert's eye left the camera, confused. What was going on? Where was the wild game? He waited several seconds, gazing about, but no one gave up any information. Placing his eye back to the lens he zoomed in for some kind of a clue; he saw it!

Taken aback, he mumbled, "no way." The older woman's hands were bound behind her back. Again, Bert's eye left the camera and he looked up mumbling, *what the hell.*"

He glanced at Darcey, but she was just watching unaware of what he was seeing. Eye on the lens again he pulled back, then focused in again for a close up of the old woman's face. She looked frightened but in control.

The party of four ushered her forward onto the center of the plastic sheet.

"Dear Jesus," Bart thought, "this isn't…this just can't be."

Quinten Christenson suddenly appeared in the lens and Bart adjusted for full view of the entire crew. Not removing his eye from the pad, he reached up and increased the volume on the mike.

Focusing his attention on the bound woman, Christenson smiled; Bart caught it on film. Over the years, he had honed his skills in judging smiles, those heart-felt and real, and those that lie. This was not a lie smile; this smile was pompous and condescending. With exception of the muffled hum of a generator in some other room, the kitchen lay quiet, and the mike picked up Christenson's conversation with the older woman.

"Well Gertrude," he began, " I suppose now would be an appropriate time to answer the questions you asked over the phone a short time ago. First, just so you know, yes, I am the one who killed Carl. It was me making him scream, I was there when he cried, and there when he pissed all over himself." Blue Eyes shrugged, "and just so you know, my mother did have a child that lived, a very beautiful child...me."

Gertrude looked at the camera, then back, "I see we're being immortalized."

"Yes," Blue Eyes said, "The entire event will be on film."

Gertrude gave a nod, "Well than I may as well say it, I think you're a much bigger ass-wipe than I first thought. And I just want to say to my beloved husband," she looked into the camera and tried her best to smile, "I love you Harry, always have." Looking at Blue Eyes again she said, "and since he couldn't be here to tell you himself, this is from Carl," Gertrude spit into Blue Eyes' face.

Closing his eyes, he calmly pulled a handkerchief from his pocket and wiped. When finished, and he reopened his eyes. There was no blue, only deep dark blackness. Gertrude gasped, saying under her breath, "Dear God, where has your soul gone."

Without reply Blue Eyes ordered; "Hang her,"

Gertrude remained still and resolute as they wrapped duct taped around her ankles. When finished, they turned her upside down and attached her to the hook tangling just above her feet.

Hanging head down, face to the camera, she stared into it, frightened, but giving no fight. Her fate was sealed. And in her 71 years she had come to understand there were only two ways to go into the next world: excepting it or fighting it. And her predicament gave no choice.

The crew that had escorted her in left their positions and followed Blue Eyes to take their place in the line of kitchen-help. Chef LaFair strolled to the island where a long line of knives lay. He knew exactly the one he wanted. With it in hand he walked briskly stepping onto the plastic positioning himself in front of the old woman called Gertrude. He began cutting away her clothing until she was hanging naked. All the while Gertrude continued to stare defiant into the camera, her face strong, determined.

LaFair walked around behind her and knelt, gripping the back of her hair. When he pulled, it tilted her head exposing her throat.

Bart pulled his eye from the lens shouting, "Wait," everyone turned to stare. "I've got to tell you, "There was a shaking in his voice, "I've filmed everything from worms to world scholars, but this is bullshit. I will not tape a snuff film. This is cold-blooded murder and I want no part of it."

His hands clasped behind his back; Blue Eyes strolled casually to Bart. "Mr. Smith," he explained "please think about this. Whether you agree or not, I can assure you, you are doing nothing wrong. And no doubt you realize that what is happening here tonight is Pulitzer Prize Documentation."

Leaving one hand resting in the small of his back, Blue Eyes placed the other on Bart's shoulder. "This is your one big opportunity Mr. Smith. A real shot at the big money; a series of paid interviews, a Best-Selling Book and perhaps even a movie deal. Do not let the opportunity of a lifetime pass you by. Besides, I have left a note for authorities that you are doing this under force and have no choice but to do as ordered. Should you refuse, I shall leave you alive but turn you into a very bloody Dick-Less Cameraman.

Bart pulled his eyes to Darcy. She lifted her face and met his stare.

The room remained quiet except for the hum of the concealed generator. All eyes rested on the newswoman in the yellow pajamas. Darcy could feel their stares; they burned into her soul, waiting, eager to hear the true morality of her conscious.

Darcy Arquine took a deep breath and glanced at the old woman hanging upside down, naked and mere seconds from a horrible death. Darcy realized someday she too would be old and shriveled. The thought turned her stomach, but that age remained a long time away. Returning her attention to her camera operator she said, "Just do it Bart. "I don't like it anymore than you do, but this will hit headline news and remain top story for weeks. Just think, it could mean an end to the longer than long hours and eight-day weeks. No more living out of a suitcase. It's our ship Bart, it's here, let's sail with it."

Blue Eyes smiled, chiming in. "There you go Mr. Smith. Your boss has spoken; so back to the camera. We're running out of time."

Bart looked nervously from his boss to the man in charge of this heinous production. He shook his head, "No. I can't, and I won't."

From behind his back Blue Eyes brought up a blue handled straight razor, flicked his wrist, and the blade snapped open. Bart's eyes widened. There was no time to stop it, no time to react. The hand holding the razor arched out and slashed. To her shock and dismay, Darcy Arquine felt a sharp sting, then gripped at her throat, Blood spurted wild from her jugular striking Bart in the face and spraying the front of his shirt. Staring into his eyes, hands at her throat, yellow pajamas sopping up running blood; little, petite Darcy Arquine dropped to her knees, then fell over dead.

Bart was speechless. Blue Eyes was not. "Now, Mr. Smith, we are so close to being out of time I can no longer argue. Will you film or not?" Bart glanced down at Darcy's body and the pool of blood beneath her. Looking back to her killers face, he swallowed. And without a word gave a nod.

CHAPTER 90

Awake now, Crystal Michelle watched the big hand pull away slowly. Having been warned not to scream she listened to the stranger explain; "My name is Ever. I am a friend of your fathers and here to help, but I fear your running away may have jeopardized everything."

"Are you here to rescue the kids?" Crystal Michelle asked.

Ever nodded into the darkness, "Yes, that was the plan. Your, and Michael Cooper's parents will be here tonight. I was to rescue you and the others before their arrival. Now we have lost the element of surprise. Your running has put the others in great danger."

She apologized, "I'm sorry. I didn't know."

Ever nodded again, "That is alright. We will just have to think of something else."

"Why don't I just go back?" She suggested.

Ever shook his head. "No, you would never make it back into the house. They would most certainly catch you. Then hurt you terribly before killing you."

"You mean, rape me?"

"That would be only part of it." Ever told her.

"Look," she said, "I know I'm only fourteen, but I have an idea. If you can help get me back into that house, I can draw their attention so you can get the boys out safely."

Ever sat back and considered her idea while asking, "Where are they keeping them?"

"Second floor, locked in a room on the end facing the front."

"Guards?"

"Yes. The window is boarded up, and one is standing outside it." Ever started to say something but she cut him off. "But the good thing is, there's an opening from the attic into the kid's room. It's inside the closet."

"Is that how you escaped?"

"Yes."

Again, Ever considered her idea. "I believe," he said, "if you make it back into the house, Blue Eyes will see to it they do not harm you; at least not until your parents are there. But that would mean you once again become a prisoner, this time by yourself. And there would be no guarantee you would make it out later, alive."

"Well, I'll be honest," she told him, "I don't like the idea, but if you get the little kids out of there, it's worth it."

"If I do get them out, then I will hide them and come back for you."

"That's fine with me," Crystal Michelle told him. "So, let's do it. "

"Okay," Ever agreed, "But you must give me no less than ten minutes. Can you keep their attention that long?"

"Come on Ever," Crystal Michelle grinned into the darkness, "I'm a teenager."

CHAPTER 91

They took Gertrude off the hook and wrapped a blanket around her. Cutting the tape free of her ankles they walked her back through the same door from which she had come. Others had already stripped Darcy Arquine and taped her ankles. Now she hung upside down in Gertrude's place.

Blue Eyes approached the new hanging corps and squatted in front of it. The female reporter's cold hazel eyes seemed to be staring into a lifeless upside-down world.

"Well Ms. Arquine," Blue Eyes said with a soft tone, "I did have other plans for you; however, all is well that ends well. I'll see you at dinner."

Quinten Christenson rose to face the line of cooks and chefs. Turning to Top Chef LaFair he gave orders, "Okay Chef, get to butchering. We need those Steaks by midnight, and you now have but several minutes to get it done. He turned again. As for you Mr. Smith," he said walking to where he was standing, "please get back to filming. And when the choice steaks are cut, I will have them laid out on the table and will require a close up of them. Please, insure your trained eye catches their exquisite color and perfect shape.

"Where is the old woman?', Bart asked."

"She is fine and will remain so as long as you cooperate. Besides, I may let her go. So, think of it this way. You have already caused the death of one woman, and now, by doing what you're told, you may save the very life of another."

Christenson put his hand on Bart's shoulder again, "You understand you will be joining us for dinner tomorrow, do you not?"

"No. I will not be able to do that."

Christenson removed his hand and folded his arms. Turning to stare at the hanging corps of Darcy Arquine he said. "Now just look at that beautiful specimen of fine meat. Won't that prove much tastier than that from a tough skinned flabby old bag?" Bart was growing pale as he stared. Darcy Arquine's intestines, heart, lungs and other organs were already piled on the plastic sheet below her head.

CHAPTER 92

From the edge of the woods, Ever studied the activity around the house. Things looked as though they were nearly back to normal. He was confident the three who had come across the field after the young girl were now deep into the woods searching with intense focus. They would not return without her, at least not until they had exhausted themselves.

His observation of the house did reveal an increase in guards: now two in the back, three in the front and one on the balcony. He guessed Blue Eyes was not too terribly concerned over the girls escape but did want her back.

At this point Ever realized that the original plan he and Bob Lemus had privately formed, was not by definition, lost; it just needed a bit of tailoring. He would have to get the girl safely back into the house if she were to stay alive, at least for a while longer. The young teen really had no idea what she was facing if caught.

Together, side by side, they left the woods, crawling across the open field toward the house. Ever was pulling a black canvas bag beside him. The bright moonlight created a world of eccentric shadows ideal for concealment; however, Ever understood even the slightest glimpse of movement could cost them their lives.

When at the edge of the field fifty yards from the back of the house, Ever placed the bag carefully into a brush pile and whispered, "You stay here and wait for my signal. I will wave for you to run for the back of the house." She nodded. "If something happens to me," he continued, "try and get back into the house and not get caught. Do not go back into the woods. You understand?"

Again, Crystal Michelle nodded. She watched as Ever rose from the ground and ran for the side of the house. He had a gun in one hand and some kind of a long knife in the other.

Once in place he moved to the corner and looked quickly around to the back. Two guards were standing beneath a tree, chatting. He guessed them to be forty feet or less away. His weapon was fixed with silencer, but he hesitated to use it. If he shot one and missed the other, there might be time for a radio call or the return of gunfire alerting everyone in the house and on the grounds.

Following a glance up into the night sky; he felt sufficient time remained before daylight, but not before the guards in the woods or those here at the house discovered them.

He thought things out. Shadows created by the trees in the yard darkened the area significantly. He could gap the distance between himself and the two guards before they realized he was not one of them. Frowning, he accepted the only option available.

Positioning his hand-held weapon and Vamp Bat behind his back, he rounded the corner and walked confidently toward the two chatting away. They paused and waited for him as he approached, but by the time they realized he was not one of them, it was too late.

Raising his automatic Ever emptied the clip, its steady ping, ping, ping ensured they would be calling no one. But these were vampires, so despite the fact he had used special rounds from the store; he would take no chances, swinging the Bat twice he be-headed both. Quickly replacing the clip in his weapon, he dashed back to the corner of the house and waved for Crystal Michelle.

She sprinted to his side. For the second time that night Ever modified the strategy. Hurriedly, they climbed up the tree Crystal Michelle had descended earlier. Jumping onto the roof they hastily maneuvered in through the window making their way to the hatchway door above the bedroom closet.

Ever put an ear to it and heard only the quiet sound of children chatting. Believing no one but the kids were in the room he gripped the hatch and pulled up. It did not budge. They had obviously nailed it. But to Ever that was little more than a nuisance.

Gritting his teeth and with a determined grip he pulled once more. This time with remarkable strain. Crystal Michelle could hear the soft screeching as nails began pulling free. Soft rays of light streaked out from the ever-widening edges below it.Eyes wide Crystal Michelle shook her head in disbelief.

The hatch pulled free, and more light poured into the space.

Setting the lid aside Ever dropped quickly through the opening. Startled, the boys turned when he came into the room. Crystal Michelle was right behind him. Michael smiled wide running into Ever's arms. Following with a return hug Ever put a finger to his lips to insure their silence and quickly rustled them all into the closet.

Crystal Michelle climbed back into the attic and Ever handed the three boys up through. He then pulled himself up and they made their way to the window, across the roof and down the tree. Little Ronnie rode piggy-back clinging tight to Ever.

On the ground, the body and heads of the two guards still lay motionless. The only sound was that of insects singing unbiased into the fast-passing night. The whippoorwill had fallen silent; perhaps something in the woods had frightened it. That concerned Ever. Whispering to Little Ronnie, he said, "You hold on tight, we have to move quickly."

Ever understood the vital importance of vanishing into the woods without being seen or before the dead guards were discovered. Crystal Michelle grabbed Michael's hand and Matt assured them he could make it on his own; so Ever nodded with a whisper, "Okay than, here we go."

Together they scurried into the field, dashing and darting from brush patch to brush patch, always waiting and watching before the next run. Michael was praying without ceasing, repeating to himself again and again, "if God before you, who can be against you, if God before you, who can be against you." And to Michael's delight, God answered his prayer just the way he wanted, at least so far. They were suddenly huddled at the edge of the woods.

CHAPTER 93

Ever knew not one minute could be wasted. Kneeling he faced the children and whispered, "Now we must enter into the woods. It is important we remain quiet and move quickly, no talking and hold on tight to each other's hand. There are three men in their searching for Crystal Michelle, they want to hurt her, and now they will hurt you too, so we must be noiseless and sneak past them. Are you ready?"

All nodded. Ever looked one last time across the field to the house: so far so good. He helped little Ronnie onto his back, stood, then took Mat's hand, Crystal Michelle grabbed his other than Michael's. Ever in the lead, they plunged like a connected line into the waiting woods.

Inside the blackness, the night creatures continued with their loud perturbing noises. The treetops blocked out most of the moon and for Crystal Michelle and the boys it was nearly impossible to see. Moving in a single line, they followed blindly behind Ever; but his eyes were not like theirs, genetically his were a human marvel, functioning normally but to the Vampire standards.

Setting the pace Ever moved steadily adjusting his speed for the sake of the seven-year-old. As ordered, all remained quiet, careful not to talk or yell; even when branches slapped or scratched at their face and hands.

The dark woods seemed an endless trek with Michael feeling as though he were being half-pulled, half-drug. His little legs were working overtime to keep up. Somewhere along the way, the Whippoorwill returned and was once again calling out into the night.

Then like the flash of a black bulb exploding, a dark form running parallel through their line snatched up Michael, disappearing instantly with him. Crystal Michelle yelled, "Oh my God."

Ever stopped turning and asking with a whisper, "What is it?"

"They took Michael. He's gone."

Ever shook his head. "We must keep going. They know we are here. Quickly, both of you grab my belt, we are almost there."

The woods weren't wide. A small clearing lay close to where Ever's truck sat. It was parked along a narrow dirt road cut through an open field. He increased their speed almost to a run. Mat struggled to keep up but held his own. Then they burst out of the woods and into a clearing beaming with moonlight. The truck sat parked to the left sixty feet, only seconds away. But Ever stopped suddenly with Chrystal Michelle and Mat bumping into him.

Leaned casually against the truck were three men; two with arms folded and a third holding Michael by the collar of his pajamas. Ever recognized two but was unsure of the third. All were Vamps. Of that he was certain.

Kneeling: Ever let Little Ronnie climb off his back and took Crystal Michelle by the shoulders, "You know how to drive?" He asked. She nodded. "Here," he handed her his truck keys. "It's locked. They will want to kill me first, then come for you and the boys. I will engage them, during the fight, get the kids into the truck and drive fast. This road will take you to the main highway, there you will come to a gate. It will be locked. Do not get out of the truck. Just crash through it and turn right. The highway will take you straight into the city. Once there, find help."

Crystal Michelle shook her head, refusing. "No, there are three of them, you need our help."

Ever smiled, holding the grip on her shoulders. "I know you are fourteen, and I trust you, but this is how we must do it; there is no other way." He gave her a reassuring nod then stood to his feet..

Facing the three that were waiting, he listened as the one holding Michael spoke out through the moonlight. "Ah yes, Everton Maus", he said with a grin. "We know of you. Even Aluka speaks of your skill. We have decided to fight you one at a time, I will go first," he made a shrug, "of course my colleagues will be disappointed and jealous when I kill you. But I burn for the recognition of killing the famous Ferret. He lifted Michael by the collar pulling his neck near his mouth, "now drop your Sidearm to the ground, you may keep the hand-held weapon. I want this to be fun."

Ever pulled his sidearm but held it saying, "You have my word. Let the little one come over here to the others, and I will drop it, and then, trust me, I will indeed promise you a very fun time."

"Honor does come with your reputation." the one holding little Michael said. He let go of the collar allowing him to run to Crystal Michelle. Ever dropped the gun then began his walk toward the three men, "You know," Ever said as he approached, "it is an insult and unfair that I fight you one at a time. For me you make this a child's game. None of you are my equal, it will take all three to match me. However, because you are obviously friends, I feel it only right to let you decide which one wants to die last."

CHAPTER 94

Inside the mansion, Bart Smith had vomited three times interrupting his filming. Chef Lafair had gutted, skinned and cut Bart's boss into sections, and was now selecting only the finest of cuts for the Charcloue family's secret marinade.

Bart didn't give a damn about a Pulitzer Prize; he just wanted to get out, to run; go someplace where no one in the world could find him. He wanted to get drunk and stay drunk for a very long time.

This was all so evil, so make believe, yet real. It was true horror, no game, no gimmicks. He worked in news; he knew this sort of thing really happened in the world, even here in the United States, but never, not in a million years did he ever think it would happen to him. Bart was scared as hell. And Burt did not want to die.

CHAPTER 95

Ever gripped the rubber embossed handle of the Bat firmly; he loved this weapon, had trained regularly with it since its inception. Already a martial artist, a master in six forms, he had incorporated the weapon into five of the styles.

Although not overly worried he was facing three opponents, one thing concerned him... it would take but one simple error, just one foolish mistake and the children would be theirs. These Vamps were freelancers; they would not, and probably did not know the truth about Blue Eyes: his power and influence. These men cared only that he had hired them for pay, and yet crossing him for the shared sexual delights of a young teen, and the delicacy of not one, but three young child delicacies would far outweigh the monies promised.

If Crystal Michelle did not get the boys into the truck and escape, these Vamps would drain them all with the little ones first; children were a true Vamp delicacy. Then Crystal Michelle following her sexual horror would be drained; and for the rest of their remaining lives the Coopers and the Parks would forever face sleepless nights of torturous mental anguish.

Ever reached the three men and stopped at a distance of twenty feet. He would have liked a greater distance from the truck but did not want to alert them of their plan.

Following several seconds of studying Ever's posture, the three left the vehicle forming a circle around him. Apparently, they had taken him up on making this a sporting game for Ever.

They too had knife weapons; one wielded a Japanese Samurai Sword: he positioned himself to Ever's right, another held a long-handled axe resembling an ancient decapitation tool: he positioned himself behind Ever, and the third, twirling and spinning it in arrogance, worked a weapon similar to the Bat Ever carried. He stopped in front of Ever slightly to his left. Ever knew he would be the one to watch closest.

Poised, Ever lowered his eyes as if studying the ground at his feet; then did not move nor look up. His blood stream was filling with adrenaline, his mindset was to kill and survive. The Ferret's brown eyes had constricted and redirected to peripheral vision; his hearing elevated to an advanced Vampire state. Everton Maus looked like a frozen statute, but for those who knew him, or had dared challenge him; they understood how he had earned the appellation: Svelte-of-Iron.

Crystal Michelle watched with her heart pounding. She wanted to collect the boys and run for the truck. But long ago, her dad, in addition to driving home the importance of not procrastinating, had also instilled the value of patience – no matter what they want of the mind; a cool head, a calm demeanor, and the acceptance of fear were the ingredients of survival, and down through history the staples of heroism.

Although scared and facing panic, she knew they had to wait; not take a step until the fight was well underway.

As for Ever she thought; '*so much for one at a time. Freaking cowards*!

The Vamp from behind moved first: Ever saw it in the eyes of the man in front. Immediately Ever spun raising the Bat in time to catch the downward swing of the long-handled ax, deflecting it to the right and spinning at the same time swinging the Bat full around; it sliced through the axe man's neck severing his head. Ever spun one more time and stopped, poised in a martial arts stance, waiting. But the other two remained fixed, staring at their colleague. The headless torso stood for several seconds before falling onto the grass. Eyes filled with surprise and anger; the remaining two worriers looked from the body to Ever.

Maintaining his posture, Ever stretched out his hand, palm up, motioning with his fingers that he was waiting. The vamp with the samurai was a traditional, he raised the blade, handle to his ear and began circling. The samurai was not a weapon strange to Ever; he was not a master in the art but had studied it sufficient to perform many of its Kata.

The samurai vamp moved slowly with eyes locked, deep in concentration. The other vamp began moving as well in the opposite direction: his weapon similar to Ever's, stretched out parallel at his side with free handheld open-knifed at his chest. Ever knew these two were pros, without doubt master's in their arts; the way they moved, working together in unison and grace, each calculating and deeply focused.

He wanted to tell Crystal Michelle to get moving, dash for the truck and get the hell out of there. But she remained, not moving, waiting! Ever knew she was staying because she cared, but it was the wrong thing to do. He cussed at her delay, and it came with a price; the samurai slashed downward, he blocked it with metal clanging metal but the tip of the samurai sliced open his shoulder; it stung but would heal quickly. The other vamp slashed out with his Bat-like weapon, Ever ducked, the samurai swung again, Ever warded it off and again the ring of metal against metal echoing into the Louisiana night.

Always Ever moved to ensure they did not get behind him. Blade crashed against blade, steel against steel sending sparks into the gray still moonlight. Around and around, they moved, warriors of perfection, swinging and blocking, waiting for that reckless opening; that one careless mistake. And it would come. It always came.

The position was right, Ever squatted kicking out for a sweep. The man with the Bat-like weapon slammed onto his back but rolled away quickly, Ever sprung to his feet blocking another swing from the samurai.

Suddenly out of the night came a new sound. It wasn't the clang of steel or roar of the truck starting and spinning away to safety; it was a soft echoing ping; then came another. The man with the samurai paused looking down at his chest; blood was slowly soaking the front of his shirt. Following a quick glance at his friend who had been the first to die, lying motionless opposite him, his shocked gaze moved to the teen girl still holding Ever's automatic weapon. His knees buckled and he dropped face first into the grass.

The last remaining vamp tossed his weapon to the ground. Crystal Michelle redirected Ever's auto to his chest, "You get out of here," she said, "go back to the house and leave us alone."

The Vamp smiled into the gray-light, "Sure, but I'll be back for you little girl." And when I do, I'm going to bleed you while I fuck you into a mythical land of pain and pleasure."

Crystal Michelle made a sour face, "You're a-real-sick-0. The only thing fucked here is you; well, your dead friends anyway. Now go, get your disgusting gutter-filled mind out of here!"

Following a flippant grin, the Vamp turned and began walking toward the woods.

"Wait," Ever called out after him, "one last thing." The Vamp stopped and turned to face him. Ever approached and when within reach, did a split-second backward whirl- swing with the Bat.

The vamps head fell to the right side tumbling off the body. Behind him, in the golden light of the moon, Ever heard:one "yuck", one "awesome" and one "gross but so wicked cool!" Little Ronnie was just speechless.

CHAPTER 96

Cain knocked on the door of the upstairs bedroom. No answer. He inserted the key and unlocked it. The young boy wanted to apologize for his behavior earlier; to make up and play some games with the boys. After giving it thought, he had come to realize an attempt to escape was a reasonable thing to do; after all, they were being held against their will. Had the situation been reversed, he would have done the same.

When he entered the room, he stopped at the threshold and looked about. No one! At first, he began to grow angry, then remembered they had nailed the attic door closed following the girls escape. He smiled, "You guys are hiding on me, aren't you?"

Excited, Cain moved to the old bed and looked quickly beneath it, no one. One place remained. They were huddled at the far end of the tiny closet. "You're in the closet," he said, "here I come."

Once there he looked in…no one! He looked up into the ceiling; the hatch was torn away. His eyes began turning black and little seven-year-old Cain screamed… "May Satin damn you Michael Cooper."

CHAPTER 97

Ever unlocked the passenger truck door and opened it. The kids scrambled in, and he closed it behind them. Then he hurried around to the driver's side and slipped in behind the wheel. The truck started immediately, and he hit the gas, spinning the vehicle in a circle and pulling onto the dirt road leading out.

In the beginning when he and Bob had formed the idea of a rescue, he had given the project a fifty-fifty chance; now, although not entirely out of the woods, no pun intended, he was feeling a cheerful twinge of liberation.

Driving at a great speed, he covered the half mile to the waiting locked gate quickly. It came in site, moonlight reflecting off its metal rails. Just as he had instructed Crystal Michelle, he would crash through it.

Then out of the moonlit night came an explosion. Thunderous, it shook the truck followed by the sound of metal clanging. The vehicle jerked, the engine died, and they rolled to a gradual stop.

Ever took a deep breath. With the vehicle sitting less than fifty feet from the gate, he pulled the sidearm Crystal Michelle had gladly returned. Climbing out he popped the hood. In the moonlight, the engine appeared to be intact. Moving to the side, he knelt and glanced beneath; the oil pan was missing. Climbing to his feet he looked back over the road behind them; dark remnants of engine parts cluttered the road.

A vamp came charging out of the shadows for a tackle, but Ever moved quickly shooting him in the head. The body dropped near the left front tire. Ever spun, waiting; but nothing else happened.

Ushering the kids out of the truck he told them, "Hurry, we must continue on foot and have three miles to reach the city." Kneeling he helped Little Ronnie onto his back adding; "Others are no doubt already on their way here. I will have to push you along."

Climbing over the gate they hurried onto the road. "Following a deep breath Ever said, "Now my young friends, we must run till we can run no more."

CHAPTER 98

Blue Eyes knew the children could not have ripped open a nailed hatch; it had to have been someone strong. He put every available vamp on the hunt knowing their search would be for one of their own kind. His orders were clear, "no one harms the children, and whoever it is with them, there is a hundred-thousand-dollar reward for bringing him back to me, alive. I say it again, under no circumstances are you to hurt any of the children and I want them all back here within the hour, now go!"

Blue Eyes was fuming, pacing the floor and mumbling. Not counting Chef LaFair and his six assigned kitchen helpers, he had begun with a hired crew of sixteen supposedly baddest of the bad-ass Vampires. "Now," he said to the remaining Vamps around him, "I already have two dead in the back yard and three missing, and not one of them answering their radios," he threw up his hands, "and it's not even fucking midnight."

His eyes black, his fists clenched, he knew without the children Clayton Cooper would never agree too killing him; "Son of a bitch" he screamed into the room, "son of a bitch, son of a bitch, and son of a bitch."

Cain sat watching his father, never before seeing him this angry. "Father," he asked, "why is it you are not sending out the demons? They are here in great numbers."

Blue Eyes answered still pacing, "Because they can do little unless possessing a..." stopping abruptly, he looked at his son, "you know, my little genius, you just might be on to something. Praise Satin, you are indeed learning so well."

Cain moved to his father's side and the two hurried to the kitchen. The killer's eyes were nearly blue again. At the clap of his hands LaFair and the six helpers stopped what they were doing to gather around him. "Who here," Blue Eyes asked promptly, "is an atheist, and does not believe in the existence of God?"

LaFair and the others exchanged glances, wondering why he was asking such a personal question, fearing the incorrect answer might put them on the dinner table. "Come on," Blue Eyes snapped, clapping his hands again, "it's a simple question people." Three apprehensively raised their hand; one was LaFair.

Blue Eyes glanced at his son, he wanted to smile but held it. "Okay," he said. "I have an attractive proposition for two of you, Chef LaFair, your skills are too valuable here, this will not apply to you. But you two," he said redirecting his attention, "I will give you five hundred thousand dollars each for - and this may sound ludicrous - the rental of your soul."

The two glanced at one another, agreeing that ludicrous did in fact explain such a strange request. "For five hundred thousand dollars," Blue Eyes continued, "all you have to do is simply consent to loaning me your soul that my demons may work with you."

The two again glanced at one another. One of the two, the woman Journeyer Chief said, "we are atheists, we do not believe in demons any more than we believe in a God. As for the soul, perhaps there is a form of existing energy in the end, but certainly no soul. We cannot loan to you something we do not have?"

Blue Eyes smiled. "Well than, by appeasing me you will make a lot of money with nothing to lose, right?" Following a mutual pause, they both agreed with a show of remaining apprehension,

"I apologize for taking away two of your staff, Chef LaFair," Blue Eyes said, "but pressing matters have arisen."

The couple introduced themselves as Pete and Alice. Pete was tall, somewhat rotund with a salt and pepper go tee. Alice was short, perhaps five six, small framed and petite, but soon her limitations would be of little importance.

Blue Eyes and Cain led the couple out of the kitchen and into the study, where seven years ago, Janis Barr and agent Clendes had faced a demon-possessed vagabond. Barr had killed the possessed man, but only after a near death-struggle.

Pete and Alice found the room fascinating and eloquent, despite its musky smell and thick covering of dust.

Blue Eyes whispered into his son's ear then walked away to stand quietly near the door. Once again, he had given his son a great deal of responsibility.

Little Cain approached the couple with a sober face, "would you please kneel." Trying to hold back their grin they did as requested. Once in position, Cain asked, "Now, we are going to ask Demons to come into you, to possess you, is that acceptable?" Looking at one another, they gave a nod of approval, a Five-hundred-*thousand-dollar approval*! "Please close your eyes and repeat after me." Cain said.

"Wait," Alice asked, trying to look serious, "are the demons here with us now?"

Cain looked at his father, irritated, but maintained a calm demeanor. Returning his attention to Alice he sighed, "Yes, there are thousands. You will be meeting them in just a moment."

"Oh," Alice said fighting back a smile, "I see. Sorry for interrupting."

Ignoring her sarcasm, Cain raised his voice, "Now please close your eyes and do not open them until we have completed the ceremony. We will now begin, please repeat after me: "I do here by surrender," they repeated the words, "my fleshly body to Satin and his demons," they again repeated but finding it difficult not smiling at this cute little boy acting so serious. Cain was finding it difficult to retain his growing anger. He could sense their insolent mannerism. He gave the last line to be repeated, "I swear allegiance to Satin for so long as I am possessed."

Repeating the last of the little boy's expletive, a smiling Pete and Alice opened their eyes; the smiles vanished, shock turned them pale.

Eyes wide they stared, unable to grasp. The room was filled with foul, hideous things, creatures the human mind could not think to create, and all were staring at them as if lusting. The assemblage began to chatter, moving in place as if growing fidgety; the things with wings fluttered, those that crawled rose up and the things with teeth snarled, drooling as if rabid and hungry.

Pete and Alice twisted looking in all directions; there numbers were incalculable, all restless, waiting, their chatter growing louder. Stunned, speechless, Pete and Alice looked at the little boy. He grinned, "Take them."

Everything, every manor of creature, beast and horrible thing converged on them, absorbing into their bodies like butter melting into toast. Peter and Alice screamed and screamed, their pain the most horrid imaginable. Dark thing after dark thing melded into them. And after a time, when all that had been inhabiting the room were inside them, the pain stopped.

Collecting themselves the couple rose to their feet, their outward appearance unchanged. Inside however, there were three differences: each was now void of human compassion, each possessed the strength of a hundred men, and both were no longer Atheist.

CHAPTER 99

Ever and the kids stared at the huge lighted eyes cutting sharply through the Louisiana darkness toward them. Pulling his automatic and placing it behind his back, he ordered the kids to jump and wave, to demand its attention. A direct confrontation was what Ever wanted.

When within a few feet from the dancing children, it came to a stop, sitting there idling, scrutinizing. The children ceased their antics and Ever approached the window tapping lightly. The young driver rolled it down a couple of inches and immediately the sounds of night rushed in.

The young male forced a smile, "What happened, did your car break down?"

Ever returned the smile wanting to hurry this along. "Yes, could you give us a ride into town?"

"Sure." Elaine and I", he glanced at the young girl snuggled beside him, "are going into town to a party. We could drop you off at a gas station or something."

"Wonderful," Ever said. The children crowded into the backseat and Ever slid in beside the young girl. "Looks like a Ford Fairlane, early sixties? "he said to the driver.

The driver beamed. "1966, belonged to my dad. He bought her new right off the Show Room Floor."

"How fast will she go?" Ever asked.

The young man grinned. "She'll top out at a hundred and ten when pushed."

"Let's see her do it, now."Ever said, "Truthfully, there are people after us." Watching the rearview mirror Ever saw six figures on foot dash on to the road, through the gate, and approximately a thousand feet behind them.

Vamps were fast runners. One turned spotting the car all six began a charge.Ever diverted his attention to the driver; pulling his automatic, "Go!"

The young man floored it, the vehicle tires gripped, and they shot forward. The Vamps ran with above-human speed. The car's speedometer climbed to fifty, sixty and seventy, the Vamps gaining. Not long after they hit eighty-five did the distance between them began to stretch. The Vamps slowed and came to a stop knowing it was now impossible to catch them by foot. They would return to the mansion and come back with vehicles to begin a relentless hunt throughout the city.

Ever had the driver drop down to the speed limit not wanting the police stopping them. When within city limits, he pulled his cell and punched in a number. It rang and rang, Ever made a frustrated face. Just as he pulled the phone from his ear, a voice came on…the person was quick to speak. "Ever, is that you?"

Ever nodded as he spoke, "Yes, I have them."

Bob Lemus closed his eyes, *Thank God*. Can you get them here to the house?"

"I think so, but we must make the switch quickly."

Under Ever's direction the young driver drove straight to Bob and Janis' house. The kids were immediately loaded into the Park's Van along with Nancy and Michelle. Jones drove and Clendes rode shotgun. It was decided they would take 67 North to 10 East to 432 North to the little town of Chipola and find a motel. They pulled away with everyone waving.

Ever apologized and thanked the young driver and his girlfriend then turned them loose. Janis climbed in behind the wheel of her jeep and yelled, "Well come on, we're going to miss dinner." Ever, Bob, Clay and Ron climbed in. Janis spun out of the driveway smiling, "Just like old times fellows."

Utilizing country roads, they looped back west pulling onto the dirt drive leading back to the mansion. They passed Ever's deserted truck, drove to the edge of the woods and parked. Clay looked at Janis, "Dejivu, hey."

Janis spoke softly in return, "Seven years and now it feels like only yesterday."

"Yes, but this time it's different," Ron added, "this time I'm paying him back for my mom and dad, and I owe the son of a bitch for what he had the Vamps do to Michelle. By my hand, he will die tonight."

Clay pulled his 9-millimeter and slid the slide. "This is my fight, Ron", he said, "it's me who will kill him. But I promise, when I do, I'll remind him it's for what he's done to all of us."

Bob Lemus shook his head, "You know, you're both talking horse-crap. The FBI has jurisdiction here, I'll be the one doing the killing."

Ron glanced down at Bob's leg than up into his moonlit face. "Hey," he told him, "Just because you cut that cast off your leg, it doesn't mean your back on duty with the FBI."

Grinning at the male fervor going on, Janis said, "Hey guys!" Each turned to look at her. "I have the perfect solution," she told them, "Why don't you three boy's make your way to the edge of the woods, line up shoulder to shoulder, whip out your dicks and get your jollies off, get rid of all this Incredible Hulk Testosterone. Then we can continue on with the mission."

For the first time since his arrival, they heard Ever laugh.

The only vamp-killing weapons among them were those that Ever carried: one Bat and one auto with silencer and four remaining clips of the special rounds. The rest of the Vamp weapons were in the canvas bag hidden away at the edge of the mansion yard.

Bob and Ever's original plan had Ever not freed the children- was to attend the dinner as usual. Then sometime during the festivities, one of them slip away and retrieve the bag. Now, fortunately, that was no longer the case, the children were safe and Blue Eyes held no trump cards…except Gertrude, and they weren't certain about that.

They moved through the woods at a quickened gait. The night sounds were loud, the stars bright, and along with the moon they continued through the woods with scattered patches of dim light. Vamps could be anywhere waiting; and waiting with authorization to kill everyone they needed, except of course for Clayton Cooper.

Clay understood both the legal and biblical ramifications of what he was going to do, but nevertheless, this night it was going to be done... he was sending the Blue Eyes killer to Hell.

Yes, it was what the psycho wanted, he understood that. This was the same evil wish that had brought Hell out of its darkness for the first time seven years ago. And just like now, back then the killer had left behind a dark trail of horrible deaths, unspeakable desecration and mental anguish.

For seven long years Clay had believed it was over. He had put the Blue Eyes Killer behind bars on Death Roll. And now he was back. How could that be? No one escapes from Death Roll. Not even someone with personal contacts in Hell.

As he skirted through the darkened woods Clay recalled the lines of a song they had sung so often in Church. A song that somehow brought a touch of consolation to his soul:"Hallelujah Hallelujahwe know that we win, HallelujahHallelujah we read the back of the Book, and we know thatwe win!"

Clay had come to grips with himself, realizing that if he too was destined to be cast into the lake of fire along with the rest, then so be it. At least his last thought would be that this nightmare was finally over. His family and friends would live on with an eternal peace.

They reached the edge of the woods and stopped. Each studied the house seeing the same things. There were lights inside, but no activity outside. It was likely all Vamps were out searching. Without the children, the game was all but over for Blue Eyes. He himself was probably inside wandering the halls, anxious for the hired help to return with the four Gold Chips, and hopefully before the guests arrived.

Clay felt relief that the kids were gone and safe. The only thing left to do now was anti-up with what was left and play the last hand.

With Ever in the lead, they made their way across the moonlit field. At the edge of the yard, they retrieved the black bag and quietly distributed the weapons among themselves.

All hated the Vamps and clearly understood killing them was the only viable chance of surviving. Yet, no matter what went down, once inside, who lived or who died took second place. Each approached with the same common goal... and that was to kill the Blue Eyed Bastard.

CHAPTER 100

Jones was glad to be out of the city lights and into the silk-lit Louisiana countryside; here the safety factor greatly increased. He glanced at his watch pushing the illumination button; three minutes before midnight. "So what time is it," Clendes asked. Jones told him and Clendes remarked, "party starts in three minutes."

Michael sat silent in the back of the Van, praying. He was also quietly crying. His dad was in great danger, and he couldn't be there to help. He loved him, wanted to see him again…alive; wanted his family life back to normal. God had to know how badly he hated Satin right now.

Demons and Vampires both were in that house; and all of them would be trying to kill his dad, along with Mr. and Mrs. Lemus and Ever and Ron. Wiping at his eyes, he sniffled and told the others with urgency, "We have to pray together as a group, and do it right now."

The others glanced at one another. Silently they had each prayed for Clay and the others; but to pray collectively, as a group, felt awkward.

"Except for you Mr. Jones," Michael said, "please keep your eyes on the road, the rest of us, let's bow our heads and pray for God to help dad and the others. God will take our strength and send it to them."

Following one more glance around they turned to their own furtive borough of the Van, and one by one, guided by little Michael Cooper, they bowed their head. Michael began praying aloud setting the example, and soon, without even realizing, everyone had joined in; even agent Jones, except he prayed as Michael requested, with his eyes open.

CHAPTER 101

Lying in the weeds at the edge of the mansion yard, they paired up. Group one: Cooper and Lemus, and group two: Ron and Janis. Bob and Janis agreed they're not teaming would be wise.

Group one made their way to the front of the house for entry, and group two went to the back for the same purpose. Ever remained outside to engage any Vamps returning to the house.

No one knew what kind of contrived plot waited – that was a major drawback. They did however, although diminutive know their enemy. Vamps were superior in every way, Demons could not be killed, and Blue Eyes owned a soul as dark as the eyes that reflected it, and now there existed a new force, one still in its infancy, but a power developing and growing rapidly…Little Cain.

On the porch Cooper and Bob Lemus stood on each side of the front door, their weapons raised. The door was closed. Lemus tried the handle and it turned. With a light push it opened, coming to a gentle stop against the inside wall. There was no screen-door and the threshold yawned like the open mouth of a waiting giant.

Deep shadows distorted the interior; there were no sounds and no movement. Cooper darted inside; his gun held by outstretched arms. The barrel moved left, right and up and down searching for a target. He found no movement. "Clear" he whispered. Lemus scurried in beside him.

Ten or twelve feet ahead stood the open entranceway to the long hallway leading into the dining room. Still no sound; however, with eyes adjusting they realized a dull light was glowing at the far end.It was quick, but they caught a shadow streaking across the threshold. Bob looked at Cooper and gave a nod. Together they advanced, cautiously entering the hallway.

At the rear of the building, Janis darted through the doorway and into the mansion's kitchen. Her semiautomatic with Vamp killing rounds was in her hand hanging at her side. Ron remained outside, crouched below the window in wait.

The kitchen had changed over the past seven years. When she had first entered it so long ago, it had consisted of darkness, dust, the smell of mildew and spider-webs everywhere. Now the room was clean and somewhat modernized, housing a refrigerator, freezer and strings of ceiling lights. The soft idle of a generator was sounding from some other location.

Although brightly lighted, the kitchen appeared deserted. Pots and pans hung over the original Oak-Island while on its top sat dishes, utensils, spices, staples and various food items; some opened and others waiting to be used.

On the wood counter to her right lay scattered bits and pieces of red meat and gristle It was obvious an animal of some sort had been butchered; the kitchen reeked with the rancid smell of blood.

Janis tapped the barrel of her auto on the window and Ron rose cautiously. He saw only Janis, so he joined her."No one here," she told him. "Look at the counter, something has been butchered, and not that long ago."

Rounding the island, she passed a stainless 30 Cup Coffee Pot with its dotted light aglow. She glanced at Ron, "Want a cup of coffee? It's probably made from ground bug juice, straight from Hell."

Ron took a quick look at the pot and frowned, "No thank you. What you just said...is probably more fact than fiction."

Janis walked to the refrigerator and opened the door; the light came on instantly. Fresh steaks lay in rubber-made containers, marinating. "To bad we're going to miss dinner, steaks look good," she told Ron. There were also bowls of salad covered with damp paper toweling ensuring the lettuce remained fresh and crisp. Closing the door Janis swept the room with questioning eyes. *What the hell?*

"Something's wrong here," she said more to herself than Ron. "Sure, it's cleaner now, brighter, and borrowing from the French, avant-garde. But where is everyone. All the other guests? Any guests? I's feeling far too...Blues Eyed to suit me. I don't like it."

Ron Parks agreed. "Yeah, for sure. It certainly isn't what I was expecting. So, let's move on. Find some action."

Without looking at him, Janis nodded. "Well," she said, "we have two doors. Behind door number one; *as I scarcely recall*, is the long hallway leading to the Dining Room. And door number two; *as I so very well recall*, is yet another hallway. That one will take us past the Den and a few other rooms."

Ron looked her way. "The Den, you say?"

Janis returned his look, "Yep. Better known as The Fun-time Charcloue Den.

Ron let the small trace of a smile show. "Well then. You must come to grips with the idea that tonight, right now, this very minute may be the last opportunity you'll ever have to visit this Historic Den. Is that an opportunity you want to miss?"

Janis returned Ron's almost hidden grin. Raising her weapon, she turned moving toward door number two. Just as Ron's little bitty smile turned into a quite noticeable grin, Janis told him, "You asked for it. Come on smiley!"

Leaving the door open the Kitchen light funneled in but faded quickly into near-complete darkness at the other end. With caution they moved slowly. The interior of the mansion was hot, no fans, despite their being a generator. Just within the last glimpse of remaining light, a written note dangled from a hanging string. Janis sighed, *here we go again*. Grabbing the bottom edge, she leaned in close for a look. It was handwritten and addressed to her:

Janis,

Here we are again. One more time you and the others have managed to screw things up. No, actually it's beyond that; things are 'fucked up'. Anyway, somehow you always manage to wiggle your way out of 'special, or shall we say, hazardous, situations'. This time, although somewhat a close likeness to your last visit to this Den, I think you will find this awaiting venue a bit more worthy of your knack. Still, if I were a betting man, I would put my money on that which awaits you. Enjoy!

Blue Eyes

Frowning, Janis shifted the string-note to Ron. He read it and whispered softly. "Well, I wanted action."

Janis gave a nod, "You know what they say; 'be careful what you wish for'."

CHAPTER 102

Reaching the far side of the long hallway and a brighter light, Clay and Bob stopped, weapons at the ready. Remembering the horror that awaited him here seven years ago, Clay grit his teeth with anger and disgust. He was sweating, fearing what awaited him now.

The dining table lavishly dressed in white linen lay garnished with silver and crystal dinning ware. A long Gold Candelabrum sat perfectly centered with lighted bright twinkling candles, supplying the only light in the room. There were strings of overhead lighting, but none were on.

The seating arrangement was set for nine. Although lying beneath a thin layer of shadows, Clay could see the huge Satanic Pentagram painted on the floor surrounding the table. It caused him to grit his teeth tighter.

At the far end of the table Blue Eyes was sitting relaxed and sipping coffee. Smiling he said politely, "Please Clay, do come in, and you as well Bob, of course."

Clay glanced at Bob and their eyes agreed. Weapons remaining raised, they entered the room. It appeared empty except for the killer.

"Please," Blue Eyes added, "I am the only one in the room. Come, sit and join me. Enjoy a cup of coffee, I assure you, it is one of the world's finest brews, imported directly from Paris", Blue Eyes took a sip and continued, "I first discovered its most exquisite flavor ten years ago while lunching at The Cafe Les Magots," he gave a sigh, "and to be honest, one sip and I was hooked. Been drinking it ever since," he grinned again, "yes, even while incarcerated."

A door to the right opened suddenly and Clay and Bob swung their weapons ready to fire but refrained. A tall man in a blood-stained white smock and tall chef's hat held a pot of coffee. The intruder quickly stopped, startled. "Please gentlemen," Blue Eyes told them, "It is only my Chef. Allow me to introduce you. Chef LaFair, meet my greatest opposition ever, the older gentleman dressed in his finest BLACK Tactical Gear, is retired FBI agent Bob Lemus." LaFair bowed while Blue Eyes continued, "and the other man in matching Tactical Gear is my younger brother, Clayton Cooper. Otherwise known as, Abel." Again, LaFair bowed.

"I've got Mr. Tall Hat Lafair covered," Lemus said following the Chef's final bow to Clay.

Immediately Clay pulled his attention back to Blue Eyes. "How many times do I have to say it, I am not your brother?"

Ignoring the remark, Blue Eyes swept his hand over the table, "Please, sit and have coffee. You have my word; so long as you relax and put away those guns, nothing will happen here but conversation."

Bob motioned with the barrel of his auto, "you, by him." Chef LaFair hurried to Blue Eyes and stood behind him. Approaching the table, Clay and Bob moved to opposite sides and sat, positioning themselves so as to visually cover the room.

Blue Eyes looked first at Clay then Bob," Chef LaFair will now come to pour your coffee, please do not shoot him."

The dining room was silent. Light from the candelabra shadowed their faces. And when LaFair filled their cups, the softness of gurgling coffee could be heard. When filled, Blue Eyes dismissed Lafair and he hurried back through the door leading to the kitchen.

Clay, laying his weapon on the table directly in front of him, broke the silence, "So how do we know the coffee isn't drugged? Are we supposed to trust you?"

Blue Eyes took another sip. "Yes, first because I give you my word, and secondly, because why would I drug you when you're here to complete the task you have been commissioned to do."

"Commissioned" Clay laughed "Commissioned by who, the Devil?"

Blue Eyes shrugged casually, "Why yes. It's amazing how much you've learned."

"The only commission here," Clay continued, "is that I put your ass back behind bars, and it's only fair I tell you, if I do kill you, it will not be with a ceremonial knife, and there sure as hell won't be a ticker-tape parade waiting for you. I'll send you packing to hell alright, but it will be just like everyone else deserving of the place. I've been there remembered, you sent me. I know very well what you will be in for."

Blue Eyes took a sip, "You are correct Abel…"

"Cooper to you." Clay retorted.

Blue Eyes shrugged, "whatever you wish. You are correct, however, concerning one thing. And that is I have no desire to go to hell unless it is by ceremony," he gestured with his cup and a shrug, "that is why I'd like you to say hello to an old friend."

Gertrude entered through the same door LaFair had used. She had a blanket wrapped around her. A male Vamp was holding a sawed-off shotgun to the back of her head.

They crossed the room to where Blue Eyes sat and stopped a few feet from his rear. Bob Lemus recognized the gunman, a man called Marlee. According to bureau records he worked as a cook in a Chicago restaurant. *"You are a long way from home Marlee." Bob told him. The Vamp did not reply.*

"You see Clay," Blue Eyes began again, "all of this was supposed to happen with Flair and Pageantry: beginning with a delightful dinner, stimulating conversation, and even perhaps some dancing. Then you're killing me as the final event. All would be over, and everyone goes home with their children and thus, live happily ever after…finally!" Blue Eyes took a sip of coffee, set his cup back onto the saucer then sat back folding his arms, "but just as before, you couldn't leave it alone, you had to play Hot Shot Town-Clown Cop. Now, because of it, poor innocent potty mouthed Gertrude may get herself killed just like Carl."

Clay looked to Gertrude. "You okay."

"I'm fine," she said, "still got my skin at least. Thanks, and no thanks to this piss head." She nodded sourly at Blue Eyes.

Rising suddenly from his chair, his face twisted with anger, the killer swept away a large portion of table setting, sending silver and crystal flying through the air then crashing to the floor clattering and breaking into pieces. The sound echoed through the near silence of the room.

From behind his back, he pulled the familiar Demon handled knife and slammed it on the table. "Now," he shouted, "both of you place your guns on the floor and kick them away."

Clay slowly stood to his feet staring into the madman's face, "I don't think so", he said, "I like it right here. You are…" The killer's blue eyes began their alarming metamorphosis quickly fading into blackness.

Clay knew their power. There was no time! Instinctively, no hesitation, he grabbed his nine-mil drawing the barrel directly to the chest of the monster he so hated; immediately he began pulling the trigger while walking straight to him; bang, bang, bang, bang; Empty casings flew like pinging insects, the loud report echoing through the mansion; and with every bullet searing from the barrel of Clay's weapon its impact walked Blue Eyes backward. And Clay walked with him, never missing a step.

All of the things that had happened seven long years ago raced through Clay's head as he fired, a nightmare for every bullet; each memory clawing its way up from the dark recesses of his mind, hoping to free itself from the chains that had been holding it their all these years.

Clay fired until his clip emptied and the slide locked open. From behind the dark Orbs, the things living within the killer's soul stared out. Blue Eyes did not fall. Without warning, he backhanded Clay sending him staggering backward and collapsing unconscious to the floor. He lay there crumpled and bleeding from the mouth.

In segments of seconds, Bob Lemus reasoned his fate. Blue Eyes was sauntering around the table now, moving toward him, smiling. With calm calculated aim, Bob Lemus, a decorated sharpshooter, squeezed off two rounds straight to the killer's head but both rounds missed. Bob spoke under his breath, "What the Hell?"

Whatever the things were that possessed this man, they were capable of rerouting a bullet less than four feet from its target and traveling at the speed of 1200 feet per second.

With what Bob believed to be the last few seconds of his life, he wanted to accomplish at least one final good deed. Refocusing his target, he pulled his sights to the Vamp holding the old woman. Blue Eyes was now less than two feet away and closing. Lemus fired. The vamp's head jerked and he fell backward dead on the floor.

Bob yelled for Gertrude to run just as one hand pulled the gun from his grip and the other grasped his throat. Tossing the weapon on the table, Blue Eyes lifted Bob Lemus from the floor. Bob's eyes widened.

Calling on every ounce of human strength he possessed, Bob pried at the evil vice crushing his throat. His eyes began to bulge, his face turning blue. Far too quickly his hope of surviving was waning. Within seconds he would be dead.

CHAPTER 103

Janis and Ron stood outside the closed door of the Den It was a new door; the one before it had been pretty much demolished during her last visit. Despite having heard gunshots coming from the front of the mansion, they could do nothing, not until they cleared the Den.

Both standing to the side, Janis rapped lightly, "Hey, in there."

A voice called out immediately, "Oh Dear God… please…help… me." It was a man's voice, sobbing as he spoke.

"Who are you," Janis asked.

"I'm Bart…Smith…cameraman with TV…" his sentence ended with him suddenly screaming out in pain

Janis made a face, "Damn it."

Throwing the door open she and Ron peered in. Candlelight revealed a young pudgy man hanging upside down strung from a rafter. Naked, he was facing the doorway with hands tied behind his back. Two people, a tall middle-aged man with a go-tee wearing a brown Doo Rag Chef Hat and white Bib Apron over white shirt and pants and a younger woman in a short sleeve Yellow Chef Coat and white Half Bistro Apron over white pants. She wore no hat.

It appeared both were covered head to toe with blood, but it was difficult to know how much since they were mostly hidden behind the man called Bart. Obviously, they were smart enough not to make themselves easy targets.

Janis and Ron glanced at one another then back to Bart. The poor man's naked body was covered with small bite size chunks of flesh missing from his hanging torso. He was bleeding from most so Janis knew the insane torture had begun only recently.Janis again made a face, "Damn it."

The young woman amused to see Janis upset spoke first. Her voice was deep and raspy, sounding as if congested, "Drop your guns and come join the fun." She waved a kitchen knife as if it were a toy, then reached around and made a slice across the pudgy man's belly, Bart screamed shaking like a hooked fish, "do it, you dumb, fucking bitch," the bloody-faced woman said, "and the cock too," she added, "guns on the floor outside the door."

She and the go-teed man started giggling like little children. Janis knew the situation. Seven years ago, in this room when she had faced the demon possessed man with the strength of ten; she had nearly been killed.

It took little sense to know putting down their weapons would prove a foolish mistake. Without them, they were no match against these satanic infested humans. Yet, if she and Ron did not do as instructed, before they could reach them, they would have Bart Smith's throat cut.

The male bit Bart again, tearing another chunk of flesh from his left flank. Bart screamed jerking against the rope holding him captive. The biter chewed, smiled, then swallowed yelling "yummy." nearly drowning out Bart's scream. He licked his lips then immediately took another bite.

Bart screamed again. Covering his mouth with her hand the young woman said, "To us his cries are music, and his flesh a tasty delicacy like fine Japanese Sushi. She giggled glancing at her companion, "it must be the salty sweat." They both broke out in laughter this time.

When the sick demented humor faded, she looked back to Ron and Janis, "Now, are you going to stand and watch us eat this delicious chubby treat, or drop the guns and come in…we promise lots of entertainment before we kill you; especially you; you saucy bad ass little bitch; for you see, I too was here seven years ago."

CHAPTER 104

Squeezing slowly, methodically, Blue Eyes stared into the dying eyes of Bob Lemus - his greatest adversary ever. No one had ever come as close as Robert Langley Lemus in catching him, no one had ever placed him in chains, and certainly no one had ever incarcerated him. This man was skillful, and he hoped to see him in hell.

Bob's airway was collapsing; death was close, seconds away; his final thoughts were on the one person he loved more than life itself, Janis Barr-Lemus.

Behind the slow execution, Clay was attempting to rise. His mind was whirling and his head ringing. He could taste blood in his mouth. Struggling, he attempted to stand but fell back to his hands and knees. He could not gain his balance.

Bob Lemus's hands fell to his side, and he went limp. Blue Eyes released his grip watching his greatest contender ever, crumble to the floor. Staring down he smiled and warmly said, "It is from my heart I say, "Agent Bob Lemus, I do truly hope to see you when I arrive home.

Then leaving the body, Blue Eyes rounded the table to Clay's struggling form. Bending, he pulled him to his feet to stare into his eyes, "Well my brother, you've managed to get Bob Lemus killed too, and as you know his wife and your friend Ron are here in the house also. At this time, they are still alive, but not for long. They will die very soon, perhaps five, ten minutes tops. It is not too late for you to save them. Just simply do that which you are destined to do. We will go to the table where I will lie down, and you will plunge the knife into my heart. If you refuse, both Janis and Ron will die here along with Bob, and as for you, your wife and your son…well, let's just say this tiff will continue on."

On the far side of the table arose a short moan from the floor. Surprise showed on the killer's face. Forcing Clay along with him, Blue Eyes moved to its source and smiled at the motionless body on the floor.

Another soft moan arose, and Blue Eyes widened his smile, "Well look at this,". I swear Bobby, you are one cool cat with nine lives. You just won't die."

Clay, nearly back to being himself again, attempted to kneel and help Bob but Blue Eyes' powerful grip held him at bay, "Sorry Abel," he said, "kill me first then you can save little Bobby…and, if not already too late, perhaps the other two playing in the Den."

CHAPTER 105

Glancing at Ron, Janis knew only two choices existed: let Bart be murdered so they could safely storm into the room and kill the demon-possessed couple or put down the weapons and pray things somehow went their way. Really, they both knew they had no choice, not morally. In agreement, she and Ron placed their weapons on the hallway floor at their feet.

The blood-soaked face of the demon-possessed woman widened her smile."Now come in and close the door behind you." She again sliced Bart's abdomen to reinforce her determination. Bart cried out jerking again at the end of the rope. "Just so you know who you will be staring at you when you die," the woman added, "this body is called Alice and he is Pete." Again, she used the knife, this time slicing Bart across the forehead. The camera operator's helpless shriek ended the standoff.

Nothing said, Ron and Janis stepped through the door and stopped. Bloody Alice told Ron, "You, cock, close it before I play the fat man's belly like a violin," She raised the knife waving it playfully in her hand. Throwing Janis an unsure look Ron closed it.

Remaining a distance of eight or so feet from Bart and the two torturing him, Janis and Ron waited. They knew something had to be done soon. The puddle of blood pooling beneath Bart's head rippled steadily. Janis' jaw tightened. Pulling her eyes to the thing called Alice she forced a smile, "So, one or more of you little bastards were here seven years ago hey. Well don't get too excited, because I'm going to kick all your little evil asses one more time."

Showing their bloody teeth with laughter, both predators stepped out from behind Bart. The woman moved to stand in front of Janis and the male, Pete, did the same with Ron. Hunched as if stalking, bloody-faced Alice began moving in slow circles around Janis, sniffing her. With the demonic voice she said, "Did you know this body is a Vampire?" Two elongated teeth began extending from the roof of her mouth and she hissed, her eyes began to yellow. Janis shuttered but hid it as Alice continued talking, "not only am I superior to you, but you will also soon find I am unstoppable."

"Congratulations," Janis said beginning to circle with her, keeping her to the front, "so what does that mean to me? That I should start calling you Alice super-freak?"

"Make light of it, sweet mouth," the demonic voice said, "but you ought to know, before this body bites you and drinks very once of your blood, it's going to strip you and lick you all over; every fold and crevice."

"Fine," Janis told her still circling, "but brush and gargle first, I hate the smell of shit."

CHAPTER 106

With his iron grip still holding Clay, Blue Eyes grabbed Bob's vest collar and dragged him along the floor to the end of the table. There, despite Bob's desperate struggle to get much needed oxygen into his lungs; Blue Eyes ignored him. And through the implausible power of the dark things inside him, the killer tossed Bob's body through the air as if he were nothing but a stuffed toy.

Although a flight lasting only seconds, Bob's oxygen deprived mind flashed back to the plane crash at Baton Rouge. This time however, there were no whirling lights, no loud sounds of arriving Crash Trucks, Ambulances, Police Cars and dozens of EMS personnel. And too, there was no one sharing the ride. This time it was only him flying through an empty shadowy sky.

Then he touched down slamming merciless against the hardwood floor at the hallway entrance leading back to the parlor. The flight wasn't over. He continued sliding through the dark hall and out into the open parlor where he had first entered. Now his body began spinning crashing into a stand, sending a chair flying through the air, rebounding off the side of a couch, and finally ending the flight with hard impact into a wall at a sudden stop.

Lying motionless, he tried to curse aloud but could not. His traumatized airway was still not allowing enough air through. The swelling was subsiding, but far too slowly. He could not yell or talk, so he did the only thing he could: he reminded himself just how much he hated flying.

CHAPTER 107

Struggling to free himself Clay shouted, "You son of bitch."

Ignoring him Blue Eyes vehemently drug him to the cleared spot on the table. Once there he said, "It is time my son."Young Cain hurried out of the shadows where he had been sitting, watching everything. Approaching he smiled, "That was awesome Father, will I too possess such strength?"

"You will my son." Blue Eyes said while forcing Clay into a chair. Plucking the Ceremonial Knife from the table he forced it into Clay's hand saying, "I will no longer tolerate your defiance, Abel; or, if you prefer, Clay. We both know the truth now don't we!"

Turning, he swept away a larger portion of the tabletop, then climbed up stretching out on his back. His head turned to look at Clay, "You have caused the death of a lot of people and you're running out of friends. The knife, one more time, is in your hand. If you do not thrust it into my heart right now, or you kill me in any other way, I have left orders and a lot of money to the Vampires. They will see to it everyone you know and every living relative you have will, and I say this in French with no apologies... fucking die! It will begin with your wife and son. Now, stand and kill me like you should have done seven years ago."

Clay rose, squeezing the knife tightly in his hand. Blue Eyes moved into a sitting position removing his dress-coat and shirt to gain access to the bullet-proof vest beneath them. Disconnecting the Velcro straps, he pulled it free and tossed it aside. His chest now bare, he laid back down and placed a finger over his heart, "here," he said demanding, "right here, lift and plunge, that is all you have to do. Now kill me and save your family."

Towering over him, staring down at the psychopath who had turned his life into an upside-down nightmare of Hell, the killer who had mercilessly murdered, butchered and raped innocent people just to bring him here for this very purpose; Clay could not understand why he was hesitating.

Following a deep breath, he finally lifted the knife high and over the killer's heart; his hand was shaking. Closing his eyes Clay asked himself, *how many times have you promised yourself this would be it, this…monstrosity was going to die this time, once and for all. Just one thrust*, he told himself, *you've waited so long. END IT! Do it for Sean and Evelyn Parks, for Carl, for…* "Shit!"

It was no use; he couldn't do it. Lowering his hand, he let the knife fall to the floor.

Scurrying off the table Blue Eyes began shouting in Clay's face, sputtering as he talked, "Just as it was when I killed you in the field over two millennium ago…your weak! You obey God like a dog. You're no more a man now then you were then." Turning to the Kitchen door he yelled, "I know you have her again, bring her here."

Another Vamp drug Gertrude out from the kitchen. They moved to where the dead Vamp lay on the floor and stood, waiting for further direction.Blue Eyes pointed a finger toward the old woman, continuing to shout at Clay, "Fine, you wish to continue getting people killed, let's start with her."

Blue Eyes stormed off toward Gertrude.

Clay shouted after him, "No!"

Replying without slowing down he said, "It's too late Abel, watch as I rip her jaw from her face and bring it back to you as proof, I'm finished playing games."

Clay charged from the table to intercept, to fight for Gertrude's life; but Blue Eyes had reached her. It was at that very moment Gertrude fainted, falling across the body of the dead Vamp on the floor.

Clay reached Blue Eyes, but the killer turned and backhanded him knocking him to the floor yet again. Teeth gritted the killer stared a moment at Clay, he wasn't moving but he was still alive. Looking back to the standing Vamp he screamed, "Get that old, wrinkled bitch back on her feet!"

Feeling his lip swelling and bleeding, Clay managed to climb back on his feet, turning just in time to witness the one thing he would never have imagined. It happened so fast and so unexpected...from beneath the blanket Gertrude pulled the sawed-off shotgun the vamp had held to her head earlier. No hesitation, not a moment's pause; both barrows roared with fire and smoke, the force throwing her frail body backward and too the floor.

Side by side, the spiraling slugs tore through each of the killer's eyes exiting the back of his skull followed by flesh, blood, and bone. The impact sent him backwards falling onto the end of the table face up and legs dangling.

Little Cain cried out, "Father!" Charging to his side he scrambled atop the table knelling beside him staring into his father's face; fixated on the now dark and empty hollow sockets where once the world's most beautiful Blue Eyes had sat.

Clay listened as the young boy whispered with anguish and pain, "Father, please come back. You must die by the holy knife."But the Blue Eyes Killer was finally gone. It was over. And he was never coming back!

Climbing off the table young Cain picked the knife up from the floor, stared at it a moment, then kissed its decorative blade. Clutching it to his heart he glanced back to the eyeless remains of his father.

Although stunned from the events that had just happened Clay hurried to Cain's side. Once there he quickly snapped up Bob Lemus's automatic from the table and shot the standing Vamp three times in the chest; thankful for the creation of special Vamp killing rounds, and that the Vamp had been as in-trolled and startled at the current events as he had been.

With the Vamp down Clay then hurried to Gertrude's side where she was now sitting upright on the floor. Looking up she sighed as Clay helped her to her feet. "You okay, Gert?" he asked.

"Fine Clay, I think," she said looking deep into his eyes, "I never killed anybody before. Sure, I've considered murdering Charlie a hundred times, but never went through with it."

Clay grinned, "Well I'm glad you spared Charlie, but this time it was the right thing to do. Self-defense Gert. And you killed a murderer wanted by the FBI."

"Gertrude sighed again, "Yeah, but now I'm worried about that little boy over there."

Clay glanced at Cain. He was still staring at his father's corps. Gertrude was right, he thought, though the boy had an evil side, he was still just a child, and the disfigurement of his father went beyond what any child should have to see.

Following a reassuring squeeze, Clay left Gertrude and went to where Cain was standing. He was unsure what to say but tried. "Cain," he began while sitting down, "I know this is tough, I know you loved your dad the way Michael loves me. If there is anything I – "

"At least you still have Michael." Cain interrupted while continuing to stare at the eyeless sockets of his father.

Clay made a face. "Yes, I still have Michael, but right now I'm concerned about you. I want to help. Is there anything I can do?"

"There is one thing." Cain said. Twisting his body, he plunged the knife that was to kill his father into Clay's throat, "you die too!" He said.

Instinctively Clay's hands gripped his throat, disbelieving what had just happened. The boy had driven it all the way through. Blood raced down the front of Clay's shirt soaking rapidly into the material. Gasping for air, he managed a startled glance at Gertrude then fell from the chair.

Gertrude yelled out, "Clay!" Hurrying to his side she lowered herself to the floor struggling to feel a pulse. Her hands covered in blood; she began to cry. There was no pulse. Clayton Cooper was dead too! Enraged, her elderly hand rose to strike the boy-killer, but from behind someone grabbed her wrist.

CHAPTER 108

The demon possessed Vampire called Pete, stood in front of Ron staring into his face grinning. Ron made a sour expression; its face and teeth were swathed heavy with Bart Smith's blood and skin.

Like the snap of a snake, Pete's hands shot out gripping the back of Ron's head pulling him close and kissing him on the lips. Quickly releasing him, the crazed mutant continued smiling then broke into laughter. Ron swiped a sleeve across his mouth then made his move. With all he had, he threw a roundhouse to the side of Pete's head, then back again with an elbow. The tall vamp-demon barely budged but it did anger him.

Gripping Ron's throat it walked him backward slamming him against the wall to the right of the door; then effortlessly slid him up to eye level and held him there. Ron's feet were dangling. "You should not have done that." Bloody faced Pete said.

Moving his face close to Ron's, noses nearly touching, Pete stared into Ron's eyes, absorbed, as if searching intensely to see his soul. Ron could not stop the slobber and blood dripping from its mouth onto him. Its breath reeked.

Struggling to turn away he found it impossible to do. Peripherally however, Ron did glimpse something unusual, a hand holding an automatic weapon was slowly extending through the slightly opened door toward Smelly Pete's head. Ron could not see who it was, but approximately one foot from its target the gun fired, kicking slightly in the holder's hand and filling the den with its loud report. The bullet entered the vamp-demon's temple killing him instantly. Ron dropped to the floor just a little before Pete.

Immediately the door swung open, and Bob Lemus stood poised with weapon raised. Decisions were instantaneous, Janis ducked, vamp-demon Alice turned to look, and Bob shot her with the remaining rounds left in his clip. Alice staggered backward falling into Bart's hanging torso sending him swaying and crying out in pain.

Switching clips Bob moved into the Den ensuring everything was now clear. From the two dead vampires a horde of demons emerged storming out of the room cursing. Janis followed them to the door shouting as they marched down the hall; "I told you, you little bastards."

Jan picked up her weapon and Bob gave Ron's back to him. Gentle as possible the three cut Bart Smith down. With Ron and Bob at each side, they began a cautious trek to the dining room where the latest wonder had been the blast of a shotgun.

Outside the Mansion the sound of approaching sirens wailed through the Louisiana night. It meant Jones and Clendes had gotten everyone away safely.

Just shy of the door leading into the dining room they stopped and lowered Bart to the floor He was now unconscious; but alive. Ron peered through the small, rounded window with a furrowed brow. The dining room lay like a battlefield. Blue Eyes lay on the table face up while Clay lay on the floor beside the table. Neither were moving.

Little Cain sat Indian Style at the head of his father and Gertrude stood huddled in a corner wrapped in a blanket. There were three vamps; two dead face up on the floor, and the other sitting in a chair at the table; that one was Ever. His arms were folded, and he sat silent staring at the floor.

The sirens were close now, only minutes away. Bob, Janis and *Ron* entered warily into the dining room. Right away Gertrude spotted them and rushed to their side shouting and angrily pointing toward little Cain. He killed Clay.He killed him. That freaking kid stabbed Clay in the neck with a knife and killed him. Then, that sick bastard," her finger moved to Ever, "came along and pulled it out. Then started sucking Clay's blood."

Ron raced to Clay checking his pulse. "None!" he shouted to the others. And rose moving slowly away.

Bob glanced at Janis. His voice raspy, "Stay with Gertrude." Walking to Clay's body he squatted and checked the pulse as well. Just as Ron had said, there was not one. The wound site presented itself clean except for a thin film of blood around a small fissure where the knife had entered.

Following a deep sigh Bob Lemus stood starring down at the man who had become his friend. Was his friend; Clayton Cooper was unquestionably dead.

Sober faced he walked to Ron, "Give me your handgun."

Ron hesitated, puzzled at first, then drew a deep breath and handed it over. Bob Lemus took it and moved to where Ever was sitting. The demon-handled knife that had killed Clay lay on the table in front of him. Bob raised the weapon in his hand. "Look at me," he said with the same raspy voice. But Ever did not move, just continued gazing at his feet. "You son of a bitch," Bob said, "look at me right now."

The loud demand seemed to break Ever's self-induced trance, and he raised his head. Bob grit his teeth. Blood covered the Ferret's face; Gertrude had told the truth. "What the fuck," Bob shouted filling with rage, "What have you done Ever? Has all this brought back a thirst? And why Clay, why not someone you didn't know. All these years, clean. And now you're back to being one of them again."

From behind Bob, Ron Parks shouted, "Oh shit, look!"

Bob Lemus turned, "What?"

Ron was staring at Clayton Cooper's body. Murdered only minutes ago and verified; it was beginning to move; slowly, pulling himself into a sitting position. Confounded, Ron continued to stare. Little Cain remained sitting and watching. Gertrude held tight to Janis' arm, frightened. Weapon still raised Bob left Ever and moved back to Clay, barrel directed at his head. "What the hell," Bob said to Clay, "your dead, you were killed. How in the hell are you now alive?"

Himself taken aback, Clay climbed to his feet and touched his throat; no puncture wound, no running blood, no pain or trouble breathing. There was nothing but a small, spot of rough skin. Almost as if a scare.

Clay's shrug was one of self-puzzlement, "I know," he told Bob, "I remember being stabbed, unable to breathe and bleeding to death, then nothing; and now?"

Everyone starred at Clay in seconds of silent wonder. Ever spoke from his chair at the table, "Do not be afraid, he is not a Demon, and he is not a Vampire, he is healed." The stunned group looked at Ever, then back to Clay.

After running a hand over his horseshoe hair Bob lowered the weapon and returned to Ever, "You?" he asked.

Ever nodded; "Yes. No one knows, not even Nasif, that a few of the old ones possess this capability. We do not know how it works, only that sometimes when we drink and do not over feed, the HUK will heal much the way we do. It does not always work, today it did, and I am thankful."

Bob glanced back at Clay with a grateful nod, "welcome back." The others stood for only a second before it dawned and they rushed to Clay like a smiling mob.

Turning back to Ever, Bob offered his hand, "I'm sorry old friend. I owe you an apology and one big-time favor."

Ever took Bob's hand while moving to his feet. "I accept," he said with a smile, "and that favor; you owe me one big Bottle of Jim Beam."

Bob returned the smile. "Done."

Clay broke from the others wanting to thank Ever himself. They shook hands and gave a shared hug. Clay told him wearing the bigger smile, "And from me, Ever; you can soon expect a big Case of Jim Beam."

CHAPTER 109

Mansion grounds were now amassed with the colored lights of Ambulances, Police Cars and Firetrucks. State and Local law Enforcement Officers combing the grounds found at least a dozen scattered bodies, all of which had been decapitated. Assisting with the bagging of bodies, FBI agent Ever Maus volunteered no information as to why anyone might have killed them in such an inhumane way.

Inside, Paramedics treated everyone as needed and when child services arrived, they benevolently separated little Cain Christenson from his father's side; the brave little boy was impressively cooperative. He had insisted they allow him to watch the paramedics place his father in a body bag and carry him away.

On the way to the door, bordered between a State Police Officer and holding the hand of a young female Social Worker, Cain stopped and asked politely if he could say good-by to the others. Granted permission, he returned to where Bob, Clay and Ron stood talking.

Once by their side he stuck out his hand to Ron. He took it and Cain told him, "Tell Mrs. Parks Carla says hello. Letting go he then turned to Bob Lemus and offered his hand. Bob took it and Cain told him, "My Father wanted you to know he respected you. You presented him with invigorating challenges, at least more so than any others. But most important; he did not want you to see yourself as a complete failure; you simply were no match for his Superior Intellect. And that nearly all your failings were because of the FBI. Father understood how our Master works but the FBI all but ignore theirs. Bob glanced at Ron, "Did I just get ripped?"

Cain once again broke his shake, this time turning to Clay. With a finger he motioned for Clay to come down to his level.Kneeling, Clay told him. "I really am sorry Cain. So sorry for all that has happened to you."

Cain reached out and wrapped his small arms around Clay's neck and hugged him, holding for some time. Waiting at the door the social worker smiled warmly.

Lemus had informed her of Cain's mother, suggesting she call the New York Office for information concerning her whereabouts. Prison videotapes of her many visits with Blue Eyes had clearly shown her love for the boy.

Arms still wrapped about Clay's neck, Cain whispered in his ear, "You did not kill my father in the way he had asked. Now he is dead, and you are alive. You have no idea what you have done Mr. Cooper. Remember this. My father was and is, a man of his word."

Clay frowned; pulling back to look into the boy's face. His eyes were black like a cold night without a Moon or Stars.*Little Cain*, Clay thought in his head, *had now become Little Blue Eyes.*

The two stared for several moments before the boy's eyes faded back to a radiant beautiful blue. With the transformation completed, he returned to the social worker slipping his hand in hers and smiled, "Thank You." She returned the smile just as two men, two women, and four children came rushing through the door.

Michelle and the kids ran to Ron, and Nancy to Clay. But Michael paused at Cain's side asking, "Is it over?"

Saying nothing, Cain gave Michael an ominous smile that only he could see. Then still holding the Social Worker's hand the little boy with the most radiant beautiful Blue Eyes walked out of the Mansion with her in toe. Glancing down at the young child she pressed her lips with a sympathetic heart thinking... *so painfully traumatized, yet such a warm and loving little boy'.*

AND A Child SHALL LEAD THEM